THE CHANGELING OF THE THIRD REICH

THE CHANGELING OF THE THIRD REICH

by

Rachel Carrera

Published by Cleo's Room Publishing, Lakeland, FL, USA

Copyright 2023, Rachel Carrera

All rights reserved. No part of this book may be reproduced or transmitted in any form or by any means, electronic or mechanical, including photocopying, recording, or by any information storage and retrieval system, without written permission from the publisher, except for the inclusion of brief quotations in a review.

"The Changeling of the Third Reich" is a work of fiction. Only the generality of well-researched Nazi officials and cruel Nazi behavior, along with the names and places involving news references and historical figures contained herein are truthful. Unless otherwise indicated, all names, characters, businesses, places, events, and incidents in this book are either the product of the author's imagination or are used in a fictitious manner. Any resemblance to actual persons, living or dead, or actual events is purely coincidental.

This book is dedicated to the memories of two people I never had the pleasure of meeting:

First,

Dawn Rae Hathcox, 1949 – 1963

She was my maternal aunt who died before I was born. When I was a child and looked through old photographs, I was convinced that my Aunt Dawn was the reincarnation of Anne Frank. Both girls exhibited incredible strength with the challenges they faced. Both had enough compassion to fill the hearts of a thousand men. Both sadly died before they reached adulthood. But most incredibly, they looked so much alike, they could've been twins.

Second,

Petrus van den Boom, 1936 – 2018

A native of Holland, he was the father of a friend. From the stories I've heard of him, he was a magnificent man with a heart of gold, which is why Petrus van den Boom was the inspiration for "The Good Doctor Petteri Van Den Boom."

OTHER BOOKS BY RACHEL CARRERA:

The Changeling of the Third Reich Book II: The Reckoning

COMING SOON:

The Changeling of the Third Reich Book III: Hitler's Orphans

"Monsters exist, but they are too few in number to be truly dangerous. More dangerous are the common men, the functionaries ready to believe and to act without asking questions."

— *Primo Levi, Writer and Holocaust Survivor*

change·ling

[chānj-ling]

noun

1. A child substituted for another, most often in infancy.

Dear Reader,

Dr. Bridget Castle and her friends, family, and patients are products of my imagination. The hospital where she works is imaginary and is part of her world. However, the world in which she resides, the time period which wasn't welcoming to women in male-dominated professions, the Vietnam War along with its protestors and its casualties, the H3N2 pandemic, and most importantly, the Holocaust were very real.

I've taken great strides to research the historical events and figures, news references, medical technology available, social terminology, and even day-to-day details such as the weather, pop-culture, and the cost of living used in Bridget's story. These are accurate to the best of my knowledge.

The only thing purposefully portrayed in an inaccurate manner in this story are the referenced Auschwitz prisoner serial number tattoos. While my research shows that tattoos of prisoner numbers at Auschwitz concluded with number 202,499 by the time the camp was liberated in January, 1945, I added an 8 to the front of tattooed numbers referenced in Bridget's story so that I wouldn't accidentally duplicate a real Holocaust victim's number. If I have inadvertently used a real prisoner number, I offer my most profound apologies to that person and their family.

Warm regards,

Rachel Carrera

CHAPTER ONE

The last passenger squeezes into the crowded elevator as Bridget presses herself against the back wall and holds her breath. As the doors close, so do her eyes, and she wills herself not to swoon. *Calm down. It's just the lift. It's not the same thing.* Her palms begin to sweat as she clutches the stethoscope in her pocket, her knuckles turning white as the car descends. The doors open on the first floor, and a whoosh of cool air enters along with Bing Crosby's "Let It Snow!"

A young woman runs a hand through her frosted, pixie-style hairdo and, from her post in the circular receptionist station, says, "Goodnight, Dr. Castle."

"Goodnight, Carol. Have a good evening. I'll see you tomorrow," Bridget says in her cut-glass British accent as she crosses the lobby. As she does every day, she places her hand over her heart and tips her head when she passes the large framed photo of President Lyndon Johnson in the foyer.

Outside, she approaches her Mustang and brushes the tears from her eyelashes then tosses her lab coat to the back seat. Blasting the heat and the radio as she exits the lot, she snakes her way through the downtown Boston traffic. *Bollocks. Why does that lad have to be so stubborn?* With a sniffle, she shoves her hand between the driver's seat and the center console, producing half a pack of Butter Rum Lifesavers. She pops one in her mouth then returns the candy to its hiding place and bobs her head to Simon and Garfunkel's "Mrs. Robinson."

2   THE CHANGELING OF THE THIRD REICH

Making her way north toward Malden, her lips curl into a heartfelt smile when she approaches a Salvation Army Santa perched next to his red kettle, ringing a bell. She nods and raises her hand in a motionless wave. Snowflakes dance in front of the windshield and melt upon touching the glass. *I can't believe it's already the twelfth of December. I really need to get Jack's gift soon.*

Soon, the traffic slows to a crawl. She cranes her neck to watch the commotion as several of Boston's finest work to contain a group of hippies in the midst of a Vietnam protest. She turns down the radio to hear their cries of "Stop the slaughter in Vietnam!" Their colorful signs proclaim: "Johnson is a War Criminal," "My Brother Was Killed – For What?" and "Why Are Only the Poor Fighting This War?" A flash of movement catches her eyes before a dirty, barefooted, longhaired teenager rolls over the hood of her car and lands on the road with a thud. He remains motionless.

Bridget throws the car into park and jumps out, ignoring the blistering cold. She kneels to feel the boy's neck for a pulse when a policeman blows his whistle and says, "Get away from him, lady! These kids are no good. No telling what they'll do to hurt you."

She ignores the cop and the blood dripping down the young man's face as she lifts his eyelids and studies his pupils. "This lad isn't hurting anyone. He's unconscious, and he's got a concussion. He needs an ambulance… Hurry up; I'm a doctor!"

Her eyes narrow as the policeman slides his bloody nightstick in its holster and, in a defeated tone, says over his shoulder, "Better get a bus for this one. He's hurt."

The cop continues to corral the demonstrators as Bridget presses her hand against the victim's open headwound to slow his blood loss. She assesses his condition. *No shoes. No jacket. Smells like he hasn't had a shower in weeks. He doesn't look to be more than fifteen or sixteen years old. His pulse is weakening.*

Minutes later, the piercing wail of a siren approaches, and a Cadillac station wagon ambulance pulls alongside Bridget's car. Two medics jump out, and as one retrieves the gurney from the back of the car, the other kneels beside Bridget with a portable equipment box. He pulls out a blood pressure cuff and wraps it around the boy's arm, saying, "Hola, Dr. Castle. What have we got?"

Bridget removes a stack of gauze from the box and presses it over the boy's wound. Looking to the medic, she says, "Evening,

Alejandro. He's got a concussion. Been unconscious for nearly ten minutes now. El policía lo golpeó en la cabeza." *The policeman hit him in the head.*

The officer breaks away from the kids being loaded into a paddy wagon and kneels beside the ambulance. "What'd you say? Is he going to be okay?"

Bridget takes a sterile wipe from the box and wipes the blood from her hands as she stands and confronts the cop. "He has a brain injury. We won't know how bad until they get him down to hospital for diagnostics, but it doesn't look good." She cuts her eyes to Alejandro. "Have them send him for x-rays posthaste, and I'll be there behind you straightaway. And have them check his feet for frostbite. It looks like he might lose a couple of toes."

The policeman shakes his head and gives a disgusted snort as he stretches to his full height, towering over her. "Stupid hippies. They don't even know enough to wear shoes in winter."

Bridget bows up her chest, and scarlet patches creep up her neck. She ignores her quickening pulse. The tears gathered in her eyes cause blurry prisms to cloud her vision, and she fears she won't be able to contain her white-hot rage. "Pardon me? Who made you lord and master over everyone?"

"This badge," he says through clenched teeth, jabbing his thumb into his chest. "This badge means I'm the law; and the law says these hippies can't congregate here! They're disturbing the peace!"

"That's codswallop, you bumbling tosser! They *were* demonstrating peacefully. Or don't you know the First Amendment?"

The policeman runs his tongue over his upper teeth then spits near Bridget's feet, causing her to jump back. "What are you, some kind of foreigner or something? What kind of talk is that besides un-American?"

"I'm as American as you are. In fact, I passed a citizenship test and probably know more than you do about how the American government works. Is that what really matters to you right now and not the outcome of this lad?"

Alejandro pulls a sheet over the victim's head. "Dr. Castle, he's gone. Do you want to sign off—"

Bridget's face falls as she eyes the gurney. She kneels and feels the victim's wrist for a pulse then shakes her head. "Damn. Yeah. Send the paperwork to my office. I'll fill everything out in the morning. Have Ernie in the M.E.'s office contact the family. Make sure they do a complete autopsy and tox screen."

"Yes, ma'am. Buenas noches."

"Si. Goodnight to you too."

The police officer cocks his head back and says, "I suppose you want to put this off on me? That kid was probably higher than a kite before I ever set eyes on him. He probably overdosed."

Bridget's face puckers into a disgusted scowl. "The autopsy will let us know exactly how he died. Or who caused it. But I don't suppose that really matters to his parents. The fact is, he's young, he's dead, and there's no bringing him back. But if his bloodwork comes back clean and there happens to be an internal affairs inquiry, I'll be happy to testify. For the victim."

The cop shakes his head and spits on the road. "Damn women doctors. We shouldn't have even given you the right to vote." He spits near Bridget's feet then turns and flails his arms at the group in the wagon. "Come on, you lazy, draft dodging doves! Let's get this show on the road!"

Bridget steps back from the spit wad, and a bit of bile rises to her throat. Her fingers find their way under her left sleeve and trace the thick scar on her forearm. Her body shivers, and she watches the ambulance drive away before she situates herself in her car. She starts driving, and the boy's blood smeared across the hood of her car catches her eye. *Bollocks. Poor lad.* She blasts the radio for the remainder of her drive home.

* * *

CHAPTER TWO

Bridget pulls into her driveway beside Jack's Lincoln Continental. Admiring the metallic huron blue exterior, she recalls how difficult it was to persuade him against getting the car in the "old man chesterfield beige" he was so set on two years ago when he purchased it. She shivers as she heads to the side of the saltbox house and turns on the garden hose. She starts spraying her car when Jack steps outside.

Jack throws his hands in the air. "There you are. Where have you been? We were supposed to meet Dr. Taylor and his new girlfriend twenty minutes ago."

"Bollocks. I forgot. I'm sorry, my love. I had a rough day."

He takes the hose from her. "Get inside. You're going to catch your death out here. What happened? You hit a deer?"

"No. A teenage boy hit me."

"What? Is he okay?"

"No. He died. I just need to hose the bonnet and clean the steering wheel before—"

"No, I'll take care of the car. You go get yourself cleaned up. I told Paul we'd meet them at Pierre's."

"Oh, Jack, I'm really not up for it. I'm so knackered, and I just want to head for the kip. My day's been bloody chaos and—"

"Babe, I'm really sorry, but it's too late. I can't reach them now to cancel anyway. Please? I promise we'll make a short night of it."

She looks into his honey-colored eyes and knows she won't win. "Oh, all right. Maybe some French food is just what the doctor ordered."

"That's right."

She heads inside and hurries upstairs where she washes her face and applies brightly colored eye-shadow, black liquid eyeliner, and ruby lipstick. She pulls her amber hair out of its taut bun and styles it into a shoulder-length flip, fluffing her long bangs. Stepping to the closet, she pulls on a sweater then chooses two skirts, holding each in front of her as she angles herself in front of the cheval mirror.

A wolf-whistle causes her to spin toward the door. "Hey, good-lookin'." Jack plucks some silver cufflinks out of the dresser-top valet and hands them to her. "Help me?"

Sitting beside him on the bed, she giggles and fastens his French cuffs. "I always love this grey suit on you."

He kisses her cheek then stands and extends his hand to her. "Why? Because it brings out the silver streaks in my hair and makes me look old enough to be your father?"

"No, because it makes me look young enough to be your daughter. Which skirt?"

He taps his chin then takes one and hangs it back in the closet. "I think the houndstooth. It's wool, and the temperature's dropping."

She steps into the skirt and says, "Can you get my burgundy tights?" After pulling on her boots, they meander downstairs, grab their coats, and head outside. "Hey, you washed the whole car. Thank you."

He opens the Lincoln door for her and waits as she gets situated in the passenger's seat. Climbing in beside her, he starts the engine. "So, what happened today?"

She closes her eyes and releases a deep sigh. "It started off with a new patient. He's got a brain tumor, and he's flown in from Cologne for me to operate."

"Cologne? West Germany?"

"Right. And I guess he was surprised when he got here this morning. I've spoken to his doctor several times, but apparently, the patient was never told I was a woman. He started right away on the penis envy codswallop. He doesn't like having a female surgeon."

"Ah. Well, he's got the best; that's for sure."

"Thanks. Then there was the double amputee lad."

"The Vietnam vet?"

"Right. There's no getting around it. He needs spinal surgery if he's ever going to regain full use of his left arm. But, of course, he's feeling good and sorry for himself, and he figures, with no legs, he might as well go ahead and die anyway."

"Aww, that's too bad. I'll make sure to stop in and check on him tomorrow. Give him a pep talk."

"Thanks. He kind of got to me today. I don't know why, but it just upset me so much. Then on my way home, I drove through a protest where a cheeky cop had beaten a boy in the head with his baton. It was quite a kerfuffle. The lad rolled over my bonnet and was unconscious by the time he hit the ground. I got out to try and help, but he died within a few minutes." She reaches under her seat and produces an opened roll of Wint-O-Green Lifesavers then pops one in her mouth. She offers him the pack, and he shakes his head. Then she returns the candy to its hiding place.

Jack rests his hand on her knee. "I'm sorry, hon. We'll cut it short tonight. Here, let's see what's going on in the news." He flips on the radio then returns his hand to her thigh where she interlaces her fingers through his.

"...and the film 'Oliver!' based on London's hit musical has opened here in the States after its initial release in England. Yesterday, with just thirty-nine days left until his inauguration, Richard Nixon introduced a dozen hopefuls who will serve in his cabinet, starting with former U.S. Attorney General William P. Rogers as his Secretary of State. Also in politics, yesterday, Alaska Senator Bob Bartlett died following cardiac surgery at the Cleveland Clinic Hospital in Ohio. He will be interred in the Northern Lights Memorial Park in Fairbanks. Bartlett, just sixty-four years old, was one of Alaska's original two Senators since the state's attainment of

statehood in 1959. In other news, the influenza pandemic, widely known as the Hong Kong flu that's been sweeping the nation since September, is still claiming lives in the U.S. as the death toll tops thirty thousand..."

Bridget flips the radio off. "That's enough of the bad news."

Jack pats her hand. "I know; you'd rather have that rock and roll than to listen to anything serious." He chuckles, and she cuts her eyes sideways at him.

In her most posh British accent, she says, "If you're insinuating that I don't take life seriously enough, I think you'd better just—"

He shakes his head and pulls into a parking spot. "I'm not hinting at anything of the kind. I'm just pointing out that—"

"That I married a man old enough to be my grandfather?" Her lips stretch into a playful smirk.

He raises an eyebrow. "I wouldn't necessarily consider a fifteen-year difference in our ages enough to qualify me as your grandfather." He turns the car off, shoves the keys in his pants pocket, and hands Bridget her coat.

She pushes her arm through the sleeve as he steps around the car and opens her door. She steps out and slides her hand into his, saying, "Okay, maybe not quite my grandfather. Maybe just my father's older brother."

When they reach the entrance of Pierre's, Dr. Paul Taylor throws open the door and steps out to greet them. Crushing out his cigarette with his heel, he says, "Jack, so good to see you. And, Bridget, you look stunning." He grabs both her hands and kisses her cheek. "I love the miniskirt. I don't think I've ever seen you look so… What is it the kids say these days? So mod."

She pulls her hands from his and puts on a plastic smile. "Yes, I'm stuck in the masculine garb at work all day, so when I'm off the clock, I like to express my femininity."

They step inside and remove their coats, and Paul rests his hand in the small of his companion's back. "Doctors Castle, I'd like you to meet my girlfriend, Nadine Franklin. Nadine, this is Jack and Bridget."

Jack extends his hand to shake Nadine's. "Nice to meet you, Nadine."

Bridget nods. "It's a pleasure. We hope we didn't keep you waiting too long." She holds her breath and watches the sequins from Nadine's too-tight dress dance as her unsupported breasts bounce when she giggles. Bridget restrains herself from rolling her eyes.

Nadine clasps her hands under her bosom and squeals. In a bawdy, unmistakably Bronx intonation, she says, "Oh, listen to her, Pauly! She's from England! Oh, honey, do you know The Beatles?"

Bridget clenches her teeth and fabricates a smile. Her eyes pierce Jack's as the hostess arrives to escort them to their table.

* * *

CHAPTER THREE

The foursome is seated and given their menus. Bridget scans the entrees then closes the bill of fare and looks to Jack. "I know what I'm having."

He winks at her and says, "The usual?"

"To be sure."

Nadine's eyes grow large, and she says, "I just can't get over your darling Old English accent. Where are you from?"

Bridget bristles. "Uh, I'm from Katesgrove."

"Oh, I don't care whose grove it is, honey. What city are you from?"

Bridget shoots Jack the *she's-such-a-twit* look, and her Queen's English morphs into a Cockney accent so thick, it would make Eliza Doolittle blush. "Oh, listen 'ere, luv, don't be such a gormless pillock. Katesgrove is near Reading in the Thames Valley, to be sure."

Nadine looks between Paul and Jack then guffaws. "Oh, that's real good, honey."

Jack slips his arm around Bridget and, in a low whisper, says, "Did you just call her a stupid idiot?"

Bridget maintains her frozen smile as she nods. Her eyes narrow at Nadine. "Say, luv, where did this randy ol' bumsucker find you? Was he looking for tarts up at the dosshouse?"

Jack huffs, and his nostrils flare. "Bridget!"

Bridget cuts a sideways glance to her husband then looks back to Nadine. "Blimey, luv, I'm just having a chinwag with the old bird. You stop being all piss and wind, won't you? Get off me wick. There's no argy-bargy 'ere, is there, Nadine?"

Nadine's open jaw closes, and her face explodes into a wide smile as she cackles. "Oh, I get it! You're so funny! I just love foreign languages."

Bridget offers an insincere smile. *This bumbling twit's anorexic intelligence is going to make this a long evening.* She raises her hand to summon the waiter.

The waiter approaches and, with a genuine French inflection to his English, says, "Welcome to Pierre's. My name is François. We have several specials tonight. May I recommend the baked ratatouille or beef bourguignon?"

Jack takes Bridget's menu and stacks it with his then hands them to the waiter. "Not tonight, François. My wife and I will both have the salade lyonnaise. She'll have the filet mignon with béarnaise, and I'll have the coq au vin. Thank you."

"Oui. Tres bien. And for Mademoiselle?" The waiter looks to Nadine?

Nadine's cheeks redden. "Who, me? Oh, I don't think I'd like lime mayonnaise in my salad. I'll just have some tossed greens with French dressing and some of that raddie-toolie you told us about." Jack and Bridget cast their eyes down as scarlet splotches bespeckle Paul's neck.

Paul collects Nadine's menu and says, "The lady and I will both have the salade niçoise and the ratatouille special, please." He offers the menus to François.

The waiter maintains a professional composure. "Very good, sir. And may I suggest a Cabernet Sauvignon?"

Paul hugs Nadine to his side and says, "We'll both have the Pinot Noir."

Jack says, "I'll have a glass of the Sauvignon blanc, and my wife will have the Beaujolais."

"Tres bien."

As the waiter turns to leave, Bridget snaps her fingers and says, "Excusez-moi, François. Pourriez-vous me donner le plus grand verre de vin possible? Cette femme est un crétin."

An amused smirk crosses the waiter's face. "Ah, bien sûr, Madame. Tout suite."

As the waiter hurries away, Jack grabs Bridget's hand and stands. "Honey, let's dance. They're playing our song."

She follows him to the dance floor and succumbs to his embrace. Her eyes meet his, and she says, "Since when is Frank Sinatra's 'My Funny Valentine' our song?"

"I had to get you away from there before you made that poor woman cry. What did you say to the waiter anyway?"

"I asked him to give me the largest glass of wine possible because that woman is a moron. And as for crying, I think she's too dense to know she's being insulted."

"Where's this coming from? I've never seen you be so rude to someone."

She takes a deep breath. "I know. It's just that... Women like her... Women who act like they don't have a lick of intellect make things that much harder for those of us who are trying to break down gender barriers. What the hell is Paul thinking, dating her anyway?"

"I think he's just lonely since Veronica died. It's been almost a year."

"Yes, but he's got to be, what, thirty years older than her?"

"At least. That's probably why he likes her."

"That's why you like me." She casts him a coy glance as the song ends, and they hold hands and return to the table.

Jack holds out her chair as she sits, and she sips her wine.

Nadine's eyes twinkle. "I just love how you spoke to that waiter. So, you can speak pretty good French too? Did you learn to speak like that in France, or do they teach French in England?"

Jack rests his hand on Bridget's knee and says, "Actually, she's traveled extensively throughout Europe. And she speaks seven languages." Bridget digs her fingernails into his hand and smiles.

Nadine's hands fly to her face. "Oh, how chic! Or, as the French say, ooh la la! I've always wanted to travel, but I've only been as far as the Grand Canyon..."

Bridget forces herself not to roll her eyes as she tunes out her dining companions. *Thank goodness tomorrow's Friday. I can't wait for the weekend...*

The men talk politics when François returns with the salads and refills the wine glasses. After he leaves, Nadine's jaw drops open, and she says, "I just realized, if you grew up in England, you must have been there during the Blitz. What was that like?"

Bridget covers her mouth and coughs. "Dummkopf." *Imbecile.*

Jack pulls his wife to his side and presses his face in her hair. In a personal tone, he says, "German?"

Bridget gives a subtle nod and stabs her dandelion greens with her fork then dips them in the yolk of the poached egg topping her salad. "If you don't mind, Nadine, I prefer not to talk about such an unpleasant time. Paul, where on earth did you find this... lovely lass?" She shoves her fork in her mouth and shoots Jack a look.

Paul takes a deep breath and pulls the ashtray closer. "We, uh, met at a therapy group for grieving widows and widowers. Nadine lost her husband three months ago to the influenza pandemic. He was actually among the first round of casualties."

Jack wipes his mouth with a linen napkin. "I'm very sorry, Nadine. This H3N2 strain has been a nightmare to contain. We lost nine patients at the hospital last week alone."

Bridget takes a big sip of wine then says, "Yes, you have my condolences. Can you all believe that in less than two weeks, Apollo 8 will be orbiting the moon?"

The foursome makes idle chitchat about the space program until the entrées arrive, and Nadine looks to Bridget. "So, Pauly tells me you're a doctor. Do you deliver babies or something? I've got a friend who's pregnant, and she's looking for someone—"

Bridget cringes, and Jack holds his breath. Paul says, "Sweetie, I told you she's a neurosurgeon."

"I know, but when I had lunch with you at work yesterday, I looked for her name on the directory and didn't see a Bridget Castle listed. I thought you were just teasing me."

Bridget pokes Jack's thigh with her fork. "Actually, I often use my initials rather than my first name. A lot of people still tend to frown on female doctors. Especially specialists and those in surgical capacities."

Nadine corrects the corner of one of her false eyelashes. "Oh, I see. Well, it is really unusual that you're a lady doctor, isn't it? What made you want to go into such a manly profession?"

As Bridget tenses, Jack says, "My wife's father was a surgeon up until he retired in '65, and now he gives lectures at medical colleges across the country three months out of the year. And since he raised my wife to be equally as brilliant, she wouldn't have been happy settling for anything less." He kisses Bridget's cheek.

Nadine's eyes twinkle. "Aww, that's so romantic. How did you two ever meet?"

Bridget cuts into her filet and says, "I started attending university at Oxford, but when they refused to let women in their pre-med program, my folks and I moved to America, and I entered Emory. When I was in my third year of med school, Jack was the Head of Neurology at the Mayo Clinic, and he came to Emory to deliver a lecture."

She pushes her fork into her mouth, and Jack says, "And when she came up afterward to ask me for my autograph—"

Bridget smacks his arm. "I asked him a question about the possible correlation of congenital malformations of the brain or spine as merely chromosomal defects versus the mother's failure to exercise appropriate prenatal care during the first trimester."

A proud grin stretches across Jack's face, and his eyes twinkle. "Oh, that's right. At any rate, I was hooked. We went out on our first date that night, and the month after she graduated, we got married. We just celebrated our thirteenth anniversary this summer."

Nadine clasps her hands under her chin. "Oh, how adorable. I didn't know the Yoyo Clinic was even near Emory."

Paul's cheeks redden, and he says, "Darling, the *Mayo* Clinic is in Rochester, Minnesota. Emory is in Atlanta, Georgia. They obviously had a long-distance relationship."

Jack nods. "That's right. We visited each other nearly every month, and we ran up quite a long-distance bill on phone calls."

Nadine furrows her brow. "So, if you're both in neurology, doesn't that mean you have to compete with each other for business?"

Paul opens his mouth, but Jack holds up his hand. Jack offers a sincere smile and says, "It doesn't quite work that way. If we were both in separate private practices, yes, we would be competitors. But as it turned out, I moved to Georgia when we were married and took a position at Grady Memorial. After my wife completed her residency, she was offered a position here in Boston in a private practice, and we moved so she could have the best start to her career; however, the male physicians at the practice were very chauvinistic. In the meantime, I took a position at Saint Francis. A couple of years later, I was offered the position of Hospital Administrator which left my position open for Bridget to take as the Head of Neurology."

Nadine clasps her hands, and her eyes meet Bridget's. "Aww, well if that's not the sweetest thing."

Paul wraps his arm around Nadine's shoulders and pushes away his empty plate. "I agree. Theirs is certainly a love story made in heaven."

François appears and stacks the dirty dishes, asking, "Would anyone like dessert? Perhaps some crêpes Suzette?"

Nadine's eyes grow large. "Ooh, I'll have some of that, honey. That sounds so Frenchy."

Paul says, "Go ahead and make that two."

Jack looks to Bridget. "Soufflé?"

"Of course. Your usual?"

He nods.

She says, "We'd like the chocolate soufflé and the pear tarte tatin, s'il vous plaît."

"Très bien, Madame." He hurries toward the kitchen.

Nadine raises an eyebrow. "So, wait a minute. If I understand everything, you were talking about those chromosome defects in babies. My sister had a baby last year with that. I mean, he's mentally retarded. My sister and her husband are thinking of sending him to one of those institutions for—"

Bridget's face reddens. "No, you can't! I mean… please don't do that to the child. Don't forget when President Kennedy called for a reduction of those confined to residential institutions and asked that methods be found to return the mentally ill and mentally retarded to a more civilized environment."

The dessert arrives, and Bridget realizes the table is still silent. She takes a deep breath. "Look, folks, I'm sorry. I didn't mean to have an outburst like that. It's just that… When I was a child, I had a… family friend who was born lame. His name was Otto." *Otto Theodor.* She takes a sip of wine. "We were best friends. He was two years older than me, and he wore braces on his crooked legs. It was a birth defect that crippled him. Nothing medically could be done. His parents received a letter from the government notifying them of a new institutional program where children like him could go live and receive special training and get the medical supervision they needed."

Nadine nods. "Well, that sounds wonderful, honey. My nephew needs a program exactly like that one."

Bridget slams her fist on the table, and her soufflé collapses. "NO!" She pushes air out of her pursed lips. "I'm sorry. I mean, *please* listen. Otto's father didn't *want* to send him away, but his mother insisted. She loved Otto so much, she wanted to give him every opportunity to be normal. She begged and pleaded with her husband to allow Otto to go, and finally, her husband agreed. It was just a few weeks later when Otto's parents received a little box in the mail. It was Otto's ashes. There was a letter stating that he contracted pneumonia and it consumed him almost immediately. *Please* don't allow your sister to institutionalize her child!" She takes a deep breath and looks around the table at the dumbstruck faces of her companions. *Bollocks.*

After a long pause, Nadine says, "Oh, dear. What happened to your arm there?"

Bridget glances down, realizing her fingernails are pressed into the scar on her left arm, as a tiny drop of blood falls to the white linen tablecloth. "Bollocks. I mean, pardon me. I didn't realize—" She grabs a tissue from her purse and blots her arm.

"Did that happen in—"

Bridget pushes her untouched soufflé toward the center of the table. "I, uh, burned it reaching in the oven when I was a child."

Nadine's brow furrows. "Really? Funny, it doesn't look like a burn. And what an odd place for an oven to—"

"Fine! I got mixed up in a fraternity pledge event gone wrong. It wasn't easy being one of the only women in med school in the early fifties, and the men there often tried to make me the butt of some of their Greek initiations."

Jack pushes away his dessert. "Honey, calm down. Nobody meant anything by it."

"You're right. I'm sorry. Paul, Nadine, I hope you'll forgive me, but I had a really tough day at work. Then on my way home, I had to stop and tend to a young man who was injured and died at the scene. Jack, if you don't mind, I'd really like to go home now. I feel a migraine coming on. It was a lovely nosh-up, folks. Smashing, really. We'll have to do it again sometime." Without waiting for her husband's reply, she stands and grabs her purse. "Jack?"

Jack stands and removes three twenty-dollar bills out of his wallet then tosses them on the table. He shakes Paul's hand. "Goodnight, Paul. Nadine, it was a pleasure to meet you." He nods in her direction then follows Bridget to the foyer and helps her on with her coat. "I'm sorry about this evening, babe. I know this wasn't the best night—"

She waves her hand and says, "Think nothing of it. I just want to go home and have a long bath then go to bed." She steps outside, and the vapor of her breath condensates into tiny puffs of fog.

He opens the car door for her, and she climbs inside. As he gets situated in the driver's seat, she turns the radio knob on and pushes the button to a preset station. The riff to Iron Butterfly's "In-

A-Gadda-Da-Vida" plays, and she stares out the window, bopping her head to the music.

Jack pulls out onto the road then turns down the volume and changes the station to Otis Redding's "Sittin' on the Dock of the Bay." He rests his hand on her thigh. "I thought you had a headache. That loud music's not going to help."

She maintains her gaze outside. "Okay." She reaches in a crevasse underneath the glovebox, grabs a Five Flavor pack of Lifesavers, pops a lime candy in her mouth, then returns the pack to its hiding place.

Jack raises an eyebrow. "What, you're not going to offer me one?"

"You never want one anyway."

"Why do you always hide those things like that?"

"I don't know. It's a habit I picked up as a child, I guess." Her voice trails off, and her thoughts turn to her childhood days...

# # #

21 February 1940

Dear Diary,

Today is my ninth birthday, and you were the first gift I opened. My father keeps a diary, but he calls it a journal, and I want to be just like him when I grow up. He started the habit when he entered university in the Medical Sciences division of Oxford. That's in England. That's also where he learned to speak many of the different languages that he's been teaching me since I was old enough to talk, and that's why I'm starting by writing to you in English today. I always felt it sounded so sophisticated.

Though my parents pretended to be happy today for my sake as I did for theirs, it was not a happy day. You see, just one week ago today, Otto's ashes were sent home. I was so excited when I learned of the new government program for physically deformed children, and I just knew Otto would go there and learn to walk without his crutches.

When I saw the box wrapped in brown paper delivered in the post last week, I was positive it was a gift for my birthday. In fact, I was so certain, I didn't even bother to read the smudged name above the address. I actually thought that perhaps Otto had it sent to me. I pulled the twine off the package and tore open the paper, and that's when a note inside, covered in ash, fell out. I screamed. My parents came running, then they read the note, and they, too, screamed. And at that moment, I knew that my birthday was over before it even began. None of us have the heart to celebrate without Otto, and I can't even imagine living my life without him in it.

P.S. You were a gift from my father. We recently relocated to an attic above a machine shop that is owned by the husband of a nurse who works for a doctor that my father knows. I'm going to hide you in the loose floorboard under my bed. That's where I keep my other secret treasures.

P.P.S. My mother gave me a doll baby. I'm too old to play with doll babies. I didn't want to hurt her feelings, so I'll probably use it as a patient when my father lets me play with his stethoscope and other medical equipment.

# # #

CHAPTER FOUR

Morning light peeks through the cracks in Bridget's eyelids as the hum of Jack's electric shaver draws her from slumber. Yawning, she stretches her arms over her head then rises and pads into the bathroom.

Jack brushes the stubble out of his shaver. "Good morning, sleepyhead." He kisses her cheek.

"Guten Morgen."

"Is that German?"

She yawns. "Sorry. I guess I was still half asleep. I was having a weird dream. Good morning, my love."

"I'll go make the coffee." He closes the door as he leaves, and she showers then styles her hair into its usual taut bun at the nape of her neck.

She applies subtle, neutral-toned makeup to her cognac eyes and pale pink lipstick to her full lips. She dresses in her typical work garb: dark slacks with a sharp crease down the front, a white button-up blouse, and dark, sensible dress shoes. Grabbing her stethoscope and a clean lab coat, she heads downstairs to the kitchen.

Jack offers her a cup, and she takes a sip as her eyes scan the counter. "Thanks. I can't seem to find my keys."

He sets his cup in the sink. "I know. I took another look at your car when I went out for the paper earlier, and there are a couple of dings on the hood. I called Smitty and asked him to come pick it up and take it in to the garage. You can ride into work with me."

She downs the rest of her coffee and sets the cup in the sink. "Okay." She turns on the water and rinses both cups. "Don't forget Beverly won't be here to clean today. She's taking a long weekend because her oldest daughter is in town."

"Aw, I forgot. Do you want to come home and change tonight before we go to your parents' house or head straight over?"

She pulls her coat on, slings her purse over her shoulder, and they step outside. "I'm not sure. Let's play it by ear. I guess it depends on what kind of day I have on the floor."

He opens the car door for her and waits as she gets situated. "I'm going to talk to that veteran this morning and see how he's doing." He gets in and starts the car.

"Thanks. Hopefully that'll help." She flips down the sun visor and finds a stubby pack of Pep-O-Mint Lifesavers, popping one in her mouth. The remaining mints go into her pants pocket.

Jack smiles at her then turns on the radio and pushes the button to the news station.

"... to report that Tallulah Bankhead, the starlet whose offstage performances often rivaled her dramatic roles in theater, film, and television, died yesterday at New York's Mount Sinai Hospital of pneumonia complicated by emphysema. She was sixty-five years old. Last night, Pan Am Flight 217 crashed into the Caribbean Sea off of the coast of Venezuela. The flight, which originated in New York City, was making its final approach to Caracas. All contact with the craft was lost at 9:59 p.m., moments after the control tower gave clearance for the scheduled ten o'clock landing. There were no survivors. In a bit of good news to lighten up this dreary Friday the thirteenth, yesterday, in Washington, D.C., Ethel Kennedy, the widow of U.S. Senator Robert Kennedy, gave birth to a daughter, Rory Elizabeth Katherine Kennedy. Though the child's birth came six months after her father's assassination, it's not likely that she won't hear all about the unforgettable Senator throughout the remainder of her life. Ethel chose the unusual name Rory after King Rory O'Connor who ruled Ireland in the Twelfth Century..."

Bridget pushes the radio button to a music station, and Sonny and Cher's "I Got You Babe" plays. Jacks cuts a sideways glance her way, and she says, "Sorry. There's nothing good about a girl growing up without her father. I just couldn't listen to that."

He raises an eyebrow. "Oh-kaaay... Aww, no. Look. There's some more war protestors." He slows the car and gestures to the group of kids holding anti-Vietnam signs.

Bridget buries her face in her hands. "That's just where they were yesterday. Bollocks. I have to go see the M.E. as soon as we get to work. I want to see if that lad died from his injuries or something else."

Jack rests his hand on her knee, and her fingers find their way to his and intertwine. He says, "I understand that President Eisenhower's grandson is marrying Richard Nixon's daughter in a few days down in Manhattan."

"Oh. That's nice."

"I thought it was interesting. I never—"

"I'm sorry, can we please just not talk right now? I've got a lot on my mind. I've got to deal with that teenager's death, and I need to do some research for my brain tumor patient. I'm starting to think it's not a skull base meningioma at all but an ependymoma."

"Oh, no. Really?"

"Yeah, I think so. I'll need to research a couple of more things before I put him through any more diagnostics. He's already so iffy about having me be his surgeon, I certainly can't let him know I'm questioning his original doctor's diagnosis."

After several minutes of silence, Jack pulls into the hospital parking lot and turns off the car. "Let me know if I can help. I'll be glad to talk to your German patient and let him know what a top-notch surgeon he has." He makes his way around the car and holds her door open as she steps out.

She pops another Pep-O-Mint into her mouth and grabs her lab coat. "Thanks, but I don't think that'll help. It might make things worse, if you know what I mean. Nepotism and all."

"Sure, hon. I understand." He pulls open the foyer door for her, and they walk into the building together then part ways at the elevator.

Gene Autry's "Rudolph the Red-Nosed Reindeer" pipes through the hospital's sound system, and Bridget waves to Carol in the receptionist station then boards the empty elevator.

As the doors merge together, a hand sticks between them, forcing them to separate. "Excuse me. Going up." The doors open, and Dr. Paul Taylor steps inside. He presses a button and says, "Oh, g'morning, Doctor. I hope your headache's better today."

Bridget forces a smile. *It just returned.* "Thank you."

"Thanks again for dinner last night. Nadine thinks you're the greatest. She's coming up to meet me for lunch today. Would you care to join us?"

Not if you were the last people on earth. "Actually, I'll have to take a raincheck. I've got a busy day and a lot of research to do. Oh, here's my floor. Good day, Doctor." She steps off and hurries down the corridor.

When she reaches her office, she hangs up her purse and peacoat then plunges her hand into an urn, fishing for a pack of Wild Cherry Lifesavers. Popping one in her mouth, she returns the pack then sits at her desk and dials zero on the phone. "Yes, this is Dr. Castle. Connect me to the M.E., please."

"Medical Examiner."

"Hi, Dr. Hamilton. It's Dr. Castle. I'm calling about the teenage boy they brought in last evening."

"I was just filling out his paperwork."

"What do you have?"

"Let's see... His name was Ronald Haynes. Nineteen years old. I talked to his mother last night. Been estranged from his family for two and a half years. He dropped out of school after tenth grade. Mom said he had a history of drug use including marijuana, L.S.D., cocaine, and heroine. She said her husband asked him to leave after they caught the boy stealing money from the wall safe. Family hasn't heard from him since, other than when a neighbor's daughter got a letter from him a few months later, saying that he was living in a commune over in upstate New York."

"What a shame. Another wasted life cut short by drugs."

"Actually, he was clean."

"What?"

"His tox screen came back clean. He was negative for opiates, amphetamines, alcohol, and barbiturates. He only had a negligible amount of cannabis."

"So, his cause of death?"

"Blunt force cranial trauma. Looks like he was struck twice. The kid didn't stand a chance. He had cerebral contusions as well as intracranial bleeding and intraparenchymal hemorrhage. The medics told me you witnessed the event. You want me to make the call over to Internal Affairs?"

"Yes, please, and you might talk with Dave about preparing for a coroner's inquest. I've got a hunch they're going to deny any wrongdoing happened if the officer I spoke to yesterday is any indication of the department. Let me know when you're ready for me to sign off on the paperwork."

"I'll send it up to your office as soon as it's done. It'll be there by Monday."

"Good enough. Have a good weekend, Ernie."

"You too, Doctor."

Bridget cradles the receiver and dabs the corners of her eyes with a tissue. *Poor lad.* Her thoughts turn to the past...

# # #

5 March 1940

Liebes Tagebuch (Dear Diary),

Today I'm missing the place of my birth, so I'm writing to you in German. I was born in Heusenstamm, Germany, but we haven't lived there in ages. Heusenstamm is near Frankfurt on the River Bieber. The war has caused us to have to relocate several times.

Seven months ago, we moved to Kraków, Poland; and last week, we moved to Avignon, France. I believe the only reason we were so successful in relocating is that my father and I are so fluent in different languages and he gets along so well with everyone. (It drives my mother crazy when we speak to each other in front of her and she can't understand us.) My father is such a kind man, he easily makes friends wherever he goes. He's always been of the belief that a stranger is a friend he hasn't met yet. I'm so glad he's here to protect my mother and me from any harm. At the rate things are changing all over Europe, I wonder where we'll move next.

We're planning on traveling to Hong Kong soon, but I'm not sure when "soon" is. My parents have a friend who used to sell medical supplies to my father's office back in Germany, and he's supposed to be making arrangements for us to travel with his family. It's so exciting to think I might get to live in an English-speaking country and have the opportunity to use proper English every day, even in school. I guess my poor mother will feel lost, but my father and I will enjoy it immensely, I'm certain. At any rate, it will be wonderful to get away from this war.

No matter where we are, it's terrifying to look up into the sky when those loud planes pass overhead and wonder if they're going to drop a bomb on us. About a year and a half ago, a lot of Jewish children were separated from their parents in a transport program called Kindertransport. The children were sent from Germany, Czechoslovakia, and Austria to live with volunteer families in England. My father said this was a generous gesture, but he fears the children might never see their families again. He says he doesn't think things will get so bad that families should ever have to be separated.

I can't imagine ever living anywhere without my family. With all the relocating we've done, everywhere seeing only faces of strangers, my parents are surely the dearest things to my heart.

# # #

Bridget shakes her head as she forces her memories to stay in the past where they belong. She stands and pulls on her lab coat then buttons it. She hangs her stethoscope around her neck and shoves her keys in her pocket then turns off the light and heads down the corridor to start her research…

* * *

CHAPTER FIVE

After lunch in her office, Bridget heads to the fifth floor. Approaching Room 529, she takes a deep breath and puts on her best plastic smile. She knocks then enters the room. "Ah, Mr. Gunter Hetzel, good afternoon. How are you feeling today?" She plucks the chart from the end of the patient's bed and scans it.

The patient's English is peppered with his native German timbre; and even lying down, his imposing stature intimidates her a little. "How do you think I am? I've flown 3,579 miles around the world, away from my family, my friends, and my own doctor, to have my skull drilled open, only to find out that a *nurse* is going to be operating on me."

Bridget replaces the chart and situates her stethoscope stems in her ears. "Herr Hetzel, I can assure you I am highly qualified to perform the surgery you require. Roll over and let me listen to your back, please."

He huffs as he turns on his side, and she places the stethoscope against his ribs. "That's good. Continue breathing normally, please." She moves the stethoscope to various areas of his back. "Very good. Now, if I can please have you roll toward me, I'd like to listen to the other side."

As the patient rolls toward her, his gown opens, exposing a large, dark, triangular scar covering the side of his right buttock. Her knees grow weak, and her head spins as the flash of a long-forgotten memory floods back...

Bridget held her mother's hand, walking through the strange town, when some commotion ahead caused her to drop her diary. "Ack! Wait, Mama!" She stopped to rescue the book when the throngs of people rushing by drove her to her knees, and she and her mother were separated. Her focus remained on her beloved book, now soiled with a muddy footprint, when a bone-chilling guttural scream pierced her ears...

"Well, are you just going to stand there staring at my Arsch — *ass* — or can I cover up?"

Bridget gasps and snaps out of her daydream. "Oh. I'm sorry. I was just calculating your heartbeat and lung capacity..." *I hope this line of codswallop sounds more believable to him than it does to me.* "...to see if you're strong enough to withstand a P.E.T. scan."

"A what?"

"A P.E.T. scan. That stands for positron emission tomography. The technologist will have you drink a cup of radioactive sodium iodide, then you'll lie still for about a half hour so the machine can produce images of your intracranial tumor."

"My doctor back home already did all the tests I need."

"Your physician did do a battery of tests, but those were nearly a month ago. I'll be repeating a number of those to compare to the original results to look for any growth or changes." She sticks a thermometer in his mouth and wraps a blood pressure cuff around his arm then pumps the bulb as she takes a reading. "So, tell me about your family. Are you married?"

"No. I was engaged, but when I learned I had a brain tumor, she said it was too much for her to handle."

"Aww, I'm sorry. But you're still young. Twenty-four, right?"

"Yes."

"I'm sure your parents wish they could be here with you."

"Actually, my mother died when I was a child. Suicide. My father blamed himself, so he never remarried."

"You have my condolences. Are you close to your father?"

"Yes. He wasn't around much when I was little, but after Mutter took the pills, he spent a good deal of time with me. He wanted to accompany me here, but his doctor won't allow him to fly. He has bad lungs. He was exposed to toxic chemicals during the war when he was a soldier."

She bristles. "Oh. I'm very sorry to hear that. Well, soon we'll have you fixed up as good as new, and you'll be able to return to Cologne before you know it."

"Danke." *Thank you.*

"Nichts zu danken." *Nothing to thank for.*

The patient raises an eyebrow. "Sprichst du Deutsch?"

"Yes, I speak a little German." Bridget scribbles some notes on Gunter's chart. "Herr Hetzel, you have a slight fever. I'm going to have the nurse bring you some Paracetamol, and I'd like you to keep drinking fluids. If your fever's down tonight, we'll get that P.E.T. scan taken care of first thing tomorrow. Make sure you get plenty of rest. We want to get you healthy so you can go home to der Vater – *your father*. I'm sure he misses you as much as you miss him."

"Danke."

"You're welcome." She leaves, closing the door behind her. Tiny beads of perspiration dot her brow, and she rushes to the ladies' room. She washes her hands then pats her face with a damp paper towel. *What is it about that man that makes me so nervous?*

An announcement over the P.A. system interrupts her thoughts: *"Dr. Castle, Dr. Bridget Castle, please report to Room 502, STAT."*

"Oh, that's Craig!" She steps out of the restroom and races down the corridor. A red light flashes above the patient's door, and the loud buzzing at the nurses' station causes her to wince. She bursts into the room, and a nurse stands arm's length from the patient.

Silent tears cascade down the patient's face, and he holds a scalpel against his carotid artery. "I swear, Doc, if you take one more step, I'm going to slice my throat!"

Bridget pulls the nurse's arm and, in a soothing tone, says, "Kelly, why don't you leave Mr. Barnaby and me alone."

Kelly's eyes dart between the doctor and the young man. Hesitating, she backs against the wall and says, "Yes, ma'am." She spins on her heel and flees.

Bridget takes a step toward the bed. "Craig, you don't really want to hurt yourself. Where'd you get the scalpel?"

"One of the orderlies dropped a tray on the floor when they had me in the whirlpool downstairs. It caused such a commotion, no one saw me take it."

"But—"

"Don't you see? I'm invisible now! No one can see me with these... these stumps!" He throws back the sheet to reveal his amputated legs then returns the instrument to his neck. "My girl broke up with me as soon as she saw me. My mother cries every time she visits. My life's already over anyway; why not just let me end it?"

Bridget takes another slow step toward him. "Craig, you're only nineteen. Your life's just beginning. With your surgery next week—"

"With that surgery, I *might* get the use of my left arm. So, what! I'll still only be half a man!"

Her face flames, and she narrows her eyes. "You're not half a man! I'm sorry you lost your legs, but you're not nearly as bad off as a lot of the casualties of war that I've seen! I just treated a young man last month who lost both arms and was paralyzed from the waist down. He'll never write his own name again, never wipe his own ass, and can't even shit without someone manually manipulating his bowels!"

"Yeah, but I don't—"

She advances closer. "Shut up! I'm still talking! I'm sick of hearing about what you *don't* have! Let me tell you what you *do* have... You have full use of your right arm. You're going to have full use of your left arm after your surgery next week. You've got two parents and a sister who loves you. You've got a good-working brain when you aren't feeling so bloody sorry for yourself." She steps closer. "Your dick works! Your organs are in perfect condition. And your legs were lost just below the knee, meaning you're the perfect candidate for prosthetic limbs." She steps closer and snatches the scalpel from his grasp. "Your *only* problem, Craig Barnaby, is that you're stuck in the middle of that damn pity party where you're the guest of honor. As soon as you get through feeling sorry for yourself, maybe you'll see how many blessings you really have!"

Craig's face turns ashen. "Uh, Doc..."

"What?"

"You're bleeding."

Bridget looks down as a steady trickle of blood squishes out of her clenched right fist and splatters on the floor. She opens her hand, and the scalpel tings as it hits the tile. She grabs a wad of tissues and presses them into her palm then kicks the instrument toward the door. "Uh, please ring for the nurse." Her knees buckle, and she melts onto the chair beside his bed in slow motion. Her skin turns pallid, and the room spins on a tilted axis.

Kelly rushes in and stops in her tracks. "Dr. Castle?"

Bridget squeezes her eyes closed and nods. "It's okay, Kelly. Please pick up the scalpel off the floor and ring Housekeeping to clean up this mess. Can you see if Dr. Redding down in E.R. can see me right away? I'm going to need about a dozen sutures."

"Right away, Doctor."

Kelly rushes out of the room, and Craig's eyes brim with tears. "I... I'm really sorry, Doc. I shouldn't have— I didn't mean for you to—"

Bridget's eyes remain closed as she applies pressure to her wound. "It's okay. Think nothing of it." Her thoughts turn to another time and place when she encountered so much of her own blood...

# # #

3 June 1940

Drogi Pamiętniku (Dear Diary),

Today I'm writing to you in Polish. My father says we won't be safe in France much longer. Yesterday morning, I was helping my mother pack some of our favorite things so we would be prepared to leave whenever my father decides where we can go. We've lost so much in all our moves. We had such a large house and garden when I was a small child, filled with so much beautiful furniture and artwork. But now, we take only what we can't live without.

While I was helping pack a crystal bread plate that belonged to my great-grandmother, I stumbled and fell. I didn't want the plate to drop, so I kept it clutched in my hand as I went down. But as I hit the ground, the plate broke in half and sliced my left arm. At first, my mother was so upset about her platter that she didn't even notice all the blood.

My father had to give me twenty-four stitches in the bathroom. He said my ulnar artery was nicked and that I was lucky it wasn't severed because that would've required emergency surgery. My arm is in a sling that keeps my hand elevated higher than my heart, and he says I'll have to wear this for several days. When my mother realized how badly I was injured, she felt terrible. My arm still hurts.

# # #

"Dr. Castle, did you hear me?"

Bridget opens her eyes. "I'm sorry, Kelly. No, I didn't."

"I said Dr. Redding is tied up with a car accident. But Dr. Taylor can see you right away."

Bollocks. Not him. "Okay."

"Do you need a wheelchair?"

Bridget stands. "Don't be silly. I'll walk. Craig, you think about what I said, okay?"

"Sure, Doc. Uh, I'm real sorry you got hurt."

Bridget dismisses his concern with a wave of her hand as she heads for the door.

Kelly asks, "Do you want me to call your husband?"

"No. He'll find out soon enough. There's no need to bother him with it now."

* * *

CHAPTER SIX

After tying off eleven stitches, Paul wraps Bridget's hand with gauze. "You're lucky this wasn't deeper. You might have ended up with nerve damage."

Bridget watches a few lonely hairs on the top of his head dance as he moves, and she restrains herself from giggling. "Yeah, but I'm still probably going to have to postpone a surgery I have on the books for Tuesday. Of course, the surgery is on the patient who caused this, so I guess he'll understand."

Paul chuckles. "I predict these sutures will be ready to come out by Tuesday. Wednesday at the latest."

"That's what I expected too. That'll work out perfectly. I've got a craniotomy next Thursday, and I don't want anything to delay it."

"Well, there you are." Bridget and Paul turn to the door as Jack struts in. "I've been calling all over for you. I went down on the floor, and Mr. Barnaby told me what happened. Are you okay?"

She hops off the exam table, holding her injured hand to her shoulder. "Yeah, it's nothing. Are you ready to go?"

Jack shakes Paul's hand. "Is she telling me the truth?"

Paul pats Bridget's shoulder. "Yes, siree. She'll be good as new next week. Say, Nadine was wondering if you two might want to join us this weekend out at the beach house. I know it's too cold to take the boat out, but—"

Bridget shoots Jack *the look,* and Jack says, "Aw, I wish you would've asked earlier, but I just committed to help my in-laws with their rooftop decorations. It's going to be an all-day event."

Bridget snuggles into Jack's waiting arms and says, "Yes, and Mum and I still have to do our Christmas shopping. Sorry, Paul."

Paul nods. "I understand. It's a busy time of year for everyone. Maybe after the first."

Bridget pulls Jack toward the door. "Yes. We'll definitely consider the possibility after the new year." She rolls her eyes, and they hurry toward the express elevator. "I just need to get my coat and bag, and I'll be ready to go."

They step on the elevator, and he pushes the button. "Are you really all right? There's no nerve damage, is there?"

"No, I'm really fine. I was so worried the lad was going to off himself right there, I didn't even realize what I was doing."

"He told me you read him the riot act. And he said you really gave him something to think about. I think he's finally ready to turn himself around. I guess seeing you covered in all that blood was his watershed moment."

"Good. Then this was worth it." They reach her office, and she hands him her keys.

He unlocks the door and helps her on with her coat. She gives him her purse, and they lock up and head to the main elevator. As he pushes the call button, she looks up to the floor indicator. "I hate taking this lift every evening. It's always so crowded this time of day. It makes me feel claustrophobic, almost like I'm packed into a cattle car with an entire herd."

The doors open, they squeeze on board the full car, and she raises her eyebrows to stress her point. When they reach the first floor, the receptionist waves, and Bridget says, "Have a good weekend, Carol."

"Thanks, Dr. Castle. I hope your hand feels better."

Bridget's muscles tighten. "Everyone here's going to know what happened by Monday; you wait and see." She nods to

President Johnson's photo as they pass, and Jack unlocks the car and holds the door open for her.

After he gets in and starts the motor, he turns on the news.

"...and today, President Johnson and Mexican President Gustavo Diaz Ordaz formally ended the Chamizal dispute between the United States and Mexico when the waters of the Rio Grande were diverted into a new concrete canal. The presidential envoy traveled to the border of El Paso and Juárez to celebrate the completion of the Rio Grande channel, and they stood at the center of the newly constructed Santa Fe International Bridge..."

Bridget flips the radio off. "Can we please not do news right now?"

Jack squeezes her shoulder. "You want to talk about something?"

"No. I just have a headache. I'd like if we could just enjoy some silence for a while, if that's okay."

"Sure, babe. Anything you want. Do you want me to call and cancel dinner with your parents? I can tell them you need to rest."

"No. Let's just head right over and get it over with. I'd like to get home early and relax."

"Of course. Whatever you say."

Bridget reaches in the ashtray and grabs a roll of Butter Rum Lifesavers. She pops one in her mouth then returns the candy to its hiding place. She pulls the bun out of her hair then leans against the window and watches the colorful Christmas lights in peoples' windows and outside their homes pass at forty miles per hour...

# # #

17 December 1940

Lief Dagboek (Dear Diary),

Today I'm going to try to write to you in Dutch. I'm sorry I haven't written in a while. We left France about six months ago. We got out just before Italy invaded, and we moved to Belgium for a short time before my father decided we would be safer here in the Netherlands. He and I have been learning the language since we arrived.

I should be grateful that so many people have been so helpful and kind to us through our tribulations, but it's difficult sometimes not to feel good and sorry for myself. If Otto were still here, he'd surely tell me to focus on the positive and ignore the adverse. He was good inside like that. He was a lot like my father. I wish I could be more like them, but inside, I feel nothing but hate for that Führer! He's taken everything from everyone! How can I find anything good when the sights, sounds, and smells of war are everywhere around us? I miss my friends, my house, my kitten, and especially my brother! Plus, I'm tired of sharing a bedroom with my parents.

Hanukkah starts in one week, and even though my parents always attempt to make it a big deal for me, this year, I feel we'll have little reason to celebrate. I remember a couple of years ago, I went with my mother to visit a sick friend, and their house had a beautiful fir tree decorated with colorful baubles that glistened when the glow from the fireplace hit them. I know it's unlikely to ever happen, but I've always wished I could have a tree like that in my own house someday.

# # #

Jack kisses Bridget's cheek. "We're here." He turns the car off and winks at her. "Does your hand hurt much?"

Her cheeks puff as she blows air through her pursed lips. "No. Not much."

"You look like you're lost in thought."

"I guess I was just daydreaming. Thinking I really need to get my Christmas shopping done this weekend. Are we getting a tree this year?"

"Sure, if you want to. Last year, you said we weren't home long enough to enjoy it."

"I know, but I kind of miss it. I think we should."

A tall man with thick, grey hair taps the hood. "Hey, you two, come on in out of the cold."

He opens Bridget's door, and she stands and snuggles into his arms. "Dad, it's so good to see you."

He kisses her forehead, and his eyes crinkle as his smile encompasses his face. "We just saw you at church last Sunday. You act like we haven't seen each other all year. Hey, what happened to your hand?"

Jack walks around the car and shakes the man's hand. "It's always a pleasure to see you, Geoffrey. She had a little accident at work today."

Heading inside, Geoffrey says, "Oh? Do I need to take a look at it? I can get me bag."

Bridget says, "No, it's fine. I just needed a few sutures."

A petite woman rounds the corner, wiping her hands on her apron. "Who's got sutures?"

Jack kisses the woman's cheek. "Good evening, Ada."

Bridget heads to the kitchen, the others at her heels. "Mm, something smells scrummy, Mum."

Jack sniffs the air. "Yes, delicious, indeed."

Bridget winks at him. "I just had to take a few stitches in my hand, Mum. It's not a big deal. They'll be out by Wednesday."

Ada picks up a wooden spoon and stirs a pot of chicken and dumplings. "Not a big deal? Of course, it's a big deal!"

Geoffrey swats Ada's behind. "Stop being such a worry wart, Mummy dear. These things often happen, working at hospital. How'd you cut yourself, love?"

"I have a patient who got sent home from Vietnam after he fell on a grenade. They couldn't do much for him at the V.A., but I think I can help. He lost his legs, and he was feeling awfully sorry for himself. Somehow in aqua therapy today, he got hold of a scalpel."

Ada gasps. "And he tried to attack you!"

Bridget looks to Geoffrey and rolls her eyes. "No, of course not. He did threaten to kill himself, but I talked him down. When I grabbed the instrument from him, I nicked myself, that's all."

Ada raises an eyebrow. Geoffrey wraps his arm around Bridget's shoulders and says, "That's right, love. Remember when I worked at Radcliffe and was performing the abscess surgery in '32? The lights flickered, and I dropped the lancet. It pierced me leg and tore me new trousers. I still have the scar just above me knee."

The family laughs, and Jack hugs Bridget to his side. In a confidential tone, he says, "Your accent is so much stronger when we visit your parents."

She raises an eyebrow and winks. Under her breath, she says, "And you don't think that's sexy?"

He covers his mouth and coughs. "You're a saucy little tart."

She giggles, and Ada spoons up four bowls of dumplings. "All right, let's eat before it gets cold."

The group sits in the dining room and devours their dinner. Jack and Geoffrey help themselves to seconds, and Ada smooths Bridget's hair. "Lovey, we've put the Christmas tree up, but we saved the angel for you to put on. We know that's your favorite part. Shall we go on in there while these two gluttons continue to stuff their cakeholes?"

Bridget giggles. "Mummy, you always know how to bring a smile to my face." They head to the parlor, and Bridget unwraps the aged Christmas angel. "I always loved this when I was young. I'm so glad you kept it."

"Well, of course, we kept it. I know how much she means to you, and you're our angel."

Bridget places the angel on the tree then stands back to admire it. "It's beautiful. Oh, look at that crooked little ornament. I forgot all about that. Wasn't I about fourteen when I made that one?"

"Well, let's see..." Ada turns the ornament over in her wrinkled hand and reads the date. "Nineteen forty-five. Yes, you were fourteen that year."

Bridget lowers her voice. "Do you know we had dinner with some stupid little twit the other night, and when she realized I was from England, she actually had the nerve to ask me what it was like living through the Blitz."

Ada's hand flies to her chest, and she rolls her eyes. "Oh, no. Well, we needn't think about such unpleasantries."

Bridget stands back and eyes the tree again. "I know what's missing..." She heads to the fireplace and counts the bricks. "Let's see... Seven up, four across..." She removes a brick and reaches in the hole behind it, pulling out a red glass cardinal. "Here, let's not forget Chirpy Bird." She locates the perfect spot for the treasure on the tree then replaces the brick.

Ada provides an understanding smile. "You and those little hidey-holes. You always loved those, didn't you?"

"Yes, I believe I did..."

After the women visit and rearrange Christmas ornaments and the men play chess, Bridget yawns and stretches her arms over her head. "Oh, dear. I'm absolutely knackered. I think we'd better head home now, my love." She kisses Jack's cheek, and he stands.

He downs the rest of his hot tea and says, "I guess you're right. If we stay any longer, your dad'll only beat me again, and I'll have to sign over the deed to the house."

Geoffrey stands, his belly jiggling as he laughs. "That's right, mate. You'd better stop while you're ahead. As it is, you owe me about a thousand quid." He winks at Bridget.

Jack shakes the man's hand. "Will you take a raincheck this time?"

"Ah, I guess me daughter won't let you run too far away without paying up. I'll let you slide just this once."

Bridget links her arm through Jack's. "Mum, did you want to go shopping with me tomorrow?"

Ada kisses Bridget's cheek. "Oh, Lovey, I'm sorry, but I promised to help sell Christmas biscuits at the church's bake sale."

"That's right. I forgot about that." Bridget plucks Jack's wallet from his pocket and offers her mother a five-dollar bill. "Please buy us a couple of boxes. Jack, get my jumper, please, love."

Ada holds her hands up. "That's far too much. They're only fifty cents a box."

Jack helps Bridget with her coat then replaces his wallet and squeezes her to his side. "That's fine, Ada, just donate the rest. We'll see you both at church Sunday." He kisses Ada's cheek.

Ada returns his kiss then hugs Bridget. "You be careful, daughter. We love you. Both of you."

Geoffrey holds the front door open. "That's right. We'll see you Sunday. Goodnight."

Bridget and Jack simultaneously say, "Goodnight." They head out to the car, and he opens the door for her.

They start driving, and Jack pats her thigh. "I just adore your mom's chicken and dumplings. Did you know she was making those?"

"No. I haven't talked to her since Wednesday. I was kind of hoping she'd made bubble and squeak. You sure stuffed your belly."

He chuckles. "I told you, dumplings are my favorite. If my mom cooked like that when I was growing up, I'd have never left home."

"Mum didn't make dumplings until I was in college."

"Oh?"

"Yes. When we moved to Atlanta, the Welcome Wagon ladies brought us a big pot of chicken and dumplings. We'd never heard of such a dish, and Dad fell in love with them immediately. So, Mum found a cooking class and took lessons. And, ever since then, Dad expects chicken and dumplings at least once a month."

"Wow. Well, she's certainly mastered the art of Southern cooking. Her pecan pie is my other favorite. If we ever get divorced,

I'm getting custody of your mum." They laugh, then he flips on the radio as The Beatles belt out "Hey Jude."

The air leaves Bridget's lungs, and her face puckers into an angry scowl. She snaps the radio knob. "Turn that bloody rubbish off!"

Jack raises an eyebrow. "Rubbish? I thought you loved the Fab Four."

"Not *that* song."

His brow creases with curiosity. He rotates the knob back on, and the chorus plays. "What's wrong with this one?"

She elbows his arm hard and pulls the knob off the radio as she cuts off the power. "I said NO!"

He raises an eyebrow. "You're not kidding, are you?"

Tears form in her eyes, and she turns toward the window. "No. I'm not."

"What's wrong with 'Hey Jude'?"

She spins toward him, her face aflame. "Stop saying Jude!"

His eyes narrow. "Why? What's wrong with you?"

"I just don't like the word Jude, all right? It means Jew."

"I think it's actually a song about John Lennon's kid. I heard that's his nickname or something."

"It's the German word for Jew."

"Are you serious? That's not even pronounced the same, is it?"

She rolls her eyes and purses her lips. "In German, it's pronounced *yoo-deh,* but it's spelled the same, and it means Jew."

"Oh. Sorry." He presses his lips together as he maintains his focus on the road.

After a long moment of silence, she lets out a deep sigh. "No. I'm sorry. I just saw a lot of people wearing those stars with Jude printed on them when I was a lass. A lot of the children came over to England in the Kindertransport."

"But I didn't think they had to wear those yet when—"

Her nostrils flare. "Are you seriously questioning what I witnessed firsthand while your ass was sitting over here in the middle of Farmland, U.S.A.?"

He shakes his head. "No. No, not at all. Sorry, hon." His voice lowers to a mumble. "I lived in downtown Baltimore. It wasn't quite a farm."

"What?"

"Nothing. I'm sorry."

She folds her arms and sniffles as she gazes out the window...

# # #

25 December 1943

Dear Diary,

It's shortly after midnight, and I know the ink is going to be smeared by my tears. I don't think I'll ever be able to stop crying! Four nights ago, on the first night of Hanukkah, my father gave me a little glass cardinal. It was the most beautiful thing, and we named it Chirpy Bird. My mother said we were silly, but she still laughed with us when we made bird calls. It was the best night ever.

The next morning, a loud, urgent knock came at the door. We didn't know who it was, but I just knew in my gut that it would be bad. My father told my mother and me to hide behind a secret panel in the back of the broom closet, and we stayed there hugging each other for what seemed like hours. We don't know how they located us, but we heard the soldiers ask my father for help. They knew he was a surgeon, and they said they had a friend who had been shot and needed assistance. We heard the man moaning in pain, saying he didn't want any filthy Jew to touch him and that he'd rather die, but the other soldiers insisted.

My father operated on him on our kitchen table. My mother and I remained as quiet as church mice as we listened to the whole thing, and the soldiers said that if their friend didn't make it, they'd shoot my father right then and there.

Nearly an hour later, we listened as my father sewed up the man, and the other soldiers cheered. Then they fired a shot – I imagine at my father – and we heard the door slam closed. After several more hours of silence, my mother and I felt it was safe to leave our hiding spot, so we crawled out of the closet and were greeted with blood splattered everywhere! We found the spent bullet my father removed in a tin cup with some bloody gauze and his surgical extractors. The contents of his medical bag were strewn about, and a spray of blood covered the back wall.

Because my mother is nearly six months pregnant, she swooned and nearly passed out. I don't believe we'll ever see my father again, and now I'm concerned for my mother's health too. How much more do we have to lose before everything's gone?

# # #

Jack pulls into the driveway and squeezes the back of Bridget's neck. "Babe, we're home. Am I forgiven?"

She laces her fingers through his. "I'm sorry. I shouldn't have snapped at you like that."

He kisses the back of her hand. "There's nothing to forgive. You had a left-footed day, and you had every right to snap. I love you, my darling."

She cups his face in her good hand and gives him a long smooch. "Flattery will get you everywhere..."

* * *

CHAPTER SEVEN

The next morning, Bridget wakes when the doorbell rings. She pulls on her bathrobe and slides her feet into her slippers then heads downstairs. As Jack closes the front door, she raises an eyebrow. "Morning. Who was here?"

He kisses her cheek and heads to the kitchen. "Smitty brought the Mustang back. It looks good as new." He pours two cups of coffee then sits at the table and cracks open the newspaper. He scans the page for a moment then knits his brow. "Oh, no. A Colonel Francis McGouldrick went missing when his B-57 collided with another American plane during a night strike over Laos. Aww, poor guy's only thirty-six years old. He has a wife and five daughters."

She sits across from him and slurps her coffee. "Bollocks. I hate war with such a passion."

"I know you do, babe. We all do. You want some breakfast?"

"If I say yes, you're not going to respond with, 'Me, too, why don't you make us some?' are you?"

He chuckles. "You know me too well. I'll cook. It won't be as good as yours, but I know you're limited with your injury."

She stands. "Thanks. I'll have dippy eggs and soldiers, please, love. And maybe some bangers?"

"Okay, soft-boiled with toast strips for you, and scrambled for me. And sausage for two. I guess I can manage that." He stands and opens the refrigerator.

"I never doubted it." She blows a kiss in the air as she makes her way to the stairs. "I'll go shower and get dressed. I want to hit the stores before they get too crowded." She takes one step up then does an abrupt U-turn and makes a beeline for the sink. She opens the lower cabinet and pulls out a rubber dishwashing glove then fumbles through the junk drawer until she locates a roll of masking tape. "I almost forgot... I need you to help me seal up my hand, please..."

After breakfast, Bridget takes her plate and egg cups to the sink then kisses Jack's cheek. "I'll be back before dinner. Maybe we can go get a pizza or something." She straightens the belt of her drop-waist dress, admiring the brown paisley design, then smooths her tights. Her boot heels click as she heads toward the door.

"Sure, anything you like." He follows and helps her on with her coat then hangs her purse over her shoulder. "Are you sure you don't want me to come along and carry your bags for you? I don't want you to use that hand."

"I'll be fine. Besides, I don't need you snooping and trying to see what I buy you before Christmas."

He wraps his arms around her waist and kisses her forehead. "All right. I just might find some secrets of my own around here today. Maybe I'll head over to your parents' house and see if there's any chicken and dumplings left. Drive safely."

She rolls her eyes and waves as she hurries through the crisp, cold air to her car. She backs out of the driveway then pops a hidden Wint-O-Green Lifesaver in her mouth and flips on the radio.

"...Protests and student strikes at the University of Panama that followed the military takeover of the Central American nation hit their climax early this morning when the nation's de facto dictator and Commander of the Panamanian National Guard, Omar Torrijos, sent the Guard's red beret troops in to close the campus. The troops arrived around two this morning and began occupation of all buildings, marking the first time that the university has been seized by the military..."

She pushes a pre-set station button, and the chorus to Van Morrison's "Brown Eyed Girl" plays. Her heart flutters. *I remember when Papa used to call me his little brown-eyed girl...*

# # #

3 July 1943

Querido Diario (Dear Diary),

Tonight, I'm writing to you in Spanish because that's the language my father and I used for our private talk today. As you know, we've been here in the Netherlands for the past three years which is the longest we've stayed anywhere since this dreadful war started. It's also the largest place we've lived in since we left Germany.

We've been cramped in this little cottage behind a medical office belonging to the Good Doctor Van Den Boom who befriended my father when they were medical students together. There's a bedroom where I sleep on a mattress at the foot of my parents' bed, then a bathroom with a sink and commode (we sponge bathe in the sink on most days, and on the weekends when the office is closed, there's a washtub that we can use and pour into the floor drain to get a hot bath). The kitchen is the largest of the three rooms, and once a week, my parents send me there to read or listen to the radio while they spend time alone in the bedroom. (They don't realize I know what they're doing!)

Anyway, today, my father took me to the kitchen to talk while my mother took a nap. He asked that we speak in Spanish so she wouldn't understand us if she woke. I've been hearing them argue a lot recently when they think I'm asleep, and I feared he might be telling me they were getting a divorce. (I actually knew someone back in Germany whose parents got a divorce. It was a dreadful ordeal.) What my father told me was not as frightful, but it was just as shocking. He told me I was going to be a big sister! I guess with the war still going strong and with us having to live in hiding, it's just about the worst timing for this to happen. I could tell he did not think it was a good idea, so I held back my enthusiasm.

I think he thought my guarded reaction meant that I was worried my parents wouldn't love me as much, and he assured me they both had enough love to go around. He even told me, no matter if the baby was a boy or girl, I'd always be his first little brown-eyed girl.

When we were alone, he used to always call me that when I was younger until, one day, he just stopped. Come to think of it, I can't remember him calling me that since we learned of Otto's death. I think a big piece of his heart died with Otto. So, you see why I can't possibly let him know how excited I am about this baby? Perhaps this will be just the thing we need to help all our hearts heal after losing Otto, and it will give us something to smile about during this time of such upheaval and uncertainty.

P.S. In case you don't know it, Dear Diary, since I've spent so much time alone in the kitchen, I recently located a hole in the wall behind the ice box. I've now moved you and my other treasures there where you will be safe. Before that, I was hiding you and my other special things in a cigar box in the top of the closet.

# # #

Bridget parallel parks around the corner from Faneuil Hall then inspects her face in the rearview mirror. She fans her red-rimmed eyes and blinks away her tears. *Can't believe I was crying and didn't even realize.* She takes a deep breath, grabs her purse, and steps out of the car.

As she heads down the sidewalk, a ruckus at the corner causes her ears to perk. *What's going on?*

A chorus of chants of "We don't give a damn for Uncle Sam! Bring the G.I.s home from Vietnam!" grows louder as she nears the cross-street. Shrill sirens approaching from behind her cause her to jump and nearly fall as three police cruisers pull up to the commotion.

She freezes in place as the cops jump out of their cars and attempt to break up the congregation of anti-war youth. The kids stop chanting when a girl bows up her chest to a policeman and shouts, "Bombing for peace is like fucking for virginity, pig!" She spits in his face. The officer grabs her arm and twists it behind her back, forcing her to her knees. She starts a refrain of "Hell no, we won't go!" and others soon join her, drowning out all voices of any peace officers attempting to do their jobs.

An officer gets on the P.A. system of his squad car and says, "All right, that's enough! You are not allowed to gather here. You can either go peacefully, or you can all spend the night in jail."

Several protestors charge the policemen, yelling, "Leave us alone, pigs! We have the right to be heard!" and, "The Man can take us away, but he can't keep us down!" Soon, many of them throw their signs through the storefront windows, and the sound of smashing glass and excited hoots and howls drown out the police's attempt to subdue the mob.

Bridget takes a step backward. *This won't end well. Those kids outnumber the cops by at least four to one.* She reconsiders her plans for the day when the earsplitting, thunderous purr of more than a dozen motorcycles slows to a stop near the turmoil. *I need to get out of here!*

She spins on her heel and smacks into the chest of a bearded, leather-clad hooligan wearing a patch over his left eye. His stench of beer and body odor coax a bit of vomit to her throat, and she steps back. Her fingers absentmindedly find their way to the scar on her forearm, and she says, "Uh, excuse me. I'm sorry."

Two more bikers join the first and form a semi-circle around her. The mere weight and girth of each of them overwhelms her, and her face blanches. "Um, I'm really sorry but I need to leave."

One of them ogles her from head to toe then tweaks her breast. Heat rises to her face as she jumps out of his grasp. Another smirks and says, "Ooh, the citizen doesn't want to be fondled by you today, Ox. Maybe she'd rather step into the alley and pull a train."

The men cackle, and Ox grabs her bandaged hand. Pain shoots up her arm, and her palm throbs as the fire of his grip grows tighter. Her purse drops to the ground, and she manages to squeak out a yelp. Her heart threatens to beat out of her chest as Ox pulls her toward the entrance to the alley. "Come on, citizen, let us show you a good time."

Her pulse races, and she's barely aware of the nearing sirens ringing in the air. The hoodlums' one-percenter patches on their sleeves catch her eye, and the hair on her arms stands on end. *That means they're outlaw bikers. Crikey!* She throws her head back and lets out a loud, high-pitched wail.

Within seconds, two policemen line up behind her, their weapons drawn. "Let the lady go, and put your hands behind your head!" one says.

The other officer thrusts her purse at her as he steps toward the remaining bikers, saying, "You, too! Hands behind your head! Now!" He pushes one of the men against the brick storefront and slaps handcuffs on the hoodlum's wrists. "Now you," he says to the third man. The third offender is quick to surrender, and he, too, is soon restrained. As the other officer deals with Ox, the first policeman looks to Bridget and says, "Aren't you a neurosurgeon over at Saint Francis?"

Her chin quivers as she says, "Yes, I'm the Head of Neurology there."

The professional anger melts from his face. "I thought so. You saved my father's life a few months ago. He had a burst aneurysm, and the E.R. doctor told us you were the best. I never got to thank you, so, uh... thanks. From the bottom of my heart."

She forces a smile, though her hands continue to tremble as she clutches her bag. "You're very welcome. Uh, I really just came down here to do some last-minute Christmas shopping, but I don't think I want to be here right now." She casts her eyes to the protesters being loaded into a police van. "I'm parked right over there. Do you think you could help me get turned around?"

The policeman gestures for another officer then hands over the handcuffed gang member. "Take these guys downtown. Book 'em on a D and D. I'm going to help the doctor back to her vehicle." He escorts Bridget to her car and unlocks the door for her. "All right, Doctor. You'll be safe now. Just go ahead and do a U-turn here, then head up to the corner. Okay?"

She wills her knees to stop knocking and says, "Yes. Thank you again. I don't know what I would've done if—"

"Think nothing of it, Doctor. Merry Christmas."

"Merry Christmas to you and your father too. Ta ta." She starts her car and manages to get turned around and to the corner without incident. She drives a couple of miles up the road then pulls over to the curb and buries her face in her hands. Her shoulders heave as she sobs. *I can't believe this is happening here!* She presses her fingertips into her eyelids and weeps.

# # #

28 March 1944

Dear Diary,

I apologize for not having written in a while. My mother and I relocated again last week. Of course, you probably know by now that my father is no longer with us. We didn't feel safe in our cottage, so we moved into the attic at the Good Doctor's house. It's actually a one-room apartment, and we felt secure there while Mama's pregnancy concluded.

Last week, we left Amsterdam and headed for the home of a friend of the Good Doctor's in the country. I was holding Mama's hand when, out of the blue, a commotion caused us to become separated. I tripped and fell, and of course you know that I dropped you, Dear Diary, in the street when a loud shriek paralyzed me with fear. But we safely made the rest of our journey, and here, I am able to go outside to the barn after dark. That's where I like to reflect on things, record my thoughts, and look at my treasures that I have hidden in the cigar box in a bucket down at the bottom of a dry well.

Anyway, I just wanted to tell you that tonight on Radio Oranje, the Dutch Minister of Education and Cultural Affairs, Mr. Gerrit Bolkestein, asked for all Jews who were currently occupying the Netherlands to keep a record documenting their experiences. He said whenever the Netherlands becomes liberated, diaries and letters about this war will be collected and probably published.

I know I haven't been diligent about writing all that's happened, so I'd like to start by documenting one of my most vivid, earliest memories of war. It was the autumn of 1938. I was seven years old, and we were still living in Heusenstamm, Germany. Some Jewish teenager in France apparently became enraged when he learned his parents had been exiled to Poland, so he shot a German diplomat in the face. (I'd like to do that myself!)

To retaliate, Joseph Gobbels, the Führer's propaganda minister, got a lot of people riled up against the Jews, and starting in the late hours one night and continuing into the next day, the Nazis torched and vandalized hundreds of synagogues and thousands of Jewish hospitals, delicatessens, bakeries, business offices, schools, houses, and cemeteries throughout Germany. A hundred Jews were killed in the rampage, and a short time later, tens of thousands were arrested and taken away.

While all this was going on, the Nazis ordered the Gestapo and the street police and firemen to do nothing to interfere in the riots unless any fires got out of control and threatened Aryan property. Because there was so much broken glass from shattered or blown out windows of the storefronts littering the streets afterward, the night was called Kristallnacht or Night of Broken Glass. To add insult to injury, the despicable Nazis held the Jewish people in the community responsible for the damage littering the streets, and they imposed a collective fine of a billion marks!

Even though I was so young when this happened, the reason this is such a vivid memory for me is that Papa's medical office was destroyed that night. Even though Papa had already renamed his clinic after one of his non-Jewish medical partners, the Nazis heard that a Jew worked there, and they looted the office then burned it to the ground.

When Papa learned what was happening, Otto and I were already asleep, so Papa carried us to the cellar. Our house was within walking distance of the downtown district where Papa's office was, so when things started getting really violent, we woke and heard everything.

Mama was so terrified, her body shook hysterically, and at one point, she started screaming. That's when Papa did something I'd never imagined he was capable of: He threw a glass of water in Mama's face! The mere sight of him acting so abusive made me cringe, but Papa and Mama both explained later that he was only trying to shock her out of her hysteria so she would keep quiet in case the S.S. or the Nazi Army was casing the street by our house.

We were forced to stay in the cellar for two days while the Nazis' vicious attacks continued. Afterward, one of Papa's partners went with him to peruse the damage. When Papa got home, he wept so hard, I feared he might never stop. And seeing my papa sob like that terrified me. I'd never seen him weep before then, and the only other time I ever saw him cry since was when Otto's ashes were sent home. Papa was always so strong and immediately found the silver lining to any situation, but it was obvious that, in that moment, not just his big heart, but his spirit was broken. And that was a much more painful sight than all the broken glass in the world.

# # #

CHAPTER EIGHT

After Bridget composes herself, she drives to the Mass Pike then heads to Framingham. Jefferson Airplane's "White Rabbit" comes on the radio, and she turns up the volume. She croons along with Grace Slick and drums her hands on the steering wheel, ignoring the searing pain in her palm. By the time she takes the exit, a growing crimson spot stains her bandage. "Crikey. I better go to the chemist's and get some new dressing."

She pulls up to a drugstore and buys a box of gauze pads, a package of dressing, and a roll of medical tape. When she returns to her car and unwraps the wound, two stitches have ripped out. "Bollocks. I'll have to take care of this soon. But first, I shop."

She dresses the wound and heads to Mammoth Mart. After combing every aisle and navigating the crowd, she heads to Zayre then tackles the Shoppers World mall. As she moves between stores, her palm throbs, and a new scarlet stain appears on the thick bandage.

She takes her final purchases to the cash register and winces as she plucks her Master Charge out of her wallet. *I hope this queue moves along quickly. This is really starting to hurt now. I can't believe that monster grabbed my bandaged hand of all places. I'd like to get him in a dark alley one night and give him a lobotomy.*

She carries her boxes and bags to her car then sets them on the ground while she digs through her purse. *Got to get the boot open.* Unable to locate her keys, her wound soon soaks the bandage, and her chin quivers. She fights to hold back her impending tears until the floodgates open. She dumps her purse on the trunk of her car but doesn't spot her keys. "No, no, no, no! Not this!" She holds her hand above her heart in an attempt to slow the bleeding as she shoves the loose items back in her purse with her left hand. "Dammit!"

A shopping mall Santa approaches her and says, "Ho ho ho! Hello there, Dr. Castle. Do you need some help?"

Bridget looks up and catches her reflection in the window of the car parked next to hers. A chunk of her hair flips backward, and smears of mascara make her look like a bandit. She sniffles and says, "Uh... Hello. I'm sorry, I don't—"

Santa pulls his beard down. "I'm Marty Gibbs. I used to be an orderly over at Saint Francis. I moved to General a few months ago. What happened here? You lose your keys?"

"I guess they must have fallen out of my purse while I was inside shopping."

"Oh, and your hand is bleeding. Here..." He pulls a handkerchief from his pocket and offers it to her.

"Thank you." She wraps the cloth around her hand and sniffles.

"Well, don't give up hope. Here, maybe you left them in the car." He steps to the driver's window and shades his eyes with his hands as he peeks inside.

"Or perhaps I left them in the boot— er, uh, the *trunk* when I brought out some parcels between stores. I guess I'll have to call my husband to bring me the spare set."

"No, they're right here on the floor. Hold on; let me see what I can do." He jogs to his car a few spaces away and opens his back door. He pulls out a hanger from the backseat window hook then twists it to a long wire with a loop on the end. He returns and fishes the wire through her window until he hooks it onto the interior lock post. After three attempts, he pops the lock, opens the door, and drops the keys in her hand. "Here you go, Doc. Can I help you load your packages? That wound looks pretty bad. Maybe I should drive you to the hospital."

She blinks away her tears and smiles as he arranges her packages in the trunk. "No, Marty, but thank you so much. I'm heading over to hospital right now. I had sutures yesterday, and a couple of them ripped out earlier. I'll be fine until I get there."

"Are you sure?" He rests his forearm on the roof of her car as she situates herself behind the steering wheel. "I'm off Santa duty now. It's no problem."

"No, really. Thank you for your help, but I'll be fine now."

"Okay, then. Merry Christmas."

"You, too, Marty. And a Happy New Year." She starts her car and heads toward the Mass Pike. *Bollocks. I hope this blood doesn't ruin my dress.* To take her mind off the day's bad luck, she flips on the radio and helps The Mamas and the Papas sing "California Dreamin'" then joins The Rolling Stones in "Paint it Black." By the time she pulls into the hospital parking lot, she finishes accompanying The Byrds in "Mr. Tambourine Man."

She parks and removes some fresh dressing from the pharmacy bag and loops it around the blood-soaked bandage and handkerchief. *Doesn't look like they're too busy today in Emergency anyway.*

She heads in through the E.R. entrance and stands at the receptionist's desk with Johnny Mathis's "Winter Wonderland" being piped throughout the floor. "Good afternoon, Marcia. I'm sorry I'm such a mess. Is Dr. Redding on duty, and if so, is he tied up right now?"

Marcia's hand flies to her chest, and she knits her brow. "Oh, my goodness! Dr. Castle, you've been in an accident. Let me page him for you. Here." She picks up the phone and pushes a tissue box toward Bridget. "Dr. Redding, Dr. Glenn Redding, please report to the E.R., STAT."

Moments later, Dr. Redding rushes into the E.R. reception area with a paper napkin tucked under his chin and half of a four-tier Dagwood sandwich in his hand. "Marcia, I told you I was on lunch. What's up?"

"Dr. Castle was in a car accident!"

Dr. Redding yanks the napkin from his shirt and tosses that and his sandwich in the garbage can behind Marcia's desk then rushes to Bridget's side. "An auto accident? What happened?"

Bridget and Glenn head toward a vacant exam room, and she says, "I'm afraid Marcia got things mixed up. I had a run-in with a patient and a scalpel yesterday, and Dr. Taylor sutured it up. Today, I was out shopping and bumped it. It looks like two stitches pulled out." She unwinds the dressing from her wound.

He prepares a povidone-iodine bath in a stainless-steel bowl and places her hand in it. "I see. Well, I'm sure we can get you fixed up as good as new in no time. Let me go get some supplies while you soak your hand." He exits the room and leaves Bridget alone with her thoughts...

# # #

21 February 1942

Caro Diario (Dear Diary),

It's my eleventh birthday today, and I'm writing to you in Italian because I met the most darling little Italian girl this morning. As you know, Dear Diary, we've been living in a small studio that sits just behind a medical facility. My father met Dr. Van Den Boom, the doctor who owns it, while they studied medicine together at Oxford. My father always refers to him as "the Good Doctor," and he is truly a gem. In fact, he even brings me a little bag of dropjes every time we see him (which is salty licorice and is very popular here in the Netherlands).

This morning before dawn, a little Italian Jewish girl was brought in by her grandmother. The girl's family had been checking out a new hiding place in the attic crawlspace of a bakery down the street, and while the child was unattended, she somehow fell through a plate glass window of the baked goods counter. The Good Doctor ran out to our cottage and asked my father to assist with mending the girl's injuries and to see if he thought she needed surgery. He wanted to have the help to work quickly so the girl and her grandmother could get back to their hiding place before the sun came up. (The Good Doctor is not Jewish, but he is certainly a blessing to those of us who are!) My father immediately woke me and asked me to accompany him to work on the girl so that I could be his medical assistant. I must stress that he did not call me a nurse.

He grabbed his black bag of medical instruments and supplies, and I put my shoes on and was honored to be asked to participate. I've always dreamed of working side-by-side with my father in our own surgery someday. We got over to the office, and the little girl was nearly hysterical from so much blood soaking the blanket wrapped around her. She kept muttering, "Sto per morire! Sto per morire! I'm going to die!"

I prepared an iodine saline solution and cleansed the wounds on her arms, legs, hands, torso, face, and scalp. Both my father and his friend plucked shards of glass from her wounds and sutured her lacerations, and I felt so proud whenever they asked me to hand them an instrument or some more catgut. My father said I was a natural born practitioner, the way I kept the child calm and professionally observed the procedure without flinching at the sight of so much lost blood and torn tissue.

The poor girl needed more than three hundred sutures. I hate to think how bad her scars might look once her wounds heal. But even though my heart was filled with compassion for my very first patient, I was on top of the world getting to help my father with his work. This will always be the most exciting birthday of my life.

P.S. We finished sewing up the little girl – her name is Giovanna – just as the sun peeked over the horizon. The Good Doctor successfully drove them back to the bakery without the Gestapo seeing them.

# # #

CHAPTER NINE

Dr. Redding returns and examines Bridget's palm. After giving her a shot of local anesthetic, he begins repairing her wound. "Did you say Paul stitched this up? He usually does better work than this."

"I probably just made him nervous. You know, boss's wife and all."

"Yeah, that and the fact that he's so preoccupied with that little hairdresser he's been dating. What's her name? Nadine?"

Bridget snorts and rolls her eyes. "Oh, yes, I've had the pleasure of meeting her. What a chippie."

He chuckles, and his eyes crinkle at the corners. "You don't say. I just met her in passing when she came up to have lunch with him recently. Paul was trying to get Gloria and me to go out with them. I had to make up an excuse. I can just hear Gloria chastising him for dating someone young enough to be his daughter's babysitting charge."

"Tell me about it. I tried to have an open mind, but she just rubbed me the wrong way. Women like her just make it so much harder for women like me to be accepted as professionals. Say, do you know if they're still having Santa come visit the pediatric floor next weekend? I purchased a few gifts today that I wanted to add to the donation barrel."

"Yeah, that's next Saturday. Today they're having some kind of children's carolers group from the Catholic Church come sing for the patients. I also heard what sounded like a bell choir warming up when I was up there earlier. I think they're hosting a little party up in the Community Room when the singing is over." He ties off the last stitch in her palm. "Here, I had to go over some of Paul's work, and I added four more where the two pulled out. You shouldn't have any more problems. The part that stayed closed looks like it's already starting to heal nicely. But it probably wouldn't hurt for you to take some Penicillin as a prophylactic measure since you opened it back up today. I'd hate to see it get infected."

She hands him a roll of dressing as he places a small stack of gauze pads over his work. "Yeah, I was thinking the same thing earlier when it happened. I've got a craniotomy patient in from West Germany this week, and I don't want anything to delay his procedure."

"You want me to write you a script?"

"No, I've got a full bottle in my office. I'll head up in a little while and get them. Thanks so much, Glenn. Um, by the way, if you don't mind, can you please not mention to my husband that this happened? He hasn't changed my dressing yet, so he won't know the difference. But I don't need him fussing over me." She stands.

He pats her shoulder. "Not a problem. Tell Jack that Gloria and I would love to have you two over for cocktails soon."

"I will. He'll be thrilled. Thanks again. I'll see you later."

He begins clearing the surgical tray. "See ya."

She treks out to her car and selects a few packages then heads back into the building. She winds her way past the cafeteria to the lobby and hops on the main elevator where she rides up to the seventh floor then makes her way to her office.

After hanging her coat and purse, she digs through her medical bag for a Spear-O-Mint Lifesaver then replaces the hidden pack and pops the candy in her mouth. She pulls a makeup bag out of her desk then steps over to the wall mirror and fixes her face and hair. With her racoon mascara gone, her hair flipping in the right direction, and her hand clean and feeling better, her lungs deflate in a contented sigh, and she manages to smile at her reflection.

She replaces her cosmetics case then sifts through another drawer for a bottle of antibiotics. She shoves the bottle in her purse and spreads the packages from her car out on the coffee table. She plucks five Barbie dolls and five G.I. Joe dolls from the lot, stuffs them in a canvas shopping bag, and heads out to the elevator. She rides down to the sixth floor and strolls toward the Community Room. Echoes of the children's chorus singing "Carol of the Bells" along with the bell choir dinging their handbells in perfect unison warms her heart. She places the dolls in a collection barrel then slips into the festively decorated room as the song comes to an end, the bells reverberating their final note.

The crowd of patients and hospital staff applauds, and a priest offers an invocation then invites everyone to help themselves to refreshments. Bridget scans the room and waves to a few co-workers then grabs a cup of eggnog and a sugar cookie. She starts to leave when she notices Craig Barnaby laughing with one of the candy stripers. The girl flips her blonde ponytail over her shoulder and bats her eyes at him.

Bridget's lips curl into a sweet smile. When the candy striper caresses Craig's forearm and Craig reaches for her hand, a pang of guilt overtakes Bridget, and she feels almost naughty for peeking on her patient. She takes two gingerbread men and a sugar cookie from the cookie plate and wraps them in a napkin then slips out of the room before anyone can approach her.

She jaunts back upstairs to her office and finds an envelope under her door. She tears it open, sits at her desk, and reads the enclosed report then grabs two giftwrapped boxes from the coffee table. She stops at her desk and jots names on the tags on each of them then ventures down to the fifth floor. She heads to Room 529, knocks, and enters without waiting for a reply.

"Good afternoon, Herr Hetzel," she says with a cautious smile. She sits in the chair next to the patient's bed and notices him writing in a small notepad. "What's that you're working on?"

"Just my reports. I like to keep a record of my vitals. It might come in handy in the future."

"Oh. I was just up in the Community Room watching the children's performance. I was hoping to see you there."

He waves his hand and rolls his eyes. "I have no desire to waste my time listening to a bunch of off-tune Kinder try to sing."

She places the stack of napkin-covered cookies on his bed tray. "Well, I brought you these anyway. I just got your P.E.T. scan results. They look good. Your meningioma has only grown half a centimeter since your last test in Cologne."

"And that's good? Sounds like *der Blödsinn* to me." He unwraps the cookies and shoves a gingerbread man in his mouth, snapping its head off.

"It's not *nonsense*. Before you got here, I reviewed all the tests your doctor sent, and from what I could see, I was afraid your tumor was an ependymoma and not a meningioma. But since the growth isn't as rapid as I anticipated, I'm hopeful that I'm wrong."

"Wait a minute. So, I fly halfway around the world for a *nurse* to drill through my skull, and you don't even have an idea of what you're looking for? What kind of *der Unsinn* is this?"

Heat rises to her cheeks. "Herr Hetzel, I can assure you this is not *drivel*. With a tumor like yours at the base of your skull, it can be any number of things. No doctor will know for certain until it is excised and biopsied for malignancy. If, indeed, it were an ependymoma, you would almost surely be facing cancer eradication treatments in your near future. If it's a meningioma, after your surgery, you'll most likely be able to leave this experience in your past and move on with your life with no further complications."

"Yeah, well, we don't even have cancer in my family, so I don't know why you think this is an epo-moma or whatever you said anyway. I don't know why my doctor back home couldn't have just done this himself and—"

She stands and towers over him. "Because your doctor is unerfahren – *inexperienced* – with the level of skill it will take to remove a tumor so close to your brain stem and spinal cord. I have that experience. Your doctor knows this, which is why he sent you to me." She takes a deep breath and sits back in the chair.

His eyes dart to her bandage. "Looks like you won't be ready to operate on anybody with those hands."

She clenches her jaw. "I assure you everything will go according to schedule."

"I don't even see how this happened. Why did I get a tumor anyway?" He pops the sugar cookie in his mouth, and crumbs fall on his chin as he munches.

"Have you lived in Cologne your whole life?"

"No. I grew up in the north part of the country."

"Hmm... Near Hamburg?"

"What? Why does that matter?"

"Was it near Hamburg?"

"Yeah. So what?"

"Neuengamme Concentration Camp was near Hamburg."

His eyes narrow. "So what! What does a bunch of no-good Jews from long ago have to do with the current state of my health?"

The muscles in her neck tense, and she strains to maintain a professional composure. "Because, Herr Hetzel, Neuengamme used prussic acid – you might know it as hydrogen cyanide – to kill its prisoners. Any toxic substance like that used on such a grand scale can't stay contained. It likely seeped into the ground and nearby bodies of water. Even when the bodies were cremated, the ashes that spread on the wind would have carried a toxicity..." Her voice trails off, and a knot forms in her stomach. *Not to mention the smell. The necrotic smell of burning flesh when the ashes poured down on us like rain...*

"So, you're saying that this thing in my head may have been twenty-four years in the making?"

"Yes, that's exactly what I'm saying." *And from the hatred in your heart, it couldn't have happened to a more deserving soul.* She clears her throat, stands, and places one of the gifts on his tray. "Here, I bought you this. I know you're having a hard time being away from your father during holiday. I was hoping it would help cheer you up. I'm sorry to cut this visit short, but I need to go. I'll see you Monday."

# # #

27 July 1945

Dear Diary,

I know it's been forever since I've written, but so much has happened, and I feared I would never see you again. I was arrested in the Netherlands last September, and I was sent to places so horrible, I can't even think about describing them yet.

Actually, I can. As a Jewish girl, I was not raised to believe in the place the Christians call Hell. But now that the war in Europe is over, I've actually attended a Lutheran church with some new friends and learned a little bit about this place called Hell. And I have no doubt that those places where I was sent were the very entrance points to Hell!

Throughout my ordeal, I realized that since the vile Führer Hitler was named Chancellor just weeks before my second birthday, hiding, fleeing, and persecution took up so much of my youth that I never really got to experience life as a child. And now, those are years that I will never get back. I'm hoping I can enter adulthood without always looking over my shoulder or being afraid.

Of all the horrors I've witnessed these past months – and they were countless – the wails of people being beaten, starved, tortured, riddled with vermin or disease, and missing their loved ones will echo in my ears for as long as I live; and the stench of mass murders, the foul odor of diseases in epidemic proportions, and the burning efflux of ash and smoke caused by bulk cremations are smells that I fear will never leave my nose.

P.S. After eight long months, the British Army liberated me and those who were with me. Once my health was restored, I returned to the Netherlands, and that was when I found you, Dear Diary, right where I'd left you. And in case you didn't know it already, I'm now living just outside of Reading, England. It makes me proud to think I might be able to attend the very classes my father did at Oxford someday.

# # #

CHAPTER TEN

Minutes pass before Bridget's pulse returns to normal. She sneaks down to Room 502 and smiles when Craig Barnaby is not in his bed. Her face lights up. *He's still at the party. Good for him.* She jots a quick note then leaves a gift on his bed tray with the note tucked under the ribbon.

She makes her way back to her office, grabs her coat and purse, then locks up and heads downstairs. She unlocks her car and examines the hood. *Smitty really did do a nice job. We'll have to give him a nice bonus for Christmas.* She looks to the sun then checks her watch. *Four-thirty.* "Bollocks! Jack's going to be hungry soon." She starts the car and taps her toe in time with Nancy Sinatra's "These Boots Are Made for Walkin'" then helps The Hollies sing "Bus Stop" as she travels toward Market Street.

She parks near the same corner she parked at earlier when Destination: Faneuil Hall was on her radar and waits to get out of her car until a group of tourists pass. She hurries to tag along at the rear of their group, hoping for safety in numbers and that she won't encounter a repeat of this morning. As they reach the statue of Samuel Adams, they stop walking, and the tourists start buzzing in French, wondering where they're supposed to go. Bridget clears her throat and directs them to their location then bids them *adieu* as they part ways.

She scans the area and relaxes as soon as she spies three police officers stationed around the courtyard. *Good. I can pick up a pizza and be home before Jack goes begging Mum and Dad to feed him.* She strolls into Quincy Market and weaves through the crowd until she reaches Romano's Pizzeria. She enters and locates the cashier station.

The cashier looks up and straightens her wire-rimmed eyeglasses. "Dr. Castle, you... You didn't call in an order, did you? We've got new help in the kitchen and—"

Bridget waves her hands. "Buonasera. *Good evening.* No, I didn't call, Mrs. Romano."

"Oh, did you want a table? We've got a booth open in the back."

"No, thank you. I've been shopping all day and hoped to pick up a medium mushroom and black olive pie to take home so Jack doesn't think I'm trying to starve him."

Mrs. Romano chuckles. "Oh, the famished husband routine. I'm familiar with that one also. I'll take care of your order myself. I'll throw some breadsticks in, too, to keep him happy. It'll be about twenty minutes. If you like, I can get you a drink while you wait. A Coca-cola or a nice glass of Chianti, perhaps?"

Bridget fishes her wallet out of her purse and passes a five-dollar bill to the woman. "Aww, that's so sweet of you, but if you don't mind, I think I'll go walk around a bit and see what stores I might still need to hit before Christmas gets here. You can keep the change."

"Of course. You come back in twenty minutes, and I'll have your pie ready."

"Will do. Grazie. *Thanks.*" Bridget zips her purse and hugs herself as she leaves the market building and steps out into the Faneuil Hall courtyard. The breeze kicks up her dress, and she smooths the skirt down over her tights. *Brrr. It's getting colder.*

While deciding which way to turn, a familiar smell tickles her nose. Goosebumps cover her arms, and the hackles on the back of her neck stand on end. She sniffs the air and follows her nose around the corner to what was, as of the first of October, a vacant shop that was recently the home of one of her favorite haunts, Steeden's Bookseller, owned by Mr. and Mrs. Blamey from Manchester.

As she trails the phenomenal scent of homemade sour dill pickles, matzah ball soup, and gravlax, coupled with the slightest hint of rugelach, her mind is transported back in time… *It smells like home.* She closes her eyes and inhales as a contented smile tugs at her lips.

A woman wrapped in a black shawl bumps into Bridget and says, "Oy! Pardon me, Miss." She rushes away before Bridget can see her face, and she enters the former bookseller's storefront.

Bridget's face blanches. *Was that—No, it couldn't be.* As she steps closer to the shop, a man flips the light off inside and disappears into a backroom. Heat rises to her neck as she pulls on the locked door, and a handwritten sign in the lower window catches her eye: *"Coming Soon: Kugelman's Delicatessen."*

She shades her eyes and stands on her toes as she peeks inside the dark store; but the only thing she can make out is a glass counter in front of the light peeking through the gap under the backroom door. With the sweet and tangy aromas swirling around her head, the air leaves her lungs, and she becomes paralyzed in a place between the present and the past.

# # #

2 March 1944

Cher Journal (Dear Diary),

Today is my father's forty-fourth birthday. Of course, we haven't seen him in more than two months, but my mother says we mustn't give up hope. (Since when did she become so filled with optimism? That was always his role, while she was the ever-doubtful naysayer.)

I'm writing to you in French today because my father always said French was the language he most adored. I'm now the proud sister of a beautiful boy named Josef Wilhelm who was born on the twenty-ninth of January, and I got to help Dr. Van Den Boom deliver him! Mama wanted to name him after Papa, and so did I, of course. But she said that she had talked at length with him about it, and Papa felt it wasn't fair to name that child after him when his first son Otto didn't get to share his name, so he's named after a man who Papa used to know. (Otto was named after Papa's brother who died of small pox a couple of weeks before Papa was born. In retrospect, it seems like kind of a bad omen.)

Despite having only the food and ingredients that the Good Doctor Van Den Boom is able to get for us with the food rationing coupons he gets from the black market, my mother still managed to make many of my father's favorites for today's celebration. She's been working for days on her beloved sour dill pickles, and tonight, she made latkes with applesauce, buckwheat knishes, and her special braided challah bread that we all adore. And for dessert, my father's favorite cinnamon chocolate babka.

The Good Doctor and his family even came up to the attic and joined us for the banquet. My mother has hardly let our sweet Josef Wilhelm out of her arms since his birth a month ago, and I know this is because she's afraid he will cry and the Gestapo will hear the noise and come to inspect. Which is why it struck me as so odd that she would make all these foods because their wonderful aromas must certainly waft on the wind and will be carried for miles.

Of course, everything was delicious, and as always, it was beautifully prepared. Still, I could hardly choke down more than a few bites. I just miss my father so much, and today, having this feast without him was only a painful reminder that I'll probably never see him again. I wish I could be more like him and Otto and apparently like Mama now, too, and find the silver lining. Maybe someday...

# # #

Bridget gasps when the light under the backroom door turns off, and she checks her watch. *Bollocks! It's been half an hour.* The moon peeks over the horizon, and a bitter wind whips past her legs. She races back to the pizza shop then heads for home.

When she gets to Malden, she places her hand on the lukewarm pizza box in the passenger seat as she makes the turn onto her street. As she slows to pull into her driveway, her eyes grow large, and her jaw drops open.

Multi-colored lights trim the eaves of the house. The family room curtains hang open, and an aluminum Christmas tree sits in the window with a rotating color wheel projecting various colors onto the tree. She steps out of the car and grabs the pizza and breadsticks. "Where did he ever find a silver tree?" She approaches the house, a goofy grin plastered on her face, when the door swings open, and Jack steps out holding a sprig of mistletoe over his head.

Jack wiggles his eyebrows. "Well, hello-ho-ho, stranger. I didn't realize you'd be gone this long. Give me a kiss." She plants an eager kiss on his lips, and he takes the pizza from her. "Here, babe, you shouldn't be using your hand."

"Thanks. I'm sorry it's not very hot anymore. We'll have to heat it in the oven. It looks like you've had a busy day."

He wraps his arm around her waist as they head inside. "I've kept myself occupied. You said you missed the festive atmosphere when we didn't decorate last year, so I wanted to make up for that. Did you get all your shopping done?"

Her head turns as she inspects the plastic holly leaf garland hanging in the foyer. "Most of it. What did you do here?"

He takes her purse from her shoulder and slings it on the kitchen table then helps her remove her coat. He slides the pizza in the oven and turns it on. "Come on; let me give you the tour."

Taking her hand, he leads her to the family room where the spinning color wheel whirrs as it projects jolly colors onto the tinsel tree. "I bought that this morning over at Grants. Your dad dropped by after lunch and helped me with some stuff. Come on in here..." He pulls her to the den where two stockings hang from the mantle, a trio of ceramic caroling nuns sits on top of the television, and ceramic elves hugging candlesticks adorn the coffee table.

Her nose twitches at the pine aroma growing stronger as she nears the freshly cut fir tree, overloaded with handfuls of silver icicles, wrapped with gold tinsel, and overfilled with multi-colored glass ornaments. "We have two Christmas trees? Wow, you really went all out, didn't you?" She giggles at the electric candoliers in most of the downstairs windows and the mistletoe springs hung in all the main doorways.

A proud grin stretches across his face. "Yup. Come here; the tour's not over." He pulls her through the dining room where a nativity scene sits on the buffet, and Santa and Mrs. Claus salt and pepper shakers decorate the tabletop.

As the sightseeing excursion concludes back in the kitchen, she smiles at a span of clay reindeer pulling a candy dish sled across the table. "We'd better check the pizza. We don't want it to burn." She opens the refrigerator and hands him a jar of dill pickles. "Can you open this for me?"

He takes the pizza out of the oven and raises an eyebrow. "Pickles? With pizza?"

She shrugs her shoulders. "I came across a new deli while I was waiting for Mrs. Romano to gather our food. The smell of pickles got stuck in my nose, I guess."

* * *

CHAPTER ELEVEN

After hours of attempting to ignore the steady buzz of Jack's snore, Bridget falls into a fitful sleep. She dreams of the morning's motorcycle gang accompanied by a band of Nazi soldiers being led by Gunter Hetzel. "Citizen, we've come to get you," Gunter says, a sardonic grin spanning his face. "You won't get away from us this time." All the men hoot and howl as their straight-legged march propels them closer. Multitudes of hungry rats, the massacred bodies of men, women, and children piled high, and mountainous stacks of children's shoes, baby clothing, sheared hair, human bones, and extracted human teeth prevent her from escaping.

As the men grow nearer, she tucks her chin down and realizes that the red silk nightgown she wore to bed has been replaced with a threadbare, lice-infested, striped uniform with a compulsory yellow double triangle badge sewn to the chest. Her hands fly to her scalp, and her fingertips trace over stubble and scabs where her beautiful crown of silky, amber hair that once earned her the nickname Rapunzel from her brother Otto formerly grew. Something crawls across her wrist, and she yanks her hands from her head, causing the sleeve of the ill-fitted uniform to slide back. Her attention is drawn to her left arm. An arm with no muscle tone, no hair, protruding joints of her elbow, wrist, and fingers with her skin stretched taut across her bones. The number 853942 tattooed on her forearm starts off hazy then comes into focus. Her pulse quickens. "Noooo!" She rubs the number with her fingertips, to no avail. She starts scratching and clawing at the marking, but her efforts prove futile. As she digs at her skin, the bare ring finger of her left hand catches her eye. "My ring! My ring from Papa is gone!"

She falls to her knees and sifts through the dirt to hunt for her lost token, but the shadows of her assailants forming a semi-circle around her blocks out the sunlight. She looks up as each of them raise their right arms in a Nazi salute, and in perfect unison, they chant, "Heil Hitler!"

Her face contorts into a look of abject horror, she clenches her hands into fists, and she throws her head back, unleashing an ear-piercing wail loud enough to wake the dead. The world turns black, and she can't see even her own shadow. The stench of death and the sounds of her tormenters cackling dwindle to silence, and the chirping and hissing of the blood-hungry rats ebbs to a familiar droning snuffle. As she hugs her knees, the sweet-scented, silky folds of her nightie tickle her arms, and she realizes she's sitting up in bed with Jack and his usual nocturnal sounds at arm's length. *Oh. It was just a dream.* As she attempts to straighten out the bedcovers and get comfortable, the moistness of her face, neck, and breasts, soaked with sweat, prevent her from relaxing. *Bollocks.*

She creeps out of bed and pulls a clean nightgown from the bureau drawer. She grabs her robe and slides her feet into her slippers then tiptoes downstairs to the powder room and gets undressed. Using a washcloth, she gives herself a sponge bath from the sink – *just as we did at the Good Doctor's cottage* – then changes into the fresh nightie.

She heads to the kitchen, wraps a sour pickle in a napkin, then sneaks into the living room and grabs the latest issue of *Reader's Digest*. She glides back upstairs to the guest bedroom. "There's no way I'll ever fall back asleep after that." She fluffs up a couple of pillows, stretches her legs as she leans back against the headboard, flips open the magazine, and munches the pickle as she reads an article by Ann Landers entitled "You Can't Tell a Kid by His Age."

When she finishes the essay, she considers reading an article about the benefits of yogurt then tosses the publication aside. She wipes her fingertips on the napkin and smooths the bandage on her hand. *Hmm. I just don't think I can sleep yet.* She opens the drawer of the bedside stand and pulls out a roll of Five Flavor Lifesavers. She pops a pineapple candy in her mouth and moseys over to the closet. She sorts through some dresses and shoes, the overflow from her main closet, then reaches in a pocket of last year's coat and finds an unopened box of SweeTarts. She opens the box and pours out a few of the sour candies. She selects a purple one to suck, and the rest go in her bathrobe pocket as she eyes the top shelf. "There it is." She grabs an umbrella and uses it to slide an octagonal hatbox off the ledge.

She blows a layer of dust off the top then heads to the bed and opens the old Dobbs Fifth Avenue box. Her fingers glide over wads of tissue paper, and she holds her breath as she plucks the filler from the container. With a determined crease in her brow, she removes item after item until she reaches an article wrapped in layers of worn tissue. She clutches the item to her chest, sits back against the headboard, and inhales a faint musty scent as she unravels the aged paper from the treasure.

With the tissue removed, she runs her fingertips across her wooden cigar box. She opens the box and unfolds a lace handkerchief, yellowed with age, wrapped around a dog-eared and faded blue and white gingham book she once loved more than life itself. *My diary.* Her fingers find their place in the journal and pull it open as if they have a memory of their own. She holds her breath as she reads the entry...

# # #

21 February 1941

Liebes Tagebuch (Dear Diary),

Today is my tenth birthday. In the past, my father has been successful in having one of his old medical partners from Germany keep many of our valuables and sell them when we need money to give to the people who have helped keep us hidden from the Gestapo and the Nazi soldiers. We've been very lucky.

When we lived in Poland and were forced to stay in a ghetto, one of my father's doctor friends learned of our predicament and connected us with a priest who helped us escape to France. We've been fortunate to stay so well hidden that, since Poland, we haven't had to walk around with the badges and armbands or be afraid of being plucked from the streets into the waiting hands of the police.

But I've heard my parents talking in hushed whispers lately, and I know that they fear that our money is running out. (I know the Good Doctor Van Den Boom is so kindhearted, he won't hesitate to use his own money to help us. But my father is a proud man, and he would hate to feel as if we were such an imposition.) It's because of my secret knowledge of our finances that, when I opened my birthday gifts today, I felt almost sick to my stomach.

My mother gave me her most treasured possession – a hand-tatted lace handkerchief that was made by her grandmother on her mama's side. I've always admired it. I know the reason she gave this to me was that she wasn't able to get out and shop for something new, and I feel horrible about her giving up something so dear to her heart.

When I opened my father's gift next, I was positively stunned. It was a small, navy box lined with white silk and dark blue velvet. Inside, I found the most beautiful silver ring I've ever seen! It was shiny and new. Its band fits perfectly around the third finger of my left hand, and the design is of a pair of hands holding a heart. I'm not talking about the Irish Claddagh ring with two hands holding a valentine-shaped heart with a crown. I mean, this was an actual, anatomically correct human heart. Inside, an inscription reads "Love, Papa." I asked Papa where he ever found such a unique treasure, and he said he had it made for me because I would always hold his heart.

I feared this must have cost far too much money for our meager budget. However, I knew enough not to question my parents about our finances. Because of these sacrifices my parents made for me today out of their love for me, I'll never part with these gifts. In fact, I'll keep them hidden in the cigar box with my other special treasures and save them until my dying day.

# # #

Bridget sniffles and realizes her cheeks are damp. She grabs a Kleenex from the bedside table and wipes her eyes then lays the open book across her lap and touches the handkerchief. *At least I still have you.* She takes a deep breath, pops a green SweeTart in her mouth, and flips the book's pages to another entry.

# # #

10 September 1945

Dear Diary,

I've been enrolled in school here in England for several weeks now. A tutor worked with me when I got here, and as it turns out, all the schooling that my parents gave me while we moved around Europe paid off. I took a placement examination and actually came out two grades ahead of where my age would place me. Because of this, my tutor was able to pull some strings, and I was able to skip ahead, right into the eleventh grade!

After so many years of living on the run and witnessing such horrors, it finally feels like things are moving in a really good direction, and I don't want to stall the momentum. I know this means I'll have to work extra hard, but I know I can do it, and this will propel me to university and subsequently to study medicine all the sooner.

When I got here, I told you how I returned to the Netherlands after being liberated from the camp, and that was when I found my box of treasures right where I kept them. I used to look over the contents of that box every day while we were hiding.

I doubt I'll ever forget each and every item that was so dear to my heart: The snapshot of Otto holding me on my first birthday, the photograph of my parents and Otto and me the day before Otto left for the rehabilitation facility, my mother's handkerchief that belonged to my great-grandmother, my heart ring, the French bookmark that belonged to my father when he studied medicine, a crayon picture of a pony that Otto drew for me when I had the measles, my Chirpie Bird ornament that my father gave me only days before he was taken, and a gold cufflink with a tiny diamond in it that belonged to my father's father. (When the other one was lost, Papa said I could have it for my treasure box.) I like to keep most of these items in a purple velvet bag that belonged to my mother. She said on their first anniversary, my father gave her a bottle of expensive French perfume, and it came in that drawstring bag. (It still smelled of the heavenly fragrance several years later.) The only thing I didn't have in my collection of my sweetest memories was a photograph of my dear baby brother, Josef Wilhelm. But of course, how would I when we could never take him to get a portrait made?

The night I was arrested, about an hour earlier, I started reading some previous entries in you, Dear Diary, and was looking over photographs and my other belongings. I'd placed my heart ring on my finger while I traveled down Memory Lane with my treasures, and that's when I heard the soldiers downstairs. I quickly stuffed you and everything back in the cigar box and shoved the box in its hiding place between the beams in the barn. I tried to sneak out the loft window to hide, but an S.S. man was on the ground waiting for me.

I was whisked away and loaded onto a crowded boxcar that smelled of urine, vomit, sweat, excrement, and death. We were packed in so tightly, there was standing room only, and I didn't recognize anyone, not that there was much light to make out anyone's face anyway. As the train rolled toward Destination: Unknown, I hugged myself in the freezing night and tried to ignore the wails of my terrified companions.

Sometime during that first night on the train when I woke from sleeping while standing, sandwiched between numerous others, I realized that I was still wearing my beloved heart ring. There were already whispers among the travelers that whatever valuables we had might be taken from us, so I squeezed past some of the people and made my way to the wall where I removed my precious ring and stuffed it between the slats of the boxcar. I hoped that someday I'd be able to find it again.

By the time the train stopped three days after our journey started, many of my companions had died. I planned to memorize the number of the boxcar so that perhaps I could locate it later and retrieve my ring; but the soldiers that unloaded us hurried us along the platform toward the camp that would be my new home: a place known as Auschwitz-Birkenau. When I realized just how many of us were dead when the car was opened, I only had a moment to glance back and see the numbers 8761 painted on the side of the car. Then they marched us through an iron gate that said "Arbeit Macht Frei" – "Work Sets You Free."

I mentioned where I had hidden my ring to a couple of girls close to my age because I hoped that saying it out loud would help me remember. But after we were all indoctrinated to our new home in Hell, I rarely had the opportunity to even think about my beautiful little ring again.

# # #

Bridget closes the book and blows her nose. "Wow. I shouldn't have read that. It just brings it all flooding back as if it happened only yesterday." She sniffles as she repacks the hatbox and tidies the room before she yawns and heads back to her own bed.

* * *

CHAPTER TWELVE

The smell of coffee and toast nudges Bridget from her slumber. She yawns and stretches her arms over her head before brushing her teeth and padding downstairs to the kitchen.

Jack pours a cup of coffee and sets it in front of her as he steals a kiss. "Ah, there's my beautiful bride. Good morning."

She yawns and slurps her coffee. "Morning."

He sets a plate of fried eggs, toast, and bacon in front of her. "Here you go." He sits across from her, opening a jar of jam.

She raises an eyebrow. "Thanks." Yawning, she stabs an egg with her fork until the yolk oozes out.

"I noticed you weren't in bed last night. Was I snoring again?"

She narrows her bloodshot eyes. "I don't know what you could possibly have inside your throat that the rest of the world doesn't have that causes you to make those dreadful noises when you sleep!"

He purses his lips and cracks open the newspaper. "Sorry, dear. Next time, why don't you just give me an elbow in the ribs, and tell me to shut up?" He scans the paper and shoves a slice of toast in his mouth.

Her cheeks flush, and she lets out a loud sigh. "I apologize. I didn't sleep well, and I shouldn't have snapped like that. Thank you for the eggs. They're delicious."

He pours cream into his coffee. "How's your hand feeling? We should change the dressing before we head out to church."

The muscles in her neck tighten. *Bollocks! I forgot to take my antibiotics last night.* She sighs. "Oh, uh, it's feeling just fine."

Without looking up, he nods. "Good. Huh. Looks like Margarete Klose died yesterday."

"Who?"

He folds the newspaper in quarters and reads aloud: "Margarete Klose, the German operatic mezzo-soprano who reached international fame in the 1930s and 40s as the lead for Richard Wagner musical dramas as well as operas written by Giuseppe Verdi, Richard Strauss, and who was most famous as a Bach and Lieder singer, died unexpectedly in Berlin yesterday. She was sixty-nine years old."

She rolls her eyes and huffs. "And why do you think I would possibly need to hear about an opera singer from Berlin? Have I ever indicated that I held any interest in the bloody opera?"

He takes a deep breath and turns the page. "Looks like Elvis is vacationing in Palm Springs."

She leans on her elbow and scowls. "And, again, is Elvis on my list of must-know-abouts?"

He flips to another page and scans it. Through clenched teeth, he says, "It seems Lucy is attempting to get Schroder to smooch with her for Beethoven's birthday."

"What the hell do I care about—wait, what?"

"*Peanuts...* You know, Charlie Brown. The comic strip. I figure if you don't want to hear the real news, you might be happy with the funnies."

She covers her eyes with her hands, and her shoulders undulate up and down.

He pushes the newspaper aside as his face grows dark with concern. "Aww, I'm sorry, hon. I was just kidding. I didn't mean to upset—"

She peeks up and bursts into a fit of laughter. "I'm sorry I'm being so shirty. I'm just absolutely knackered. Honestly, I feel like skipping church and going right to Bedfordshire."

He chuckles. "Shirty? That's cranky, right? I love how your British slang really kicks in when you're tired. I think I learn something new each time. Do you really want to stay home? I can call your parents and tell them—"

"No. I promised Mum we'd be there to help her oversee the orphans' toy collection being loaded on the truck. She's so proud of chairing the committee, I don't want to disappoint her by not going to see all the donations she's gathered."

He takes their dishes to the sink and links his hand through her elbow. "Okay. You're the boss. Let's head on up and let me change that dressing on your hand..."

* * *

CHAPTER THIRTEEN

As the church service concludes, the pastor brings Ada to the lectern, and her chest swells as she reads the report of how many toys were collected for each age group. When she announces that the 1968 toy drive has been the church's most successful since their inception of the Toys for Orphans crusade began in 1951, the sanctuary roars with applause, and Bridget's eyes pop open, jolting her from her unexpected catnap. *Bollocks! I hope no one saw me.* Her tweed dress makes her arms itch, and her feet already ache in her high heels. Feigning a smile, she longs for the moment she can snuggle under the covers in bed and down a mug of hot cocoa before taking a much-needed snooze.

After numerous rounds of "Peace be with you," the congregation is dismissed, and Bridget and Jack follow Ada and Geoffrey outside behind the building where a large, empty moving truck awaits. Ada unlocks a storage shed, then Jack and Geoffrey start bringing crates of toys from the shed to the loading area behind the truck. Three men soon join them and form a human chain between the shed and the truck, each passing a box to the next. Bridget stands back with Ada as she supervises the bucket brigade.

Bridget covers her mouth and yawns. "Sorry, Mum. I didn't sleep well last night, and I guess it's catching up to me."

Ada hugs her daughter to her side. "Well, you're still young. You don't need all that beauty sleep anyway."

They giggle until a teenage boy rushes out the back door and shoves a note at Bridget. "Dr. Castle, the hospital phoned. They said it was urgent that I find you and pass the message."

Bridget scans the paper. "Oh, no. There was an accident. Looks like a child fell off a statue and may have a brain injury. I have to go. Jack, you get a ride with Mum and Dad. I need my car keys."

He digs in his pocket and tosses the keys to her. "Do you want me to go with you?"

Already in motion, she waves and, over her shoulder, says, "No. I'll call you later." She rushes to her Mustang and adjusts the seat. As she speeds toward the hospital, she turns on the radio. The world news plays, and she changes the station to find a local update.

"...at the Charles Sumner monument in Harvard Square, when they set their daughter, two-year-old Susan Donna Turner, on the pedestal near the bronze feet of the sculpture to take a photograph. The child was rushed via ambulance to Boston's Saint Francis Hospital. It is unknown at this time how extensive her injuries are. In other news, your favorite department store and mine, Jordan Marsh, is featuring a twenty percent off sale on select merchandise starting tomorrow and continuing through Friday, December twentieth..."

Bridget flips the radio off and guns the accelerator. "What were those parents thinking?" She lets out a long sigh. "I guess I don't have any right to judge them. I don't know what happened or how bad the child's injuries are." Her tires squeal as she peels into the emergency parking lot. She grabs the keys and unbuttons her coat as she races into the building. "Where's the Turner child?" she asks the receptionist.

Dr. Redding catches her eye and waves. "Bridget, we're in here."

Bridget hurries to the exam room. "What have you found so far?" After washing her left hand and the fingertips of her bandaged hand, she removes a small flashlight from Glenn's lab coat pocket then checks the unconscious child's left pupil. The girl's chocolate brown eyes show no sign of life. Bridget checks the toddler's right eye. "Acute pupillary dilation. Have you run x-rays yet?"

"Yes, we just finished. Roger's going to run the films up here as soon as they're ready. The paramedics had to defibrillate her on scene."

"How many times?"

"Once."

"Vitals when she got here?" She grabs the stethoscope from around his neck.

"B.P.: one-sixty over one-fifteen, pulse: one fifty-five."

Bridget sticks the stethoscope stems in her ears and leans over the child as she listens to the toddler's heart and lungs. She uses care as she moves the child's hair with a pen, inspecting her scalp. "I don't see any lacerations or scalp tears. Bollocks, where's Roger with those films?"

"He should be back any time now. If you have to operate, what about your hand?"

"I don't know. Let's just get a look at the diagnostics first and play it by ear from there. Have you met the parents? Did they say how it happened?"

"Yeah, Dad set her on the statue pedestal. Wanted to get a photo. Mom was supposed to stand beside her and hold the child up, but the wind blew, and she turned away to keep her hair from blowing. It happened in a split second. The girl leaned forward and landed on the crown of her head. I called your service as soon as I heard about it from the paramedics before they bought her here. I guess the service tracked you down pretty quickly because we only had her about fifteen minutes before you arrived."

She nods and peruses the patient's chart. "Okay, very good. Can you please call for a nurse? I need someone to run up to my office."

"Sure." He activates the intercom on the wall. "Nurse Linda to E.R. Three, STAT."

Bridget makes some notes on the chart as Linda steps into the room. "How can I help you, Doctors?"

Bridget pulls the keys from her coat hanging over the chair and tosses them to Linda. "Can you please run up to my office? I'm going to need my lab coat, my stethoscope, and my medical bag. You'll find them in the storage closet. And in my top desk drawer, there's a leather stick barrette. Oh, and there's a pair of Birkenstocks under my desk. Can you grab those, too, please?"

"Yes, Doctor. Right away." The keys jingle as Linda makes a beeline for the express elevator.

Glenn raises an eyebrow. "Sandals in the middle of winter?"

Bridget rolls her eyes. "I can't stand around in these stilettos all day. Every bone in my feet'll be broken. You want to point me toward the parents, and we'll see if they've got anything else?"

"Sure. I've got them in a private waiting room. Didn't want the press to hound them." He accompanies her down the hall then leaves her with the victim's family. "I'll go check the status of the films."

Bridget extends her hand to shake the father's then, remembering her injury, rescinds the offer. "Good afternoon, folks. My name is Dr. Castle. I'm going to be evaluating your daughter and possibly performing surgery. I'm waiting on some test results right now. Can either of you tell me exactly how she fell?"

The father stands and paces in front of his chair. "I guess it was my fault. I picked her up and set her up on that statue to take a photo. While I was looking at the camera settings, she just toppled over." His voice cracks.

The wife scoots to the edge of her chair. "No, it was my fault. A gust of wind blew, and I didn't want my hair to be mussed for the picture, so I turned away from it. That's when she fell. I'm just... I'm a horrible person, that's all! If anything happens to my baby, I'll never forgive myself."

Mr. Turner sits beside his wife and wraps his arm around her shoulders. Bridget pulls a chair in front of them and sits. "Mr. and Mrs. Turner, I'm not here to debate any fault in the matter. From a medical perspective, I just need to know what happened. When she hit the ground, was there blood? Did she scream? Cry? Was she conscious? How long was it until the ambulance arrived? Did either of you attempt to move her body?"

The parents look at each other then at Bridget. Mrs. Turner's hands tremble as she says, "I didn't see her fall, but from what it looked like immediately after, I think she landed directly on the top of her head."

Her husband nods. "Yes, that's what happened. She leaned forward, almost in slow motion, and by the time she hit the ground, she was upside down. I thought I heard a crack, but there was no blood anywhere. I tried to catch her but... She didn't even make a peep. I—to be honest, I thought she was dead." He buries his face in his hands and sobs.

Bridget nods and looks to the wife. "I'm sorry to put you both through this, but it is important. Did either of you move her before the paramedics arrived?"

Fresh tears well in the mother's eyes. "Well... yes. I mean, she's our baby, and I wanted to comfort her. When my husband ran to find a pay phone and call an ambulance, I fell to my knees and scooped her into my arms. I rocked her back and forth and kissed her forehead and told her everything was going to be all right. Oh, I just can't believe this nightmare is really happening!"

Glenn sticks his head in the door. "Dr. Castle, we have the films."

Bridget stands and takes a box of tissues from a nearby coffee table, offering it to the couple. "Okay, well, someone will be out soon to keep you abreast of what's happening. I promise I'm going to do everything I can for your child. Goodbye." Her high heels click as she hurries back to the exam room.

Shoulder to shoulder with Glenn, Bridget shoves two x-rays in the light box, stepping closer to inspect them. She scratches her head and flips her hair out of the way. "Are there any more views? The parietal isn't damaged at all."

Glenn removes the films and replaces them with two more. "Yeah, we took images of the temporal and occipital."

The nurse returns with Bridget's items. "Dr. Castle, will there be anything else?"

Bridget slides her arms through her lab coat and kicks off her Sunday shoes, trading them for the sandals. "Yes, could you please take my coat, purse, and shoes up to my office?"

"Of course."

"Thanks, Linda. You can just leave my keys at the reception desk." Bridget gathers her hair at the nape of her neck and manipulates the leather tab over it then pushes the stick of the barrette through. She tucks some stray hair behind her ear then steps closer to the light box. "All right. Let's see..." She shakes her head. "I can't see anything. Both temporals look fine. Give me the occipital views."

Dr. Redding switches out the films, and they both lean in to inspect. Bridget removes a pen from her pocket and taps the left film. "There it is. Look there. Right on the median nuchal line. That's not a linear fracture; it's a depression fracture. There's no way around it; I'm going to have to go in. We need to get her prepped right away."

"But your hand. Maybe Jack should step in on this one."

She flips on the lights. "Jack hasn't done this type of pediatric procedure in more than five years, and we don't have time to waste. We'll just have to remove the dressing and double glove my hand. You go have someone get us a room ready. I'll tell the parents." She leaves with a determined gait.

She flings the door of the waiting room open and stands in front of the couple. "All right, I've identified the problem. Your daughter has a depression fracture. That means she most likely landed on something or something struck the back of her head on the way down."

The father clears his throat. "Uh, what does that mean?"

"That means we operate. Now. There's no time to waste. If it were just a linear fracture, we could hold off, and she'd probably be fine. But with a depression fracture, the skull has been broken, and with her still being unconscious, my bet is it's pressing on her brain. I won't know for certain until we get in there."

The mother's hand flies to her chest. "How long will the operation take?"

"Mrs. Turner, I won't know until I open her up and see how much damage there is, but it'll be a minimum of four hours. A nurse will be in periodically to keep you posted." Bridget hurries out then flees to the doctor's lounge and phones her parents' house.

"Hello?"

"Mum, it's me. Is Jack there?"

"Yes, we brought him home to feed him. We heard about the accident on the news. Is the little girl going to be okay?"

"I don't know. I need to operate. Just tell Jack I'll see him later. I've got to go."

"All right, Lovey. Good luck."

"Thanks, Mummy." She cradles the receiver and heads up to the second-floor procedural area where she finds a nurse. "Amy, are they prepping the little Turner girl yet?"

"Yes, Doctor. She's in Prep-Room Three."

Bridget heads to the Prep-Room and peeks her head in as the child's head is being shaved. Pecan-colored curls fall to the floor, and Bridget's breath catches in her throat. *Bollocks. I hate this part so much.*

# # #

9 October 1945

Caro Diario (Dear Diary),

I've been doing well in school. In fact, so far, my grades are among the top three averages in four of my classes. The only class I don't particularly care for is physical education. It's not that I don't want to get out there and play or do the exercises they require. But I feel so self-conscious undressing in that locker room, and the showers that offer little privacy almost send me into a panic. I'm 5' 2" tall, and before I was arrested, I weighed 109 pounds. After being liberated, I weighed 62 pounds. I've gained nearly 25 pounds since then (or almost 2 stone as they say here), but I'm still underweight, and the sight of me without clothes makes the other girls stare. Of course, my short hairstyle doesn't help, either.

I'll never forget the day I arrived at Auschwitz-Birkenau. The men and women were sorted into different groups. We were then registered and assigned a number. There was a lot of confusion during the process with the guards barking orders in German, and so many of the other prisoners didn't understand them or know how to respond. I don't know what made me speak up, but all of a sudden, I found myself translating several conversations in different languages. One of the S.S. men pulled me aside and whispered to another of the higher-ranked guards who pulled me from the queue and pushed me to the front of the group. He whispered to the registration clerk, and only later did I learn that my multi-lingual ability earned me the position of being an official translator for the registration process.

From that point on, I was known only as number 853942. Next, I was tattooed with this, my new moniker. The tätowierer – tattooist – was a young Jewish boy not more than sixteen or seventeen years old. I could tell he was horrified to have to puncture my skin, but he was more terrified not to. His eyes silently pled with me to forgive him. We were then assigned barrack numbers and given our work detail.

After that, I was ordered at gunpoint to remove all my clothes. (We all were.) My hair was sheared by another prisoner who was apparently still outraged at the way her own crowning glory was shorn when she arrived because she didn't hesitate to cut my scalp and pull fistfuls of hair as she snipped them off. Next, another woman with a razor finished shaving my head and all my private parts. I'd never been so humiliated!

Calcium chloride was then rubbed into our heads (which stung our open cuts and eyes) and was meant to "kill the filthy vermin of the lice-infested Untermenschen – sub-humans," as one S.S. man put it. We were then forced into a large, dark room where we were shivering and attempting to cover our nudity before streams of icy water rained from the ceiling to either cleanse us or torture us further.

Of all the degradation, humiliation, and debasement I faced (we all faced), I believe the experience of having my hair shorn and shaved – the mere shock of witnessing such a barbaric act, the ghastly sight of the large piles of all our hair being saved for use somewhere else, the desperate pleas of so many women and girls crying and begging to keep their hair, the urgent whispers of the barbers attempting to silence them before the guards killed them on the spot, and the sharp sounds of so many pairs of scissors clipping away so fervently was an event that will remain carved in my mind like stone until my dying day.

# # #

An orderly clears his throat behind Bridget. "Excuse me, Doctor. I just brought you some sterile scrubs to the washroom."

Bridget shakes her head at the ghosts of her past. "Thank you. Do you know what operating theater we'll be using?"

"Yes, Suite Two."

"Very good." Bridget heads down to the washroom, removes her bandage, and washes her hands. She changes into her aqua-colored scrubs, stores her wedding rings and clothes in a locker, then scrubs her hands and forearms again. Using a stiff brush, she winces when the surgical soap works its way into her wound. *Wow, that smarts.* She keeps her hands above her elbows as the circulating nurse assists her with her hairnet, cap, and mask.

Bridget follows the circulating nurse into the surgical suite entrance, and the nurse dries the surgeon's hands with a sterile towel. The nurse stretches two pairs of sterile gloves over Bridget's hands and offers her a gown. Bridget slides her arms in the sleeves, and the circulator steps behind Bridget and pulls the gown around the doctor's torso, tying it in the back. After the nurse tucks Bridget's gown sleeves into her gloves, Bridget nods and says, "Thank you. Is everyone ready?"

"Yes, Doctor."

Bridget heads over to the operating table. The scrub nurse rolls a tray of instruments beside Bridget. The patient lays prone with her face positioned through a hole in the table.

Bridget nods to a man seated by the patient's head. "Ah, Dr. Dick Spurgeon, my favorite anesthesiologist. It's always good to see you here. I'm glad you were available today."

Dick holds a face mask and hose over the patient's mouth. "Likewise, Dr. Castle."

Bridget takes a deep breath. "Scalpel." The nurse places the instrument in the doctor's hand, and Bridget makes the first incision. "Folks, we have a twenty-seven-month-old Caucasian female named

Susan Donna Turner. Susan and her family were in town this weekend, sightseeing in Harvard square, when the family stopped to pose for a picture with the Charles Sumner monument."

The scrub nurse peeks over Bridget's shoulder and says, "I spoke to the family briefly when they got here. They said Charles Sumner was the wife's grandmother's great uncle, and they were getting the picture for Grandma. Such a shame…"

* * *

CHAPTER FOURTEEN

Nearly eight hours later, Bridget's lungs deflate as she exits the surgical suite. She and Dick head down the corridor together, and he says, "Nice work, Doctor."

She manages a weary smile. "Thanks. You too. I'd say little Susan is a very lucky girl today." They reach the express elevator, and she stops walking. "I'll head down and talk to the parents."

"All right, Doctor. Goodnight."

"Night." Bridget takes the elevator to the first floor and gasps when the doors open to Jack and Dr. Redding standing there. "Oh, what a surprise. What are you doing here, love?" She kisses Jack's cheek.

He wraps his arm around her and rubs her back. "I've been here for a couple of hours. I wanted to drive you home. I knew you'd be exhausted. How'd it go?"

"A lot better than I expected. I think she's going to—" A commotion at the reception desk causes them to turn.

"But, Miss, it's my granddaughter!"

"Ma'am, I'm sorry. It's the hospital's policy not to allow children in the visitor's area. You're going to have to—"

Jack cocks his head back. "Excuse me. What's going on, folks?"

The guest, holding a sleeping toddler against her chest, directs her attention to Jack. "Sir, my granddaughter is having surgery, and my daughter asked me to come up and sit with them. We're staying in a hotel, and there's no one there to watch Melissa here. I *had* to bring her."

The receptionist says, "Yes, Dr. Castle, and I tried telling her that we have policies which—"

Jack holds up his hand, shushing the employee. "Ma'am, is your granddaughter the child who fell at Harvard Square?"

"Yes, I've been waiting for hours to know how she's doing."

The child in her arms wakes and turns toward Bridget. In a sleepy voice, she says, "I want Mommy."

Bridget locks eyes with the child, and her voice catches in her throat as she whispers, "Sie sind Zwillinge."

Jack raises an eyebrow. "Pardon me?"

Bridget clears her throat. "I said they're twins. She's Susan's identical twin, isn't she?"

The grandmother nods. "That's right. When we were at the square today, I was holding Melissa, here, up on the statue while her mother was holding Susan. Is… is Susan out of surgery?"

Bridget gestures toward the waiting area, saying, "She's in recovery right now. Come with me. I was just headed over to talk to her folks."

The entourage follows Bridget to the lounge. Bridget offers a triumphant smile and says, "Mr. and Mrs. Turner, Susan did very well. She's in recovery. You'll be able to see her in about an hour, but only for a couple of minutes. She needs her rest."

Tears stream down Mrs. Turner's cheeks. "Then she's going to be okay?"

Bridget grabs a fresh box of tissues from a cabinet and offers it to the family. "She had an external occipital crest depression fracture with secondary hemorrhage and edema of the cerebellum and brainstem. I'd say we got in just in time."

Mr. Turner shakes his head. "I'm sorry, what?"

Bridget cups Melissa's face with her hand and gestures with her finger to the back of the child's head. "The crest, what we call the median nuchal line, is a little ridge back here in the center of the skull that divides the left and right sides of the head. A depression fracture is a broken piece of skull that pressed inward and lodged against the brain. The fracture stretched from here down to the rear of the foramen magnum, which basically is a hole in the skull base where the spinal cord connects with the brainstem. Understand?"

Mr. Turner nods. "I think so, yes."

"If her brain would've had time to swell more, we'd likely be having a very different conversation right now. We relieved the pressure and drained the hemorrhage. When you see her, she's going to have a drainage tube which I'll remove in about a week if everything goes as planned. Her head is bandaged, and she's wearing what we call a halo vest traction brace. It looks scary, but it's necessary. Basically, a metal hoop is secured to her head and affixed to a vest to stabilize her cervical spine and to keep her immobile and prevent any further neurological damage. She also has a lot of facial bruising as a result of the surgery. We're going to need to keep her in the Pediatric I.C.U. for at least five days. During that time, she'll be on anabolic steroids to keep the swelling down, and she'll have to take an anticonvulsant to make sure she doesn't have a seizure. Okay?"

Mr. Turner stands and offers his hand to Bridget. As they shake hands, he says, "Thank you, Dr. Castle. When we got here and they told us a lady doctor was coming—Well, I must admit, I didn't have much hope for my little girl. I was wrong. I'm really sorry." He scoops Melissa into his arms. "Missy, thank the nice doctor for helping your sister."

"Thank you, lady."

Bridget gets lost in the child's chocolate pools identical to her sister's.

# # #

20 October 1945

Liebes Tagebuch (Dear Diary),

School is going great. In fact, everything in my life is wonderful. At least it was until this morning. I went out on a shopping excursion – my first real time leaving the house all by myself except for school – when I found a little cart that sold flowers. I was feeling so happy being out and about town that I decided to stop and pick up a bouquet of asters for the house.

While I was digging through my change purse for money, two little girls – identical twins – accompanied their mother to the cart. While their mum talked with the flower cart owner, the girls started playing near the road, and one fell into the street. I was so lost in their identical coffee-colored eyes, I almost didn't realize a car was coming. I dropped my asters and my purse and scooped the child up just in time as the car sped by. The girl looked at me as I set her down, and she said, "Thank you, lady."

It was such a simple phrase, but it brought back so many horrendous memories that I immediately fled and raced all the way home, leaving my money and flowers behind! I certainly couldn't talk to anyone about what troubled me, so I decided to tell you, Dear Diary, instead. (You've always been so good at keeping my secrets.)

I already told you that when I first arrived at Auschwitz, the Nazis were interested in my ability to speak multiple languages, and they assigned me to be a translator for the incoming prisoners. At first, I was hesitant to do anything that might help those bastards in their quest to reach the Final Solution. But then one of the ladies in my barrack told me that I'd better cooperate or they'd likely kill me.

It wasn't long before I realized that I had an advantage over them: I knew what the prisoners were saying, and I could warn them about certain things such as telling the registrar that they had certain specific skills, even if they didn't. Doing these little things certainly saved many of them from the gas chambers or other abuse. At least I felt good about contributing something toward the anti-Nazi cause.

But then came the day when a train came in, and many of the prisoners looked positively ill as they disembarked. I quickly realized they were dehydrated and were suffering from heat stroke. (Even though winter was almost upon us, they were packed in so tightly, it was obvious from their red faces and soaking wet clothing that their insides were baking.) Before I even had time to consider that I might get in trouble for speaking my mind, I heard myself calling for ice and water (as if such luxuries existed), and I instructed the victims to remove all their unnecessary clothing so they could lower their temperatures.

One of the S.S. men grabbed my arm and pulled me to the side. He dialed a phone then covered his mouth, whispering as he spoke.

Before I knew it, he told me to follow him. He took me to a building across camp where he said I would be an assistant to a Dr. Josef Mengele. The guard said he'd overheard me talking to one girl about why her menstrual cycle had stopped. Another time, he witnessed me counseling a man about eating cockroaches when he was hungry and telling him all the diseases he could catch if he continued to do so. The guard said Dr. Mengele would appreciate someone with such a large medical vocabulary and multi-lingual skills to help him in his work. I was actually foolish enough to feel flattered.

It wasn't until the guard left me there that Dr. Mengele told me about his theories on why using twins as human lab rats was going to prove to be a genius idea because they would be the perfect subjects, having one as the control subject and the other as the test subject. It was my job to translate his commands to the unsuspecting children.

Once I realized just how perverse and disdainful his ideas of "experiments" were, I also realized that if I dared to disobey him, I would likely wind up on his dissection table sooner rather than later. That sick demon subjected those poor children to purposeful injections of diseases and blood and semen and even chloroform to stop their hearts. Every week, the little ones lined up naked, and he would measure every part of them then have me translate what he wanted them to do while a nurse took their blood. Oddly, the twins were allowed to keep their hair so the doctor could measure it each week and see if there were differences. He tested these children for human endurance and the lengths one might take to survive.

I heard tell around the camp that once, he even shot two eight-year-old twin boys in the neck and autopsied them right then and there to resolve a quarrel with some other doctors as to whether the boys were infected with tuberculosis. (They weren't.) I also heard that he performed an operation on a set of Roma twins wherein he cut and sewed them together to create conjoined twins.

Dr. Mengele frequently got the children to do what he wanted by telling them that if they cooperated, they would go see their mama. (I especially hated him for this particular lie. It was so cruel!) And when the children didn't speak German, he wanted me to tell them this falsehood too. I wanted to tell the children that their mothers were dead. That they would be better off if they, too, provoked the crazy madman and got themselves killed instantly so that at least they wouldn't have to endure any more of his insane barbarities. But in the end, I couldn't bring myself to say that to the little kiddies. So, I, too, told them to head down the hall to the lab and do as they were told so they could see their mamas.

Every night after I had to fib to these children like this, I would have nightmares and lose sleep. The last time I translated this brutal falsehood before I was transferred away, one pair of identical girls, maybe three years old, looked over their shoulder at me with their big, brown eyes as they proceeded down the corridor on their death march, and the one on the left said, "Thank you, lady." I felt as if I had been punched in the gut, and in that moment, I wished I could trade places with them. And I wished more than anything that I had the power and opportunity to kill that psychotic demon bastard, Dr. Mengele!

# # #

CHAPTER FIFTEEN

Late the next morning, Bridget wakes to the sound of voices. She wipes the sleep from her eyes and checks the clock beside her bed. "Ten o'clock. Wow, I overslept." She scurries to the bathroom and manages to cover her hand with her dishwashing glove then showers. She manipulates her hair into its usual low bun for work, applies her neutral-shaded makeup, and dresses in her conservative slacks and blouse before heading downstairs. Jack closes the front door and winks at her. "Good morning, beautiful."

She furrows her brow as she digs through her purse. "Where's my keys?"

He folds his arms across his chest. "Good morning to you, too, dear. You're looking very handsome today."

"Sorry. I can't believe I overslept so late. I need to get going. Have you seen my keys?"

"You didn't oversleep. I turned off your alarm."

Her eyes pierce his. "How could you do that? I have a lot on my schedule today. Do you know where my keys are or not?"

"I assume they're in your office at work. And you're welcome."

She taps her forehead with the heel of her palm. "You drove me home in your car. I forgot."

"Right. Because you were so tired and had such a long day after getting so little sleep. I called us both in late this morning so you could catch up on your rest. Go grab some breakfast, and we'll leave whenever you want."

"I'm sorry. Thank you, my love." She heads to the kitchen and grabs a banana. "Who was at the door?"

"Which time? First, it was a Fuller Brush salesman. I was just getting rid of him when Beverly pulled up. She wanted to get an early start cleaning since she missed a few days last week, but I told her you were sleeping. I sent her to the store with the food list."

She bites off a chunk of banana then spreads some peanut butter on the next bite. "Good. Is there coffee?"

"We're all out. We can stop on the way."

She shoves the last bite in her mouth and grabs her coat. "All right. I'm ready."

As they head out to Jack's car, they wave to their neighbor across the street. Jack says, "Morning, Mrs. Arnold. Any word from Barry yet?"

The woman shakes her head and stuffs her newspaper in the pocket of her bathrobe. "No. He was still in Saigon, last we heard, and the mail isn't always reliable. We just keep praying."

"All right. Please keep us posted. We'll be thinking about him." He opens the door for Bridget. "Okay, you want me to stop for coffee?"

"No, I'll just grab some at work." She yawns and looks out the window as he starts the car. They back out of the driveway, and he turns on the news.

"...and yesterday, David Jacobs, the British lawyer known for representing celebrities such as Liberace, the Rolling Stones, Judy Garland, and the Beatles' manager Brian Epstein, was found hanged in his home at Hove in Sussex, England. He was fifty-six years old. In a more humorous event, at least to some of us, Philadelphia Eagles fans who attended the final home game in a season with eleven straight losses became so enraged at the team's performance in yesterday afternoon's game against the Minnesota Vikings that they booed and threw snowballs at Santa Claus. Frank Olivo, a fan already

dressed as Santa, was recruited to portray Father Christmas during halftime after a previously planned Christmas pageant was canceled due to the poor condition of the field..."

Bridget's heavy eyelids close as the car slows to yield to a group of war protesters.

The muscles in Jack's neck tense as the wail of a siren grows nearer. "Uh oh, looks like the cops are coming to break up the commotion. It's too bad the kids can't find some way other than standing in front of businesses to make their point..."

Jack's voice ebbs, and Bridget's mind succumbs to sleep. Her dream transports her to Auschwitz with Gunter Hetzel dressed in an S.S. uniform. He points a handgun to her back and pushes her along to Dr. Mengele's office. As they enter the empty room, Gunter spins her around to face him. He unbuckles his belt and aims the weapon at her forehead. "Lie down and lift up your skirt!" Too frightened to protest, her hands shake as she complies with his order. He reaches between her legs, and his sadistic grin morphs into a look of utter disgust. "Monatsblutung! Du ekelhaft Hure!" *Menstrual blood! You nasty whore!*

Bridget lets out a yelp as her head jolts up and she awakens. She feels Jack's eyes on her, and heat rises to her cheeks. "Sorry. I guess I dozed off." She wills her heart to stop its ferocious pounding. *Bollocks, that dream was just like when it really happened. I wonder if Herr Hetzel is the son of that guard. They look so much alike.*

# # #

12 November 1945

Drogi Pamiętniku (Dear Diary),

Today was a Monday in every sense of the word! When I arrived at school, I realized that I'd forgotten the chemistry report I'd been working on all last week. The instructor allowed me to bring it in tomorrow without losing credit because he knows what a diligent student I am; but him announcing that in front of the class only made them resentful towards me, especially since they are so much older than I.

When I went to Phys. Ed., the girls were supposed to do drills, one of which was running up and down the steps on the stands, while the boys played rugby. After a particularly strenuous drill, I sat for a moment to catch my breath while I pretended to tie my shoes. The girl's coach (who reminds me too much of the Bitch of Bergen-Belsen, the female S.S. guard who always walked around with that scary dog and ordered it to attack people) kept blowing her whistle at me and screaming at me to get up on my feet. (Little does she know, with all I've been through, she doesn't intimidate me a bit.)

When I was done tying my shoes, I stood to resume my drills. A few seconds later, I heard laughter, and I turned around to see what was so funny. The girls were pointing at me, and the boys had stopped playing and were all coming closer to look at me. It made me feel almost as self-conscious as the first time I had to strip when I arrived at Auschwitz.

I had no idea what was so funny, but one nice girl named Shirley ran to my side and whispered to me that I had started my menstrual cycle. It made me remember the first time I ever got my period when I was eleven. Mama had already educated me on what to expect, and she'd even shown me how to fold up rags and pin them inside my undergarments so I'd know what to do when the time came. But Papa said the first time was a special occasion, so he asked Dr. Van Den Boom to purchase me some storebought sanitary supplies. When the Good Doctor returned with a story of how difficult it was for him to locate them due to the war shortages, I never dreamed I could encounter a more humiliating event. (What made the event even more embarrassing was that the Good Doctor brought me a large, valentine-shaped box of chocolates rather than the little paper sack of dropjes he usually gave me.)

I know I never even told you about my coming of age, Dear Diary, because, back then, in my eleven-year-old mind, my reproductive organs were a thing of privacy to be kept to myself. But after all I've seen and lived through since last year, I don't usually encounter many things that frighten or embarrass me.

After I arrived at Auschwitz, I had only one cycle before they stopped completely. When it came, of course, the S.S. didn't provide any sanitary supplies, and one of the older lady prisoners told me how I could sneak into the uniform shed and steal a uniform top and shred it into rags which I could reuse.

So many women were treated as if they were even worse than sub-human when they walked around camp with blood running down their legs. But I know for a fact that the messiness of it saved more than a few women from enduring medical experiments, experimental surgeries, and even from rape. I know the latter because an S.S. guard attempted to molest me until he learned I was having my cycle; then he was repulsed.

But back at school today, I was a bit alarmed to hear that my cycle had returned. After all, I've been in a state of amenorrhea for over a year now. So, if I would have gotten my cycle today, despite the bit of mental discomfort it may have caused, its arrival might have actually been a reason to celebrate. But that was not the case. As it turned out, one of the boys had poured red paint on the bench as a trick to see if one of the girls would sit in it. My gym bloomers were ruined.

# # #

Jack eases into a parking place, and he and Bridget head inside the hospital. On the way in, she nods to President Johnson's picture. After retrieving her keys from the emergency receptionist's desk, Bridget hugs herself as they wait for the elevator. The canned music of Jimmy Boyd belting out "I Saw Mommy Kissing Santa Claus" echoes down the corridors. When the car stops at the seventh floor, Bridget pecks Jack's cheek and says, "Have a good day, my love." She yawns as she heads toward her office.

After dumping her purse, coat, and an extra pair of shoes in her office, she makes a beeline down to the sixth floor Community Room and pours a steaming cup of coffee. A smile comes to her face as she watches a group of Boy Scouts and their den mother sorting toy donations into groups according to age and sex while a troop of Girl Scouts wrap the gifts in festive paper and ribbons for the hospital's Pediatric Ward. She peeks at the activities until her cup is empty, then she refills it and heads back to her office.

She yawns and slaps her cheeks to try to wake up. *I can't believe I'm still so exhausted.* She sits at her desk and steeples her fingers, resting her forehead on her hands. Moments later, she jerks her head up and snorts. "Bloody hell. I can't do anything if I'm sleeping on the job." She slurps her coffee then raises an eyebrow. "What's this?" Across the desk sits a small, wrapped box with a gift tag that reads *"From Your Secret Admirer."* A smile crosses her lips as she tears off the paper. She giggles aloud at the sight of the Christmas Storybook of Lifesavers. "Jack, you silly old bean. I love you." She tears through the cellophane and phones Jack's office as she removes each roll of candies from the book.

"Hello. Jack Castle here."

Her heart flutters. "Well, hello, Dr. Castle. I just called to thank you for the lovely gift."

"Hmm, your voice sounds vaguely familiar... Who is this, please?"

She chuckles. "Ah, it's a dark and mysterious woman who holds the key to your heart."

"Oh? Let's see... Is it Carla? Oh, no, Sally, right? Or maybe it's Barbara or Judy?"

"Well, maybe. Or perhaps I dialed wrong. Was this Jack Castle? Or did I dial Donald or Richard by mistake?"

Jack lets out a loud belly laugh. "You're cute. Did you get your coffee?"

"Yes, two cups. I think I need it intravenously. I can't wake up."

"Oh, no. Well, we'll make an early night of it tonight so you can catch up on your sleep. I can wait around and drive you home again if you like."

"No. But would you stop and pick up some Chinese take-out on your way home? I suspect I won't feel up to cooking."

"Of course."

"Thanks. And thank you for the Lifesavers. I wish they had coffee flavored."

"Uck! That sounds disgusting. Hold on, hon... What? Oh, okay... Hon, I have to get going. There's a Board Member here with a gift basket, and he wants to give it to me in person."

"Well, aren't you the special one? All right, my love. See you later."

"Okay, hon. Bye bye." He hangs up, and she cradles the receiver.

She stands and hides each of the dozen rolls in separate places throughout her office. Popping a clove-flavored candy in her mouth, she stretches her arms above her head. "All right, I need to wake up. I guess I'll go check on little Susan first." She locks her office and heads down to the elevator. She hums along with Wayne Newton as "Jingle Bell Rock" plays in the lift then steps off at the Fourth Floor Pediatric Ward.

She takes a tangerine Lifesaver from her pocket and pops it in her mouth as she reaches the nurses' station. Her eyes open extra wide as she attempts to disguise her exhaustion. "Good morning, Brenda."

"Good to see you, Dr. Castle. Hardly morning anymore. We're waiting on the lunch cart to come so we can make rounds."

Bridget's cheeks flush. "Right. I got a late start today. How's Susan Turner doing?"

"She's doing well. She had a bit of a rough night, but we got her to drink some apple juice this morning, and she's managed to keep it down. She's still quite groggy."

"Yes, that's to be expected. I wanted to keep her partially sedated until she starts to heal and we see how things are going. What room is she in?"

"Four-eleven."

"Very good. Thanks for your help." Bridget makes a beeline for the child's room and pulls her stethoscope out of her lab coat pocket. "Well, hello there, Susan. It's good to see you. My name is Dr. Castle. Can I use this to listen to your chest?" She inserts the stems in her ears and presses the instrument against Susan's torso.

"Mommy. Where's Mommy?"

"Aww, your mummy will be here soon, and your daddy too. Visiting hours start at noon, and they're going to come see you when the nice nursey has your lunch ready. Okay?"

Susan's thumb finds its way to her mouth, and she begins suckling as her heavy eyelids flutter closed.

Bridget straightens the child's covers and makes a notation in the patient's chart. *That's right, you sleep, little one. Sleep for the both of us. I wish I could curl up there and join you.* She stifles a yawn as she shoves her stethoscope back in her pocket, and she makes her way to the elevator. She rides up to the fifth floor and heads to Room 502.

She knocks and heads in, stepping aside for the food service worker delivering the patient's lunch. The employee leaves, and Bridget sits in the chair next to the bed. "How are we doing today, Mr. Barnaby?"

Craig lifts the cover off his plate and grabs his fork. His cheeks redden, and he casts his eyes down. "I never thought I'd hear myself say this again, but I feel good. Really good, actually. I'm looking forward to having my surgery and going home. My dad said he's got a job lined up for me in his buddy's motorcycle repair shop as soon as I want it."

"Really? That's wonderful. I told you your possibilities are limitless as long as you have the right attitude."

He stabs an asparagus spear and shoves it in his mouth. "Yeah, I know you did. I think when I saw your, uh, hand bleed like it did, I, uh, really had a wake-up call. I, uh... I'm really sorry about that."

Her eyes twinkle, and she squeezes his wrist. "If my injury was responsible for such a turn-about in you, then it was worth it. But, um..." She tilts her head and raises her eyebrows. "I was at the Children's Choir Party the other day. I saw you with a certain lovely candy striper. Could that be part of the reason for your new attitude?"

He scoops up a bite of mashed potatoes and attempts to conceal a grin. "You busted me. Her name's Lisa. She just turned eighteen, and she has a brother in 'Nam who's M.I.A." He slaps his thigh. "And she doesn't even seem to be phased about these things being gone." He wiggles his stumps under the sheet and shoves the potatoes in his mouth.

"Well, that's terrific. I'm just so happy for you, Craig." She holds up her bandaged hand. "I had to perform an emergency craniotomy yesterday, and while I was able to do all I needed to, I would feel more comfortable if we postponed your procedure until Wednesday instead of tomorrow. I should have my sutures out by then."

"Sure, Doc, whatever you say."

"Well, I think this Lisa's a keeper. You're certainly in an agreeable mood these days."

He slurps his hot tea. "Actually, if I wouldn't have been such a prick, you wouldn't have gotten hurt. I mean, I know it's my fault, and I'm real glad you were able to save that little kid yesterday. I saw it on the news."

"Oh? Well, I'm glad too. It really doesn't even hurt anymore, but I'd still prefer to wait an extra day to be sure. You seem like you've got something else you want to talk about."

He casts his eyes down and twists the stem of his apple. "Uh, yeah, I uh, I just wanted to say you were right about something else too."

She raises an eyebrow. "Oh? And what was that?"

"When you said my dick works. You know, that I had a lot to be thankful for."

"I beg your pardon?"

"I mean, I haven't had any, you know, feeling *down there* since I got back from 'Nam. But Lisa's been coming up to visit me every afternoon after her shift ends these last few days, and, uh... Well, let's just say, it's waking up down there. You know what I mean?"

Bridget suppresses a grin as she stands and pulls her stethoscope out of her pocket. "Yeah, I know what you mean. And I'm very happy for you. If you'll lean forward and let me listen to your lungs, I'll leave you with your lunch and let you get ready for your visit later with Miss Lisa."

He beams as he leans over his tray.

She performs a quick pulmonary examination and pats his shoulder. "All right, Craig. You can relax now and enjoy your meal. I'll pop in and see you tomorrow, and the next day, we'll get that left arm of yours working properly again, okay?"

"Thanks, Doc. Oh, and thanks for the electric shaver and shaving kit. I know those Norelcos are expensive. That was so generous of you."

"You're very welcome. I hope you liked the English Leather that came with the set."

"I've never used it before, but it smells really good. Lisa likes it."

"Ahh. Well, good."

"And I caught the hint."

"The hint?"

"You got me English Leather because you're English. If you were getting me something to remember you by, I think you changing my life by slicing your hand to keep me from making such a stupid mistake is going to stick with me a lot longer than the aftershave will. But I do thank you. From the bottom of my heart."

"Well, you're very welcome. I know it's rough being in hospital, especially over Christmas. Listen, I'll check in with you tomorrow. Eat your lunch."

"Okay. Thanks, Doc. See ya."

She waves as she pulls the door open. "Ta ta." She starts toward Room 529 then stifles a yawn as she spins on her heel and scurries to the elevator. *Must have coffee before I deal with Gunter Hetzel and his attitude today.*

* * *

CHAPTER SIXTEEN

Bridget rides down to the first floor and follows the sinuous corridor. As she approaches the cafeteria, an unpleasant fragrance assaults her nose. *Ugh! Smells like fried aubergine.* As she rounds the corner, the menu board comes into view, and her suspicion is confirmed by the *"Daily Special: Eggplant Parmigiana"* sign. *No, thank you.* She grabs a tray and heads to the end of the line.

As she mentally hums along with Dean Martin's "Baby, It's Cold Outside" playing throughout the lunchroom, the man in front of her steps backward, bumping into her.

He spins to face her, the muscles in his neck tense. "Excuse me. I'm so sorry—Bridget. I didn't realize it was you. I apologize. I thought I was about to get splashed with hot soup up here."

She dismisses his concern with a wave of her hand. "It's no problem. How are you doing, Ernie?"

"Good. Hey, I've got that report on the Haynes kid ready for you to sign off on. I also contacted Internal Affairs at the police department and gave them a heads up. I told them I'd deliver a copy as soon as I get your John Hancock."

"All right. I'll stop by the morgue after lunch and sign it then."

"Great. Hey, would you like to eat with me? Dave was going to join me, but his wife showed up and needed his help loading a Christmas tree into her station wagon, so he took an early break."

"Sure, I'd be happy to dine with you."

"Good." He steps up to the food service worker. "I'll have an eggplant special and a hot tea, please." He peeks over his shoulder at Bridget. "You?"

She winces and wrinkles her nose. "None for me, thanks. I'll have the chicken pot pie and the largest cup of coffee you have."

The server giggles as she passes their plates under the glass. "Your beverages will be down by the cashier. Have a good day, Doctors."

Ernie takes his dish and winks at the lady. "Thanks, Miss. You too." He slides his tray down the rail and grabs a bowl of warm apple crisp. Bridget takes a slice of sour cream pound cake, and they make their way to the cash register.

The cashier rings up Ernie's lunch and sets a steaming cup of tea on his tray. "That's a buck ninety-one today, Dr. Hamilton."

He takes a five out of his wallet and nods at Bridget. "I'll get Dr. Castle's too."

Bridget says, "No, that's not necessary."

"I know it isn't, but I'm doing it anyway. Here you go." He nudges the bill at the cashier.

The cashier keys in the amount of Bridget's items. "Okay, that'll be $4.17. Out of five." She counts out his change then sets a large cup of coffee on Bridget's tray.

Bridget smiles and splashes some creamer into her cup then sprinkles in two heaping spoonsful of sugar from the bowl next to the register. "Thank you. And thank you, too, Ernie. I appreciate it."

He leads them to an empty table then waits for her to sit. "No problem. I'm just happy to have the company today. My wife's been up in Montpelier since last week. Her dad fell on some ice and broke a hip, and she went to help out my mother-in-law. And my cooking isn't the greatest, so I've kind of been living out of the cafeteria here. You know, working with the stiffs, it's usually nice to go home and have someone to talk to. But with Maggie away..."

"Oh, no; I had no idea. I'm so sorry. Please give Maggie my best when you speak to her. You know, you could've come and stayed with Jack and me. We've got plenty of room, and a lot of the time, our cleaning lady starts dinner for us before we even get home."

"Aw, thanks. I wouldn't want to impose, and I'm hoping Maggie'll be home soon. If she's not here by Friday, I think I'll drive up and surprise her for the weekend."

"Well, next Wednesday's Christmas. Surely, she'll be home by then, no?"

"Actually, we usually visit her family for the major holidays. Maybe I'll just take some vacation time and head up early. I don't know. How's the pot pie today?"

"Mmm, very good. The crust is delicious. Very flaky. You like your aubergine?"

He raises an eyebrow. "Excuse me?'

She giggles. "Sorry. Your eggplant."

"It's wonderful. You want a piece?"

The muscles in her neck tense. "Uh, no, thank you. Personally, I can't stand it." She sips her coffee. "Speaking of delicious, this coffee is the best..."

After lunch, Bridget accompanies Dr. Hamilton to the morgue in the basement. She reads and signs the witness portion of the M.E.'s report on Ronald Haynes then helps herself to the coffeepot on the counter. "Thanks for taking care of this. I really hate when the police have it in for all the teenagers just because a few might be bad."

He stuffs the report in a manila envelope. "I don't think all cops feel that way. I've got a cousin who's been on the force for more than twenty years and—"

"Please don't misunderstand. I'm not saying *all* cops are dirty. It just seems like I've seen a lot of Vietnam protesters come through the emergency room over the last couple of years, and when all they want is peace, it's kind of ironic how often they end up on a slab."

"Well, you've got to admit, a lot of those same kids come through my department already on a slab because they're putting dope in their body, either shooting it up, snorting it, smoking it, or eating it."

"I'm not saying drugs aren't always involved. I know that sometimes—"

"That's what I'm talking about. The hippies we get through here, more often than not, they're tripping on something. Even this Haynes guy. He came up clean, but why was he living in that commune? Because his parents had enough of him doping up and stealing their money to support his habit."

Heat travels up Bridget's neck to her face. "I think we're talking about two different subjects. Yes, drugs are bad. No contest. No, not all police officers are bad. In fact, most aren't. But the handful that are seem to get away with more than just a once-in-a-lifetime lapse in judgment."

"Doctor, with all due respect—"

"I'm talking about a slow motion attempt at genocide. I think a lot of people – policemen – they look at these teenagers with the long hair, the dirty clothes, and the beads and crazy outfits, and they judge that instead of what's inside."

"Okay, so there may be some bias there. I'll give you that. But genocide? That's a bit extreme."

Bridget squeezes her hands into fists, and her nails dig into her palms. She winces when a fingernail pierces her wound site. "Ernie, please don't forget that I grew up in Europe when a fairly unknown man named Adolph Hitler rose to power in a short amount of time. He, too, started off judging a small group of people for the way they looked, the way they behaved, the way they dressed… The way they worshipped."

Ernie's neck reddens, and he blows air out of his puffed cheeks. "Oh. Gotcha. I see where you're coming from. Sorry, I know you've traveled all over Europe. I bet you've probably even seen the site of one of those extermination camps, huh?"

She takes a deep breath. "Uh, yes. As a matter of fact, I've seen more than one."

He winces. "I sure stuck my foot in it, didn't I? You probably witnessed the Blitz firsthand, too."

# # #

9 September 1940

Cher Journal (Dear Diary),

We're in Belgium now in a town called Ghent. We're staying in a small, secret room in the back of a bakery that belongs to the family of one of the medical students my father knew from university. I hate when we have to hide, but at least it always smells so good here, and there's always plenty of delicious food. My father doesn't think we'll be here for long.

After we left France, Belgium wasn't even on our radar because of how they were blitzkrieged by the Nazis back in May. But our plans to get to Hong Kong seem to have disintegrated. The Jewish family who offered to allow us to travel with them have backed out on their proposal. They feel it's too risky to include more people on their journey. My mother and I were terribly upset when we learned this, but my father, the eternal optimist, says there must be something better in our future.

After the Nazis succeeded in taking Poland last year, they spent a good amount of energy on their Blitzkrieg missions to overtake a lot of smaller European countries. But this past weekend, we listened to the radio after the bakery closed and were shocked beyond belief to hear how Germany is blitzing England with their Luftflotten.

Last month, when Birmingham and Liverpool were attacked, we kind of hoped the evil Nazis might have realized they were in over their heads; but on Saturday night, the aerial branch started their lightning warfare against London, dropping more than 272 tons of high explosive bombs. This is terrifying!

# # #

Bridget presses her lips together and nods. "Yes, well, speaking of German dictators, I have a cranky German patient I need to go see, so if you'll excuse me…" She tops off her coffee again.

Ernie smiles and opens the door for her. "If I don't see you soon, you and Jack have a Merry Christmas."

Her face softens. "Thanks. And thanks again for lunch. And I meant what I said... If you'd like to come out to the house to stay until your wife gets home, or even just for a meal, we'd be happy to have you."

"I appreciate the offer. I'm going to call Maggie tonight and see where things stand. But I'll keep it in mind. Thanks."

"All right then. Ta ta." She rushes toward the elevator and presses the call button. When the car arrives, she steps on and taps her fingertips against her thigh in time to Nat King Cole singing "All I Want for Christmas is My Two Front Teeth."

The thought of dealing with Gunter Hetzel causes her eyes to roll. She gulps her coffee and exits at the fifth floor. As she passes Room 502, she peeks in Craig Barnaby's room, and her heart swells at the sight of Lisa sitting next to him, dealing a deck of cards. They both laugh, and Bridget realizes she's been watching them longer than she intended. *Oops!* She takes a deep breath and forges down the corridor.

* * *

CHAPTER SEVENTEEN

Bridget stops at the nurses' station and tosses her coffee cup in the garbage. "Afternoon, Maryann. How's Mr. Hetzel getting along today?"

The nurse takes a deep breath and cuts her eyes down the corridor to the patient's room. "He's... about as satisfied as ever. You know, between the scratchy sheets, the too-thin blankets, the non-German television channels, the bland food, and all, I don't think he's going to be giving us a three-star review anytime soon."

"Ah. Well, it's good that at least he's still able to communicate all his dislikes. With his tumor, he's experiencing changes in his vision and memory, not to mention weakness in his arms and legs. So, let's just focus on the positive, okay?" *Even if he is a big tosser.*

"I'm sorry, Doctor. I'd still like to set his bedpan about six inches out of his reach, though."

Bridget stifles a giggle. "Well, let's not resort to that type of behavior." *Yet.*

The nurse blushes as she turns away and stacks some file folders. "Of course."

They both jerk their heads around when a loud ruckus comes from Room 529. Bridget says, "I've got this," as she rushes to the room. She opens the door as a full lunch tray flies across the room, and a female staff housekeeper ducks to avoid being struck.

The patient's face grows scarlet as he points at the older woman. "Die Juden sind unser Unglück!" *The Jews are our misfortune!*

Bridget's breath catches in her throat. *That's just what the Nazis used to say!* She steps around the woman and says, "Herr Hetzel, you must calm down immediately!" She pushes the patient's shoulder until he lays against his pillow. "Getting so upset is not good for your health." She takes her stethoscope out of her pocket and inserts the stems in her ears. Pressing it against his chest, she listens to his thumping heart.

His eyes narrow at the woman cleaning the food off the floor. "Die Juden sind unser Unglück! You need to get her out of my room! I won't eat food prepared by no damn Stück!"

Ein Stück... That's what the Nazis used to tell us... that we were of no more value than a stick. Bridget's blood boils, and she struggles to maintain a professional composure. She casts a passing glance at the woman then turns her full attention back to the patient. "Herr Hetzel, undoubtedly your brain tumor has caused you to become delirious. This is a Catholic hospital, and you are not back in Nazi Germany. I really need you to calm down and relax. Your blood pressure is dangerously high."

The cleaning woman stands and sets some broken pieces of a plate on her cart.

The patient points at the woman and sits forward. "Dammit, she's a Jew! Ein unnütze Esser!" *A useless mouth!*

Bridget's eyes narrow. *Damn. The Nazis used to call us that, too. He's positively got to be the son of one of those guards!* "Herr Hetzel! That's quite enough! Sie müssen sich hinlegen und ruhig sein!" *You need to lie down and be quiet!*

The cleaning lady steps closer to them and peeks around Bridget's shoulder. Grey hair frames her amber-flecked cognac eyes, moist with tears. The woman's hand flies to her chest. "Mein Gott! Tochter, it's really you!"

Bridget reads the woman's nametag. "Helen... Kugelman. Ma'am, this patient is under my care and—"

Gunter points at the old woman. "She said Tochter! She called you her daughter. She's a nasty Jew, and so are you!"

Bridget removes her keys from her lab coat pocket and unlocks a cabinet near the patient's television. She removes a glass vial and loads a syringe. "Mr. Hetzel, she called me doctor. Not Tochter. Now, I've warned you, you need to relax." She rubs a cotton ball soaked in alcohol on his upper arm. "I'm going to give you something to help you get the sleep you need so we can stay on track with your upcoming surgery." She injects him, and his muscles go limp within seconds.

She disposes of the syringe and steps closer to the woman. "Ms. Kugelman, come with me, please. We can't have you upsetting the patients. Mr. Hetzel needs his rest."

They step into the corridor, and Bridget pulls the woman by her wrist into a janitorial closet across the hall. She closes the door and pulls the string on the lightbulb. As the light flickers on, she spins and confronts the woman. "Who are you?"

"Renate, mein Tochter. I thought I'd never see you again. And look at you! You're a doctor. Your papa would be so proud."

Bridget bristles, and tears form in the corners of her eyes. "I— I'm not Renate. My name is Bridget." Her proper British accent slips to one with German undertones as a lump forms in her throat. "And look at you... I see you go by Helen now."

"Sweet girl, you know I always prefer AnneHelene. But in America, they favor Helen. I can't believe, after all this time, I've finally found you! My darling girl, I can finally hold you in my arms just as I've held you in my heart all these years." Helen throws her arms around Bridget and pulls the doctor to her bosom. Tears cascade down the woman's cheeks, and she sniffles.

Bridget ruffles at the woman's touch. "I... We can't..."

The P.A. clicks on, and an announcement plays throughout the hospital. "Dr. Castle, Dr. Bridget Castle, please report to E.R. Two, STAT."

Bridget steps back, resting her hand on the doorknob, and her Queen's English returns. "Sorry. I have to go. Come to my office at four o'clock this afternoon. It's room 722. Okay?"

"Jah, I'll be there." Helen clasps her hands together under her breasts, and her elated smile grows wider.

Acid wells in Bridget's gut as she rushes toward the elevator. *What a thing to happen! I can't believe this, after all these years.* She steps into the empty car and stabs the first-floor button with her index finger. *Wow. I never thought I'd see that face again in this lifetime.*

# # #

30 April 1944

Lief Dagboek (Dear Diary),

I hate this day with a passion! Even more than the Nazis, today, I hate my mother, and I vow to never forgive her for what she's done. We stayed at the country house with the friend of the Good Doctor Van Den Boom for just four weeks when, all of a sudden, this morning when I woke, Mama told me that we had to leave. I quickly gathered my little suitcase with my meager belongings, and I ran to get my treasure box from the bucket in the well. Mama gathered her things and bundled Josef in his blanket, then we made our way down to the carriage house where our host hid us in a space under a secret panel in the floor of his dairy delivery truck.

We squeezed in tightly and held each other in the dark. When we got to a checkpoint, we held our breath and prayed little Josef wouldn't cry or whimper while the truck was inspected. We were all so silent, I swear, our own heartbeats sounded like rolling thunder. After a few minutes, the truck was cleared to pass, and we rode silently for what felt like hours, crammed in there like sardines, with only two holes drilled underneath the vehicle's carriage to allow us any fresh air.

Finally, we heard the sounds of livestock as the truck slowed. It was actually exciting to think we might get to stay at another farm where we could go outside after dark from time to time like at the last place. When the truck pulled into the barn, our host let us out. As I stood there taking in the surroundings, Mama handed me my suitcase and kissed my cheek. She said, "Let me look at you. Now, kiss Josef Wilhelm. There's no telling when we'll all see each other again, but I shall carry you in my heart each and every day, my beautiful daughter." I didn't understand what she was saying when our host looked at his pocket watch and motioned for her to get back in the truck.

"What are you talking about? Where are you going?" I screamed through my tears, but Mama pulled the back doors to the wagon closed and kept her palm pressed against the glass as the truck started and pulled away. I tried to run after her, but my new host grabbed my arm and told me to stay hidden. His wife pulled me to her bosom and tried to comfort me. She said my mama didn't feel safe where we'd been staying, and the chances for our survival would be greater if we hid separately.

I don't know if that's true but, frankly, I don't care! I'd rather die as a family than live spread out across the globe. At least little Josef gets to keep his mama. I hope I don't forget what he looks like. My heart is shattered into a million pieces, and I will never forget what my mama did to destroy this family! Nor will I ever forgive her.

# # #

CHAPTER EIGHTEEN

The elevator doors open, and Bridget rushes down to the Emergency Department. Dr. Redding waves her into the trauma area, saying, "We have a fifty-three-year-old Caucasian male, hit by a car while he was walking his mail delivery rounds in Back Bay on Newbury Street. Name's Dale Bivens. The car wasn't traveling fast, but the victim hit his head on the sidewalk. He's been unconscious since he got here. He's already been to x-ray."

Bridget takes a flashlight out of her pocket and examines the man's eyes. "His left pupil is dilated. Affirmative on the concussion." She inserts her stethoscope in her ears and listens to the patient's heart.

An orderly races in and says, "Here's the films, Doctor." He shoves a set of x-rays at Glenn then hurries out.

Glenn turns off the overhead light and flips on the light box. He pops two x-rays in front of the lamp. Bridget stands next to him and inspects the images. "Look. There it is in the left temporal. A hairline, closed linear fracture. Not more than an inch long."

The patient stirs, and his eyes flutter open. "Wha—what happened? Where am I? My shoulder and head hurt." He tries to sit up then collapses back to the bed as he winces. "Oooh."

Glenn shakes the man's hand. "Hi. I'm Dr. Redding. You have a sprained shoulder and a head injury, sir. We had to call in our neuro-specialist to make sure you were okay." He steps aside as Bridget moves closer to the patient.

128   THE CHANGELING OF THE THIRD REICH

Bridget rests her hand on the patient's arm. "Mr. Bivens, my name is Dr. Castle. You're at Saint Francis Hospital. Do you remember what happened?"

"Yeah, I, uh... I was delivering the mail and, uh... I took lunch and then started down Newbury Street when, uh... Wow, this is embarrassing. I can't seem to remember. I'm sorry."

"No need to apologize, sir. You were struck by a car. You have a minor skull fracture and a bit of a concussion. I'm going to order you a P.E.T. scan so we can see how swollen your brain is. Okay?"

"What's that?"

"Now, don't worry. It's nothing, really. You'll drink a little cup of liquid, then you'll have to lie still for a half hour or so while the machine does all the work. Then I'll get the results and see what we're dealing with. If it's nothing major, we'll just plan on keeping you here for a couple of days for observation, then we'll let you go home." She writes a note on the patient's chart. "I'm going to leave you in Dr. Redding's capable hands. If you have any family we need to notify, Dr. Redding will make sure someone calls them for you."

"Uh, thanks. I would like to call my wife and let her know where I am."

Bridget looks to Glenn. "Have them scan him STAT, and call me as soon as the radiology report is ready, okay?"

"Will do. Thanks for your help."

She waves to the patient and makes her exit. As she hurries to the elevator, she attempts to focus on Bing Crosby's "Silver Bells," but her thoughts keep wandering back to the Netherlands. *How could Mama think I'd ever want to see her again after she threw me away?*

She boards the empty elevator and jabs the button for the seventh floor. *If I ever had children, you can bet I'd never choose between them. I'd never play God, deciding which might stay with me and which might be sent away.*

The doors open, and she bites the insides of her cheeks to keep from sobbing. *I'll be damned if I shed one more tear over the woman who threw me away as if I were an object worth no more than a stick – ein Stück! I wonder if she realizes that her callous decision decided my life's fate, and less than sixteen weeks later, I was arrested and shipped to one stop east of Hell!*

She storms down the corridor to her office, throws open the door like a hurricane-force gale, and slams it shut. She opens a file cabinet drawer, grabs a pack of Wild Cherry Lifesavers, and shoves two candies in her mouth. She scowls as she sits at her desk and flips open a medical journal, thumbing through each page without stopping to read any particular item.

Over the next hour, her breathing returns to normal, and she manages to read an article regarding the current status of Philip Blaiberg, the recipient of the second successful human heart transplant earlier in the year. She comes across a months-old report on the subject of the state of irreversible coma establishing the paradigm for defining brain death. *This is from August. Did I ever read this?*

She starts perusing the publication when a knock at the door startles her. *Bollocks!* Her hand covers her racing heart. "Who is it?"

The door opens, and Dr. Redding steps in. "Hey. I have the P.E.T. scan results for Bivens." He offers her a manila envelope then sits on the corner of her desk and thumbs through the desk's clutter. "Last summer's Harvard report? It's a little late for spring cleaning, isn't it?"

She opens the test results and scans the first page. "Yeah, well, I was, uh, busy." She chuckles. "Oh, oh, this is good. It's only a mild concussion. This is what? Monday?"

"Yes. The sixteenth."

"Good. Well, I see no reason to keep him here past Wednesday. Has he been admitted yet?"

"Yeah, they're working on getting him a room."

"Okay. I'll talk to him when I make rounds in the morning. You can go ahead and let him know we're cutting him loose Wednesday if nothing further develops. I want him on bed rest for a week, and no work until the new year."

He stands. "Sure. I'll write it up and let him know. It's almost four. You cutting out soon? I thought I just saw Jack down in the front lobby."

She looks at her watch. "Yeah. I've got something to take care of, then I'm going home too. I'll see you later. And thanks for bringing this up right away."

"No problem. Goodnight." He opens the door and gasps when an older woman raises her hand to knock. "Oh! Excuse me, ma'am. You startled me. Are you in the right department?"

The woman cuts her eyes to Bridget. "Yes, I'm looking for—"

Bridget steps forward and pulls the woman by the wrist. "She's here to see me, Glenn. She's interviewing as a possible substitute for my cleaning lady at home next month. Beverly's daughter's getting married in Florida in January."

"Oh, that's right. Okay, then. Goodnight, ladies." Glenn closes the door behind him, and Bridget turns the lock.

She steps backward and gestures to the twin guest chairs in front of her desk. "Go ahead and have a seat."

The woman's face glows with obvious joy, and her eyes twinkle. "Renate, I can't believe it's really you."

"Yeah, well, I told you before, my name's Bridget."

"Oh, you use your middle name Brigitte?"

Bridget sits behind the desk. "No, not Brigitte. Bridget. I changed it when I moved to England after the war. I'm surprised you recognized me after all this time."

The woman reaches for Bridget's hand, and Bridget bristles and recoils. A pink blush creeps up the woman's neck, and she folds her hands in her lap. "How could I not recognize mein own Tochter? I was afraid I'd lost you forever."

Bridget's eyes fail to match her tight, plastic smile. *Lost me? You threw me away like rubbish!*

The woman takes a tissue from her cleavage and dabs her wet cheeks. "How long have you been here in America?"

"About twenty years. What about you? I haven't seen you here at hospital before."

"No, I should say not. I started work here last week. After the war, I came to America and moved to Rochester, hoping to locate you. I know you and your papa always dreamed of working at the Mayo Clinic someday. So, I got a job cleaning bedpans there, hoping that if you ever made it there, I'd find you."

"Oh?"

"Yes. While I was there, I took some classes to learn the English. It really made me miss you and your papa. The way you two always slipped in and out of whatever language enticed you always amazed me at how you both adapted with such ease."

"I see. Well, you were apparently a good student. Your English is remarkable." *Too bad you didn't care to learn it while Papa was alive.*

"While I was working there, I met a nice man. A patient. He's originally from Stuttgart. His name is Maurice Kugelman, and he owns a string of delicatessens."

Bridget holds her breath. *The new deli at Faneuil Hall. It was her.*

"So, Maurice and I eventually got married, and I explained to him that I was there searching for my daughter. He suggested that we don't just limit ourselves to the Mayo Clinic but try other major hospitals throughout the country. So, he opened a deli in Chicago, and we went there for a couple of years while I took a job at a couple of the hospitals there. When that didn't produce any results, we moved to New York, and he opened another deli while I worked at three different hospitals searching for you. We decided to try Boston next, and we got here about two months ago. After I helped him set up the sandwich shop, I applied to work here. You know, Maurice lost his wife and all three of his daughters at Dachau, so he's been very encouraging and hopeful that I would locate you someday. He's a lot like your papa with his eternal optimism. I can't wait for you to meet him. I just know you'll both love each other to pieces."

"Yeah. Well, about that—" The phone buzzes, and Bridget jumps. She picks up the receiver. "Pardon me. Dr. Castle's office."

Jack's voice evidences his surprise. "Hi, hon. You haven't left yet?"

In a sharp tone, Bridget says, "Would I be answering my phone if I left?"

"Yeah, listen, I'm at Great Wall, and I don't think you ever told me... Did you want the cashew chicken or the pork lo-mein?"

She squeezes her eyes closed and rubs her temple. "Actually, I've been wanting to try the crab fried rice."

"Oh, that sounds good. I'll get that too."

"And don't forget the eggrolls."

"Right. Okay, Miss, please change the General Tso's to two orders of the crab fried rice."

Bridget huffs. "You forgot the eggrolls!"

"Oh! And two eggrolls... Okay, hon, it'll be ready pretty soon, I'm sure. There's no one else here. Are you going to be done soon?"

"Yeah, I'm on my way."

"All right, see you at home. Love you."

"You too. Bye." Bridget cradles the receiver and turns her attention back to Helen. "All right, well, uh, that was my husband, and he needs me to hurry home so we can have dinner. I'll have to talk with you another time."

Helen's face explodes in an excited smile. "Oh, I'd love to meet him. Is he a doctor too? Do you have children?"

Bridget tucks her hands under her desk and squeezes them into tight fists. In a low, guarded tone, she says, "No. No children. And, yes, he's a doctor. He's the administrator here. You probably already met him when you interviewed for the job."

"Well, I could go pick up Maurice, and we could come over and meet you after your meal. We could light the second candle tonight, just like we used to."

"What are you talking about?"

"Your Hanukkah menorah. The second candle. That's tonight."

Bridget's fingers find their way to the tattoo scar on her forearm. "Yeah, well, I don't do that anymore. And I'm sorry, but you can't meet my husband."

"What?"

"I mean, not yet. Listen, I really need to get going." Bridget stands and heads to the coat rack. She removes her lab coat and pulls on her peacoat. "Meet me back here tomorrow at noon. We'll have lunch and talk then. Look, please don't tell anyone you know me. I, uh, I'm sure you understand the complications of me being a female surgeon in a male-dominated profession. You can respect that, can't you? Please don't make things more difficult for me." She slings her purse over her shoulder and rests her hand on the doorknob.

Helen stands. "Oh. You're a big-time doctor, and your mama's just a cleaning lady. That's okay. I do understand, really. I'm very proud of your success. My heart is just brimming with love for you, mein Tochter. I'll be here at noon tomorrow with bells on. I can't wait to tell Maurice that my search is finally over." She throws her arms around Bridget and pulls her close. She kisses both of her daughter's cheeks then touches Bridget's chin. "Such a beautiful girl. You've always been such a beautiful girl. Was für ein Segen!" *What a blessing!*

Bridget remains frozen in body and in time. *You didn't even embrace me like this the day you let me go. Why am I such a blessing? To assuage your guilty conscience?* She restrains herself from blurting her thoughts and says, "I really must go."

Helen steps backward into the corridor and fans her eyes. "Yes. Yes, of course. Mustn't keep a hungry man waiting. I'll count the seconds until I see you tomorrow."

Bridget turns off her office light and locks the door. She looks over her shoulder and lowers her voice. "Right, then. Noon tomorrow. Good evening." She strides toward the executive corridor with a purposeful gait, knowing Helen won't be allowed to follow her.

As she enters the restricted area, she peeks over her shoulder, and Helen is no longer in sight. Jack's receptionist says, "Dr. Castle, if you're looking for your husband, he already left for the day."

Bridget feigns surprise. She snaps her fingers, saying, "Oh, that's right. I forgot he was leaving early today. Thanks for your help, Bonnie. Have a good evening."

Bonnie looks up from stacking carbon paper in between stationary. "No problem, Doctor. Enjoy your night." Without breaking her stride, she rolls the stack into her typewriter and clips the carriage release lever closed.

The clicking of the typewriter echoes down the hall as Bridget heads to the elevator. When she squeezes into the crowded car, she hugs herself and wills her body to stop shaking. *This whole experience is surreal. How am I ever going to explain things?*

The doors open, and she remains oblivious to the Fontane Sisters' "It's Beginning to Look a Lot Like Christmas" being piped throughout the lobby. She keeps her head down as she forges toward the door.

Carol waves from her perch at the reception desk. "Goodnight, Dr. Castle."

Bridget ignores the comment as well as President Johnson's photo as she rushes to her car. She starts the engine then peels out of the parking lot and into the stream of traffic. *What am I ever going to do about this?*

# # #

15 April 1946

Dear Diary,

Today marks one year since I was liberated from Bergen-Belsen. So much has happened since then, I can't even begin to describe all my good fortune. Mummy and Dad have been so generous with me and in helping me to achieve the best of everything life has to offer. They love me, and I adore them.

After the woman who gave birth to me threw me away like rubbish, and then I was arrested while she and my baby brother lived a grand life together in safety, probably in Hong Kong where she knew life would be free of Nazi terrors, I never imagined I would even survive to see my fifteenth birthday, much less that I'd be living in a large home with my own room, two parents who are devoted to my care, and with so many comforts I haven't known since I was a small child.

But even with all the reasons I have to celebrate my life now, I still don't know how I can ever forget that fifteen days from today will mark two years from the date I was made to be an orphan by my mother's own hand. If my papa was still alive, he would surely hate that woman as much as I do for all she did to tear our family apart. She'd better hope she stays put in Hong Kong and that I never see her face again as long as I live. At least little Josef, who is two now, is safe and probably doesn't know yet what a monster his own mother is. I hope he at least knows someday that he once had a big sister who will always love him.

# # #

CHAPTER NINETEEN

Bridget pulls in her driveway and parks beside the Continental. Her pulse races, and tears burn behind her eyes. *Jack will surely hate me for keeping this from him all these years.* Her stomach churns as she enters the house and hangs up her coat.

Jack peeks around the corner from the kitchen. "Hi, sweetheart. I didn't hear you come in. Hurry up. Dinner's still hot."

She takes a deep breath and bites her lip as she follows him. *Bollocks.* He kisses her cheek, and she sits across from him and opens her box of rice. She forces a smile. "Mm. Smells good."

"Yeah, I don't even think I've heard of crab fried rice before. I can't wait to dig into this." He shoves a huge forkful in his mouth, and a wide grin spreads across his face. "Wow! This is amazing. I think I've found my new favorite here."

She casts her eyes down and forces a small bite in her mouth, not really tasting anything. "Mm hm. Glad you enjoy it."

He shovels in another bite and raises an eyebrow. "What's wrong? I thought for sure you'd tell me I didn't find my favorite here; *you* found it for me." He chuckles.

She sighs. "Oh. Yeah, that's good."

"What? Bridget, what's wrong?" He chomps off a bite of eggroll then pushes his plate aside and grabs her hand. "Hey, you're shaking." He flips her hand over and feels her wrist. "And your pulse is racing. Are you getting sick? Aw, I hope you haven't been exposed to that flu."

Her chest heaves, and her chin quivers. She pulls out of his grip and buries her face in her hands. "I'm not sick. It's just—I just did something that—I have something to tell you, and I don't know if you'll ever be able to forgive me." She starts sobbing, and a lump forms in her throat.

Jack's face blanches, and he furrows his brow. "What? What do you mean you *did* something? You're not stepping out with Ernie Hamilton, are you?"

A look of confusion washes over her. "What? Eww, are you serious? Why would you ask me such a crazy thing?"

"I don't know. I heard you two had lunch together today. I know his wife's out of town. He's probably lonely and—"

She winces and waves her hands in front of her face. "And he's about eighty pounds overweight, bald, and has chronic halitosis! What the bloody hell are you thinking, accusing me of cheating on you? I've never even considered it, despite you being such an old codger."

His shoulders relax, and he chuckles. "Well, then what's so horrible you don't think I could forgive you?" He caresses her cheek then plunges his fork into a hunk of crab.

She blows her nose and takes a deep breath. "I just—there's something I haven't told you. It happened a long time ago, years before we met. I wasn't trying to keep it from you, but I just couldn't—"

"Hon, whatever it is, it can't be that bad. Let's enjoy our dinner while it's still warm, and you can tell me after."

"No. If I wait any longer, I'll lose my nerve altogether. I have to tell you right now."

"Oh-kaaay. Then tell me. If it's something from when you were a girl, I'm sure it can't be so bad that it's got you this upset. Just calm down and spit it out."

"That's what I'm trying to do. I need you to please keep your cakehole closed and let me get it out in my own way. Okay?"

He heaves a bite of food in his mouth and nods. "All right. I'm all ears."

"My mother showed up at hospital today."

"What? I thought she had that committee meeting at the Women's Club this afternoon. Is she okay?"

"No, not Mummy. My mama."

"But Ada's—"

"Please shut up, and just let me say this!"

"Sorry. Go ahead." He nibbles his eggroll.

"Look. I wasn't born in England. I was born in Heusenstamm, Germany. The people who gave birth to me aren't Geoffrey and Ada Anderson. My parents were Dr. Jens Eckhard Breitman and AnneHelene Denenberg Breitman. And my name wasn't Bridget. I was born Renate Brigitte Breitman."

He nods and shovels a bite of rice in his mouth. "Okay."

"Okay? I spill my guts, and all you have to say is, 'Okay?' What's wrong with you?"

He shrugs. "What do you mean what's wrong with me? You told me to shut up and let you explain. I'm just listening, waiting for you to tell me everything before I form an opinion."

She steeples her fingers under her chin and closes her eyes. "All right. Well, my father – my papa – was a brilliant surgeon. I had an older brother, Otto, who was born with crippled legs. And soon after Hitler became Chancellor, he initiated a program to round up all the children with mental and physical handicaps. That's when my brother, my best friend, was sent to one of those institutions where they said he developed pneumonia and died a short time later. Of course, now I have no doubt he was exterminated upon arrival. He probably never even spent one night there." Grabbing a napkin, she sniffles then dabs her eyes and pinches the bridge of her nose.

He rubs her arm. "I'm so sorry, hon. I had no idea your little friend Otto was actually your brother."

She sniffs and nods. "I know you didn't. Anyway, we were exiled and sent to live in a ghetto, and with my papa's many friends all over Europe, we managed to go into hiding, and we did all right for ourselves. I mean, considering all the other—I, uh, guess I forgot to mention that I'm Jewish too. Which is why we were always on the run from the Nazis." Her shoulders heave as she sobs.

He scoots his chair closer and hugs her to his chest. "Shh. It's okay, sweetie. That's all in the past. Please don't cry."

She pulls out of his embrace and waves her hand. "No. I'm not done. We were supposed to travel to Hong Kong where it was safe for Jews. My papa paid for our passage, and we just had to wait until the other families were gathered for us to all be ready to go. But the man who got my papa on board with this plan, the man who my papa paid most of our savings to so that we could go, he ended up keeping Papa's money and said there was no room for us in his convoy." She takes a sip of hot tea.

He offers her an eggroll, and she waves her hand. "No, thanks. Anyway, a couple of months before my thirteenth birthday, some soldiers came to where we were hiding. One of them had been injured by the Resistance, and they needed my father to operate right away to remove some shrapnel or something. My mother and I hid in a broom closet until they left. My mother was pregnant, in her second trimester, and we stayed in that filthy hole in the wall for hours without making a sound until those bastards left. And after Papa saved their friend's life, they bloody killed him!"

In a low whisper, Jack says, "I'm so sorry."

"We had to move to a safer location where my mama gave birth to a baby boy. His name was Josef Wilhelm. He was such a sweet baby, he hardly ever made a peep. Mama and I were so frightened that he might cry and the Gestapo would hear us, that she kept him in her arms nearly every moment of every day, so he never really had the need to fuss."

"Wow. I always thought you were an only child."

She rolls her eyes. "Would you listen to what I'm trying to tell you, please? We moved again shortly after my brother was born. Then by the time he was three months old, my mama told me we were in danger, and we had to leave. We hid in a hollowed-out cubby of a milk wagon while our host took us to an old farm out in the country. Then when we got there, my mama kissed me goodbye, and she took my brother and left me there. I had no idea why she didn't want me anymore, but I suppose she and Josef found another passage to Hong Kong. That was the last time I ever saw or heard from her until today."

He stands and throws his food containers in the garbage then sits beside her. "Wait, so that farm was in… England?"

"No. It was in the Netherlands. I lived the life of an orphan there for about five and a half months before I was arrested. I was sent to Auschwitz-Birkenau. That was in early September of '44. I was there just over two months before I was transferred to Neuengamme in late November. Shortly after the first of the year, I was sent to the Bergen-Belsen Camp. There, I was liberated by the British Army in April of '45."

His face blanches, and he winces as he grabs her hand. "Damn, babe. Three camps?"

"Yeah. So many of us were dying of murine typhus and were covered with fleas and vermin, and all of us were literally walking skeletons on the verge of starving to death that when the soldiers who liberated us saw our conditions, they were immediately appalled. I, personally, witnessed several of them vomit at the mere sight of us. Many of the soldiers attempted to do a kind thing and handed over whatever rations they had to the prisoners, but I knew that wouldn't go well."

"Oh, no. Their stomachs exploded."

She nods. "I tried to warn them, but no one wanted to listen to me. They were hungry, and they wanted to stuff their faces with real food instead of the occasional potato skin and cabbage water soup we were used to. One of the supervisors in the Royal Army Medical Corps listened to me, though. He took a real interest in me and wanted to know how I came to have so much medical knowledge. I told him that my papa was a surgeon before he died and how my dream was always to be a surgeon just like him. He told me that he and his wife had a daughter who was less than one month older than me, and she'd been killed in the Blitz nearly four and a half years earlier."

"I see."

She rolls her eyes. "No, I don't think you do. That doctor, the couple who lost their daughter in the Blitz, they were Mum and Dad.

They adopted me. They took me in and treated me as if I were their own child from the moment we met."

"Okay."

"Why the hell do you keep just saying, 'Okay?' What's wrong with you? I lay a bombshell like this on you, and you have no reaction?"

"I don't know. I guess it all seems so surreal. I'm just trying to digest everything you're telling me. I mean, I guess I don't quite understand the problem you had today at work."

She rubs her temples. "What don't you get? The woman who threw me away like garbage ran into me today and said she's been looking all over America for me. What am I going to do?"

"What do you mean what are you going to do? She's your mother. You're going to call her and invite her over here, and we're going to get to know her and see where your brother is. Maybe he lives close too."

She swipes her hands across her face and lets out a long, deep sigh. "You're not understanding! That's exactly what I cannot let happen. Don't you see?"

"I guess not. Explain."

"Blast it, Jack. Before I got to England, Mum was in a state of deep depression. She was all but catatonic since the loss of her child. The girl's name was Hazel Bridget, and the moment Dad brought me in the house, Mum perked up and called me Hazel. She called me her dead daughter's name! I'm a *changeling;* don't you see? Dad obviously brought me there to take the place of the child they lost. They loved me and nurtured me and cared for me. They moved halfway around the world when the school there wouldn't let me study medicine because of something as stupid as my gender. And they never asked for anything in return. I can't betray their loyalty by welcoming back another parent who, by the way, I vowed to never speak to again because she tossed me aside when times got tough. I've never spoken to Mum about anything concerning my past – about being German or Jewish or even having had brothers or parents. I could tell immediately from the moment we met just how much pain she had been through because I recognized that same starved-for-love look I had myself. I knew never to correct her when she accidentally called me Hazel, and I changed the spelling of my middle name to Bridget when I took their last name in the legal courts. For all intents and purposes, I *am* their daughter. *Theirs.* Not Mama's. Not any longer."

Jack looks at his watch and stands. "Look, babe, it's almost a quarter 'til six. Let's table this for a while. You're getting yourself worked up, and it's almost time for the National Christmas Tree Lighting." He reaches for her hand and intertwines his fingers in hers. "Come on." He leads her to the den and turns on the television then wraps his arm around her shoulders as they sit on the couch and wait for the TV to warm up. "Look, we got here just in time."

They watch as President Johnson lights the tree then addresses the crowd. He says a prayer for peace and reconciliation abroad and tranquility at home. The President's daughter and grandson sit on the stage along with several other dignitaries. The seventy-four-foot-tall Engelmann spruce glistens in majesty as the four thousand blue and green lights twinkle against the darkness of the waning crescent moon.

Jack smiles and says, "Isn't that a gorgeous sight? I'm sure glad we splurged and got the color TV when it was on sale last month."

Bridget stands and flips the television off then sits in the recliner perpendicular to him. "It looks bitter cold out there to me. And the President sounds like he's trying to get sick. So, back to my problem..."

"It doesn't sound like much of a problem, hon. Your parents – the Andersons – know you were born to another family. Certainly, they wouldn't begrudge you allowing your mom and brother back in your life."

She bows her head and wipes her teary eyes. "To tell you the truth, I didn't even ask my mama about Josef."

"So, you'll ask her when we see her. You've got all the time in the world now."

She narrows her eyes. "I already told you I want nothing to do with that woman! And why don't you seem more surprised about any of this?"

"What?"

"You heard me. I just told you you're married to an imposter, that our entire life together has been a lie, and you don't even have a reaction? What the bloody hell's wrong with you?" She throws a decorative pillow at his head.

He scoots closer to her and takes her hand in his. His eyes search hers, and he takes a deep breath. "Honey, I... What you told me wasn't a surprise. At least a lot of it wasn't. Geoffrey already told me about you being in Bergen-Belsen when he found you, and he told me that he and Ada adopted you."

Fresh tears well in her eyes. "He told you that? Why?"

"He told me the night I asked him for your hand. He said your past was painful and that you never wanted to talk about it with him, so he didn't imagine you'd let me know anything about it if you could help it. And he cautioned me not to push you to bring it up unless or until you wanted to. I'm sorry if I did the wrong thing by not letting you know what I knew."

"Oh. Wow. I have no idea how to process all this. Bollocks, my head is splitting."

"Well, look, now that it's all out in the open, where's your mom staying? Do you have her number? Let's plan a get-together."

"What's wrong with you? I already told you no! I won't do that to Mum! I have a lunch scheduled with my genetic mother tomorrow, and I'm going to tell her to go away and never contact me again. Then I want you to fire her."

Scarlet patches creep to his face. "What? No way! I can't fire my own mother-in-law. There's no reason for that. I won't do it!"

She jumps to her feet. "That woman is *not* your mother-in-law! Ada Anderson is your mother-in-law. You don't even know this woman!"

He narrows his eyes and steels his jaw. "I'm beginning to think I don't know you!"

"She doesn't need the job! She as much as said so. She's only working there to look for me. And now she found me."

"But—"

"But nothing! This conversation is over! This isn't your call to make. She already gave me away, and we said our goodbyes. That chapter of my life is closed, and I have no intention of opening it again."

"Bridget—"

"Enough already! I've got a splitting migraine, and I'm going to bed. You can sleep in the guest room. I don't need your big locomotive nose snoring and keeping me awake. Goodnight!" She storms out of the room and up the stairs. Moments later, she slams and locks her bedroom door then curls up under the covers in her big, lonely bed. *I'll never forgive you, Mama. Never.*

# # #

31 August 1944

Drogi Pamiętniku (Dear Diary),

I'm writing in Polish today so my host family won't be able to tell what I'm writing if they happen to find you. Yesterday was four months since Mama left me here. I'm convinced she took Josef to Hong Kong and has started a happy, new life for herself. Maybe she met someone who didn't want to take on the responsibility of raising another man's daughter. Maybe Josef is small enough that Mama's new husband can pretend he is the baby's real father, and I would just be a painful reminder that she had a life before. Whatever she's doing, I hope she's suffering. I hope she is haunted by the ghosts of Papa and Otto and that she never has a good night's rest again.

The host family here act as if I'm a nuisance to them. They're hiding seven other children whose parents either died or were arrested, and they treat us as if we are their personal servants. The only time I get to spend writing in you, Dear Diary, is when I offer to muck the horse stalls or milk the cows. At least then, I get to climb up into the loft and spend a few minutes each day sorting through my treasures and reviewing my previous entries of happier times when Papa was alive and when my family was together and we loved each other and when the only things we hated were the Nazis.

I'd give anything to be on the run or even in a ghetto with all of them again, with Otto still alive, and before Mama turned so evil. It seems I always long for what I can't have.

# # #

CHAPTER TWENTY

Unable to get comfortable during her fitful attempt at sleep, Bridget tosses and turns until dreams transport her back in time. She awakens in the observation clinic in Dr. Mengele's office, sandwiched between nine other prisoners. She props herself up on her shaky elbows and realizes her body is consumed with fever. Looking around the dimly lit ward, she recognizes the other patients as subjects of the doctor's perverted experiments. *What happened? Why am I here?* She swipes her hand across her sweaty face, alerting her as to just how much her skin hurts. *It burns. What's going on?* She collapses back to a supine position and tries to recall what events led to her being there. *I don't remember getting sick.*

She scratches her upper left arm and yelps. *Oww!* Pushing up her striped sleeve, she uncovers a pus-filled injection site surrounded by hot, scarlet rings. "Whoa! He injected me with something."

The girl next to her, covered with oozing, red bumps, opens her mouth and reveals grey, broken teeth. In an urgent whisper, she says, "He injected all of us with something. That's why you're here. If you don't shut up and act like you're asleep, he'll come back in and shoot you with something else!"

The door hinges squeak, and Bridget closes her eyes and lies motionless. Footsteps grow closer, and she holds her breath. *Who's that?* After moments of muffled sounds, someone places a cloth-wrapped bundle under her hand. The person's touch lingers, and Bridget resists the urge to peek and see who it might be.

"Hurry up! Get out of here!" The gruff, familiar voice of an S.S. guard makes Bridget's heart skip a beat. Something grazes her brow, then she peeks though one eye and spies Gunter Hetzel standing at the door, pointing at the female prisoner carrying a basket. "I said that's enough! Go!"

The woman hastens her pace, leaving Bridget unable to see her face. *Who was that?* As soon as the door closes and the lock turns, the patients all come to life, sitting up and unwrapping the rat-chewed, filthy cloth packages delivered by the prisoner. Bridget finds three bread crusts and two raw potato peels in her pack. She peeks at the girl next to her and counts only one of each.

The girl shoves her potato peel in her mouth, and her broken teeth chew with the same eagerness that all the hungry prisoners share. She looks to Bridget and says, "Someone important must like you. You got extra."

Bridget's cheeks redden, and she slips her largest crust to the girl. "Here, you take it. You've been here longer than me."

As the sounds of the patients' munching ebbs, the door opens, and the shadow of a female S.S. guard blocks the sunlight streaming in behind her. In a loud, firm voice, she barks her command. "Greife sie an, Hund! Töte sie!" *Attack them, dog! Kill them!*

Bridget gasps as the woman unleashes a vicious German shepherd, and the dog bounds over to the first cot and starts devouring the patient. Bridget sits up and tries to shriek, but no sound comes out of her mouth. The guard's laughter grows louder, and her face comes into view. At that moment, Bridget realizes the guard's face is Mama's. "Noooo!" The dog jumps toward her, and she rolls out of its snapping jaw and onto the floor with a thud.

Bridget sits up and looks around the dark room. *Bollocks, what a dream.* She pulls herself up and rubs her hip. *Oh, that's going to leave a bruise.* She turns on the lamp beside the bed and eyes the empty spot where Jack usually sleeps. "That's right. He's in the guest room." Squeezing her eyes closed, she wills her heart to stop racing. *Calm down. You're okay now. That's in the past.* She opens her eyes and takes a deep, purposeful breath, filling her lungs to capacity, then slowly empties them. *That's better. If my mind can take me back to such horrors, it can also take me to my own private Brigadoon. I don't need to keep revisiting those ghosts.*

She looks at the clock. "All right. Quarter after six. I might as well get ready for work." She showers and dresses then heads downstairs. As she passes the guest room, the steady buzz of loud snoring permeates the door. She chuckles. *That chainsaw nose is louder than a hoover.*

She heads to the kitchen, grabs a banana, and jots a quick note: *"J.- Couldn't sleep. Left early to catch up on work time missed yesterday. Love you. xoxo -B."*

She gets in her car and watches the house as the upstairs window lights up. *Jack's awake. His own snoring probably woke him.* She slips the car into reverse and backs out to the street, when a black POW-MIA flag flying in the neighbor's yard across the street catches her eye. *Aw, bollocks. The Arnolds must've heard something about Barry. Aww, that's too bad. He's a sweet kid. I better go over there tonight and see if they need anything.* She flips on the radio.

"...and last night, the five hundred and thirty-eight members of the electoral college cast their ballots. In a shocking twist, Dr. Lloyd Bailey, a Republican elector from North Carolina, cast his vote for George Wallace rather than for President Elect Richard Nixon. This upset gave a slight change to the projected numbers, allowing Richard Nixon three hundred and one votes rather than three hundred and two. George Wallace received forty-six rather than forty-five votes from his pledged electors. And Hubert Humphrey maintained all one hundred ninety-one of his..."

She turns the station. "Who cares? We already knew who won the race." She turns up the volume and bebops along with The Beatles as they sing "Hello, Goodbye," then she croons with Bobbie Gentry as she belts out the "Ode to Billy Joe."

She pulls into the hospital parking lot next to a brand new, Gulf blue VW Beetle with the Monroney purchase label still in the rear window. *Nice car. Too bad they were designed by Adolf Shitler.* As she collects her clean lab coat, stethoscope, and purse, she stands and waits as Carol steps out of the new vehicle. "Morning. That's a lovely blue Bug."

Carol's proud smile lights up her face. "Oh, Dr. Castle, you're here early today. My husband gave it to me last night. It's an early Christmas present. Isn't it the grooviest car ever? I just love it so much."

"That's certainly a very generous gift. I'm sure you'll enjoy it for many years." Bridget shoves her hands in her pockets as a few snowflakes flutter down from the grey-white sky. "Brrr. It's going to be cold today." The women hurry inside.

As Bridget waits for the elevator, she taps her toe, keeping in time with the Trapp Family Singers warbling "Little Drummer Boy" throughout the lobby. The car arrives, and she heads upstairs to her office.

Seated behind her desk, she sucks on a tangerine Lifesaver and reviews her daily patient reports. As she concludes, she yawns and stretches her arms over her head. "What was I thinking, not stopping for coffee today?" She grabs some cash from her desk drawer and heads downstairs to the cafeteria.

She purchases a large coffee and a cherry Danish, and as she stirs sugar and cream in her drink, Dr. Paul Taylor approaches her. *Great.*

He knits his brow as he nears her. "Doctor, I'm glad I caught you. I went upstairs to find you, and Bonnie said she thought she saw you heading down here."

"Oh. I'll have to thank her." She sips her coffee and maintains a plastic smile. *What now? You want me to go have a girl's day with that twit Nadine?*

"I escorted a patient in last night... Actually, it was Nadine's grandmother. She fell off a stepstool when she was decorating her tree. I admitted her and diagnosed a sprained hip, but she's been complaining of a headache ever since. Nadine and I stayed the night with her. Around four this morning, she started getting dizzy; and shortly after that, she was nauseous."

The muscles in Bridget's neck tighten, and she furrows her brow. "Oh, no. We better order a P.E.T. scan, STAT."

"Already did. The radiologist gave me the report a few minutes ago. That's why I was looking for you." He offers her a large envelope.

She bites into her Danish then sets the pastry and her coffee cup on the counter and scans the report. "How old did you say she is?"

"She's seventy-two. She's generally in pretty good health except for some mild hypertension. Lives alone. Has all her faculties."

Bridget nods and flips the page of the report. "Okay. Yeah, we're going to have to go in there and drain. This subdural hematoma is eleven millimeters in the parietal. You'd better go reserve a surgical suite. I've got a couple of things to take care of. I'll meet you down there in half an hour."

"Okay. I'd like to assist."

"I was certain you would. I'll see you, Paul." She thrusts the report at him and grabs her coffee and Danish then rushes to the elevator. She chows down her snack, guzzles the coffee, and calls down to the Emergency Department as she reaches her office. "Is Dr. Redding in, please? This is Dr. Castle."

"Of course, Doctor. Please hold..."

"Dr. Redding here."

"Glenn, it's Bridget. Listen, I need a favor."

"You got it. What's up?"

"If you're not busy, I need you to come up to my office and remove my sutures. I have a surgery this morning, and I'm sure they can come out now. I'd take care of it myself, but, you know, it's my right hand..."

"Oh, yeah, no problem. I'm between patients right now anyway. Let me grab some instruments, and I'll be right up."

"Okay, thanks. Bye." She hangs up and grabs a piece of stationary and an envelope from her drawer. She takes the silver ballpoint pen from her desk set then taps her temple as she formulates the note in her mind. She nods and writes:

Dear Helen,

I'm sorry I won't be available to meet with you today. The fact is, I'm sorry you wasted your time looking for the daughter you threw away all those years ago, but I don't want to see you at all. Not today and not ever. I would appreciate you telling Josef that I do love him and wish him well; but since you didn't care to be a mama to me any longer, I found parents who wanted me and loved me and would never think of abandoning me like you did. Since the only reason you took the job here was to attempt to reconcile with the child you gave up, there is no longer any reason for you to maintain your employment here, and it would be much more comfortable for us both if you left quietly. I'm sure I can get you an excellent letter of recommendation for you to obtain other employment if you so desire.

Regards,

Dr. Bridget Castle

She stuffs the letter in the envelope and seals it without review. She writes "Helen Kugelman" on the envelope and slides it under the telephone as a knock comes at the door.

The door opens, and Glenn steps in. "Hey. You ready for me?" He sits across from her.

She extends her palm across the desk. "Definitely. Thanks for coming up."

"No problem. I was on my way to go check on Bivens unless you're headed down there."

"I'll check on him this afternoon. Do you know his room number?"

"Five-eleven." He cuts the bandage off her hand and examines the wound site. "Hmm, this has healed nicely." He lifts each suture with sterile forceps then snips them with surgical scissors. Afterward, he removes each with tweezers then cleanses the site with antiseptic. "There you go. Nice healing, Doctor."

She giggles as she stands. "Thank you. Nice sewing, Doctor."

He heads toward the door and rests his hand on the knob. "I know I don't have to tell you this, but make sure to finish your Penicillin."

She nods and pats her lab coat pocket, causing a pill bottle to rattle. "Thanks. I'm already on it."

"Okay. Good luck on the surgery. Was this one on the books?"

"No. I've got a seventy-two-year-old female who took a fall last night, and she needs a single parietal burr-hole craniostomy."

"Ouch."

"She's Paul's girlfriend's grandmother. He's going to be assisting."

"Oh. Double ouch. Well, good luck to you and the patient."

She presses her lips together, and her eyes twinkle. "Get on out of here, you. Thanks again."

He raises his hand in a motionless wave as he heads down the corridor. "No problem."

She returns to her desk, takes the envelope from under the phone, and stares it. "Okay, AnneHelene, Helen, whoever you are. Time for me to let go of the past once and for all." She tapes the note outside of her door, locks up, and heads down to the second-floor procedural area.

As she enters the Prep-Room, the patient's head is being shaved. Tufts of short, white fuzz fall to the floor, and the hum of the shaver pierces Bridget's ears. She approaches the patient, and the woman extends her hand to shake Bridget's.

Paul rubs the woman's shoulder and says, "Grandma Fran, this is Dr. Castle. She's the one who'll be doing your surgery. Dr. Castle, this is Nadine's grandmother, Fran Alexander."

Bridget shakes the woman's hand. "Good to meet you, Mrs. Alexander. We'll have you feeling as good as new in no time."

The woman allows her hand to linger in Bridget's. "Oh, my. I'm pleased to meet you. I've never known a lady doctor before. I appreciate you helping Pauly with my surgery."

Bridget offers a polite smile. "Yes, ma'am. Dr. Taylor, I'll see you inside. What theater are we in?"

"Suite One."

"Very good." She makes her way to the washroom. As she lathers her forearms and hands then scrubs them with a brush, her mind's eye pictures the shavings of the patient's hair dropping past her shoulders to the ground, and long forgotten specters come back to visit...

# # #

2 January 1946

Lief Dagboek (Dear Diary),

Happy New Year. Today, Dad took Mummy and me to have a family photo made. On our way home, the car ran out of petrol. We were only about three blocks from the house, so we decided to walk, and Dad was going to get a petrol can and walk back after lunch. This shouldn't have been a noteworthy event, but some snow flurries started to fall. I guess seeing those white flakes land on Mummy's dark grey coat kind of took me by surprise. It was like one of those flashback memories long forgotten, only something triggers it, and it all comes flooding back and threatens to drown you.

It reminded me of a time a couple of weeks after I arrived at Auschwitz. That infernal music was playing. The musicians, skinny, bald, and haggard, played for hours every day out near the entrance gate, no matter what the weather. I was doing my job as the interpreter for the newcomers, and for some reason, that day, I found it particularly difficult to maintain concentration with that blasted music playing over and over. (In retrospect, I suppose part of my problem was that I had been without much food for nearly two weeks since my arrest, and the hunger pains still stabbed my guts like daggers.)

Anyway, I was talking to a middle-aged Roma woman who had just stepped off the train, and she was frantic because her husband had died en route, and his body had been used as a bench by the other prisoners. I was attempting to calm her down because I knew if she didn't stop screaming, she would be shot. I felt especially bad for her because she reminded me of the photos I had seen of my papa's mother, older with white hair and wrinkles around her eyes. I kept my eye on her as she was tattooed and stripped of her clothes and her dignity. And then her snow-white hair was shorn from her head and her body.

And as she left her hair behind and attempted to conceal her nudity as she was escorted with the others to the delousing shower, it started to rain – only it wasn't rainwater, but ashes, and the silvery ashes from the crematorium rained down on her shoulders and mixed with the bits of her white hair that still rested on her back and shoulder blades.

By then, she was so defeated that she didn't even attempt to brush them away. So, when that day came rushing back this morning when the snow hit Mummy's coat, I started to hyperventilate. I became dizzy, and the next thing I knew, I blacked out, and Dad caught me before I hit the pavement.

Of course, I couldn't tell Mum or Dad what happened or why I had such a horrific flashback, so I just fibbed and told them that I'd been so excited about the photos that I hadn't eaten a proper breakfast, and the walking made me lightheaded. It's bad enough when I dream about that Nazi hell at night, but to have these memories invade my mind during my waking hours, sometimes, I feel as if I was never liberated, and this is all just another part of the Nazis' cruel torture. Why can't these old ghosts stay dead and buried?

# # #

CHAPTER TWENTY-ONE

After discovering and correcting an additional minor complication, Bridget exits the surgical suite shortly after two o'clock. As she and Dr. Taylor remove their scrubs, Paul says, "That was some amazing work, Doctor. Nadine will be so relieved you caught that extra bleeder before it got out of hand. I know she'll want to take you to dinner and a show or at least do something to repay your kindness."

Bridget washes her hands. "That's what I get paid to do. There's no need for any extra gratitude. What's an extra burr-hole? A couple of hours here or there? I'm just glad Mrs. Alexander was in such good health that she was able to withstand the surgery. A lot of people her age wouldn't have been so lucky."

"Yes, I know. It was a real treat getting to watch you work. The last time I got to assist with a craniostomy was in my second-year of residency, and there was a thirteen-car pile-up on the Mass Pike."

"Thanks, Paul. I always believed the brain is a fascinating organ, and we'll probably still be learning new things about it for the next thousand years. If you'll excuse me now, I really need to get caught up on my rounds. I'll check in on Mrs. Alexander tomorrow when they get her transferred back upstairs. I'll see you later." She pushes open the swinging doors to the scrub room and rushes down the corridor, hoping to avoid being roped into another get-together with Nadine.

As she reaches the elevator, a cleaning lady backs off, pulling her cart, and Bridget holds her breath. *No, please don't be her.* The woman turns and offers a perfunctory nod and polite smile as she makes her way toward the surgical suites. Bridget's lungs deflate. *Good. I don't want to have to have a showdown to explain my letter. Maybe Mama'll just take the hint and go away sooner rather than later.*

She ducks her head and makes a beeline to the back stairs. *I don't want to risk running into her. Certainly, she's read my note by now.* She heads up a flight of stairs then stops at the third-floor landing. She fishes a dime out of her pocket and peeks out the door to an empty corridor. She steps across the hall to the physical therapy gymnasium and locates a payphone. Dialing the hospital's main line, she disguises her voice with a Spanish accent. "Hola, may I speak to the Housekeeping Department supervisor, por favor?"

"Of course, please hold…"

"Saint Francis Housekeeping. Martha Grady speaking."

"Hello, Señora Grady. Can you please tell me if AnneHel—I mean if Helen Kugelman has left for the day?"

Some papers rustle, and Martha says, "May I ask who's calling? I'm afraid I can't give that kind of information to just anyone."

"Oh, uh, yes, of course. I'm her next-door neighbor, and there's a problem at her house. I, uh, I think maybe a water pipe burst. I don't know how to reach her husband."

"Oh, dear. Hold on… Hmm, I'm afraid we're too late. She signed out early today with a personal emergency. My goodness, I don't know who you can call. Have you tried the fire department?"

"What? Oh. Si, that's a good idea. Gracias. Thank you very much." Bridget hangs up the phone, and her heart threatens to jump out of her throat. *Bollocks. I should feel a lot happier about this than I do. I guess throwing away your closest family member and not having any regrets comes more easily for her than it does for me. Or it just shows I'm more human than she ever was. Oh, well. It's water under the bridge now anyway.* She heads to the elevator and rides up to the fifth floor.

She stops at Room 502 and peeks in the window. Craig and Lisa trade playing cards and laugh. Bridget knocks and enters the room. "Good afternoon, Mr. Barnaby. You seem to be in good spirits today. Are you ready for your big day tomorrow?"

Craig's eyes twinkle, and he grabs Lisa's hand. "Yes. Actually, I can't wait. Doc, I'd like you to meet Lisa McIntosh. She's, uh... She's my girl." He and Lisa exchange glances.

Lisa extends her hand to shake Bridget's. "I'm pleased to meet you, Doctor. Craig's told me what a miracle worker you are."

Bridget raises her eyebrows. "Oh? A miracle worker, eh? Well, I think Craig's something of a miracle himself. It's good to see you both so happy. Craig, will your parents both be here for your surgery in the morning?"

Lisa twists her fingers in his. "Yes, his parents and I will be waiting together. I took the day off so I could spend it with them."

Craig's cheeks flush. "What can I say? She adores me." The couple laugh, and Bridget giggles.

Bridget pulls her stethoscope out of her lab coat pocket and steps around the bed. "Very good. I firmly believe that the bigger support system you have, the faster you'll heal and redefine your limits. All right, let me just have a quick listen, then I'll leave you two to your card game." She conducts a swift pulmonary exam then makes a notation in the patient's chart. "All right, Mr. Barnaby. Looks like everything's in order. I'll see you in the morning. Glad to meet you, Miss McIntosh."

She steps down the hall to Room 511, then knocks and enters. "Good afternoon, Mr. Bivens. It's good to see you awake."

Dale sits forward and adjusts the pillow behind his back. "Hey there, Doc. You just missed my wife. She had to get home to get dinner started."

Bridget inserts her stethoscope stems in her ears. "Oh, I'm sorry I missed her. How are you feeling today? Is your head giving you any pain?"

"A little bit."

"Well, with a brain injury, some discomfort is to be expected. Lean forward, please, and let me listen to your lungs."

She listens then replaces the stethoscope in her pocket and takes out a flashlight. "Good. Now, I'd like you to follow my finger with your eyes." She moves her index finger back and forth, up and down, then shines the light in each eye. "Your left pupil's still slightly dilated. I'm going to have the nurse give you some Paracetamol with your dinner, and that should ease some of your discomfort. If your pain becomes unbearable, we can start you on a low dose morphine drip, but I really hate to resort to that unless it's absolutely essential. You otherwise look good, and I anticipate you'll be discharged tomorrow."

"Thanks. That's what Dr. Redding told me too."

She makes a note on the patient's chart. "Good. All right, then, sir. You take care, and I'll see you tomorrow."

"Thanks, Doc. Goodnight."

"Goodnight."

She heads to the nurses' station and leans on the counter. "Afternoon, Maryann. How's our favorite patient today?"

Maryann winces. "Who, Mr. Hetzel? Cranky as usual."

Bridget suppresses a smile. "That's not what I meant."

"Sorry. I know. He's stable. At least he is now. His vitals were good an hour ago. He didn't eat much breakfast or lunch. That cleaning lady who he blew up at yesterday brought him some flowers this morning, and he yelled at her something fierce."

Bridget's stomach tightens as a wave of acid wells from her gut. "Helen Kugelman? She brought him flowers?"

"I guess that's her name. It's the woman who he yelled at yesterday when you were in there."

"Why'd she bring him flowers?"

"I don't know. They spoke in German, then he started screaming at her again. He threw the vase at her, and it shattered. I sent her away and asked her not to return to his room. That was early this morning, and by the time his breakfast came, he said he wasn't hungry. I left the tray with him, and about an hour later, he still hadn't touched much of anything, but he vomited coffee grounds."

"Oh, no. Just the once?"

"Far as I know, yes, ma'am."

Bridget shakes her head. "Hematemesis means there's coagulated blood somewhere. My guess is it's a gastrointestinal ulcer, and his hot temper isn't helping matters. I'm going to order a full set of G.I. x-rays right away, and I'll possibly have Dr. Slater give him an endoscopy in the morning. Can you please call down and make the arrangements for radiology, pronto? Have them send the results up to my office STAT."

"Yes, Doctor."

"Good. I'll go let him know what's going on while you arrange transport." Bridget taps her fingertips on the countertop then heads to Room 529. "Afternoon, Herr Hetzel. How are you feeling?"

"I feel like the Grim Reaper is just lurking around the corner, waiting for me to let my guard down." He closes his eyes and winces as he presses his hand under his ribcage.

"It looks like you're having a lot of abdominal pain. I understand you had an episode of vomiting blood this morning. How long has that been going on?" Her eyes scan the room for the hint of flowers. *I wonder what they argued about.*

He shakes his head and clenches his jaw. "About a month, I guess."

She reviews his chart at the end of the bed. "I don't recall your doctor mentioning anything about bloody vomit."

"I never told him. It didn't seem relative to my head problem."

"Well, as I told you before, if your tumor is a meningioma, it's probably not related. If it's an ependymoma, vomiting is actually a symptom. But in your case, I have a strong suspicion you're dealing with an ulcer. So, I've ordered up some tests, and if that's the case, we'll deal with things accordingly."

"If it's a Geschwür – *an ulcer* – then it's not related to my brain tumor, and I'll thank you to stick to the job of worrying about my tumor and nothing else!"

"Herr Hetzel, if it's a bleeding ulcer, you may find yourself short on blood during your cranial surgery which could put you in a dangerously risky predicament. Furthermore, if it's an ulcer severe enough that it causes you to vomit, and if you have the need to vomit after your surgery, not only will it certainly cause excruciating pressure on your brain, but the results could prove to be fatal. Understand? Now, the nurse has ordered a wheelchair, and you *will* be getting x-rays in a few minutes. And as a precaution, I'm ordering Dietary to send you a light, bland evening meal, and I want you to eat everything. I'll see you later."

Bridget scribbles a note on the chart and hurries out of the room. She heads down to the fourth-floor nurses' station. "Afternoon, Brenda. How's Susan Turner today?"

"Good afternoon, Doctor. She's doing well. She managed to eat some applesauce for breakfast and some cottage cheese and Jell-O for lunch. Her parents are in there with her now."

Bridget smiles. "Good. Let's keep her on a soft diet for a while longer, then we'll try some boiled chicken and rice. Do you know what's on board for her dinner?"

The nurse reads a clipboard. "Looks like mashed banana and mashed turnips."

"Okay, that's perfect. I'll go check in with her, and I'll see you tomorrow."

"Thank you, Doctor. Have a good evening."

Bridget proceeds to Room 411. "Good afternoon, Turner family. How are we feeling?"

Mrs. Turner gestures to a picture book and says, "Very good, Doctor. Susan feels good enough today to hear her favorite story, 'Lyle, Lyle Crocodile'."

Mr. Turner turns the page and says, "Yes, good enough to listen to us read it fifteen times."

The adults laugh, and Susan says, "More! Read more!"

Bridget steps closer and pulls her stethoscope out of her pocket. "Hold on a moment, princess. Let's let me just listen to your heart." She listens to the girl's chest and back then shines her flashlight in the child's eyes. She makes a note in the chart and says, "All right, Susan, everything looks just the way it's supposed to. You keep being a good patient, and we'll see about getting that drainage line removed soon. Goodnight, folks."

"Goodnight, Doctor. And thank you." Susan's mother grabs the girl's hand and squeezes it as she nods at Bridget.

Bridget leaves the fourth floor and heads down to the cafeteria. She hums along to Bobby Darrin singing "O Come All Ye Faithful." As she gets there, she encounters a janitor mopping the floor and says, "Afternoon, Harold. It's good to see you back. Did you enjoy your vacation?"

He stops working and leans on his mop. "Yes, ma'am. That bed-and-breakfast was just as nice as you said it was. The missus and I had the time of our lives. She just told me last night she wants to bring you some of her special spiced rum cake before Christmas gets here."

"Aww, that's very sweet of her. Thank you. I'll look forward to seeing her. Well, I'll let you get back to your work." She heads to the counter and waves down a food service worker. "Excuse me, Nancy... I know you're closed and getting ready for the dinner crowd, but I was in surgery and missed lunch. Could I possibly get a sandwich to take back to my office, please?"

"Of course, Dr. Castle. We have some nice roast beef today. We have egg salad. We have ham and Swiss. I know you always enjoy the tuna salad. We've got some corned beef left if you want a Reuben. Or I can make you a submarine sandwich."

Bridget holds up her hand. "That all sounds wonderful, but I just want something fast and easy. How about the egg salad on whole wheat?"

"You got it. You want some chips with that?"

Bridget rests her hand on her belly. "Oh, I'd better not. I'm afraid I haven't burned off all last month's Thanksgiving delicacies yet. Do you happen to have any sour dill pickles?"

"Of course. Hold on..." Moments later, Nancy returns with a sandwich and two large pickle spears on a paper plate. "Here you go, Doctor. Would you like me to make you some coffee or tea?"

Bridget nods to the red, orange, and purple punch cascading down the glass walls of the triple beverage dispenser and says, "Some orange drink would be just fine, thank you."

Nancy fills a large paper cup adorned with blue and green atomic starbursts. "Here you are. It's nice and cold."

Bridget slurps a sip and nods. "Thank you. This really hits the spot." She takes three one-dollar bills out of her pocket and sets them on the counter. "Thank you so much, Nancy. Keep the change. I'll see you tomorrow."

"Wow, thanks! Goodnight, Doctor."

Bridget stifles a yawn as she makes her way up to her office. She opens the door and steps over a manila envelope. She sets her food and drink on her desk then picks up the envelope and freezes as she eyes a small piece of scotch tape stuck to her door. She fingers the remnant then peels it off. *Well, what's done is done.*

She sits and takes a bite of her sandwich as she reads Gunter Hetzel's radiology report. "Bloody hell. Peptic ulcers." She picks up the phone and dials. "Yes, this is Dr. Bridget Castle. May I speak to Dr. Slater, please?"

"Yes, ma'am. Please hold..."

"Dr. Slater speaking."

"Steve, hi, it's Bridget."

"Hey. What's up?"

"I've got a patient scheduled for a craniotomy Thursday. He's got a five-point-nine-centimeter meningioma which technically could be an ependymoma. I won't know for sure 'til I get in there. It's a skull base growth, and he's flown in from West Germany for the procedure. Problem is, this a.m., he started coffee ground vomiting. I just sent him for G.I. x-rays, and the report tells me we're looking at three large ulcers. Two gastric, one duodenal."

"Ah, and if his gut's bleeding, he runs the risk of losing too much blood in surgery, so you want me to work my magic and see what I can do for him right away."

"Yes, please."

"All right. Send his file down, and I'll do what I can."

"Thanks. His name's Gunter Hetzel. He's in five twenty-nine. I'll send the report down to your office posthaste."

"Sounds good. I'll get a gastroscope in there and take a look. We'll start him with an antacid, but be aware that if it's severe, that might not do anything. In which case I might need to go in and remove part of his gut."

"Which would postpone my surgery. I really can't afford to put this tumor off any longer, Doctor."

"Well, I don't know what to tell you. You might want to get some blood from the bank ready on standby for your surgery to go off as scheduled, and I can get to him once he's recovered enough from that. But if he's tossing coffee grounds, his gut's bleeding, and he's headed for trouble."

She sighs. "Bollocks. I guess you're right. I'll alert the bank. You go ahead and scope him, and let me know what you find, okay?"

"Will do. We'll talk tomorrow."

"Thanks. I have surgery at nine in the morning. I'll be available all day after that."

"Sounds good. Send me that report."

"You got it. Bye." She cradles the receiver. "Bollocks. This is the last thing I need to tell Herr Hetzel."

She eats a bite of pickle then slides the radiology report back into the envelope and heads down to the executive suite. She stops at Jack's door and says, "Hey, Bonnie. Is my husband in his office?"

Bonnie looks up from her typing. "Hmm? Oh, no, ma'am. He left nearly two hours ago. He said he had something important to tend to."

"Oh? Any idea what it was?"

Bonnie chuckles. "Doctor, you know how tight-lipped he is. I have no idea. Though, if I were to guess, I'd say he might be doing some Christmas shopping."

Bridget raises her eyebrows. "Ah. I bet you're right. Hey, do you think I could have one of your runners take this report down to Dr. Steve Slater's office?"

Bonnie takes the envelope from Bridget. "Of course. It'll be down there in about fifteen minutes."

"Thanks. I appreciate it. Have a good evening."

"You, too, Doctor." Bonnie resumes typing.

Bridget strides back to her office and eyes the thin strip of adhesive where the scotch tape affixed the note to Helen. She runs her fingertips over the residue and takes a deep breath. *Bollocks. I wish I would've made a copy of what I wrote. I hope I did the right thing.*

# # #

13 May 1941

Liebes Tagebuch (Dear Diary),

Today was the absolute worst day of my life! The Good Doctor Van Den Boom's wife brought a picnic dinner to our little cottage, and the entire van den Boom family came along to celebrate the doctor's son's thirteenth birthday. The boy (his name is Ambroos) is so full of himself! He took every opportunity to flaunt the fact that his family has money and that mine doesn't.

I tried to tell him that we had plenty of money before the war started, but he said that didn't count because, without his father's help, my family would be living back in the ghettos with the rodents. Then he started calling me mouse, and he wouldn't stop his merciless teasing. I finally had enough, and I told him that he was no better than the vile Führer Hitler! Then I reminded him that his father wouldn't' have even passed his medical examinations if it hadn't been for my father helping him study when they were in university, so he should attribute his father's wealth to my father's intelligence.

As soon as the words escaped my mouth, the whole room grew still. Dr. Van Den Boom was the first to speak. He gave a nervous chuckle and said, "Well, she's right about that, Ambroos. If Jens wouldn't have spent hours tutoring me, I wouldn't have passed half my anatomy or clinical pathology tests."

The veins in Papa's temples bulged, and he refused to even look at me. I was so embarrassed that I allowed my mouth to hurt the man who has been nothing but kind to us just because his son behaved so boorishly, and I immediately regretted my actions. As soon as the Good Doctor and his family left, my father took me to the bedroom and told me he'd never been so disappointed in me. He said that with so much these days that is beyond our control, our mouths are one of the few things that are within our control. He said that my words have the power to heal or the power to hurt, and I'd better learn the difference. He said the Führer used poisonous words to fill millions of hearts with hate, and the way I behaved today was no less venomous than that and served no other purpose than to inflict pain. He also said that if I ever hope to make it as a doctor, I'd better grow a thicker skin and learn to ignore unkind remarks and focus on the bigger picture.

My father has never spoken so harshly to me. He's never uttered a word of any dissatisfaction of any kind with me or with anyone, as far as I know. He has always found something good to say, even in the most awful of places we've been and ordeals we've faced. And I, his only living child, actually repulsed him today!

I didn't realize until that moment that I had so much power – so much hatred inside me just waiting to boil out. Papa said he still loved me – that he would always love me – but that in the moment that I said such an ugly thing to Ambroos, Papa's heart ached with the thought that I would choose to be so... common.

I lamented my words as soon as I saw how they had hurt the Good Doctor Van Den Boom, but later, seeing how deeply they sliced through Papa's heart, in that instant, I would have gladly cut my own tongue out and thrown it in the fire if I could only take away the pain I caused my beloved father, my hero. I hope I can, one day, gain back his respect. Until that time, my life will not be worth living.

# # #

CHAPTER TWENTY-TWO

Bridget's heart weighs heavy in her chest as she drives home. She tries to stop overthinking her decision to shun her mama. *I can't risk hurting Mum and Dad, even if Mama's reason for abandoning me isn't as Machiavellian as is seems. How could I ever ask them to share my love when they gave me all of theirs?*

She turns up the radio and sings "The Shoop Shoop Song" with Betty Everett, croons "The Last Time" with The Rolling Stones, and belts out "I Am a Rock" with Simon and Garfunkel.

She turns down her street, and her neighbor's POW-MIA flag flaps in the wind. She turns off the radio, and her face grows somber. "Oh, that's right; I have to go over and check on Mr. and Mrs. Arnold and see what's going on with Barry."

She pulls in beside the Continental and raises an eyebrow at the familiar thirteen-year-old Armstrong Siddeley Sapphire parked off to the side. *What're Mum and Dad doing here?* She collects her purse and shivers as she steps out of the car, the frigid wind whipping through her. *Crikey, it's getting colder. Maybe we'll have a white Christmas.*

She reaches the porch and pulls a piece of paper off the door. *What's this?* Unfolding it, she reads Jack's clumsy handwriting: "You're certainly good at leaving notes today." She crumbles it and heads inside. *I'm not amused.*

"We're in here, Lovey. Won't you join us?" Geoffrey says from the kitchen.

Bridget hangs up her coat and purse and follows her nose to the source of the delicious aroma of fish and chips. "Mmm. Where's Mummy?" She kisses Geoffrey's cheek and sits beside him at the table.

Jack sets a plate in front of her and gives her a quick peck then sits on the other side of her. "It's just us. Uh, we wanted to—"

Geoffrey slides the malt vinegar bottle to her. "We had something to talk to you about, Lovey."

Her face blanches. "Is Mummy all right? She's not sick, is she?"

Geoffrey licks his thumb. "What? No, she's a tough old bird. She wouldn't dare get sick. She's just fine. I'm here to talk about... I want you to tell me what happened at work yesterday."

She stops spritzing her plate with vinegar and narrows her eyes at Jack. "I guess it wouldn't do me any good to tell you nothing happened. It seems Mister Blabbermouth has already opened his cakehole and sang like a canary, eh?"

Jack's lips stretch into a tight line. "Let's not twist things out of proportion."

Geoffrey rests his hand on Bridget's. "Lovey, Jack told me about your mother searching for you. You can't break her heart by refusing to see her."

"But you and Mum are—"

"Mum and I love you, and we always will. Nothing could ever change that. You're our daughter. But you have other family too. And it's not right to deny them the opportunity to share your love."

She buries her face in her hands and takes a few deep breaths. "But I don't want to betray Mum. I know when you two lost your Hazel, Mum was heartbroken."

"That's right, love, but your being there helped heal our broken hearts. Nothing will diminish all the good you did for us."

"But—"

"But nothing. No one's asking you to love anyone any less. There's plenty of love in a person's heart to go around for a lifetime."

"But—"

"Listen. Mum and I loved our dear Hazel with all our hearts. And we always will 'til our dying day. When you came, we fell in love with you, and we also quickly grew to love you with all our hearts. That didn't take away from our love for Hazel. It just took away some of the pain of losing her and replaced it with the joy of having you."

She sighs and pushes her plate aside. "I don't think it matters anyway. I wrote my mother a very harsh letter this morning, telling her I didn't want to see her. I told her I wasn't able to forgive her for throwing me away like she did."

"Listen—"

"No, Dad, you listen. You have no idea what my so-called mother did. What she put me through the last six months before I was arrested. I woke up one morning, and she announced that we needed to pack immediately because we had to relocate. We hid while our host transported us, and when we reached our destination, we got out of the car, she kissed me, and that's when she dropped the bomb on me that she and my baby brother were going somewhere else. That I would be staying there without them. And just that quick, she got back into the car and left. She threw me away like rubbish! And I hate her for it."

Geoffrey squeezes her wrist. "Lovey, I've never asked you to talk about your life before we met. I figured it was something so personal, you wanted to keep those memories to yourself. Maybe that was wrong of me. If you've been walking around feeling angry and hurt for the past twenty-three years, then I was definitely wrong not to have tried to allay those feelings."

"There's nothing you could have said to make me feel any better about what she did. Don't you understand? Only a *monster* would leave their thirteen-year-old child with strangers while they moved on to greener pastures and forgot they had a family. How can I ever forgive such a horrid deed?"

Geoffrey takes a deep breath and presses his lips together. "Your papa would."

Goosebumps cover her arms. "What did you say?"

"You heard me. Jens would've forgiven AnneHelene."

The color drains from her face, and a cold shiver travels up her spine. "How did you know who—"

Geoffrey pulls a folded envelope from his breast pocket and pushes it toward her. "I'm truly so sorry, Lovey. I should've told you from the beginning who I was, but you were so frail when I got you out of Bergen-Belsen. And when you agreed to come home with me and Ada took a look at you and seemed to finally have a reason to live, I... Well, I just didn't want to have anything ruin what we had. It was selfish of me, I know. I hope you can forgive me."

Bridget's fingertips graze the edges of the worn Air Mail envelope, and when she unfolds it, her breath catches in her throat. "That's... that's my papa's handwriting."

"Yes. Jens and I went to university together. We were good friends. Of course, he was a good friend to everyone he knew. He was impossible not to like."

She nods, and her hands tremble as she lifts the flap of the envelope. "What's in here?"

He takes the letter from her and unfolds it. "Do you want me to read it to you?"

She attempts to say yes, but all that comes out of her mouth is a hoarse squeak. Jack squeezes her shoulder as Geoffrey clears his throat.

In a clear, strong voice, he reads:

2 December 1943

My Dear Geoffers,

How are you and your beautiful Ada doing these days? My lovely AnneHelene is with child. If we should have another daughter, I've asked that we name her Hazel as a remembrance of your darling girl. Renate is doing well, despite the efforts of the Führer to achieve his Final Solution. We've actually been staying in a cottage owned by our old classmate, the Good Doctor Petteri Van Den Boom. He's been a kind and generous host, and I dare say I don't know how we would have ever lasted so long without him. My family and I have been so blessed to have been the recipients of so much kindness from so many friends and acquaintances I made while at university with you.

Ever since we lost Otto, my heart has had a void in it – an affliction of which I'm sure you can relate. But since I learned of the coming of this new child, that void is being replaced with such love that I can't help but fear that something might happen to wake me from this wonderful dream. By that, I mean, how many blessings is it right for one man to claim as his own?

Dear friend, I am writing to ask you a favor. As you know, AnneHelene and I have been doing all we can to keep our little family together and to keep our darling Renate as far away from this war as possible. But with all that's happening around us, with so many Jews being arrested, we fear that we may not be able to stay together much longer. I know you offered to take Renate back when the Kindertransport was moving children to the safety of the U.K., and now, I wish I would have taken you up on your generous proposal. She's such a sweet young lady, and I have no doubt that she'll be a fine surgeon someday. She'll probably make the likes of you and me look like numbskulls with all the talent she has, as well as her strong driving passion to practice medicine.

The bottom line is, I'm writing to ask you the favor of taking Renate and raising her as your own. I'm not sure how I can get her to you just yet, but if AnneHelene and I are arrested, we'll both feel much better if we don't have to worry about the children. Once the baby comes in another couple of months, AnneHelene and I have already decided that we will need to find someone to take him or her until this war is over and we can rebuild our lives in freedom. While I hate the thought of losing the children – we both do – we agree that they will probably fare better if they go to non-Jewish homes and live without us, at least until this nightmare comes to an end.

I know this is a huge undertaking to ask of you, but because you are one of my dearest friends, I consider you the brother I never had. Of course, you remember me telling you that my actual brother died only days before my birth, so as far as blood family goes, neither AnneHelene nor I have anyone. And the truth is, I can think of no one else that would help educate Renate and encourage her to be the surgeon she is meant to be. So many of our classmates would scoff at the idea of a female physician, but I'm convinced that, someday, women will outnumber men in many professions and not just in medicine.

Thanking you in advance for your kind consideration of this matter.

I remain,

Your dear friend and brother,

Jens

Silent tears stream down Bridget's face as Geoffrey folds the letter and stuffs it back in the envelope. She sniffles, saying, "So, that's why you came to find me at Bergen-Belsen?"

Geoffrey blows his nose on a napkin, making a honking sound, and shakes his head. "No, child. I was in Italy with the Royal Medical Corps when that letter came, and Ada never opened me mail. By the time I read it several months later, I was unable to make contact with Jens, and I assumed — that is I hoped that he had made other arrangements, and you were all safely tucked away elsewhere. I was unable to reach Petteri to give me any further details. When the British Army liberated Bergen-Belsen, I was sent in for medical duty after we realized how horrid the conditions were there. When we heard reports that some of our soldiers fed their rations to the newly liberated prisoners and literally watched them gorge themselves to death, and that more than half of the survivors were barely holding on due to the outbreak of typhus, we knew we had to get in there as quickly as possible. When I got there and you were among the people taking charge, trying to convince people not to take the food being offered to them, I had no idea who you were. I mean, I was just amazed at your obvious medical sense, not to mention your will power and self-restraint, not wanting to stuff yourself after having been starved for so long. When you told me your name was Renate Breitman, I wasn't sure if you were indeed the daughter of me friend or if the name was purely a coincidence."

Geoffrey sips his beer. "It wasn't until weeks later when I took you home... Ada and I would just hold each other and watch you sleep on those early nights with us, not believing our good fortune of having a new daughter to love, and... well, Lovey, you talked in your sleep. You talked a lot of Otto and your parents and Dr. Van Den Boom. Once you mentioned him, I knew it was no coincidence. I knew then for certain that you were Jens Breitman's little girl. I never told your Mum. Never let her read this letter, either. I locked it in the safe and kept it hidden away all these years. After a few months, you stopped talking in your sleep. You gained weight. Your hair grew back. We had that tattoo removed from your arm. And you acted as if you were reborn. And I guess I got caught up in the fantasy because, to me, you were me flesh and blood daughter. There was no time I could remember before you were there. I'm so sorry I never shared this with you before. I hope you don't hate me." He wipes his nose, and a single tear rolls down his cheek.

Bridget stands and throws her arms around his neck. "Hate you? I love you more than ever! I mean, I always loved you since the day you asked me to come home with you. But to know now that you knew my papa and were actually the man he *chose* to have raise me if he couldn't... It's like fate stepped in and made sure we were placed together. But... I don't even understand how this could be. You studied medicine at Université de Caen."

"Actually, Lovey, I *graduated* from Caen. But I attended university at Oxford until the summer of '24. As you know, me mum was from France. After me father was killed in the Great War, she started missing home. She moved back to Normandy when I entered university. In '24, she suffered a stroke, and I transferred to be nearer to her. But Jens and I remained close. He even came to visit me over Christmas holiday that year. And, after me mum passed the following spring, I returned home to England and did me residency alongside Jens and Petteri."

She blinks away a tear. "My papa frequently spoke of his university roommate named Geoffers, but I never knew the man's last name, and of course, I never dreamed it was you."

"Well, Geoffers was a nickname only Jens could get away with. He was a sterling chap, to be sure. But me point, Lovey, is that your papa and mama had already planned to separate you and your sibling from them to keep you from harm. It sounds to me like they discussed this at length before he wrote me this missive."

She casts her eyes down, and her cheeks grow warm. "Oh. I guess you're right."

"So, it sounds like your mama was only carrying out your papa's wishes after he'd already been arrested."

She raises an eyebrow. "He wasn't arrested. He was killed. It was the twenty-second of December, 1943."

Geoffrey nods. "Lovey, I'm just trying to tell you, please don't dismiss your mama without hearing what she has to say. You might be surprised at why she felt she had to do whatever it was she did. Keep in mind, even though you were an exceptionally intelligent and mature child, you were, in fact, a child. And you were dealing with the emotions of a child. And then to add insult to injury, it was only a short time later, wasn't it, that you were arrested and walked through the Gates of Perdition? Don't you think that may have compounded your feelings of betrayal?"

"No. Maybe. I don't know. I was so furious with my mama from the moment she left me, I never considered anything other than she wanted to be rid of me."

"Well, do you think if that's the case, she'd have spent the last decade or two searching for you halfway around the world?"

"I guess not. But it's too late. I wrote her a horrible letter this morning and all but told her I hated her. I've been having second thoughts ever since, thinking that my papa would be so ashamed of me if he knew what I did. But she's already read it."

Jack pulls a sealed envelope from his breast pocket and slides it across the table to her. "Are you talking about this letter?"

She looks at him with red-rimmed eyes. "How'd you get this?"

"I went down to your office when I heard you got called to surgery. I ran into Helen on my way, and I snatched the letter off your door before she saw it. I told her you were tied up, and she told me she needed to reschedule your meeting anyway because she needed to leave due to some kind of emergency with her husband's restaurant. I introduced myself, and we spoke for a few minutes before she left. She really seems like she loves you, babe, and I don't think she has any idea of what you've been thinking about her. I came home afterward and called your dad to see what he thought. I explained how torn you were about not wanting to hurt him or your mum."

Geoffrey rubs her shoulder. "That's right, Lovey, and Mummy and I want you to see your mama and welcome her into your life. We know that doesn't mean you'll love us any less. Listen, love isn't like a pitcher of water. You don't just fill a few glasses full then run out of liquid and let the other glasses stay dry. It's a bottomless urn that runs freely, and you can fill each new glass until it's overflowing without ever having the fear of it running out."

She pinches the bridge of her nose and sniffles. "That's a really beautiful analogy, Dad. Thank you. Thank you for... just thanks for everything!" She falls into his waiting arms and warms herself in his loving embrace.

Jack picks up a strip of cod and says, "All right, you two, the fish and chips are cold, but I, for one, am not going to let that keep me from this delicious treat." He shoves the fish in his mouth and smacks his lips as he chews.

Bridget stands and takes everyone's plate to the stove. "Let me reheat these in the oven. I'm sorry I've made such a fuss. Jack, I really appreciate your rescuing that letter before my mama read it. Thank you, my love." She turns on the oven and scrapes the plates onto a cookie sheet then sets it on the rack.

Jack takes a deep breath. "Denk nicht daran, mein Schatz."

Bridget's face blanches as she spins to face him. "What did you say?"

"I said, 'Think nothing of it, my darling.' At least that's what I tried to say."

"Yeah, I know *what* you said. But you said it in German."

Jack's eyes dart between Geoffrey's and Bridget's. "I, uh, guess with everyone else coming clean, I have a confession to make too." He extends his hand to her.

She intertwines her fingers through his, and he pulls her to his lap. She holds her breath. "What is it?" *Bollocks, he better not tell me he's a former Nazi soldier or something!*

"I, uh, I wasn't born in Baltimore. I was born in Munich. My birthname was Jakob Ernst Cassewitz. I was Jewish. Mein Vater – *my father* – worked as a book binder for Eher-Verlag... You might know them as Eher Publishing. When they published *Mein Kampf* in the summer of '25, Dad came home and announced that we had to get out of Europe. My mom's brother had recently moved to America and purchased a soft drink factory in Baltimore. Dad made arrangements with him to take a job at his bottling facility, and we left Germany the week of my tenth birthday in '26. My family changed their name to Castle, and as soon as we got here, we started attending Catholic mass. We never told anyone we were German or that we were Jewish because, once we relocated, we embraced our lives as Americans, and we never looked back."

A deep crease settles in Bridget's brow. "So, all this time, when you act as though you don't understand me..."

"I honestly don't understand you most of the time when you speak German. Like I said, I was barely ten when we left, and my father forbade us from using anything but English from that point forward. I only remember a few random words and phrases. I really never meant to keep it from you. But when Geoffrey told me you were a European Jew and that you'd been through so much you probably wouldn't want to bring up your past, I was afraid if you learned that my family got out in time, you might resent me or... I don't know. You might reconsider marrying me because I might be a source of bad memories or something."

Tears cascade down her cheeks, and she sniffles.

He offers her a napkin, saying, "I'm really sorry, hon. Please don't hate me."

"Hate you? How could I hate you? You only did what your family expected of you. A lot of Jews escaped and pretended they weren't Jewish anymore. Besides, I can hardly hold against you what I'm guilty of myself."

Geoffrey stands and opens the oven door. "Well, I, for one, think it will be unforgiveable if me fish and chips get burned, and if you haven't noticed, me stout is empty. Will you get me another pint, love?"

The group laughs, and they make small talk over dinner.

* * *

CHAPTER TWENTY-THREE

Bridget and Jack hold hands as they sit in the Arnolds' living room while Mr. Arnold reads the telegram informing them that Barry was prepping for an operative in the Mekong Delta when the Viet Cong got wind of the operation and moved in. They took several prisoners, and Barry was thought to be among those captured.

Bridget squeezes Mrs. Arnold's wrist. "I'm so very sorry. I know it isn't easy getting such news."

Mrs. Arnold dabs her eyes with a handkerchief and sniffles. "Thank you, Dear. You're right; it isn't. Especially when the military is so vague with details."

Mr. Arnold folds the telegram and slips it in the envelope. "Hon, I told you they aren't allowed to release more information because it could compromise—"

"I don't care! That's my baby over there. I want him home. I don't care about any of their military secrets."

Jack bows his head. "I'm sorry, folks. You know, after the Japanese bombed Pearl Harbor, my brothers and I wanted to enlist. Long story short, Uncle Sam said I had flat feet, so they wouldn't take me. But both of my brothers were shipped overseas. One was captured as a P.O.W., and the other was killed in the Battle of the Bulge. I just... I just want you to know that I understand how difficult it is to wait and keep your hope alive."

Mr. Arnold clears his throat. "Oh, I had no idea. I'm very sorry. Do you mind if I ask what happened to the P.O.W.?"

Jack nods. "His plane was shot down while he was flying in some supplies. He was captured and kept in a German Stalag until the end of the war. Now, he practices veteran's law out in Albuquerque. So, I'm sure Barry will turn up soon. After all, it's the season for miracles."

Mrs. Arnold wipes her eyes with the corner of her apron and says, "Yes, that's right, isn't it? Thank you both for coming over to check on us. It means so much. But if you don't mind, I have a headache. I think I'd better lie down."

Bridget and Jack stand, and she says, "Of course. We understand. Please don't hesitate to let us know if we can do anything. Goodnight."

The men shake hands, and Jack holds the door open for Bridget. "Please keep us posted if you hear any more news." They head out, and he wraps his arm around his wife's shoulders as they hurry across the street. "Wow, the temperature's really dropped, hasn't it?"

"I'll say. I was hoping you'd build us a fire."

"Good idea. If you'll make us some hot cocoa." He opens their front door, and they step inside and remove their coats.

She rubs her upper arms and shudders. "It's a deal." Catching his hands in hers, she steps close to him. "By the way, thank you."

He kisses her forehead. "For..."

"For rescuing that letter I wrote and for getting Dad over here to talk to me. Having him bring that letter from my papa was just... It was like a miracle. I never had any idea they knew each other."

"Yeah, that was pretty astounding, wasn't it?"

"You mean, you didn't already know Dad and my papa were friends?"

"No, he only told me you'd been in Bergen-Belsen. I had no idea about the rest. Like I told you yesterday, I never even knew your little friend Otto was really your brother. Hey, let me get started on that fire. It's cold in here." He swats her behind on his way to the den.

A while later, they snuggle on the couch and sip cocoa as they watch *It Takes a Thief*. The crackling and warmth of the fire lulls Bridget into a state of relaxation, and by the time *The Doris Day Show* starts, she drifts into unconsciousness.

When she awakens, she's in Auschwitz, standing at attention in front of Dr. Mengele and holding her bony hands over her small, bare breasts. Her upper arm throbs at the injection site, though her fever has dissipated, and she's been allowed to leave the observation clinic. Dr. Mengele examines the scarlet rings still present on her bicep. "Hmm, does this still hurt?" He plunges his thumb into the bull's eye as he maintains his steely focus on her face.

She holds her breath and refuses to display a reaction to the fiery pain. "Nein, Doktor."

He raises an eyebrow and tosses her threadbare striped uniform shirt to her. "Very good. Get dressed. You're leaving."

She pulls her shirt over her head and scratches her protruding ribs where a flea bites her. "Leaving, sir?"

"I've selected twenty children. Ten boys, ten girls. They'll be sent to Neuengamme so that my colleague, Dr. Kurt Heissmeyer, can use them in his research to find a cure for tuberculosis. I've chosen four caretakers to accompany them for transport. Two of these women are nurses from Poland. One is a Hungarian chemist. And one, who I'm sure you will find particularly interesting, is a Polish doctor. A female physician, if you can imagine such a preposterous thing. The children I've selected are Polish, Italian, Dutch, French, and Yugoslav. You'll be going along to translate for the caregivers and for Dr. Heissmeyer. And you'll do *whatever* he asks of you. Understand?"

"Jawohl, Doktor."

As they are paraded to the boxcar, Dr. Mengele asks the unsuspecting children, "Who wants to go and see their mama?"

Bridget holds her breath and forces herself not to exhibit a reaction to the doctor's cruel lie. *Bastard! May God strike him dead where he stands.*

After being stuffed into the cattle car, the train pulls away, and Bridget peeks out the door crack. For a brief moment, she can swear she sees Mama, bald and thin, weeping and waving at the train. *It can't be her. She's in Hong Kong.* When Auschwitz is no longer in sight, she remembers her beloved silver ring and starts searching the slats of the car to see if it could possibly be the same train that brought her to her first stop in Hell. Her efforts are for naught.

When the train stops, Gunter Hetzel, dressed in his S.S. uniform, stumbles as he pulls open the door. He winces and grabs his ribcage, falling to his knees. "Help me, Doctor! It hurts!"

Bridget steps onto the platform and kicks him in the gut. "Help you? No, Herr Hetzel, I won't help you. You deserve every ounce of pain you feel and more. I told you the prussic acid here would cause you problems. That's probably why you have those ulcers."

Gunter narrows his eyes. "If your papa was here, he'd help me. He was a *real* doctor. He cared about everyone. He'd certainly be ashamed of you if he knew how you turned your back on your own mama. What a horrible daughter you are! You shouldn't even be alive, Bridget. Bridget..."

"Bridget? My name is Renate."

"Bridget. Bridget, wake up. Bridget." Jack shakes her shoulder. "Honey, let's head up to bed."

Her eyes flutter open, and she gasps at the sight of him. "Oh, bollocks. I think I was having a dream."

"It sounded more like a nightmare. You were moaning and holding your shoulder. Are you all right?" He extends his hand to her.

She yawns and places her hand in his. "Yeah. It was nothing. I guess I can't stop thinking about Barry being a prisoner of war." She averts his gaze. "Wow, it's already after ten. I need to get to bed. I've got surgery in the morning."

As she snuggles beside Jack, his nightly sawmill opens for business, and she fights the impulse to pinch his nose. *What the bloody hell does he have up there?* She waits fifteen minutes to see if the noise might ebb, but it only grows louder. She pulls on her robe and heads to the guest room.

As she gets settled in bed, her brain refuses to relax. "Bollocks. Now, I can't sleep." She flips on the bedside lamp, opens the closet, and locates her stash of SweeTarts. She pops an orange one in her mouth and pulls the hatbox off the top shelf.

She takes the box to the bed, unpacks the layers of tissue, and pulls her treasure box from the belly of the container. She holds her breath as she opens the cigar box and pulls out a violet, velvet bag, worn with age. She closes her eyes as she inhales the faint, sweet smell of Mama's French perfume. She pulls the drawstrings and opens the mouth of the bag. Using the same delicate care she would when operating on a patient's brain, she pulls out the photo of her parents and herself with Otto. Her hand flies to her heart as she inspects every inch of the paper. The sepia photograph shows Otto smiling. He holds Bridget's hand, and her adoration of her big brother is evident in the way she looks at him. Her parents stand behind the children with their arms around each other, and Mama's head rests on Papa's shoulder. *We all looked so happy.*

A tear rolls down her cheek, and she wipes it on her sleeve before it can fall on the photo. She sets the snapshot aside and plucks out the French bookmark. Her index finger traces the drawing of the Eiffel Tower under the phrase "Bienvenue à Paris!" – *Welcome to Paris!* She takes a deep breath. "Oh, Papa, I miss you so much. I never meant to hurt you."

She sets the bookmark aside and unfolds a yellowed paper. Her lips curl into a smile as the whimsical artwork drawn by Otto causes her mind to return to the time she had the measles and Otto asked her what she wished for to make her feel better. She told him more than anything, she wanted her very own pony, so Otto drew a purple pony with his crayons and had the horse prancing through a patch of blue and yellow flowers under a pink sky. Her fingertip traces his signature printed in the lower right corner, and a lump forms in her throat. "My sweet Otto, you were always my hero."

She sniffles as she refolds the paper and reaches in the bag. She pulls out the gold cufflink and recalls how she used to pretend that the diamond in it was actually a rare jewel that belonged in the crown of some queen or king who had offered a tidy reward for its return. Her fingertip traces the M monogramed in the gold, and she smiles at the memory of how she used to turn it upside down and pretend it was a W for Windsor Castle. She imagined she would return the jewel to its rightful owner, and the royal family would be so grateful, they would take her and her family into the safety of their castle where Hitler and the war couldn't touch them. She shakes her head at the silliness of her childhood fantasy.

She comes to the photo of Otto holding her on his lap for her first birthday. Though the photo is monochrome, in her mind's eye, she can see the carnation pink streamers and magenta balloons, and her heart smiles at the silly paper party hats worn by herself and her older brother. She can clearly see Otto's ginger-colored hair, his full, pink lips, his rosy cheeks, and his bright green eyes with cocoa-colored flecks. *Just like Papa's.* "Otto Theodor, you'd have been three and a half here. I wonder if our sweet brother Josef Wilhelm looked like you at that age. I wish more than anything I had a photo of him."

She dabs her eyes with a tissue and repacks her treasures in the bag. Next, she unwraps her mother's handkerchief from her beloved diary then opens the book and turns several pages until she reaches what she's looking for. She holds her breath as she reads the entry.

# # #

22 November 1945

Querido Diario (Dear Diary),

I didn't realize what day this was until I was in chemistry class. Some of the students were complaining about having so much homework, and the professor said, "Aww, you poor, poor babies. Who wants to go and see their mama to cry about the mean teacher giving too much work?"

The way he asked who wanted to see their mama gave me a sudden flashback of when Dr. Mengele told me I was being transferred to Neuengamme. I remembered fixating on the wall behind the doctor because I refused to ever look him directly in the eye. There were Xs over the month of November until that day, the twenty-second. Though that was only one year ago today, it feels like a lifetime ago... Yet, sometimes, it's all as fresh in my mind as if it happened only yesterday.

I'd all but forgotten what happened when we were leaving and the train pulled away... I peeked between the crack by the door, and I could've sworn I saw my mother waving at me. I mean, I know it wasn't her. She was so thin and bald, her cheeks and teeth protruded from her face, and her hips and breasts had all but disappeared. I know we all looked like walking skeletons, but I couldn't imagine that Mama hadn't made it to Hong Kong with Josef by then.

At any rate, the whole event today reminded me of what a bastard Dr. Heissmeyer was. He may have even been worse than Dr. Mengele. He hypothesized that the injection of live tuberculosis bacilli into subjects would serve as an inoculation against the disease, and he used the children I traveled with as human lab rats!

Soon after we arrived, he ordered me to load the syringes with the bacterium. The thought of partaking in something so evil made my empty stomach churn. The only thing that saved me from having to actually participate in this precipitated mass homicide was that an S.S. guard came in looking for assistance. His lower abdomen was hurting something fierce, and he was sweating despite the cold weather. I knew right away he was suffering from acute appendicitis or perhaps even a ruptured appendix, and Dr. Heissmeyer was too busy with the children to stop and help.

So, the S.S. guard asked if I could give him something for the pain, and I was tempted to give him a shot of the tuberculosis bacterium. But then I thought of Papa and what a good doctor he was and how, even on his dying day, he risked his own life to save one of the Gestapo. I remembered how much it had hurt him when I was so cruel to Ambroos van den Boom, and I recalled how many times my father used read me the Hippocratic Oath and tell me that there was nothing more important than keeping one's word when having taken such a solemn vow, no matter what the circumstances.

Now that Papa's gone, all I have left of him are my memories, and it's been my solemn desire since he died to make sure I honor him in all I do. So, I treated the guard as humanely as I would hope he'd treat me. I gave him something for his pain, and I alerted Dr. Heissmeyer of my suspicions about his appendix. The doctor took him into surgery a short time later and said my diagnosis was correct: The appendix had ruptured.

It made me proud that all my father's coaching had paid off. If only now I could find a way to forgive my mama because I know that's the one thing that I can never do; yet that's the one thing my papa would surely insist upon.

# # #

CHAPTER TWENTY-FOUR

Early the next morning, the spicy scent of cinnamon tickles Bridget's nose, and she wakes with a smile on her face. *Mm, I smell sweet rolls.* She showers and dresses then hurries downstairs.

Beverly refills Jack's coffee cup then slides a fresh cup in front of Bridget, saying, "Good morning, Dr. Castle. I made your favorite holiday rolls." She offers her the platter.

Bridget plucks a bun from the plate and stirs cream and sugar into her cup. "Mm, they smell heavenly. You're here early."

"Yes, ma'am. I have to leave early for a special church service this evening. My youngest grandson is in the children's program. He's a wise man."

Bridget's face lights up. "Congratulations. That's going to be a real treat for you. Why don't you make a short day of it and leave after lunch?"

"Are you sure, ma'am?"

Jack sips his coffee and nods. "Of course. There's nothing more important than family. You can borrow our Super Eight if you like. It's better than the old eight-millimeter, and I've got a couple of extra rolls of color Kodachrome film you're welcome to use. Each cartridge records for fifteen minutes."

Bridget says, "Yeah, and you can take the reel-to-reel recorder to capture the audio if you want."

Beverly's eyes sparkle with obvious excitement. "Really? Aw, that would be such a blessing. I could really surprise my daughter with a recording like that. Her husband's still in Laos, and she's having a difficult time trying to keep him in the loop with the kids growing and asking all their questions about the war. My granddaughter's fifteen now, and she was arrested last weekend at a peace rally down in Cambridge. She's hanging out with the hippies, and her mother's fit to be tied."

Bridget winces. "I'm sorry to hear that. She could put her energy to better use if she'd come be a candy striper at hospital and work with some of the veterans we get from the V.A. Then she could see firsthand just how much they, too, hate this war. These rolls are delicious. May I have another?"

Jack passes the platter to her and creases the newspaper in front of him. "Oh, wow, listen to this…"

"Yesterday afternoon, Mary Flora Bell, age eleven, was sentenced to life in juvenile detention after she was convicted of the murders of Martin Brown, aged four, and Brian Howe, aged three, in Scotswood, a district in the West End of Newcastle upon Tyne. Earlier this year on May twenty-fifth, the day before her eleventh birthday, Miss Bell strangled Brown in a derelict house. It is believed that she acted alone. Two months later on July thirty-first, she and a friend strangled Howe in the same Scotswood area. Miss Bell carved an M into the boy's abdomen, cut his hair, scratched his legs, and mutilated his genitals. Justice Cusack, who presided over the case, described Miss Bell as dangerous and said she posed a grave risk to other children. She was sentenced to a Red Bank secure unit in Newton-Le-Willows, Lancashire."

Jack sets the paper down and sips his coffee. "That's incredible. Can you imagine what a monster this child would be in a few years if she hadn't been caught?"

Bridget shudders. "Sounds like she's already a monster-in-the-making. Makes me wonder what her parents were like. I don't think being detained at Her Majesty's pleasure is going to make a difference other than getting her off the streets. She could use some intense psychotherapy if she has any hope of getting back on track. Well, if you two will excuse me, I have surgery this morning, and I've a lot to do beforehand. Beverly, good luck to your grandson. Jack'll get you the camera and recorder before he leaves." She kisses Jack's cheek, takes her cup and plate to the sink, and heads upstairs.

After brushing her teeth, she bundles up and scurries out to her car. She scrapes the ice off the windshield and starts the ignition then flips on the radio. She sings "Magic Carpet Ride" with Steppenwolf, "Harper Valley P.T.A." with Jeannie Riley, and "Carrie Anne" with The Hollies.

As she nears the hospital, the traffic slows, yielding for a group of long-haired kids holding a war protest demonstration at the corner of Boston Common. The kids carry colorful hand-painted poster board signs with slogans such as "Get Out of Vietnam Now!" and "End the War Before It Ends You!" Bridget catches herself smiling at the organized way the peace activists are making their ideas known without infringing on anyone's rights. *They aren't interfering with businesses today. Hopefully they won't get arrested this time.*

As she drives past, she removes a glove, toots her horn, and holds her fingers up in a V. Many of the kids return the peace symbol to her, and her heart warms as she shoves her hand back in her mitten.

She pulls into the hospital parking lot and rushes inside. *Brrr!* She nods at President Johnson's photo and smiles as she passes Carol's desk then pushes the elevator call button. "Morning, Carol. You still enjoying that new car?"

"I sure am, Doctor. It's the hippest car I've ever had."

"You're a lucky young lady. Have a good day." Bridget steps on the elevator and rides up to the seventh floor then hurries to her office. As she steps in, she picks up a manila envelope from the floor and tosses it on her desk.

She removes her hat, coat, and mittens then turns up the radiator as she pulls on her lab coat. She takes a roll of Clove Lifesavers out of an extra pair of shoes in her closet, pops a candy in her mouth, then hides the roll again. She thumbs through the file folders until she comes to what she's searching for. *Ah, Mr. Gunter Werner Hetzel. Let's see what we can do for you this morning.* She takes the file to her desk and sits on her foot as she leans over the file and starts reading.

"Hmm. Blood type's AB negative. All right. Let's see what Dr. Slater found." Opening the manila envelope, she winces. "Aw, bollocks. Blah, blah, blah. Twenty-four-year-old male. Blah, blah. Peptic ulcer disease. Two gastric ulcers, three centimeters each. One duodenal, one-point-five centimeters. Blah, blah, blah. History of hematemesis. Active bleeding. Administered G.I. cocktail for dyspepsia at five this morning and prescribed Bismuth Subsalicylate. Partial gastrectomy recommended as soon as possible. Bloody hell!"

She opens her top desk drawer and fumbles inside for a Pep-O-Mint Lifesaver. She sucks on the candy as she dials the phone.

"Blood bank. Arthur speaking."

"Arthur, you're just the man I was looking for. This is Dr. Bridget Castle. I've got a bit of a situation I need help with."

"Sure, Doc, what is it?"

"I've got a surgery on the books for tomorrow, and it looks like I'm going to need to reserve a few pints of AB negative. He's high risk."

"Hmm, I'm not sure if we have much AB neg in stock. Let me see... Okay, we have nine pints on hand. Will that do?"

"Yeah, hopefully, that'll be fine. I'm scheduled for Theater Three at nine in the morning if you can please mark them for standby."

"You got it, Doc. Take care."

"You too. Thanks." She hangs up the phone and checks her watch. "Quarter after eight. All right, I'd better go get this over with." She tucks Dr. Slater's report in the patient's file folder and stuffs the folder back in the drawer then heads down to the fifth floor.

As she steps off the elevator, Nat King Cole crooning "Chestnuts Roasting on an Open Fire" is drowned out by the piercing, inflammatory shrieks of a woman, the slamming of items against a floor or wall, and the husky roar of an undeniably angered Gunter Hetzel. His voice echoes down the corridor. "Halte sie von mir fern!" *Keep her away from me!* The sound of glass breaking proceeds, "Lass diese Juden nicht wieder in meine Nähe!" *Don't let that Jew near me again!*

Bridget races down to her patient's room. Two nurses hold meal trays in front of their faces like shields, and an orderly attempts to roll the bedside tray out of the patient's reach. Mr. Hetzel grabs his coffee cup and throws it against the wall, causing it to shatter and splash liquid on the wall and floor.

Bridget's face turns crimson, and she edges into the room in front of the others. "Herr Hetzel, du hörst sofort mit diesem Unsinn auf!" *You stop this nonsense right now!* She unlocks the drug cabinet beside the TV and loads a syringe.

The patient's tawny hair falls in his eyes as he gnashes his teeth. "You keep that woman away from me! I don't want her coming near me again!"

Bridget plants herself beside him and swats at his side as she rolls him over and throws back the blanket. His triangular scar peeks out as she swabs his right hip and plunges the needle into his flesh. "Here, this will help you calm down and get the rest you need."

"I mean it, Doc. You see that scar on my ass? A Jude – *Jew* – did that to me, and I *don't* intend to allow myself to be marred any further by any such Untermenschen – *sub-human!*"

As his eyes meet hers, she sees him not in his pale green hospital gown but in a full Nazi uniform decorated with numerous medals. She blinks her eyes, and he's back to being Herr Hetzel, a young patient succumbing to the effects of the sedative. His eyelids flutter for a moment then close, and his clenched hands open as his muscles relax. His chest rises and falls as his breath comes slow and steady.

The orderly begins picking up the broken glass from the floor, and one of the nurses says, "I'll go call Housekeeping."

Bridget pulls the other nurse aside. "What happened to cause this episode?"

The nurse says, "When Foodservice brought his breakfast, they dropped a bowl of oatmeal on his floor. I guess they called down to Housekeeping to clean it up, and that new lady was the only one available. I was standing right out there. She was perfectly pleasant. Told him, 'Good morning,' and started cleaning the mess. He immediately became enraged. He threw his apple juice glass at her, and it hit her in the head."

Bridget's face blanches. "Oh, no. Was she injured?"

"Her forehead was bleeding. My guess is she probably needed a couple of stitches. I sent her right down to Emergency and thought I'd try to get the mess cleaned before someone else got hurt, but he was carrying on so, it's like he was a madman. You got here about a minute later. You saw how he was. He's crazed."

Bridget shakes her head. "He's dealing with a brain tumor that affects his judgment, and I just got a report telling me he needs G.I. surgery for some bleeding ulcers. He's in a lot of pain, and I'm sure that his pain plus being in a strange country with no family or friends isn't helping. His surgery with me is scheduled for tomorrow, so let's just do what we can to get him though the rest of the day. He'll probably sleep until after lunch with what I just gave him." She makes a notation on the patient's chart and takes a look at the sleeping man. "All right, I'm scheduled for surgery right now. I'll check back on him later."

"Yes, Doctor. Good luck."

"Thanks." Bridget ducks out and treks down the hall. She peeks in Room 502 and nods at the nurse making the empty bed. *Good. Craig's already downstairs waiting on me.* She gets on the elevator and heads down to the second floor.

She heads to the surgical waiting area and smiles at how comfortable Lisa looks sitting with Craig's parents. She takes a deep breath and steps in front of them. "Good morning, Barnaby family. I see Craig's already getting prepped. Do you have any questions about his surgery?"

Mrs. Barnaby grabs Lisa's hand and says, "I think Craig explained it pretty well. You're doing two surgeries, right?"

Bridget nods. "There are two procedures involved. Technically, it's just one surgery. A discectomy and a laminectomy. Basically, I'm removing the herniated disc in his cervical region, as well as the lamina, which is the part of the vertebrae that protects the spinal canal. I need to remove the lamina so I can get to the disc. Once those are gone, he'll have about a four-week recovery time, some physical therapy, and his left arm will feel like new again. Understand?"

Mr. Barnaby chuckles and scratches his head. "I can't say I understand, Doc, but my son says you're the best, and that's good enough for us. Thank you for all you're doing for him."

"Ah, Craig's a special young man. Okay, so, I'm going to go on back and get ready. This surgery takes about three hours, give or take. A nurse will be out to keep you updated sometime around the halfway point. All right? Mr. and Mrs. Barnaby, Lisa, we'll see you folks later. Bridget waves then heads to the washroom.

# # #

5 January 1943

Liebes Tagebuch (Dear Diary),

Last night, the most amazing thing happened. Papa was reading an Agatha Christie book to Mama and me when we heard a noise at the door. At first, we feared it was the Gestapo. Papa sent Mama and me to hide behind a secret door in the broom closet.

We were terrified that he would be shot or arrested. But after only a few minutes, he told us to come see what it was. A skinny hound dog had apparently been struck by a car then wandered to our door. His back end was crumpled, and Mama said the most humane thing we could do would be to put the pup out of his misery. I started petting it, and it licked my hand. I fed it some bread and butter, and the poor thing acted as if it hadn't eaten in a month.

I begged Papa not to kill it, and he said the dog would need extensive surgery to get it well enough to walk again. I reminded him that if anyone could perform such a miracle, he could. I know most people wouldn't care so much about an animal they didn't even know, and they might even say such extensive surgery isn't worth it for a mutt. But my papa loves all living things. Plus, I knew he'd jump at the chance to put his surgical skills to use, not to mention take the opportunity to allow me to see such an intricate procedure up close. So, he told me he'd need a surgical assistant, and he and I sneaked over to the Good Doctor's office and anesthetized the animal.

What happened next was nothing short of a miracle! Papa actually performed a modified spinal fusion surgery where he screwed a damaged vertebra to a healthy one. It took us nearly four hours. I've never seen such delicate work up close, and it made me proud to know he had the skill to perform such a feat. He said I was a big help and he couldn't have done it without me.

This evening, we told the Good Doctor Van Den Boom about it, and he said he'd be happy to take the hound back to his house to recuperate. He said his son, Ambroos, would love a dog. Right now, we're still keeping our fingers crossed that the dog recovers with no further damage. I'll let you know how it turns out.

P.S. 8 March 1943 – Dr. Van Den Boom said our dog passed away last night. Papa said he wasn't surprised because the dog was so weak to start with, his body may have not been able to withstand the surgery. But Dr. Van Den Boom assured me that he was a happy animal until the end. I'm so glad we were able to extend his life and show him some love, even if only for a while.

# # #

CHAPTER TWENTY-FIVE

Bridget checks the wall clock as she washes her hands. Looking to the anesthesiologist, Dr. Dick Spurgeon, she says, "Wow, it's already half past one. Good work, Doctor."

Dick offers her a towel as he dries his hands. "Thanks. It was a pleasure as always."

She dries her hands, grabs her lab coat, and heads out to the surgical waiting lounge. The group, glued to the TV, is engrossed in a breaking news bulletin. Bridget steps behind them and strains to hear the report.

"...and early yesterday morning, twenty-year-old Emory student, Barbara Mackle, was taken at gunpoint from a Rodeway Inn in Decatur, Georgia where she was staying with her mother, Jane Mackle. The student was sick with the Hong Kong flu which is still slamming the nation, and Miss Mackle's mother drove up from the family's home in Coral Gables, Florida to care for her daughter and bring her home for the holidays. The suspect, a Caucasian male in his mid-twenties, posed as a detective to gain entry into the room. His accomplice, a Caucasian female in her mid-twenties, though some eye-witness reports say it was another young man, chloroformed, bound, and gagged Jane before kidnapping Barbara. Action News has just learned that Barbara's father, Robert Mackle, is a successful land developer in Miami..."

Bridget clears her throat. "Pardon me, folks."

Mrs. Barnaby jumps in her seat. "Oh, Dr. Castle. How's Craig?"

Bridget's smile matches her twinkling eyes. "His surgery was a success. He's going to be in recovery for a couple of hours, then he'll be moved back up to his room. If you want to go grab some lunch, you'll probably be able to slip in and sit with him for a few minutes when you return before visiting hours end. No more than ten minutes, though. He needs his rest."

Mrs. Barnaby stands and hugs the surgeon. "This is our Christmas miracle! Thank you so much, Doctor. You've really made such a difference in our baby."

Mr. Barnaby stands and shakes Bridget's hand. "Yes, indeedy. I don't know what we'd have done without you. Well, you and this pretty little thing." He squeezes Lisa to his side. "Between the two of you, Craig's got a whole new lease on life. Thank you."

Bridget tips her head. "Well, you've got an amazing young man. I'm glad everything worked out as planned. Now, if you'll excuse me, I have to be somewhere, but I'm sure I'll see you again in the coming days."

Mr. Barnaby raises his hand in a motionless wave. "Of course. Thanks again, Doc. Merry Christmas."

"Merry Christmas." Bridget waves as she leaves the lounge then makes a beeline for the elevator. She heads down to the first floor and hums along with Elvis as he belts out "Blue Christmas." She rushes over to the Emergency Department and finds Dr. Redding clearing a tray in a trauma room. "Hi, Glenn. How's it going?"

"Oh, hey. I just had a kid with hypothermia. He fell through the ice over at Chestnut Hill."

"What? It's not cold enough for the whole reservoir to be frozen over. How was he skating?"

"No, it wasn't an ice-skating incident. The water was frozen around the edge, and a group of teenagers started jumping on it, trying to get it to crack. This kid slipped and fell in; then he was too prideful to go home and get some dry clothes on. He'd made it all the way over to Faneuil Hall until he couldn't walk anymore, and his buddies abandoned him. Someone called his parents, and by the time his dad found him, the kid's hands and feet were blue. I sent him up to four for hemodialysis to rewarm his blood, but I'm afraid he still might lose a couple toes."

"Aw, bollocks." Her mind floods with memories of Bergen-Belsen when prisoners were punished by being made to march in place, naked, in the snow, until they dropped; then their lifeless bodies were left there until the next day as a warning for the others to not step out of line. She shudders and hugs herself.

"Hey, are you okay? You look like you've seen a ghost."

"Huh? Oh, sorry. I guess I was just—my mind just wandered for a moment. Uh, I came to ask you about a woman on the housekeeping staff. Her name's Helen Kugelman. One of my patients injured her, and I heard she might have needed sutures."

"Oh, yeah. The woman from your office. She's a sweet lady. I gave her three stitches on her forehead. She's going to have a nasty bruise for a while, but luckily, the laceration is near her hairline so the scar shouldn't be too noticeable."

"I see. I just wanted to make sure she didn't get hurt too badly. Do you know if she went back to work or—"

"I told her it'd be a good idea to rest, but I don't know if she left or not. As soon as I finished with her, we had a tourist group bus accident come through here, and we were backed up for a couple of hours."

"Eww. Not too bad, I hope?"

"Nah. Nothing severe. Mostly just a few contusions, a few sprains, and a couple of whiplash. Actually, we could've used you here. They were Japanese, and we had a hell of a time trying to communicate with them."

The muscles in her neck tighten, and she sucks air through her teeth. "Oh, I'm afraid I wouldn't be of much help there. I haven't learned any languages from the Orient yet, though I'm not opposed to trying someday."

"Really? It's so fascinating how easily you pick up different languages. I have a difficult enough time getting along when my wife's family comes down from Quebec and they start in French. I can understand them early on, but then they get to going so fast, I can't keep up."

She giggles. "Well, I bet they can't set a broken femur or stitch up a stab wound, so you've certainly got your own strengths."

She checks her watch. "Hey, I just finished surgery, and I need to hit the cafeteria before they close. I'll talk to you later, okay?"

"Sure thing. Take care."

"You too." She scurries out of the department and makes her way down the winding corridor to the cafeteria. She whistles along with Stevie Wonder singing "What Christmas Means to Me."

As she nears the lunchroom, she stops to read the specials board. *Hmm... Do I want turkey and stuffing? Or lentil soup?*

As she debates her choices, like nails on a chalkboard, a familiar laugh comes from behind her. "There she is! Look, Pauly, it's Doctor Bridget."

Bridget holds her breath. *Bollocks.* Turning to face Nadine and Paul, she forces a smile. "What a surprise."

Paul raises his eyebrows. "Well, isn't this perfect timing? We were just up visiting Grandma Fran, and we were talking about you."

Nadine grabs Bridget's arm. "Yes, were your ears burning?"

If they were, I might have had a warning that you two were here. Bridget's body tenses. "Uh, no. No, they weren't."

Paul pulls a pack of cigarettes and a lighter from his breast pocket. "Well, as long as you're here, will you join us for lunch?"

Nadine clasps her hands together. "Yes, it's the least we can do for you."

Crikey. "Um, actually, you know, I'd love to, but I've got a really tight schedule this afternoon, and I'm just picking up something to take back to my office. I've been in surgery all morning, and I have some research to do before I make my rounds. So, thanks for the offer, but I'm afraid I'm in too much of a rush right now. Maybe some other time. Excuse me." Bridget flees to the counter before they can respond.

She picks up a tray and slides it down the rail. "Can I get a bowl of the lentil soup with a slice of that thick buttered bread?"

The food service worker offers a smile as she nods. "Of course, Doctor." She stirs the soup with a long-handled ladle.

"Actually, can I get it to go? I need to do some work up in my office."

"Sure thing. Just let me find the lids. What would you like to drink?"

"Hmm, a Coke would hit the spot."

"All right. I'll bring this down to the cashier."

"Thanks." Bridget hurries to the cashier station and pulls two one-dollar bills out of her pocket.

The cashier takes the money and says, "Okay, Doctor, that's a buck twenty-two out of two... All right, you get seventy-eight cents back, and here's your food." She slides Bridget's food across the counter and passes her a stack of napkins. "Have a good evening."

"Thanks. You too." Bridget peeks down the line at Nadine and Paul then ducks her head as she hurries out of the cafeteria. *That was close.* She rushes to the elevator and holds her breath until it arrives. She rides up to the seventh floor and breathes a heavy sigh of relief once she's locked in her office.

She slurps a spoonful of soup and phones the Housekeeping Department.

"Housekeeping."

"Hi, this is Dr. Castle. You have a new employee, Helen Kugelman. Can you tell me where I can find her right now?"

"Oh, uh, Helen had to go home. She was hurt on the job today, and the E.R. doc wanted her off her feet until tomorrow. You want I should give her a message?"

"Um, no, that's okay. Thank you anyway."

"Yep. Good evening, Doctor."

Bridget's lungs deflate, and she dials Jack's office.

"Administrator's office. How may I help you?"

"Bonnie? It's Bridget. Is Jack around?"

"No, I'm sorry. He left for the day."

"Really? How long ago?"

"He told me he was going to lunch around noon. About an hour later, he phoned and said he wouldn't be back today."

"Huh. And he didn't say where he was?"

"No, ma'am. I'm sorry."

"All right, then. Thanks anyway."

"You're welcome. Goodbye."

Bridget hangs up and tears her bread in half then dips it in her soup. *Wonder where he went now?*

She finishes her lunch then heads down to the fourth-floor nurses' station. "Afternoon, ladies. How's Susan Turner today?"

The nurse adjusts her cap. "She's doing remarkably well. She ate all her breakfast and lunch and asked for more. She doesn't even seem to notice the halo anymore. She keeps asking her parents to read to her and where her sister is."

Bridget nods. "Excellent. That's better than I expected. Let's go ahead and try her on some boiled chicken for dinner."

"Yes, Doctor. I'll call Dietary right away."

"Very good." Bridget heads into the patient's room where the child's parents are reading a storybook. Bridget clears her throat. "Wow, Susan, that Lyle Crocodile sounds like a very smart cookie."

Susan giggles, and Bridget grabs her stethoscope and listens to the child's lungs. She looks in the girl's eyes and mouth with a flashlight then steps to the corner of the room with the parents. "Mr. and Mrs. Turner, I want you to know I can't tell you when I've seen such a quick recuperation. Normally with Susan's type of brain injury, she might experience loss of coordination, digestive problems, trouble swallowing, or problems with other automatic functions. At this rate, I anticipate she'll be ready for her first functional evaluation by early next week which is about a week ahead of schedule."

Mrs. Turner clasps her husband's hand and says, "Really? What wonderful news! Thank you, Doctor."

Bridget makes a note on the patient's chart. "I've ordered some boiled chicken for her dinner. I want to see how she handles solids."

"Oh? Okay, great. Thank you."

"All right, you folks take care, and I'll see you tomorrow. Goodnight, Susan."

"Bye bye."

Bridget heads up to the fifth-floor nurses' station. "Afternoon, Kelly. I need statuses on Bivens, Alexander, Barnaby, and Hetzel."

The nurse flips over a page on her clipboard. "Okay, let me see... Mr. Bivens is doing very well. Vitals are good. No complaints other than a slight nagging headache. He ate all his breakfast and lunch. His wife's in there with him right now."

"Good. Let's go ahead and cut him loose. If you'll type up his discharge papers, I'll sign off when I finish my rounds. Restrictions are no lifting more than ten pounds, no driving, no heavy equipment, no alcohol, Paracetamol for pain, no work until further notice, plenty of bed rest, and follow-up in ten days."

"Yes, ma'am. Mrs. Alexander is having some cognitive difficulty, and she hasn't had much of an appetite. Also, I went in to check on her after Dr. Taylor left. Her language is garbled, and she seems to be confused."

"Bollocks. Any fever?"

"Yes, one hundred point one."

"Uh oh. Okay, I'll take a look at her. What room is she in?"

"She's in 514. Also, Craig Barnaby woke up briefly but fell asleep again almost immediately. His vitals are good."

"All right, that's fine. He's told me that he doesn't usually do well with anesthesia, so I'm sure he's just sleeping it off. And Hetzel?"

Kelly rolls her eyes. "He woke up from the sedative you gave him about an hour ago, and he's been a real pip ever since. He refused to touch his lunch, and he won't let me near him to get vitals. Every time any of us even try to go in there, he raises Cain and yells like his bed's on fire."

"Okay, well, he's not the first grizzly bear we've ever treated. I'll see what I can do."

Bridget heads to Room 511. "Mr. Bivens, I understand you're getting a little tired of us here. You think you'd like the scenery better at home?"

Mrs. Bivens's face lights up. "Really? Dale, did you hear that? Can he leave today, Doctor?"

Bridget removes her stethoscope from her pocket. "Well, let me have a listen to his lungs, and I'll see what I can do." She listens to his chest and back then shines a flashlight in his eyes. "Here, keep your head still and follow my finger with your eyes." She moves her finger left, right, up, and down. "Very good. Well, I don't see any reason to keep you here. I've already got Kelly typing up your discharge instructions. You need to listen to everything she tells you and get plenty of rest. No exceptions. If you still feel wonky after a couple of days, call my office. Okay?"

"Yes, thank you, Doctor."

"Okay. I want you to make an appointment to come back and see me in ten days, all right? So, just hold tight for Kelly, and you folks have a Merry Christmas."

Mrs. Bivens stands. "Dr. Castle, thank you so much for all you've done for Dale. I was so scared when I learned he'd been hit by a car."

"Well, you take good care of him, and I'm sure he'll be just fine."

"Oh, I will. Say, I just love your accent. Are you from England or Australia?"

"I'm from England. I lived about an hour and a half away from London in a little town near Reading."

"I just wondered because you said 'my', not 'me'."

"Pardon me?"

"You told Dale to follow *my* finger, call *my* office. I used to spend summers with my aunt in Newcastle, and she said 'me' all the time."

Bridget raises her eyebrows. "Ah, then that explains it. Folks in Northern England do say 'me'. My dad's from Manchester, and my mum's from Liverpool, and they both say 'me' also. But I always lived in the South country. I guess my accent was influenced by someone in my childhood who taught me several foreign languages."

"Huh. You learn something new every day. Well, thank you, Doctor. Merry Christmas. And as my aunt would say, 'cheerio'."

Bridget giggles and wiggles her fingers as she waves. "You folks take care and have a happy holiday. Ta ta."

She heads across the hall to Room 514. "Good afternoon, Mrs. Alexander. How are you feeling today?"

"Nadine, honey, could you please call the children in from out back? They've been outside too long."

Bridget slips her stethoscope stems into her ears and steps closer. "Mrs. Alexander, I'm Dr. Castle. I'm going to listen to your heart." She presses the instrument against the woman's chest. "Sounds like you're wheezing. I'm going to need to look in your throat." She inserts a tongue depressor and shines a light in the woman's mouth.

"Nadine, get that thing out of there! The dog's been playing with it."

Bridget shakes a thermometer and sticks it under the woman's tongue then feels the patient's wrist as she waits. "Mrs. Alexander, I need you to keep that under your tongue for a minute. Your pulse is rather fast. Have you been feeling okay today? The nurse said you didn't eat much. Is your stomach upset?"

The woman's face blanches, and a gurgling noise emanates from under the covers.

Within seconds, Bridget's nose burns, and she holds her breath. She lifts the blanket and steps backward. "Mrs. Alexander, you've had a little accident. Let me see this..." She reads the thermometer. "A hundred and two point three. Mrs. Alexander, I'm afraid you've got the flu. Just hold on, and I'm going to get a nurse to come help us." She presses the buzzer, and moments later, a nurse steps in.

The nurse's eyes grow large, and she winces. "Oh. We've had a little accident, haven't we?"

Bridget washes and dries her hands then nudges the nurse into the corridor and steps out with her. "I believe Mrs. Alexander has H3N2. We need to quarantine her. I know that Dr. Paul Taylor and his fiancé have been visiting her. I need you to contact him STAT, and tell him to let his supervisor know he's been exposed. He's going to have to get checked before he'll be allowed to work anymore. And let him know Mrs. Alexander is quarantined, so they won't be able to visit again until further notice. Understand?"

"Yes, Doctor."

Bridget removes a prescription pad from her pocket and scribbles a note. "Start her on I.V. fluids, and let's get her something for her diarrhea and nausea. Okay?"

"Of course, Doctor. Right away."

Bridget steps down to Room 502 and peeks in. Craig's chest rises and falls as he sleeps. She steps over to the bed and listens to his heart then takes his pulse. *He's doing just fine.* She makes a notation on the chart at the end of his bed and tiptoes out.

She heads down to Room 529 and knocks then walks in. "Good afternoon, Herr Hetzel. How are you feeling?"

Gunter winces as he pulls himself to a seated position. His pale face and bloodshot eyes add to his weary demeanor. "I want to go home. I don't care about this damn surgery anymore. This Krankenhaus is killing me. Es ist voller Juden." *This hospital is killing me. It's full of Jews.*

"Nein. I've told you before, this is a Catholic hospital." She cleans and shakes the thermometer beside his bed then sticks it under his tongue. "Your doctor in West Germany sent you halfway around the world to me because he knows I'm qualified to help you." She removes the thermometer. *One-oh-one point seven. Bollocks.* "Herr Hetzel, how's your appetite?" Bridget stares into his jade irises where flecks of russet seem to dance as they hypnotize her.

He rubs his eyes, breaking the trance. "My stomach hurts too much to even think of food." He presses his fingertips between his ribs and recoils.

"Well, I really hate to have to tell you this, but you have a fever. Which means that we can't possibly do your surgery tomorrow."

"What? But you promised I'd be well and able to get out of here before February third."

She writes on the patient's chart. "I don't believe I actually gave you a date. Does something special happen on February third?"

He cringes and repositions himself in the bed. "Yeah. That's my birthday. But it's also the anniversary of the date mein Mutter – *my mother* – killed herself. I *must* be with mein Vater. He doesn't do well on that day. You know... die Niedergeschlagenheit." *Heaviness of spirit.*

"I understand. It's very difficult to lose a loved one, and sometimes, it seems as though we never get over the pain. I'm truly very sorry. But that's why I know your father will want you to get yourself healthy so you can get home and be with him for many years to come. And with your fever, we just can't operate yet because that could put you at greater risk of infection."

"So, what do we have to do?"

"First, I need to make sure you don't have the influenza that's going around. I'm going to get you started on an I.V., then I'm going to call Dr. Slater to see what kind of meds we can give you to reduce your fever. I'm worried the Paracetamol might affect your ulcers and make matters worse."

"And then what?"

"If your fever turns out to be nothing, we'll move forward with your surgery on Friday. If there's something more to it, we'll have to wait and see what's going on. Okay?"

"Habe ich eine Wahl?" *Do I have a choice?*

"No."

"Well, I guess then my fate is in your hands. You just make sure and keep that maid away from me. I don't need her kind smelling up my room with her stench."

Bridget clenches her hands info fists. *You bloody wanker. I'd really like to punch you in your ulcer-infested gut right now. Or give you a lobotomy.* She scribbles a note in his chart and opens the door. Without turning back, she says, "I'll call down to Dr. Slater right away. Goodnight, Herr Hetzel."

She gnashes her teeth as she pulls the door closed, then she heads to the nurses' station. She signs off on Mr. Bivens's release then says, "Kelly, please start an I.V. on Mr. Hetzel, and treat him as if he's quarantined. I'm going to call Dr. Slater and see what he recommends for the patient's fever. I really hope he doesn't have the flu."

Kelly grimaces. "Oh, do you think he does?"

"I'm not sure. But if you don't mind, I have somewhere I need to go after I talk to Dr. Slater. Could you please call downstairs and cancel Mr. Hetzel's reservation for Theater Three tomorrow? See if you can tentatively reserve it for Friday morning. I'll know for sure after we get his fever under control."

"Yes, Doctor. Right away."

"Thanks. Have a good evening." Bridget heads down to the third floor to Dr. Slater's office. She knocks and waits a moment before walking in. "Afternoon, Steve."

"Bridget, what a nice surprise. How's our German patient doing? Ready for his surgery tomorrow?"

"Actually, that's why I'm here. He spiked a fever. No appetite. His stomach hurts, but no vomiting or diarrhea so..."

"So, it's probably his ulcers causing pain."

"Right. But I have another patient who's positive for H3N2, so I'm hoping that doesn't makes its way to Herr Het—I mean Mr. Hetzel. He can't afford to postpone things much longer."

"Have you given him anything yet?"

"Just I.V. fluids, so far."

He stands. "Okay, well, I'll go take a look at him and see what's going on. For future reference, you can give him up to a thousand milligrams of acetaminophen, and it won't hurt his ulcers. But I appreciate your checking with me first. I may need to give him another G.I. cocktail. And I'll see that he gets a shake for dinner. He should be able to digest that without incident." He checks his watch. "It's almost four. Are you going to be here much longer? I can come see you once I examine him."

She sucks air through her teeth. "Ew, I'm sorry. I actually have an appointment I have to get to. Maybe I can meet you early in the morning?"

He peeks at his appointment book and turns the page. "Sure, I'm free in the morning. I have a surgery at eleven, but before that, I'm available. You come on down when you get in, and we'll see what we can do to get Mr. Hetzel back on track."

"Thanks. I appreciate your help." She tucks a loose strand of hair behind her ear and rests her hand on the doorknob. "All right, I'll see you tomorrow."

He chuckles. "Yeah, and if we can get that Shylock maid to leave him alone, maybe we can get his ulcers under control before I have to operate."

Her heart skips a beat, and patches of crimson creep to her face. "Pardon me?"

"Certainly, he's told you about the Heeb who's been coming in his room, upsetting him."

"What?"

"Sorry. Normally, I try to keep my opinions to myself, but it turns out my uncle was in the same regiment as Hetzel's grandfather. My uncle was recruited into Hitler's Army when he was just a seventeen-year-old kid. He started out patrolling the streets but eventually got promoted and was in charge of keeping inventory records at Buchenwald. From the letters he wrote my mother, the damn Kikes in that camp were so unruly, he feared he'd lose his job or be jailed if he didn't figure out how to keep 'em in line. He only did what other guards were doing, and after the war, he moved to America and took a job driving a cement truck in Hartford. He had a wife and three kids and was doing well when he applied for a bank loan. Then probably some Jew banker tipped off the government or something, and he was extradited back to Germany in '62. He was tried and convicted for war crimes against humanity, and he's still there serving out a twenty-year sentence."

Her stomach churns, and a wave of nausea causes her to feel faint. "Oh. I had no idea." *I had no idea what a racist wanker you are!*

"Yeah, well, that's why I get so livid when those damn Jews start talking about how they were starved and all that drivel. My uncle told me none of that happened, and he knew firsthand. I mean, come on. A Holocaust? Mass genocide? No. The only people they even put in those camps were the ones who refused to be deported and started all the rioting to try to ruin the Aryan businesses and properties. I mean, I can see why that Heeb maid ticks him off so much. It's just a cruel reminder of all his family's had to endure."

"I, uh… I'm sorry, Steve, I'm not feeling very well right now. If you'll excuse me."

"Oh, yeah? You do look kind of green. I sure hope you don't have that flu. As a matter of fact, I feel a little headache coming on too." He rubs his temple then shakes his head. "All right, you take care, and we'll talk tomorrow. I'll go up and see Hetzel now."

"Thanks." She steps into the corridor. Her hands tremble as she pulls the door closed, then she hurries to the elevator. As she reaches the seventh floor, she stops at the executive restroom and vomits. *Bollocks. I can't fathom how some people are so ignorant that that they still believe the Holocaust never happened.*

# # #

23 December 1945

Dear Diary,

I'm so angry tonight, if I didn't know better, I'd swear at one point my blood was literally boiling! Mum and Dad wanted me to attend the young people's Christmas party after church services today. I didn't really want to, but I wouldn't disappoint them for anything, so I stayed.

After we had cake and cookies and punch, our Sunday School teacher, Miss Welch, gathered us in a circle and asked us to tell what we were most thankful for. Of course, I have no idea what Christmas traditions generally involve, so I just stood back and let other people take the lead. Other people were saying things like they were thankful for their boyfriend or girlfriend or for the gifts accumulating under their trees or that the Blitz hadn't killed their loved ones. (Can you believe that only one person who spoke before me said that they were thankful that the war was over?)

When it got around to my turn, I, of course, didn't want to say what I was really thankful for... That Mum and Dad adopted me and even moved to a different town and changed churches so none of their old friends and neighbors would know I wasn't really their daughter. That they love me like my own mother apparently never did. That my diary was right where I'd left it and I was able to get it back once I was liberated from Bergen-Belsen. That my hair is finally starting to grow back and look semi-normal, and that Dad took me to hospital to get my hideous tattoo removed. No, I couldn't say any of that, so I simply said I was thankful that all the concentration camps had finally been liberated.

What happened next was something I never thought I'd ever hear in my lifetime... A boy named George Welford laughed and said there was no such thing as concentration camps! He said they were just made-up fantasies of an overactive imagination used as propaganda to defeat the German army. He said his father has a cousin in America who worked for Henry Ford, the automaker, and that Mr. Ford was who convinced him that the Germans wanted nothing more than to gain control of Europe. He said they never persecuted the Jews, the gypsies, the homosexuals, the Jehovah's Witnesses, or the people with mental illnesses or with physical deformities (like my poor, dear Otto). He said that he's seen proof (whatever that may be) that there were no such things as gas chambers, and that no one was ever starved to death. Honestly, I think he'd still be there spouting off all this rubbish if Miss Welch wouldn't have shut him down. But I heard at least two more boys ask George to tell them more about his theories after the teacher was out of earshot.

As soon as Miss Welch became preoccupied with refilling the punch bowl, I sneaked outside and vomited in the snow! I then hid in an alcove until Mum and Dad came to pick me up. Can you believe there are actually such idiots in the world who live in such denial? As the playwright John Heywood once said, "There are none so blind as those who refuse to see."

# # #

CHAPTER TWENTY-SIX

Bridget drums her fingertips on the steering wheel as she heads toward Faneuil Hall. The Lovin' Spoonful's "Summer in the City," Johnny Rivers's "Secret Agent Man," and The Doors' "Light My Fire" warm her and help take her mind off her white-hot rage ignited by Dr. Slater.

As she searches for a parking space, her pulse quickens. *I hope you can forgive me, Mama. Actually, Papa, I hope you can forgive me for harboring so much hatred toward Mama all these years. I know that no matter her reasons for doing what she did, you'd want me to find a way to forgive her.*

She parallel parks and grabs her purse then shoves her hands in her coat pockets as she walks with a determined gait toward Kugelman's Delicatessen. As she reaches the door, her heart sinks to her stomach. *They're closed.* The *"Coming Soon"* sign in the window pops against the dim background of the darkened store. She sniffs the air but smells only the faint garlicky aroma wafting over from Romano's Pizzeria. She shades her eyes and peeks through the window, hoping to spot an emergency telephone number, but nothing jumps out at her. *Bollocks.*

As she heads back toward her car, an idea sparks, and she hastens her pace. "Maybe I can get Jack to call H.R. and get Mama's home address."

"You talking to me, lady?" An unshaven, unkempt, middle-aged gentleman scratches his protruding ribs and coughs into his shoulder as he leans against a lamppost.

Bridget eyes his thin jacket and threadbare jeans, hardly enough to keep the cold out of his bones. She stops walking and grips her purse to her side. "Sir, it's too cold for you to be out here tonight. Do you have a place to sleep?"

He blushes and hangs his head. "I was staying over at the V.A., but they're full."

"Then you're a veteran?"

"Yes, ma'am. U.S. Air Force. I was in the Flying Tigers during W.W. Two and then flew in injured during Korea. I retired as a Major after I took some shrapnel in my shoulder."

"Do you work?"

"Back in '54, I took a job down in New York as a navigator for PanAm and did pretty good there until this year. But in April, my only son was killed in 'Nam. Then in June, my wife got sick and passed away. Then in September, I was hospitalized with the flu, and I missed too much work, so they let me go. I came up here to see if I could find work at the Logan Airport, but nothing was open."

"Wow, I'm so sorry. Do you mind if I ask, what was wrong with your wife?"

His voice quivers. "Breast cancer. It apparently went undiagnosed for a long time. Once we found out about it, all we could do was make her comfortable. I took off work to spend all the time I could with her. She went about four weeks later. I was devastated. I tried to keep up with all the bills, but she accumulated so much expense in such a short time, and then with her funeral and our son's…" He shakes his head and sighs. "Anyway, I lost the house, trying to keep up with all the financial obligations. I just couldn't do it."

"I'm so sorry. I know how hard it is losing someone you love. But, say, I have a friend who's in charge of the aircraft marshallers out at Logan. Would you like me to make a call for you and see if he can use you?"

"Are you serious?"

"Of course."

"But you don't even know me."

"Listen, I've been helped by more strangers than I can even count. What's your name?"

"Pete. Pete Keene."

She takes a notepad and pen from her purse and writes his name. "Okay, Major Keene, I'll give my friend a call and tell him to expect to hear from you next week after Christmas. So, until then, let's see what we can do to get you in from the cold."

Tears leak out of the corners of his eyes. "Are you kidding me?"

"Why would I make a joke about something as serious as your health and wellbeing? You look trustworthy. You're just down on your luck, but I believe we can remedy that. Come with me." She takes his arm and steadies him as she leads him to Romano's.

As they enter the restaurant, Mrs. Romano pushes her eyeglasses up the bridge of her nose, saying, "Buonasera, Dr. Castle. How are you doing this evening? You didn't call for a reservation."

"No, not tonight, Mrs. Romano. I'm actually in a hurry to get home, but I wanted to ask you a favor."

"For you, anything. What can I do for you?"

"My friend here, retired Air Force Major Pete Keene, has a job interview next week at Logan. But until then, he could use some food and a job and a place to sleep. Temo che non sopravviverà alla notte fuori con questo tempo. *I'm afraid he won't survive the night outside in this weather.* I know you often hire extra kitchen help and let them stay in your garage apartment, and I was hoping..."

"Ah! Of course. For any friend of yours, only the best. You like lasagna, Major?"

His eyes dart between Bridget's and Mrs. Romano's. "Well, yes, of course I do."

"Good. You go sit at table seven, and I'll get you some lasagna, a big salad, and some of my special cannoli for dessert. Oh, and I believe we have a warmer coat that'll fit you in our lost and found."

Pete's eyes glisten with tears. "Oh, I... thank you. Thank you both so much. I don't know what to say."

Bridget shakes his hand and slips two twenty-dollar bills and her business card into his palm. "Don't say anything. Knowing you're warm and fed is all the thanks we need. My number's on that card. You call me if you need anything else. And my friend at Logan will call you here at the restaurant. Okay?" She looks to Mrs. Romano.

Mrs. Romano's eyes twinkle as she says, "Of course that'll be okay. He's going to start work here tomorrow, but tonight, Major, you fill your belly and warm your bones. You understand?" She grabs the man's shoulders and nudges him toward table seven. "Don't you worry, Doctor. We'll take good care of your friend."

The man peeks over his shoulder. "Thank you so much. Both of you. You're truly an answer to my prayers."

Bridget wiggles her fingers as she waves. "Take care, Major." As soon as he sits, she nods her appreciation to Mrs. Romano then treks outside and hurries to her car.

As she heads home, she sings along to the radio. When "Hey Jude" comes on, she changes the station. Every other preset station has commercials, so she turns the dial until she reaches a Big Band station and pauses on Glenn Miller crooning "In the Mood." *Aww, Papa loved that song.* When Kay Kyser and His Band start singing "Three Little Fishies," tears cascade down her cheeks. *Mama used to love the melody to that one, but she couldn't understand the lyrics. I remember how Papa tried to use the tune to inspire her to learn English, but she just couldn't catch on. Or wouldn't.* As the fishie trio spots the shark and starts to hightail it back to the safety of their meadow pool, the high-pitched wail of sirens drowns out the remainder of the song. Within seconds, blue and red flashing lights speed toward her, and she pulls over to the side of the road and watches as they pass in the opposite direction.

Crikey. One, two, three... seven squad cars! Three ambulances. Two fire trucks. I wonder what happened. This certainly can't have a happy ending. She turns the radio knob, seeking a news report, but she can't find anything involving local traffic.

After the emergency vehicles pass, she merges back onto the road and turns the radio off for the remainder of her drive. "I really need to find Mama and talk to her. What if she sensed how angry I was and she's avoiding me? What if she knows how much I've resented her and she's already talked her husband into scrapping the deli idea and moving back to New York? Or Chicago or Minnesota? She could always tell what I was thinking, even without my saying it. I'll never forget that time she knew how livid I was at her during Rosh Hashanah when I had so much trouble finding the words to confess my ire..."

# # #

12 September 1942

Cher Journal (Dear Diary),

Yesterday evening was the beginning of Rosh Hashanah. Obviously, there was no way we could attend synagogue (we haven't in many years), but the High Holy Days are so important to my mother, that my father and I do all we can to accommodate her keeping up the customs. Of course, this is the holiday when we ask forgiveness from those we may have wronged.

Just as I have for the past two years at this time, I waited for Mama to ask for my forgiveness. You see, ever since Otto left, I've been furious with her for insisting that he be sent to the government facility where he died. He used to get so excited when the High Holy Days came around, and this time of year always reminds me so much of him that I feel as though my heart may burst from the sheer volume of pain it holds. He always looked forward to the feast Mama would prepare, particularly the apples and honey and Mama's delicious braided challah bread. And I'll never forget just how sweet his little giggle sounded each time the shofar (ram's horn) was blown.

So, last night, by the time we were ready for bed, I was especially upset with Mama for, once again, not having asked for my forgiveness for her role in Otto's death. I put on my nightgown and slipped into my bed. This was one of those times when I particularly resented not having my own room because I wanted to pull the covers over my head and scream like the dickens! But since we all share a bedroom, of course that couldn't happen.

I was lying there alone in the dark when Mama came in, sat beside me, and started smoothing my hair like she did when I was little. It felt so good, but I was so incredibly outraged, I didn't want her touching me. I flinched and pulled away, and she asked, "Why are you so angry with me, my schönes Mädchen – beautiful girl? You're still blaming me for losing our sweet Otto? And perhaps you're wondering how you can possibly ask me to forgive all your anger?"

I was appalled! I suppose the shock of her suggestion may have shown on my face, but I was determined to maintain my resolve. "No," I said with no further explanation.

She gave me a sweet smile and said, "Oh, dear Tochter, don't tell me it's the other way around. That, in fact, you've possibly been waiting for me to ask your forgiveness because you blame me for your brother's death."

My jaw dropped open. "How did—"

"How did I know?" she asked. I nodded my head, unable to form words. She hugged me to her breast and said, "Oh, dear one, did you not think I've known these past years that you hold me responsible for losing your best friend? Of course, I knew. But you have to realize that before I can ask for your forgiveness, I have to be able to forgive myself. You see, I've missed my firstborn every second of every day since we sent him away with that government man. And from the very moment I learned of his death, I've wished nothing more than to cut out my own heart and offer it in exchange for the return of that dear boy. And now, with the High Holy Days upon us once again, my soul yearns for him more than you can even fathom. Maybe you never considered this, but from the day Otto was born, I always wondered if perhaps I had done something to cause his legs to be so crooked. I wondered if there was one particular moment that I did something wrong, and I wished more than anything I could go back in time and erase my mistake. But, sweetheart, if you want me to plead for your forgiveness, if you need me to atone for my role in Otto's death, then I beg you, please release me. Not

because I deserve it. I don't. But because you don't deserve to hold on to so much rage. My darling, I love you every bit as much as I loved – as I will always love – your brother. I would've never done anything to either of you if I thought for even a moment it could cause you even minor pain. Won't you please forgive me?"

Tears streamed down my face, and I bawled like a baby as she held me. I sobbed so hard, I couldn't even speak to tell her I did forgive her. And I didn't even get to ask her how she knew the secrets I kept locked so deep in my heart of hearts. But at that moment, in my mama's arms, nothing else was of any importance. I loved her, and she loved me, and that's all there was in the world that mattered.

# # #

CHAPTER TWENTY-SEVEN

Bridget checks her watch in the moonlight, hoping someone will still be in the H.R. Department by the time she can get home and have Jack call to get her mama's address. *I don't want to put this off another day. I want to give Mama the opportunity to explain her actions and let her know I've forgiven her, and I want to honor the kind of upstanding man Papa was by letting go of my animosity.*

As she pulls into the driveway, her forehead wrinkles as she eyes Jack's Continental and Geoffrey's Armstrong Siddeley pulled all the way up and a third vehicle, a Spanish red Chrysler Newport, parked behind the Continental. *Whose car is that?*

She fishes a Wint-O-Green Lifesaver from the glove box and pops it in her mouth. After re-hiding the candy, she grabs her purse and lab coat then pulls her hat down over her ears as she steps out into the blistering cold. Nearing the house, a familiar fragrance tickles her nostrils. *What's going on?* She accelerates her pace. As she opens the front door, the roar of laughter assaults her ears, and the pungent aroma of sour dill pickles, sour kraut, and pastrami, coupled with the sweet smell of fresh challah bread and cinnamon chocolate babka transport her back in time. *That's Mama's baking! I'd know it anywhere.*

She hangs up her purse and coat then removes her hat and mittens, when an unfamiliar masculine voice says, "And this must be Renate!" She turns to find a chubby stranger with a warm smile opening his arms to her. "Renate, I'm Maurice Kugelman. I'm so pleased to meet you. Your mama told me what a beautiful girl you are, and she didn't exaggerate." He throws his arms around her, and she succumbs to his embrace as she peeks over his shoulder at the framed photo of herself graduating from medical school, standing between Ada and Geoffrey.

Heat rushes to her face, and she pulls out of his hug. "Uh, it's nice to meet you, Mr. Kugelman. Um, I go by Bridget these days, if you don't mind."

"Of course, Bridget. And, please, call me Maurice."

Helen steps out from the kitchen, her eyes sparkling. "There she is! Mein beautiful Tochter! Come, give your mama a hug." Tears fall from her chin as she squeezes Bridget to her bosom.

Bridget quivers as she allows her years of bitter hate to melt away. She closes her eyes and holds her breath as if to preserve the moment in time. The embrace lasts much longer than the last time they saw each other before so many events pulled them a world apart. A lump forms in her throat and threatens to suffocate her. "I do love you," she says in a low whisper.

Moments later, Jack peers around the corner, saying, "Come on, you two. The kugel is burning."

Helen rolls her eyes and throws her hands in the air. "Ack! I've been making kugel for nearly fifty years and haven't burned one yet, dear son." She rushes back to the kitchen with Bridget close behind.

Bridget says, "I didn't get to see that head injury you got from Herr Hetzel. I heard you got quite the bruise."

"Ack, it's nothing." Helen dismisses the notion with a wave of her hand then pulls a dish from the oven.

Jack pecks Bridget on the cheek and hugs her. He leans into her ear and says, "I hope you're not upset, hon, but I thought the sooner we got the whole family together, the better."

Her eyes dart to Ada and Geoffrey then over to Helen. Bridget's face blanches, and she steadies herself on the back of a chair.

Geoffrey stands and pulls out a seat for her. "You feel okay, Lovey? You look peaked."

Ada squeezes Bridget's hand. She winks and says, "She's fine. She's just a bit overwhelmed to have so many people who love her in the same room. Is that it, Lovey?"

Tears stream down Bridget's face like twin rivulets, and she nods. Ada scoots closer and hugs her, saying, "There, there, dear girl. This is a day to rejoice and be happy." She lowers her voice and adds, "Dad told me you were worried you'd hurt me feelings if you accepted your mama back in your life. Darling, I know how much you love me, and me love for you will never fade. You get up there, now, and see your mama. She's missed you all these years."

Bridget nods and squeezes Ada's shoulder as she stands. "Is there anything I can do to help you, uh, Mm—Mama?"

Helen turns from the counter and fans steam from the kugel. "No, sweetheart. All that's left is for Maurice to add the Russian dressing to the Reubens, and I believe we're ready to eat." She carries a bowl of her homemade sour dill pickles to the table. "Ada, I can't thank you and Geoffrey enough for finding Rena— *Bridget* and for taking such good care of her all these years. I know that would've made Jens so happy. He always spoke so highly of you. I know at one point, we discussed sending her to live with you. I believe he even sent you a letter about it, but I don't know if we had the right address. He was so afraid you two would lose touch after the Blitz."

Geoffrey winks at Bridget and says, "Actually, I just dug up that letter yesterday and showed it to our girl. It's kind of an amazing coincidence how I ran into her at Bergen-Belsen."

Helen sits and starts dishing up the kugel. "Bergen-Belsen? I thought Dr. Mengele sent you to Neuengamme after you left Auschwitz."

Bridget's heart skips a beat, and she scoots her chair over to make room for Maurice to squeeze by. "How in the world did you ever know I was at Auschwitz? Or that Mengele sent me to Neuengamme?"

Helen looks to Maurice then casts her eyes down. She takes a deep breath and rolls up her left sleeve, revealing a tattoo of the number 849259. "The day I left you at the farm, the thirtieth of April, 1944, I had no choice. Someone had spied on our host where we stayed after we left Dr. Van Den Boom's house, and they threatened to turn them in. I wanted to keep you and your brother out of harm's way, so I begged our host to let me take you both to safety; then I agreed to turn myself in so our host family wouldn't get in trouble for harboring us."

The air leaves Bridget's lungs, and her face loses its color. "What? No! Where's Josef now?"

Helen hangs her head. "I'm afraid, dear girl, he didn't make it. After I left you, I took him to a couple that your father trusted. They owned the print shop. The wife was Jewish, but the husband wasn't. I was sure Josef would be safe there. Your father and I talked extensively about what we must do if we were ever put in this situation, and we agreed the best plan was to split up and hide separately. Anyway, late that night, I was taken into custody and transported to Auschwitz-Birkenau. By the time you got there on September ninth, I was bald, tattooed, so skinny I looked like a skeleton, and I was covered in lice. I worked at the front in Kanada, sorting and cataloging valuables. I saw you as you came in, and you looked small and so so scared; yet you still raised your voice and translated for the others who didn't understand what was happening. I wanted more than anything to run over and hug you, but I was too ashamed for you to see me like that. I knew how angry you were at me for leaving you the way I did, and I didn't want to cause a scene and have us both be shot on the spot. The couple I left your brother with were arrested about a month after I was. The wife ended up at Auschwitz, and she told me she left Josef hidden in a basket in an alcove under the stairs. She said he was bundled in that blue blanket I'd knitted for Otto with Otto's initials." She covers her mouth and squeezes her eyes closed. "I guess it's only fitting that it became Otto's brother's shroud. As her family was being dragged up the road, she said she looked back and saw the Gestapo torching her house. Our little Josef was killed in the fire."

Tears well in Bridget's eyes. She mouths a silent, "No."

Jack places his hand on Helen's back and slides a glass of wine in front of her.

Helen's chin quivers, and she shakes her head. "Thank you, son. Anyway, that woman was sent to work in the kitchen. Because we were friends, she tried to sneak extra food to me whenever she could. But once you arrived, I asked her to give all the extra she could to you."

Bridget's jaw hangs open. "That was you?"

Helen stabs a pickle with her fork and sets it on her plate. "You were my baby. What else was I going to do? When Dr. Mengele requested you to translate for him, I asked a friend of your papa's who also worked in Mengele's office to keep an eye on you. He told me that at one point, Dr. Mengele got angry with you because he didn't believe you were translating his exact words to the children, so he decided to use you as a test subject, and he gave you an injection."

Bridget absentmindedly rubs her upper left arm and nods. "That's right. I had fiery, scarlet rings on my shoulder for weeks."

"I know. I came in to feed you when you had the fever in the observation clinic. I just had to take a look at you up close. I kissed your forehead when I slipped the extra bread into your hand. Your fever was so high, I wasn't even sure if you were aware that anyone was there, but I was pretty certain you wouldn't know it was me."

"No, I didn't."

Helen rolls her sleeve higher, revealing a large, raised scar on her bicep. "Well, I learned that the doctor had plans to keep injecting you until you died. So, I asked Jens's friend if he could get Dr. Mengele to allow me to trade places with you. Since I was responsible for both your brothers being killed, I certainly couldn't see you perish too." She hangs her head, and her voice catches in her throat. "I told him he could do whatever he wanted to me and I wouldn't complain as long as he left you alone. That's when he agreed to send you to Neuengamme. I guess he figured that with your multi-lingual skills, you'd be too valuable to kill." She rolls her sleeve down.

Bridget sniffles and wipes her eyes with a napkin. "Mama, I never knew. I wish you wouldn't have—" Her chest heaves, and she begins sobbing.

Tears form in Ada's eyes, and she rubs Bridget's arm. "Aww, there, there, child. Your mama loved you so much, she'd have walked across hot coals to save you. That's what a mother does for her babies."

Bridget, seated between both women, looks to Ada then to Helen. "I just wish I would have known you were there. I'm so sorry for... for everything!" She kisses Ada's cheek then falls into Helen's arms.

Helen rubs Bridget's back. "Aww, my sweet Tochter. I didn't want to upset you with all this talk. I just wondered how you ended up in Bergen-Belsen."

Bridget sniffles and wipes her nose. She stabs her fork into the pickle bowl and takes two large pickles. "I was at Neuengamme until shortly after the first of January, then they transferred me to the Bergen-Belsen Camp. And of course, you know that's where we were liberated by the British Army in April. So, you were at Auschwitz, which means you got released in January, right?"

"Well, Auschwitz was liberated in January, but a month earlier, I was transferred to Ravensbrück. The Soviets freed us on April thirtieth. I was put in the makeshift hospital for a while, and I didn't get out until November. I went back to the Netherlands to look for you, but of course, you weren't there. But I was able to rescue a few of our things that Dr. Van Den Boom was kind enough to save for us."

Bridget's eyes light up. "Really? Like what?"

"Mostly photos. I got a few things that belonged to your father. Oh, and I got our Hanukkah menorah that belonged to Grandma Breitman."

"You did?" Bridget nibbles a pickle, and her eyes roll back in her head. "Mmm, these are every bit as fantastic as I remember them. You always made the best pickles."

"Thanks. Yes, I actually brought the menorah for you tonight and set it up in there next to your beautiful Christmas tree. I also have something else I think you might be missing."

Bridget grabs Helen's wrist. "Now that you're here, I'm not missing anything anymore."

Helen kisses the back of Bridget's hand then reaches between her own breasts and pulls out a long silver chain hanging around her neck. "Did you hide this in a train?" At the end of the chain dangles the silver ring given to Bridget by her father.

Bridget's head swims, and the room spins. "How— how did you ever find that? I thought it was gone forever."

"I was stuck in a crowded boxcar on my way to Ravensbrück. That's about three hundred and fifty miles, and by train, it was a four-day ride. More than half of us died before the second day ended, and there were so many of us packed in there, the dead couldn't even fall down. I was crammed against a wall, and the smell was making me feel as though I was going to be sick, even though there was nothing in my stomach to regurgitate. So, I managed to turn in my spot and pressed my face against the slats of the car. I ran my hand up and down over the slats just to keep myself occupied and take my mind off all the moaning and crying. That's when I felt something in between the wood. It was dark, of course, so I couldn't see, but I kept picking at the thing until this little ring popped out. I assumed it was someone's wedding band. I stuck it on my pinky finger, and when the train stopped, I swallowed it so that I could retrieve it later and see it. I know that sounds silly or maybe even foolish, but by then, I'd been deprived of so much, I just wanted something to call my own. A few days later when I passed the ring, I cleaned it, and that's when I realized what it was. No one but your papa would commission such a ring as a pair of hands holding a human heart. But when I read the words *Love, Papa* inside, I nearly fainted. I was soon able to get a needle and some thread, and I managed to sew it into the hem of my uniform where it stayed hidden until we were liberated. After that, I wore it on a chain next to my heart because that was my sign that I would find you someday and give it to you in person." She pulls the chain over her head and slips it into Bridget's eager hands.

Bridget examines the ring in her shaky palm until tears cloud her eyes so much, she sees nothing but shadowy prisms. "Thank you. I can't tell you how much this means to me."

Helen stands and hugs Bridget to her bosom. "Aww, my sweet child, I know how much you loved your papa. There's no need to thank me." She takes the necklace from her daughter and slips it over Bridget's head. "Now, you wear it next to your heart so you can feel close to your papa once more. And, everybody, let's eat! I didn't make all this food for it to go to waste. And once we're done, we have cinnamon chocolate babka for dessert." She sits and slices her Reuben in half.

Jack pulls a piece off the braided challah bread on his plate and says, "Helen, everything smells delicious! I don't know you very well, but I love you already."

Ada giggles. "I guess this *is* more exciting than me chicken and dumplings."

Jack's cheeks turn red. "What? No, I didn't mean that—"

Ada pats his hand and says, "I'm just joking, love. It's okay. Really. Helen, you'll have to share some of your recipes with me. This does smell scrumptious."

Helen reaches across the table and squeezes Ada's hand. "You, my friend, are as valuable as a diamond. I'm so happy Bridget had the good fortune to finish being raised by such good people. I know you and I only met once those many years ago, but if you'll remember, I told you then how much I liked you. Or rather, I had my Jens tell you because I didn't know the English back then."

Both women chuckle, then Ada says, "And thank you for blessing this earth with such a lovely girl. I don't know what I would've done if she wouldn't have come into me life when she did."

Maurice reaches between the women for a pickle, saying, "Honey, eat now, visit later. Isn't that what you always tell me?"

Helen smacks his arm. "That's because you don't usually be quiet long enough for anyone else to get a word in."

He bites his pickle and winks at her. "I'm just kidding. I know you've been waiting for this day for such a long time. You've got years of catching up to do. You can't possibly do it all in one sitting."

Geoffrey sips his wine and says, "No, but that shouldn't stop them from trying. Helen, this is the best kugel I've ever tasted."

"Thank you. Jens always said you were full of compliments."

"Well, he deserved all the praise I gave him and more. He was a fine surgeon and an outstanding friend. I've really missed him."

"Me too." She looks to Maurice and winks at him. "Sorry, hon. I have been twice blessed."

He returns the wink and raises his glass. "To Jens and to all our other loved ones who have gone on before us."

Geoffrey is the next to raise his glass. "Cheers!"

Everyone else follows. "Cheers!"

Bridget's heart smiles as she sips her wine. *To Papa. And Otto and Josef.*

The group makes small talk for the remainder of the meal. After everyone has cleaned their plates, Jack pats his belly and says, "Um, not to accuse anyone of anything, but I believe I was promised some cinnamon chocolate babka."

Bridget raises her eyebrows, and her mouth forms a silent O. "I don't believe you just did that."

He shrugs his shoulders and smiles a crooked grin. "What can I say? I love dessert."

Bridget smacks his wrist. "You're a pig!"

He nods. "When it comes to dessert, this you know. And I'm not ashamed to say so. Can I help you, Helen?"

Helen stands and collects the plates. "No. You sit; I serve. Tonight, this is my kitchen. Okay?" She heads to the sink and returns with the babka and a stack of small plates.

As she slices the dense, marbled cake, Jack says, "Hon, why were you so late tonight? I actually expected you about an hour earlier than you got here."

Bridget wipes the corners of her mouth and rolls her eyes. "Oh, what a day I had. First of all, I've got a patient who's developed H3N2. She's seventy-two and only one day post-surgery, but she's got all the symptoms."

Jack's lungs deflate. "Oh, no. That would be Paul's grandmother."

"Nadine's."

"Whatever. And Paul's been down visiting her, which means I have to cut him off the schedule. Crap." He digs into his cake. "Wow, this is delicious, Helen. I haven't had this since I was nine years old."

Helen offers a proud smile. "I'm glad you like it, son."

Bridget takes a bite, and her taste buds trigger instant memories of how much her father loved the special treat. "It's as wonderful as ever, Mama."

Helen nods. "Thank you."

Jack says, "So, was the flu case the only thing that held you up?"

Bridget sighs. "I wish. No, Herr Hetzel spiked a fever, so I had to postpone his surgery. I guess that opens up my morning tomorrow."

Jack waves his hands as he finishes swallowing a huge mouthful of cake. "No. I forgot to tell you Steve called you here at home. He said Hetzel's fever was because he's reacting to the G.I. cocktail. Steve thinks Hetzel's allergic to the anticholinergic."

"Really? That's interesting."

Geoffrey sets his fork on his plate. "To be sure. In fact, I just read a journal article that said that anticholinergic reactions are actually more common that you would think. They say it's not a true allergy but more of an acute intolerance."

Jack raises an eyebrow. "Really? How fascinating. I'd like to read that when you're done with it."

"I'll be sure to bring it next time we come."

Maurice pauses as he raises his next bite to his mouth and says, "How about tomorrow?"

Geoffrey says, "Pardon me, mate?"

"How about we all get together again tomorrow? Helen and I can host at our house. We're having such a good reunion, but it's getting late. Yet I know my wife won't sleep a wink until she knows when she can see you all again."

Helen blushes, saying, "That's true." She looks to Bridget. "And even though I know I'll see you and Jack at work tomorrow, we all have our jobs to do, and I don't want to embarrass you, both important people, being related to a bed pan washer."

Bridget cringes. "I'm really sorry I said that—"

"No, you were right. When I used to wash linens at the hospital where your papa worked, we had to pretend as if we didn't know each other. I knew how much he loved me, and it pained him to have to ask me; but it was best for his career. Now, you and your husband have come too far to let me get in your way. So, at the hospital, I'm Helen Kugelman the cleaning lady, and we'll keep our distance."

"But—"

"No. Don't argue with your mama."

Bridget scrapes the last crumbs of babka from her plate. "I never could win an argument with you anyway."

"That's right. Now, if you all agree, then Maurice and I would love to host dinner at our house tomorrow. For *all* of you." She looks to Ada and Geoffrey and squeezes Ada's hand.

Ada's eyes dart between Geoffrey's and Helen's, and she says, "We'd love to."

"Good." Helen stands and collects the plates then takes them to the sink. "I'll be happy to clean these dishes; but, folks, it's nearly midnight, and before the clock strikes twelve... Well... I know it's usually done at sundown, but... I'd just love if we could light the fourth Hanukkah candle together as a family." She links her arm through Ada's. "And that means *all* of us as family. Okay?"

Ada kisses Helen's cheek and says, "I'd love to. And I'll help you with those dishes afterwards."

Bridget's heart melts at the sight of both of her mothers, walking arm in arm. *I wish this night would never end.*

# # #

14 December 1941

Liebes Tagebuch (Dear Diary),

It was the first night of Hanukkah tonight, and the Good Doctor Van Den Boom and his family joined us for dinner. The Good Doctor brought me an extra-large bag of dropjes which I adore. Then Ambroos tried to get me angry by teasing me that if I ate them all, I'd probably get fat! (Mama told me later that she thinks he has a crush on me which is why he always teases me so, but I certainly don't see it.) Anyway, I learned my lesson and refused to allow his words to cause me to react.

My parents gave me the most remarkable gift, and I was so surprised... It was a Bakelite radio! Of course, a few days ago, our radio stopped working just as we were learning about America getting into the war. Papa opened it up and said since it was more than ten years old, it was unlikely, what with the war going on, that we'd be able to get replacement parts without difficulty. So, I do realize that this gift "for me" is really a gift for the whole family, especially since we live in such tight quarters. But Papa said it was technically mine, nonetheless, and it was so exciting to get such a grown-up present.

I didn't think the day could end any better, but then Dr. and Mrs. Van Den Boom gave me a book called "Evil Under the Sun" by my favorite author, Agatha Christie. I've loved her ever since I was small and Papa would read her books out loud to us and translate them into German so that Mama and Otto could understand. I was so touched that they would give me such a perfect gift for a holiday that they don't even celebrate, and they will always be among my list of favorite people. I hope that after this war ends, we'll be able to stay in touch with them forever. I have to say that, so far in my lifetime, this has definitely been one of my best Hanukkahs.

# # #

CHAPTER TWENTY-EIGHT

The next morning, Bridget dreams she's surrounded by rolling waves as far as the eye can see. She clings to a wooden pole, and as her grip slips, she finds herself perched in the crow's nest of a ship. Her eyes search the deck for anyone to help her, but she's alone. When she fears she can't hold on any longer, it starts to rain, and Frankie Ford's "Sea Cruise" blares from somewhere below. Wooden splinters stab her hands, and she lets go then falls in slow motion.

As the deck comes closer, she hits the floor with a thud and wakes up. "Oww, bollocks. Why do I keep falling out of bed?"

She pulls herself up and rubs her hip as Jack's off-key voice, emanating from the shower, wails the "Sea Cruise" chorus. She giggles at how slowly he's singing the fast-paced song. She gathers her clothes and heads to the guest bathroom where she showers, dresses, and styles her hair.

She returns to her bathroom, now evacuated, and applies her makeup then heads downstairs. Jack kisses her and sets a cup of coffee on the table in front of her. "Good morning, sweetie. Are you excited about tonight?"

She smiles and touches her cheek, still sore from all the grinning she did the night before. "Yeah. If you'd have asked me a week ago what I'd do if my mother showed up, I'd have known exactly how I'd react, and it was very different than what really transpired. Thank you for sticking your big nose in my business and getting Mum and Dad on board to support me in all this. Their blessing means so much to me." She stirs cream and sugar in her coffee and takes a sip then pulls her silver ring necklace out of her collar and admires it. "This is some ring, huh?"

His eyes twinkle. "That's a sweet tangible memory of how much your papa loved you."

"You mean my mama."

He raises an eyebrow. "But your papa gave that to you."

"He gave me the original one. This is a duplicate. Mama must have had it made later."

"What makes you say that?"

"With this one, the heart is backwards. See here… The superior vena cava is on the heart's left, not the right. Plus, the back says *'Love, Papa'*."

"Wasn't it engraved before?"

"Yes, but it was in German. It said *'Liebe, Papa'*. When I first saw it, I was hopeful it was really was the original, but as Mama told her story, I knew it couldn't be true. After four days on the train with nothing to drink other than her own urine or the sweat off other people's backs, it would be nearly impossible to swallow anything solid, much less a ring."

Goosebumps cover Jack's arms, and he shudders. "Oh, wow. Then how do you suppose Helen knew where you hid it?"

"I was thinking about that last night. At first, I thought she might've just guessed because it wasn't confiscated from me when I arrived at Auschwitz, and she knows how much I always liked to find hiding places. But then I realized that she'd have no way of knowing whether or not I hid the ring somewhere on the farm where I'd been staying. I'm guessing she must've overhead me mention hiding it when I got off the train. I recall talking about it with some other girls on the day I arrived, mostly because I wanted to make sure I remembered where I'd left it. Or perhaps I talked in my sleep when I was in the observation clinic. That's the only explanation I can think of."

"Wow. She's some kind of woman. And so are you. I still can't believe you survived three extermination camps. You never cease to amaze me." He plants a kiss on her lips then removes some

English muffins from the toaster. He flips an egg and a slice of ham on each then offers her a plate. "Here, I made us breakfast sandwiches."

"Aww, thank you, my love. I'm surprised either of us can eat a bite after last night's feast."

He sits across from her and butters the inside of his muffin. "Tell me about it. I'm going to have to walk the halls all day to work those calories off." He pats his belly then takes a bite.

She stands and grabs the phone. "Oh, I almost forgot, I have to make a call. Can you please bring me my purse?"

He stands and heads to the foyer then returns as she dials a number. "Who're you calling?"

She holds up her index finger as he sits and works on his breakfast. "Yes, is this the aircraft marshallers' office?"

"Yes, ma'am. How can I help you?"

"I'd like to speak to Lloyd Milton, please."

"Of course. Please hold..."

"Lloyd Milton here."

"Good morning, Lloyd. It's Bridget Castle."

"Bridget, what a nice surprise. How are you and Jack doing?"

"Terrific. And you?"

"I'm great. I've started exercising, and I'm feeling so much better. You'd hardly believe I had a heart attack ten months ago."

A heartfelt smile encompasses her face. "Aww, that's really wonderful. Congratulations. Hey, I'm on my way out the door, but I just had to call you and see if you can help me with something."

"You name it. What's up?"

She pulls a scrap of paper out of her purse and reads the name. "I have a friend. He's a retired Air Force Major. His name's Pete Keene. He was in the Flying Tigers during World War Two, then he retired from the military and worked in New York for PanAm as a navigator. He lost his son in 'Nam earlier this year, then his wife died unexpectantly back in June. He was having a rough time of it, then he was hospitalized with the flu in September. Apparently, he missed too much work, so they let him go. And because of his family's medical and funeral bills, he ended up losing his home."

"I see. And you were thinking I might need another marshaller."

She bites her lip and twists the phone cord around her fingers. "Well, I was hoping."

"If he's a friend of yours, I'll make room for him. Maybe I can even let him bunk at my house while he gets back on his feet. You know, with the kids gone, it gets pretty lonely there these days."

"Aww, thanks, Lloyd. You're the best. He's working temporarily over at Romano's Pizzeria. I told him you'd call him there if you were interested."

"Romano's. Got it. You know, I might just go there for lunch and meet him in person. And don't worry; I won't spoil my diet with a thick, gooey pizza."

She chuckles. "Thank you so much. I can't tell you how much this means to me. You'll have to come over for dinner soon so we can catch up."

"Okay, you name the time, and I'll be there. Well, let me go so I can make these lunch plans. I'll let you know what happens. Merry Christmas, Bridget. And to Jack too."

"Thanks. Merry Christmas to you too. And congratulations on the diet."

"I appreciate it. Bye bye."

"Bye." She cradles the phone then returns her attention to her plate.

Jack pops the last bite in his mouth and says, "How's Lloyd?"

She peppers her egg. "Good. He's been exercising and says he feels remarkably better."

"Nice. So, who's this Pete?"

"Oh, I met him yesterday. Nice old guy. Well, you heard. Lloyd's going to give him a try out at Logan."

He shakes his head. "You're something else, you know that? I suppose you got him the job at Romano's too?"

"Of course. If Mrs. Romano couldn't take him, I guess I'd have brought him home, and we'd have ourselves a new gardener for a while. It's too cold for him to be out on the streets."

He bonks his forehead with the heel of his hand. "Oh! Speaking of streets, I hit a patch of black ice yesterday and scraped my hubcap on the curb. I called Smitty, and he's going to come pick it up today and get 'er fixed. I'm going to need a ride to work."

She finishes her sandwich. "Okay. I'd like to head out soon. Are you ready?"

"Soon as I write a note for Beverly to give Smitty the keys."

She takes their plates to the sink. "Just give me a minute." She runs upstairs and brushes her teeth then applies her lipstick. She pulls her coat on as Jack meets her at the door. "All set?"

He thrusts her hat and gloves at her. "Here, you'd better take these. It's really cold today."

She stuffs the gloves in another jacket pocket and pulls her mittens out of a vase. "Let's go."

He opens her car's passenger door for her then climbs into the driver's seat and starts the engine.

As they begin driving, she lets out a deep sigh. "I just wish my papa would've lived. I wish you could have met him. He'd have loved you."

He rests his hand on her knee. "I'm sure I'd have loved him too. I really like Maurice. He seems like a genuine guy. You can tell he really adores your mom."

"I guess so."

"What's wrong?"

"I just… All these years, I've had a different picture in my head. I thought Mama and my brother were safe in Hong Kong. I feel horrible that she suffered so much, and now it kind of makes me angry that she never let me know she was at Auschwitz while I was there."

"I was thinking about that last night too. I'm not saying I know what you or anybody went through, though I have studied it extensively. Especially after your dad told me how he met you. Now, this is just my opinion, but I kind of get the feeling Helen was dealing with so much mentally, turning herself in, losing her children, then learning your brother was killed, she was probably just barely holding it together. And if she would've had to answer your questions or maybe even consider that you might've witnessed her being abused, she probably couldn't have dealt with that on top of all she was already handling."

Bridget hangs her head and closes her eyes as moments pass in silence.

He rubs her arm. "I'm sorry, babe. I had no right to speculate. I shouldn't have—"

"No. I was just thinking that you're probably right. And I guess it just hit me that my baby brother's actually dead. He never even saw his first birthday." She sucks air over her quivering lip and pinches the bridge of her nose as tears leak out of the corners of her eyes. "Every year on January twenty-ninth, I always think of him and try to picture what he might be doing to celebrate his special day, what he might look like, what his interests are. When he was a baby, he looked exactly like Otto, so when Josef would've been growing up until he was ten, I always imagined he'd have looked just like our brother."

"Just ten?"

"Otto was ten when he was sent… when he went to the… the last time I saw him."

"Right. I'm sorry. You've described him as your friend for so long, I keep forgetting he was really your brother."

She huffs, and her nostrils flare. "Look, I already apologized about—"

"Whoa! Let me be clear, I wasn't condemning you. I understand why you weren't forthcoming about your painful past. I've never held that against you. All I meant was it's just taking me a while to catch up with all I've recently learned."

She casts her eyes to her lap. "Oh."

As they exit Malden, he tunes the radio to the news.

"...and in national news yesterday, President Lyndon Johnson was admitted to the Bethesda Naval Hospital as he joined the ranks of thousands of Americans who've fallen victim to the H3N2 flu pandemic. Coincidentally, Vice President Hubert Humphrey became bedridden while visiting Phoenix and was forced to cancel his planned speaking engagements after learning that he, too, contracted the Hong Kong flu. In another influenza-related incident, actress Joan Tabor died yesterday in Beverly Hills after accidentally overdosing on influenza medication. Her acting credits include the film 'The Teenage Millionaire' and numerous television appearances. She was thirty-six years old. In more uplifting news, the American communications satellite Intelsat III F-2, cited as the most sophisticated switchboard ever built, was launched last evening at 7:32 p.m. from Florida..."

He flips off the radio. "Dang, we missed the local news. When your dad got there last night, he said he'd heard something about a multi-car pileup. I wanted to see if there were any casualties."

She squeezes her eyes closed. "Actually, I think I saw the rescue vehicles for that on my way home. That's too bad."

"Yeah. I guess we'll know something when we get to work."

"Oh! Speaking of work, I really need to talk to you about firing someone." She flips the visor down and pulls out a roll of Spear-O-Mint Lifesavers then pops one in her mouth.

He shoots her a look. "What's up lately with you asking me to fire people? First your mother, now who?"

She narrows her eyes at him. "I've never interfered in your business before my mama started working at hospital, and I had a good reason for not wanting her there."

"Okay. And now?"

"And now I have another good reason for you getting rid of Steve Slater."

"What? He's the head of my G.I. Department. He's a Harvard graduate. He's got an impeccable record. He's double Board Certified in Internal Medicine *and* Colon and Rectal Surgery. He's the best there is. *Plus,* he's a good friend. Why would I want to cut him loose?"

"Because he's also an anti-Semite."

Jack's face turns green, and he looks as if he's been punched in the gut. "What?"

She shrugs her shoulders. "An anti-Semite. You know, he hates Jews."

"Yeah, I know what the word means. How did you ever come to think this?"

"He told me."

He swerves into oncoming traffic then corrects his mistake as he keeps his eyes on her. "Are you serious?"

"As a heart attack. He gave me a ten-minute spiel yesterday about how the Holocaust never happened. He's got an uncle who was a guard at Buchenwald who's still serving out a twenty-year sentence for war crimes against humanity, and he thinks his uncle got a raw deal. Not to mention all the racial slurs he kept saying about Mama and other Jews."

Jack swipes his hand over his face. "Crap. Well, you're right. We can't have him working there, behaving like that. The Catholic church certainly won't tolerate that kind of blatant hate and racism in one of their hospitals either. I'll have to see who I can get on board to replace him before he gets wind that I'm giving him the axe. I'm sorry, hon, but I'm going to have to ask that you put up with him until I can get this taken care of."

"But it'll be soon, right?"

He takes a deep breath then blows it out through pursed lips. "If he's as bad as you say, I'd like to walk him out today; however, it's just not feasible, considering the large patient load he currently has. But I'll definitely make it a priority to have Bonnie get me all the résumés we've received over the past few months and see if I can get any applicants in for an interview right away. Hopefully the holidays won't prolong things." He pats her thigh and winks at her. "Don't worry. I'm not taking this lightly."

She interlaces her fingers through his. "Thank you, my love."

He heaves a heavy sigh. "I guess I'd better call Dean Burnetti down in the Legal Department and give him a heads-up too."

She squeezes his hand. "I'm sorry to be the bearer of bad news."

He parks, and they head toward the building then stop to inspect a flyer posted on the entrance door. Jack reads the notice aloud:

> *Thursday, December 19, 1968: Last night, a multiple vehicle accident on the Massachusetts Turnpike resulted in numerous fatalities as well as more than twenty patients left in critical condition. Many required blood transfusions. Because of this, Saint Francis Hospital, as well as other Boston area hospitals, are experiencing a severe shortage in the uncommon AB negative blood and are low in various other blood types. In keeping with the Christmas spirit, please visit our Blood Bank located on the Second Floor and donate a pint of blood. Your selflessness just may mean the difference between life and death to someone in need. For donors with AB negative or the universal O negative blood, please alert Arthur Oleson in the Saint Francis Blood Bank, and you will be moved to the front of the line. Thank you.*

Jack's face blanches. "Oh, wow. This is not good." He pulls the door open and gestures for her to walk in first.

She nods at President Johnson and waves to Carol as they make their way to the elevator. She says, "It's worse than you think. I need AB neg on standby for Mr. Hetzel's surgery."

They step aboard the empty car, and he presses seven. "Well, you're AB negative. You're going to have to donate."

She winces. "I'd just hate to do that, not knowing what I may have been exposed to in my past, you know? I'd hate to pass whatever poison I came in contact with on to anyone else."

He hugs her and kisses her forehead. "I see. But I think the slight chance of a pint of blood possibly being tainted decades ago far outweighs the risk of someone dying if there isn't enough to go around today."

She steps backward and catches his hands in hers. "You're right. I'll make sure to get down there this morning."

"Good. And even though they might not need any O positive, I'll pay them a visit today too."

They exit the car at the seventh floor, then she stops at her office, and he continues down the corridor. She hangs up her coat and hat, changes into her lab coat, and calls down to the blood bank.

"Blood bank. Arthur speaking."

"Hi, Arthur, it's Dr. Bridget Castle."

"Morning, Dr. Castle. I'm sorry I couldn't keep your AB neg on reserve. We had a humdinger of a rush last night."

"Yeah, that's why I'm calling. I'd like to donate. I'm AB negative."

"Really? Right on! Whenever you get down here, I'll slide you to the front of the line. We've already got all the chairs full and a line backed down the hall."

"Are you getting much AB neg?"

"No, not one so far. And no O neg, either. I'm hoping things pick up soon. I just got the flyers posted about an hour ago, and three radio stations have agreed to announce our need."

"Well, I'm sure that'll bring you a lot more folks as the day progresses. All right, I'll see you soon."

"Yes, ma'am. See you shortly."

"Bye." She cradles the receiver and digs a Butter Rum Lifesaver out of a hiding place in her desk. She pops the candy in her mouth then heads down to the fourth floor. She stops at the nurses' station and says, "Good morning. How'd Susan Turner do on her dinner last night?"

The nurse peers over the top of her glasses at a clipboard. "Morning, Doctor. It says here she ate every bite. She even asked for more when she was done."

"Good. Did she eat all her breakfast? I believe it's still mashed bananas."

"No, ma'am, it hasn't arrived yet. They're short-staffed in Dietary. They're running about an hour and a half behind. I guess a lot of the staff are out with the flu."

Bridget winces and sucks air through her teeth. "Oh, that's unfortunate. Will you call down and see if they can add some oatmeal to Susan's bananas? And order some more boiled chicken for her lunch with some white rice, okay?"

"Yes, Doctor."

"Good. If she does okay on these without incident, let's go ahead and order her a regular diet for dinner and see how she does."

"Sounds good. She's really doing well. If she wasn't wearing the halo, you wouldn't even know she just had brain surgery."

"That's what I like to hear. All right, you have a good day. Make sure you donate some blood when your shift ends."

The nurse holds up her arm and gestures to a Band-Aid. "Already done."

"Good job. I'll talk to you later." Bridget heads to Susan's room. A candy striper seated next to the bed sets aside the crocodile book.

Bridget gets her stethoscope ready and says, "Good morning, Susan. My, my, but you love that story, don't you? Here, let me listen to your heart and lungs." She positions her stethoscope and conducts a brief exam. "Well, your heart sounds perfect, little one."

The girl bats her long eyelashes and says, "I want Mommy."

Bridget makes a note on the chart. "I know you do, sweetheart. I'll see what I can do, okay? I understand your breakfast will be here soon. I'll check on you later. Bye bye."

"Bye. More crocodile!"

Bridget's heart lightens as she heads back to the nurses' station. "I'd like to get a special dispensation for Susan's mum to be allowed to stay with her in her room."

The nurse straightens her glasses. "But visiting hours—"

"Nurse, I don't care about visiting hours. I want the child's mother to be allowed to stay with her at all times. I want you to call and get an extra bed moved in there to accommodate her. And phone her before she comes up here today so she can plan accordingly. It can be her or the father, either one. Just let them know they both can't stay outside of normal visitation. Only one of them or the other. Understand?"

"Yes, Doctor. I'll take care of it."

"Thank you. Also, I'd like you to get her on the surgery schedule for Monday. I want to remove her drainage tube."

"Yes, Doctor."

"Good. Send a message up to my office, and let me know what time and surgical suite we get."

"Yes, ma'am."

Bridget hurries to the elevator and heads up to the fifth floor where she makes a beeline for the nurses' station. "Good morning. Can I please get a status on Barnaby, Alexander, and Hetzel?"

The nurse cringes. "Last night, Mrs. Alexander started wheezing so badly, she couldn't catch her breath. Dr. Redding was in the E.R., and he came up and looked at her. He prescribed an inhaled corticosteroid, and he ordered her an oxygen tent. She's doing a little better this morning. At least she's resting comfortably, and her vitals are stable."

Bridget shakes her head. "Okay, thanks for letting me know. I'll consult with Dr. Redding later. How about Barnaby?"

"Mr. Barnaby's on top of the world. He is so happy, it's contagious. He's been asking to see you. His vitals and appetite are good."

"Perfect. I love hearing that. And Hetzel?"

The nurse takes a deep breath. "He seemed chipper as ever early this morning when Dr. Slater stopped in to see him, but he's been his normal cranky self with the rest of us."

Bridget presses her lips together and stretches her neck. "How are his vitals? His appetite? His pain level? I hate to keep repeating myself, but the patients don't come to us for a social visit. They're in pain and not feeling their best. I want to know how he's doing with regard to his physical health, not his personality. Understand?"

The nurse's cheeks turn bright pink, and she nods. "I'm sorry, Doctor. His vitals are good. His fever broke late last night, and he's been stable ever since. He ate about a third of his dinner. I think he spent more time counting his peas than eating them. Breakfast has been delayed because of a staff shortage, so I don't believe he's been served yet. I'll keep an eye on him."

"Thank you... Listen, I'm sorry I snapped at you. I know he's a difficult man. You're doing a great job with him, okay. Keep up the good work."

"Thank you, Doctor."

"You're welcome. Have you been down to donate blood yet?"

"I called, but I'm O positive, and they don't really need me. I did call my boyfriend and his sister and her fiancé, though, and asked if they could come by and be tested. None of them know their blood type, so we don't know if they'll be helpful, but they're going to try."

"Good job. Thanks for the help. That'll mean a lot to a lot of people."

"Thanks."

Bridget taps the countertop. "All right. I'm off to see Mrs. Alexander." She stops at the janitorial closet and pulls a long-sleeved gown over her clothes, dons a head covering and a surgical mask, then pulls on some latex gloves. She steps down the hall to Room

514 and peeks inside the plastic tent covering the patient's bed. Mrs. Alexander's chest rises and falls as she sleeps, and the soothing hum of the oxygen pump assures Bridget that Dr. Redding made a good call. She takes the patient's pulse then reads the chart at the end of the bed and makes a note. Satisfied, she removes the gloves and tosses them in the garbage can then washes her hands and exits. She removes the gown, mask, and headdress then tosses them in the dirty linen depository in the closet before she strolls down to Room 502.

Her face brightens as soon as she steps in the room. "There's my star patient. How are you feeling today, Craig?"

"I'm so happy to be alive. I just... I can't explain it. I love my life."

She raises an eyebrow. "Well, that's certainly is an about-face. I'm glad to hear it."

His dimples dance as he smiles. "Yesterday, right before I went into surgery, I asked Lisa to marry me. She said yes."

"What? But you've only known each other a week or so."

"We actually kind of knew each other a couple of years ago. We went to the same high school. That's why we started talking in the first place when we met here at the Christmas party. Turns out we both had a little crush on each other back then, but neither of us ever acted on it. As for now, we both feel like, when you've met the right one, you just know it, and there's no denying it. My parents met on a blind date, got married a month later, and they've been happily married for twenty-four years. But we're not getting married until April. Lisa wants a springtime wedding. Right now, we're content just being engaged."

"Well, I couldn't be happier for you. Both of you. Congratulations." Bridget pulls her stethoscope from her pocket and listens to his heart and lungs then takes his pulse. "Everything sounds good. How's your pain level?"

"Not that bad. Nothing like when I had these removed." He wiggles his leg stumps. "So, Doc, how long did you know your husband before you knew he was the one?"

She shoves a thermometer in his mouth and says, "Under your tongue, please. Let's see, we met when I was a student at Emory.

Jack visited my campus to deliver a lecture. I stayed afterward under the guise of asking a question, but I was really hoping he'd ask me out. And it worked. We went out that night, and by the time he dropped me back at my dorm, I knew I wanted him to be the one. But he didn't actually ask me to marry him until a couple of months later when I went to visit him over summer break. And we didn't get married for another year until after I graduated." She removes the thermometer and smiles as she shakes it down. "No fever. Very good."

He wiggles his eyebrows. "Thanks. So, it sounds like you kind of believe in love at first sight too."

"I guess I do. I've been very happy with my husband, and I'm pretty sure he'd say the same about me. Not only do we love and respect each other, but we're truly best friends. As long as you two feel that way about each other, I think you'll do just fine. Anyone who puts a smile like that on your face is someone to hold onto."

His cheeks turn red, and a wide grin stretches across his face. "Yeah, that's what I think too."

She taps his bedrail. "Okay, then. I have work to do, and you have to rest. I'll see you later."

"Thanks, Doc. I mean, for everything."

She winks at him and says, "Anytime." Her heart warms as she heads out.

# # #

24 April 1954

Querido Diario (Dear Diary),

A neurosurgeon from the Mayo Clinic came to campus to lecture this morning. He's not exactly the most handsome man, but I was instantly attracted to his mind. I stayed after the symposium and waited until everyone else left, then I asked him a question to see if we had any chemistry between us. Turns out he's fifteen years older than me which is probably why I'm attracted to him — He's not juvenile like so many of the other young men my own age, and he doesn't have the slightest qualms about me being a woman and wanting to specialize in surgery. His personality is incredible (and truth be told, he reminds me a bit of Papa—and Dad, too, for that matter).

Anyway, I'm very tired, and I have an early morning of labs. But I just wanted to document something of my evening because I've got a feeling that Dr. Jack Ernest Castle is the man I'm going to marry someday. At least I hope so.

# # #

CHAPTER TWENTY-NINE

Bridget heads toward Mr. Hetzel's room but stops when Glenn, exiting Room 514, bumps into her. He pulls the mask off his face and says, "Pardon me. I was up most of the night with the car crash victims, and I only got about two hours of sleep. And after I saw Mrs. Alexander last evening, I knew we'd have to take Paul off the schedule, so that means overtime for me." He pulls off his gown and head covering and wads them into a ball.

She shakes her head. "Yeah, I'm really sorry about that. I was going to come see you in a while, though. How's Mrs. Alexander? Do you agree it's H3N2?"

"Oh, no doubt about it. You made a good call."

"I've got an idea that, with an incubation period of up to five days, she probably brought it in with her. I wish I'd have known before I operated. I'd have tried to delay surgery."

"Well, of all the surgeries you do each month, burr-holes are definitely some of your less aggressive procedures. I'm sure if you thought you could've put it off, you would have."

"That's true. I hate second-guessing myself. It's just that at her age, the procedure was risky enough without the added pain or complication of this flu."

"If I may, I'd like to suggest increasing the dosage of the antibiotics you have her on. I left you a note on her chart. I know it won't help with her flu symptoms, but I thought it might reduce her risk of surgical site infection, considering her resistance being lowered with the H3N2 diagnosis. She's breathing a lot easier now than she was when I saw her last night, so I'd like to keep the croup tent on her for a couple of days. I also had them put her on clear broth and Jell-O for breakfast and lunch then the B.R.A.T. diet for dinner. We'll see how she does on that, then tomorrow, we'll play it by ear."

"Okay, sounds good. I'll sign off on the dosage increase. Thanks for your help with her."

"It's my pleasure. Say, you want to hit the cafeteria with me? I'll buy you a cup of coffee."

"I'd actually love to, but I'm afraid I can't. I'm still on rounds, and I have to get a surgery rescheduled. And now with the blood shortage, I need to go donate."

He winces and sucks air through his teeth. "Yeah, I feel you there. I donated first thing when I got here. Well, maybe some other time. Good luck, Doctor."

"Thanks. You too, Doctor." She waves as she heads to the nurses' station. She signs off on Mrs. Alexander's medication increase then takes a deep breath as she makes her way to Room 529.

As she approaches the door, she hears a sweet, familiar voice speaking in German. *Mama?* She hastens her pace. "Mrs. Kugelman. What are you doing in here?"

Helen places a bowl of oatmeal and a glass of buttermilk on the patient's tray. "I was just explaining to Herr Hetzel that I got sent to help out the Dietary Department today because they're short-handed due to the flu. I told him I didn't mean to upset him. I only came to deliver his food."

Gunter glares at Helen. "And I told *her* I didn't want anything that's been touched by the hands of a nasty Untermenschen!" He shoves the tray and sends it rolling until the milk spills, the glass shatters, and the oatmeal bowl crashes to the floor.

Bridget scowls as she grabs the buzzer and rings for a nurse.

Helen kneels to pick up the broken glass, and Bridget says, "No! You're in Dietary today. You leave that right where it is. Herr Hetzel, my patience with you is growing very thin."

A young nurse pops in the door, saying, "Can I help you, Doctor?"

Bridget's face relaxes into a look of relief. "Si, Maria. Por favor saca a esta mujer de aquí. Inmediatamente. Este paciente es simplemente odioso para ella." *Please get this woman out of here. Right away. This patient is simply hateful to her.*

Bridget guides Helen into Maria's arms and pushes the food cart out after them then closes the door and spins to confront the patient, her face aflame. "Herr Hetzel, if you keep it up, I'm going to put you on the next plane back to West Germany and let your tumor kill you!"

He sneers. "Ah, and you had the nerve to tell that nurse that *I'm* the one who's hateful?"

Her breath catches in her throat. "Pardon me?"

"You told her to get that Jew out of here because *I'm* hateful to her… Oh, you didn't know I hable español?"

Bridget clears her throat and kneels to scoop up the broken glass. "No. No, I didn't. I apologize."

"Well, don't look so surprised. You apparently speak three languages. Why shouldn't I?"

She stands and deposits the glass in the wastebasket. "You're right. I mean, I'm actually fluent in seven languages, but I get what you mean. I shouldn't have assumed."

He drops his ire and looks genuinely intrigued. "Really? I mean, you really speak seven languages?"

"Yes."

"Wow. I mean, I speak five. I've never another Mehrsprachig – *polyglot*."

She sits in the chair next to his bed and rests her hands on her lap. "That's interesting. My father taught me from the time I was old enough to speak. It just came naturally to him, and it seemed easy to me. My mother couldn't understand a word we said." She chuckles. "Did your father teach you?"

"Nah. My Vater only spoke German until a few years ago when he had to learn English for business. My Mutter only spoke German too. When she was alive, that is. I really don't know how I was able to pick up so many foreign tongues because I wasn't exposed to much of anything other than Deutsche – *German* – except occasional television broadcasts or a couple of foreign kids in school. It's just always held my interest."

She smiles and stands as she takes her stethoscope from her pocket. "Here, sit up so I can listen to your heart." She listens to his heart and lungs then takes his pulse, blood pressure, and temperature. "Your vitals are good, and you're temperature's back to normal. I got a message from Dr. Slater that your fever spiked because you were having a reaction to your G.I. cocktail. So, I'm going to try to get your surgery back on the books for tomorrow if I can."

"Oh, you don't want to send me home to die anymore?"

She blushes. "I apologize for that remark. I didn't mean it; I just lost my temper. I just really can't stomach any kind of hatred, and it's not good for your health either. Look, if you want your surgery to be successful, you need to keep your strength up; and you can't do that if you keep tossing your meals at the staff."

He rolls his eyes. "And all I've asked was that the one woman who seems set on tormenting me just leaves me alone. I don't like Jews. Isn't that my prerogative?"

She balls her hands into fists and takes a deep breath. Through clenched teeth, she says, "Yes, you have the right to feel that way. But you *don't* have the right to abuse our employees. She's only been doing her job. And besides, I already told you she's not Jewish."

"Sure, she is. I can smell the stench of her every time she gets near me."

Bridget's face turns scarlet, and her eyes bug out of her head. "Herr Hetzel, you need to—" She closes her eyes and takes a deep breath then lowers her voice. "You need to eat. I'll have someone call Dietary to bring you some more porridge and buttermilk. Good day." She spins on her heel and storms out of the room, her insides boiling with fury.

# # #

3 October 1948

Dear Diary,

I started my sophomore year at Emory recently. Honestly, last year at Oxford was more difficult than this. These students seem more interested in having parties and stupid fraternity events than they do about realizing what an honor it is to be in pre-med. Perhaps they take it for granted since all the students in my classes are males except one other young woman. Though she aspires to be an obstetrician so she can "deliver babies," which to me just seems to patronize all the skilled women who want to go into medicine and have a real knack and desire to practice any field that a man can. They've been accepting females in the medical program here since '43, so perhaps it's not as big of a deal to them as it is to me who had to leave the Continent and move across the pond to even have the opportunity available to me.

But the reason I'm so wound up today is that my table partner (in 4 out of 7 classes) is on my wick! He's made nasty comments under his breath since we were first assigned to the same table (we're in alphabetical order). He doesn't seem to know how to speak at all unless he's being derogatory. Today, he threw a wobbler when I was the only person in our Bacteriology class able to answer correctly when the professor asked who could list the categories of pathogenic organisms.

After class, the maggot started saying (at the top of his voice) that I need to get back to the kitchen, that the only thing a woman's good for is making babies, and that I smelled of menstrual blood! That particularly annoyed me because I'm still dealing with amenorrhea. So, I guess my ire showed which, of course, made him keep it up all day. He's such a childish prick.

The only thing that prevented me from slapping his face was the memory of when Papa got so upset at me that time I allowed Ambroos van den Boom to get under my skin. I guess, though, that having learned that lesson was a good thing because the last thing I want is to give the school a reason to eject me from the pre-med program. I guess if I'm going to cut it in a male-dominated profession, I'd better learn to have a thicker skin. So, I promise not to give him the satisfaction of seeing me react, but I will definitely be venting to you, Dear Diary, as long as this little scum-sucking imbecile keeps talking.

P.S. 10 December 1948 – Turns out I don't have to worry about dealing with the little scum-sucker any longer. He was expelled today after being caught cheating (off my paper, no less!) in our Zoology class. Ha!

# # #

CHAPTER THIRTY

After work, Bridget kicks her shoes off as Jack drives toward their house. She rolls up her sleeve, peels the Band-Aid off her arm, and says, "It's too bad they couldn't use your blood, but at least there's not a shortage of O positive." She opens the ashtray and pulls out a new roll of Wild Cherry Lifesavers, taking two out of the pack. "You want one?"

He raises his fingers from the steering wheel. "No, I already told you I'm saving all my room for whatever your mother's cooking tonight. I even had a light lunch in anticipation."

She sucks on both candies and replaces the roll in its hiding place. "Maybe I should have bought you a larger belt for Christmas." She pats his belly.

He cuts his eyes to her. "Okay, so, not to change the subject but, uh, were you able to get that surgery rescheduled?"

"Yes. Tomorrow at eleven. Herr Hetzel's quite the handful, he is. We had a little run-in this morning after he threw his food at Mama again."

"He did that again? You think his behavior's related to his meningioma?"

"Perhaps, but more than that, I think his father was a Nazi swine, and the apple didn't fall far from the tree."

"Wow. Well, speaking of Nazi swine, you'll be interested to learn that I've already got two interviews lined up for Monday to replace Slater."

"Really? That was fast. You think either will be a good fit?"

"One of them is currently the head of G.I. down at Lincoln Hospital in New York. He's chomping at the bit to get up here because his father recently passed away. His disabled mother lives in Chelsea, and she doesn't want to leave her home, so he wants to be close to her."

"Aww, that's nice."

"Yeah, he'll be up here visiting her next week for the holiday, so it'll be convenient. Hey, your parents are here. I thought we were meeting them." He pulls into their driveway and nods at Geoffrey.

"No, I told them they could ride with us. I don't want them to feel like, just because Mama's back in my life, I'm casting them aside." She steps out of the car. "Mummy, you look beautiful. Is that a new blouse?"

Ada smooths her top. "Yes. I was out Christmas shopping, and I couldn't resist getting something for meself."

Bridget kisses Ada's cheek. "Well, it's stunning. Just let me change and re-do my hair and makeup, and I'll be ready posthaste." She unlocks the front door and runs upstairs.

A short time later, Geoffrey and Jack discuss Nixon's upcoming inauguration in the front seat of the Armstrong Siddeley. In back, Ada examines Bridget's face and says, "Oh, I love that plum eye shadow. It really enhances your beautiful eyes."

Bridget closes her eyelids for a moment, showing off her black liquid eyeliner. "Thank you. I got it to go with my new minidress." She turns in her seat to display her violet and white checkered jumper worn over a black, long-sleeved sweater and black tights.

Ada looks her over from head to toe. "Ah, I thought that was new. And those are the ankle boots you got for your birthday. I forgot about those."

Jack chuckles and twists around in his seat. "Ada, she already has two closets full of clothes. If she doesn't curb the shopping, we might have to build on an addition to the house."

Bridget gives a playful pout as she straightens her headband and touches her hair where it flips up, causing her shiny locks to bounce. "Oh, stop. You know I have to be stuck in drab makeup and dreary suits all day at work. When I'm not there, I like to wear all the cool colors and hip fashions."

Jack nods as a smug smile crosses his face. "See what I mean? She wants to be *hip* and *cool*. Maybe next, she'll want me to buy her a string of puka shells instead of pearls."

Bridget smacks his shoulder. "Yeah, well, maybe I'll need to get you an ear trumpet because me dressing like this makes you look like my grandfather! That's what I get for marrying a man some sixty years older than myself."

Everyone enjoys a hearty laugh until moments later when Geoffrey slows to a stop. A uniformed policeman planted in the middle of the road holds up his hand. Geoffrey cracks his window and says, "What's going on, Officer?"

"We had some war protesters out here blocking the sidewalk, and a store owner took his shotgun to them. This street's cordoned off. You'll have to make a detour."

Bridget sits forward and leans over the front backrest. "Is there a medical crew here yet?"

"They're on the way, ma'am."

She opens her door and jumps out. "I can help."

A deep crease settles into the police officer's forehead. "Ma'am we don't need any hand holders out here. We've got four kids who've been shot. Now, please get back in your—"

Ignoring him, Bridget races toward the incident scene, and Jack jumps out and follows her. Moments later, Geoffrey joins them with the policeman on his heels. "Folks, I need you to get back in your vehicle at once!"

Jack kneels by a bloody young man and feels for a pulse. "It's okay. We're doctors."

The policeman folds his arms and says, "That's all right for you two, but *she* needs to get back to the car."

Geoffrey kneels by a teenage girl and presses his fingers into her neck where blood squirts out like a fountain. "Don't be such a backward twit! I'll have you know, she's not only a doctor, she's a neurosurgeon. She's Head of Neurology at Saint Francis. This girl's about to bleed out! Where's that damn ambulance?"

Bridget kneels by a long-haired boy who doesn't look to be more than fifteen, coagulated blood pooled in his open chest. When she can't detect a pulse and his chest doesn't move, she swipes her palm across his brow to close his eyes. "This one's gone." She looks to the storeowner standing handcuffed beside another policeman, and she narrows her eyes. "I hope you're happy! All these kids wanted was peace!"

She crawls across the sidewalk to a young woman with a bloody gut. Bridget picks up the girl's wrist and says, "You're going to be just fine, pet. Don't you worry." She presses her hands between the girl's ribs in an attempt to stop the bleeding. "How old are you, love?"

In a raspy voice, the girl says, "Seventeen. How's my baby brother? Is he okay?" She gestures to the dead boy who looks like he could be her twin.

Bridget peeks over her shoulder at the kid then back at the young woman. "Now, don't you worry. Everybody's going to be just fine. I just need you to—"

The wailing of a siren grows closer and drowns out her words. Two medics jump out of a station wagon ambulance. One grabs the gurney, while the other snatches the equipment box and races toward Bridget. "What've we got, Doc?" He pulls out a blood pressure cuff and wraps it around the girl's arm.

Bridget grabs a pair of scissors and cuts open the girl's shirt. "Alejandro, she's taken a bullet to the right lung. It sounds like it's collapsed. We need to hurry."

Alejandro makes a small incision then inserts a tube into the girl's chest. Her breath becomes more stable, and Bridget helps until the wail of more sirens approaches. While Alejandro and his partner lift the girl onto the gurney, Bridget watches as Geoffrey helps another medical crew lift the girl he assisted onto a stretcher.

Bridget's chest tightens when he pulls a sheet over the girl's head. *Oh, no.*

Her eyes seek out Jack, still working on a young man. A pair of medics roll a gurney close, and Jack steps back as the two lift the boy then load him into the back of the ambulance. She looks back to the dead brother of the girl she assisted, and someone has covered his body with a sheet. A crimson spot over his heart, the size of a basketball, provides a stark contrast to the surrounding snow piled up against the edge of the road. Something colorful catches her eye, and she looks to a painted poster board sign laying in the road that says, *"Take a Chance on Peace."* Green, pink, and orange painted flowers decorate the corners, and the purple and yellow peace symbol painted under the words brings tears to her eyes.

Fire burns in Bridget's gut as she cleans her hands with a sterile wipe. She glares at the storeowner, saying, "Whatever they do to you in court, it won't be enough! Even if they give you the death penalty, your life won't make up for the two or more you've taken tonight!" Her nostrils flare, and scarlet splotches rise from her neck as she storms back to the car.

Ada rubs Bridget's shoulder. "I'm so sorry, Lovey. They're lucky you were here."

"We lost two of them. They were just babies. All of them. My guess is none of them were more than eighteen years old. With as much death as I've seen in my lifetime, you'd think I'd be numb to it, but it gets me every time."

"Lovey, that's because you have such a big heart." Ada hugs her daughter as the men get in the car.

Geoffrey starts the vehicle and turns up the heat then waits for the policeman to direct him out. "The officer apologized for his comment, love. I hope you didn't let that upset you."

Bridget shakes her head. "Thanks, Dad. I've dealt with chauvinists for years. They don't even faze me anymore. I'm just sickened that the gormless shopkeeper would shoot those kids at point blank range, and for what? They weren't robbing him. They just wanted to make their voices heard."

Jack turns in his seat. "I think the problem was that they were blocking his storefront, and he probably felt as if he was losing business."

"Yeah, well did you happen to notice the sign in his store window? He closed at six o'clock. That was about fifteen minutes after he murdered two children. How many customers could he have possibly lost in those fifteen minutes?"

Geoffrey waves at the policeman and pulls back onto the road. "I think we're all on the same team here, Lovey. You needn't prove your point to us."

She hangs her head. "Sorry."

Geoffrey makes a left turn. "Here we are in Back Bay. I think it should be just a couple more roads ahead. I do hope your dear mum won't be too upset that we're late."

Bridget slips her hand into Ada's. "My mum's right here, Dad."

"I apologize, Lovey. I certainly didn't mean to imply anything out of sorts."

Bridget says, "Helen was married to a doctor. I'm sure she'll understand why we're tardy."

They turn into a driveway, and Geoffrey says, "Well, here we are and only twenty minutes after the hour."

# # #

19 April 1942

Lief Dagboek (Dear Diary),

It's almost midnight on Sunday night, and I'm terrified. Early in the wee hours this morning before dawn, the Good Doctor Van Den Boom came to our cottage. We were still asleep, and with it still being dark outside, we might have feared it was the Gestapo. But the Good Doctor uses a secret knock when he visits so we'll know it's him. He asked Papa to grab his medical bag and go with him.

I only heard bits of their conversation, but from what I could gather, there was a Jewish boy that Dr. Van Den Boom's neighbor is hiding, and he needed an emergency appendectomy. (Papa says Dr. Van Den

Boom's dream when they were in university and residency was to concentrate on internal surgery. However, with the war raging as it is, the Good Doctor found it more practical to practice as a general physician. So, when major invasive surgical intervention beyond wound repair is required, he often looks to other doctors for assistance.)

I expected Papa home sometime after lunch, but Mama said that the Good Doctor would probably wait to bring him back so they could hide under the cloak of darkness. Still, that was hours ago, and I've been terrified that something dreadful has happened. I've been pacing the floor for hours, and it irritates me to no end that Mama doesn't even seem to be worried. She's kept her nose buried in a book since after dinner, with a silly smile plastered on her face. She says being the wife of a doctor – especially a surgeon – means you often have to be patient and wait because one never knows what they might encounter when they take on the responsibility of opening up another human being. I'm so aggravated, I could scream!

P.S. 20 April 1942 – The Good Doctor Van Den Boom brought Papa home at 3:30 this morning. Mama made them coffee while they sat down and explained what the surgery entailed. Because of the patient's family being in hiding, they were too terrified to leave or allow their son to even go to Dr. Van Den Boom's office. So, Papa and the Good Doctor had to perform the surgery in the attic of Dr. Van Den Boom's neighbor's house where the family lives. They used the family's dining table as an operating table, and they had to prop the table legs up with books so that they weren't hunkered over the boy's body for so long. Dr. Van Den Boom served as the anesthesiologist as well as Papa's surgical assistant. (I really wish I could have gone along to help!)

When they opened up the child, it seems they found that he not only needed his appendix removed, but they realized that the boy had a volvulus with a bowel obstruction, and they had to repair the torsioned intestine and assure that the blood flow returned to the area. Papa said it was one of the most difficult surgeries he's ever performed because of the lack of *available equipment and the primitive surroundings. They both hope and pray that the boy doesn't develop an infection; but barring that, they said he may just be okay.*

As for me, I was intrigued with every detail of the procedure, and Mama eventually had to tell me to stop asking so many questions because both men needed to get some sleep. I guess if I'm being honest, I have to admit that Mama was right… Being the wife of a surgeon means a lot of unquestioning patience and waiting. I hope someday I have a husband who is equally as understanding.

# # #

CHAPTER THIRTY-ONE

Bridget, Jack, Ada, and Geoffrey approach Helen's porch, and Bridget's stomach does flipflops until the door flies open. Helen, wearing a warm smile, says, "Welcome! Please come in and get the cold out of your bones. We just saw a news report about a shooting nearby, and we figured the traffic would be detoured. Can I get anyone a drink? Some wine, perhaps?"

The doctors wash their hands, and after everyone enjoys two glasses of Cabernet Sauvignon over small talk, Bridget stands and crosses the room. She examines a photo of a young Maurice with a woman and three small girls. *That must be his wife and daughters.* She spots a framed photo of Papa and herself, and her heart skips a beat. *I don't remember ever seeing this.* Her eyes move to the next photo of Mama with Otto. *Oh, I don't remember this either. Look how young Otto was.* She then looks to the next framed image: a watercolor painting of a baby boy. *He looks so familiar.* She picks up the frame for closer inspection. The child's olive eyes with copper flecks, his auburn tufts of hair, his chubby, rosy cheeks draw her in. *I know this face.* She turns toward the room. "Mama, who is this? Is it Otto?"

Helen stands and joins her daughter. "No. It's our Josef. Maurice painted it for me. He's quite the hobby artist. He studied the photos of you and your papa and Otto, then, when I described Josef, he painted it as a wedding gift to me. Since we were never able to get any photos of your brother, I've always tried to keep his image fresh in my mind. It's a good likeness, don't you think?"

Bridget studies the picture again and traces the boy's eyes with her fingertip. "Yes. It's amazing. His eyes look like Papa's. There's something about this that just hypnotizes me."

In a private tone, Helen says, "I can have duplicates of all these made for you. I know you'll want copies." She turns her attention back to her guests and clasps her hands, saying, "Is everybody ready for dinner?"

Geoffrey says, "Indeed we are. Something sure smells delicious. Helen, I hope we haven't put you to too much trouble."

Helen gestures to a set of French doors. "Let's make our way to the dining room. Geoffrey, nobody put me to any trouble. Maurice did the cooking today while I was at work."

As they head to the table, Bridget says, "Speaking of work, I think it would be best if you stayed away from Mr. Hetzel. I'd hate to see you get hurt again."

Helen casts aside Bridget's concern with a wave her hand. "Ack, I'm not worried about him. With all I've lived through, there's nothing that can ever hurt me again. I don't know what it is about him, but something just seems so familiar."

Bridget sneers. "Yeah, he looks familiar to me too. He reminds me of an S.S. guard back at Auschwitz."

Helen squeezes Bridget's shoulder, saying, "Everyone, have a seat, won't you?" She joins Maurice in the kitchen. Within moments, they return with two trays of bowls. "I hope you all like Polish food."

Ada inhales the steam coming from her bowl of soup. "What is this? It smells simply divine."

Maurice picks up his spoon and says, "It's called krupnik. It's a barley soup with smoked meat and vegetables. Everybody, dig in."

Geoffrey takes a bite and says, "Ooh, sterling job, old chap. It's jolly good indeed. I've never had it before, but I'd definitely like to have it again."

Bridget sips from her spoon and says, "I'm sorry, Maurice. I thought Mama told me you were from Stuttgart. Are you Polish?"

Maurice shakes his head. "No, I was born, raised, and married in Stuttgart, where I owned an office supply store and repaired typewriters. But a few years after the birth of our second child, my family was exiled to the ghetto in Warsaw. I learned to cook there, and though rations were scarce, I memorized a lot of what the Poles told me about how each dish should be prepared. In my deli in Chicago, I feature Polish Wednesday every week, and the customers go crazy for it."

Jack smacks his lips. "Mm, I can see why. This is certainly a delicious meal."

Maurice and Helen exchange amused glances and chuckle. Helen says, "Son, this isn't the meal. It's just the appetizer." She and Maurice stand and head to the kitchen then return, each carrying a lidded silver serving tureen.

Helen removes the lids and gestures. "This is your main course. It's called kurczak de volaille. You want to tell them about it, dear?"

Maurice brushes his hands on his trousers. "This dish originated in France, but the Poles adopted it. Basically, it's chicken stuffed with mushrooms and bread crumbs. And over here, we have our side dish called pierogi ruskie. They're dumplings filled with potato and cheese, topped with caramelized onions and sour cream sauce."

Ada's eyes grow large. "Mmm, that sounds scrumptious." She scoops some onto her plate and takes a bite, then her eyes roll back in her head. "Incredible! Maurice, you're a genius."

Maurice puffs up his chest. "You're too kind. Listen, everyone, make sure to save room for dessert. We're having sernik. That's a traditional Polish cheesecake drizzled with chocolate and powdered sugar."

Ada smacks Geoffrey's arm. "Why can't you learn to cook for me like this?"

He laughs. "Hey, you know surgeons are no good in the kitchen."

Jack chuckles and says, "Tell me about it." He cuts his eyes to Bridget and suppresses a grin.

She slaps his hand and furrows her brow in a playful pout. "Shut your cakehole, Jack Castle! I cook for you sometimes."

Helen claps her hands and throws back her head with a hearty laugh. "I know what you mean, Geoffrey. My Jens was all thumbs in the kitchen too."

Maurice snorts and says, "I don't know. He made decent enough bread at Dachau, considering what inferior ingredients he had to work with." As soon as his words escape his lips, his hand flies to his mouth, and he cringes.

Helen narrows her eyes and, through clenched teeth, says, "I thought we agreed not to discuss that tonight."

Bridget's heart races. "What are you talking about? My papa wasn't in Dachau. He was killed in our cottage in the Netherlands."

Maurice looks to Helen, and she takes a deep breath. She says, "Rena—I mean Bridget, honey, Papa wasn't killed when we thought. He was taken to Dachau. He knew Maurice there. They lived in the same barrack."

Bridget's hands tremble, and tears burn behind her eyelids. "No. No, that's not true."

Maurice hangs his head. "I'm so sorry. I shouldn't have brought it up. Bridget, your mama wanted to tell you in her own time. Please forgive me."

Bridget sucks air over her quivering lip. "There's nothing to forgive. I simply don't believe you. You must be mistaken." She takes a bite of pierogi. "This is very good. Let's talk about the food again. Did you always enjoy working with food?"

Geoffrey rubs Bridget's arm. "Lovey, they're telling you the truth."

She narrows her eyes at him, and vermillion patches bespeckle her neck. "No. No, it can't be!"

Geoffrey grabs her hand in his. "But it is. Petteri sent me something a long time ago to hold onto for you. I brought it with me tonight, just in case you or Helen wanted it. It's out in the boot of the car. Hold on." He stands and grabs his jacket then hurries outside.

Bridget holds her head in her hands, and the room spins. "I'm sorry. I don't why I'm reacting this way. I should be happy that Papa lived longer than I thought. But knowing he died in a camp..." She throws her arms around Jack and buries her face in his shoulder as she sobs.

Geoffrey returns with a case, and Maurice says, "Honey, if it helps, your papa didn't die while he was a prisoner."

Bridget sniffles. "What?"

Maurice takes a deep breath. "I better start at the beginning. My family and I were arrested in October of '42 and taken to Dachau. I had a daughter who was three, another who was five, and one who was twelve. My wife was six months pregnant. The train ride from Poland lasted a week, and my wife and girls were very weak by the time we arrived. My wife started hemorrhaging before we were unloaded from the cattle car. She was immediately put in a line with other women and children who I later learned would be executed that very evening. My two youngest were soon put in the line with their mother. I had no idea that would be the last time I would ever see them. My twelve-year-old, Ursula, was put in a women's line; and, of course, I was sent with the men."

Bridget wipes a tear from her cheek, and Maurice takes a sip of wine. He says, "Nearly fourteen months after we arrived, Ursula grew very ill. She had a fever and cough, and I just thought she'd caught a bad cold from being so emaciated and exposed to the elements. It was about a week later, around the first of the year in 1944, that a new trainload of prisoners arrived. By then, I was a kapo, a job which I loathed. I was in charge of correcting the prisoners who sorted and catalogued the valuables that came in with the new detainees. I watched as this man, who I later learned had been shot in the leg, limped off the train. He wore a makeshift tourniquet. When he was commanded to empty his pockets, he pulled out a stethoscope, a reflex hammer, and a surgical clamp. When he was registered, he said his name was Dr. Jens Eckhard Breitman. I knew then that I had to get him to help my daughter. I pulled some strings and got him assigned to my barrack. He looked at Ursula and examined her as best as he could with having no medical supplies on hand. He said that he was nearly certain that she had tuberculosis. Of course, I knew back then that TB was a certain death sentence, but it wasn't until later that I learned that the camp physicians were actually injecting people with the virus to test their experimental medicine. Though Ursula was not injected, it then became clear how she was exposed to the disease. Jens said that the best treatment would be rest and isolation, not to mention good nutrition. But, of course, none of that was possible. She continued to grow weaker and expired less than a month later. My only solace was that at least my family no longer had to suffer so mercilessly."

Maurice pulls a handkerchief out of his pocket and wipes his red-rimmed eyes. "Because your papa had been so kind, I wanted to repay him. I got him a job working in the kitchen so he would have the opportunity to gain access to a little extra food. But your papa, being the kind man that he was, never kept any extra nourishment for himself. He always held back an extra piece of bread which he gave to whatever prisoner looked to be the worst off. One of the punishments often carried out there was when someone got out of line, he or she was tied to a post, and a dog handler brought out the starved Doberman pinschers and forced us all to stand at attention and watch as the ravenous dogs literally ate the violator. One time, one of the dogs turned on the onlookers and bit a thirteen-year-old boy in the ankle, leaving a wound that nearly reached the bone. Of course, the guards thought that was hilarious. After we were dismissed, your papa actually managed to smuggle a needle and thread out of the uniform shack and sewed up the child's leg. I think, had that not happened, the boy would have surely either bled to death or died of infection."

Helen pinches the bridge of her nose and slips her hand into Maurice's. "Tell her how much he talked about his little brown-eyed girl."

The hackles rise on the back of Bridget's neck. *Mama never knew that was Papa's special nickname for me. Even if she'd have heard it, he always called me that in English, so she wouldn't have understood.* She rubs the goosebumps off her arms.

Maurice takes a sip of wine and says, "Your papa's leg healed from his gunshot wound, but he had a permanent limp. He used to talk to me about you and your mama and your brother Otto. He told me how you and he would often talk in different languages when you were holed up in tight quarters and that it drove your mother crazy not being able to understand you. He said his special nickname for you was his little brown-eyed girl, that you loved to document everything in your diary, and that you had a treasure box and what he described as a cute habit of hiding things in cubby holes. When your mama and I saw *To Kill a Mockingbird* a few years ago, I told her then that Boo Radley hiding things in the knothole for Scout and Jem was exactly how I pictured you from your papa's description." He and Helen chuckle. "Anyway, Jens told me you were excited because you were going to be a big sister soon and that he had no doubt that one day you would be a fine surgeon."

Bridget sniffles, and her voice quivers. "You said he didn't die in Dachau?"

"I said he didn't die while he was a prisoner. In April of '45, we heard rumors that the American forces were getting closer. On the twenty-sixth of the month, the S.S. gathered over seven thousand prisoners, mostly Jews, and led them on a death march toward Tegernsee. They initially selected Jens to go on that march, but I used all the influence I could and was able to convince them that I needed him to stay and help me correct the remaining prisoners. Three days later, the American forces liberated us."

Bridget's stomach lurches. "That was just a few days after I was liberated. Where did he go?"

Geoffrey clears his throat and nods to Maurice. "Lovey, your papa was severely malnourished. He had dysentery, malaria, and TB. He died in hospital less than a month later."

All eyes turn to Geoffrey. Bridget says, "Which hospital?"

Geoffrey opens his case and says, "After liberation, eleven of the Dachau barracks were converted into a hospital to house the ailing prisoners. The American One-Sixteenth Evacuation Hospital arrived there a few days later on the second of May."

Bridget raises an eyebrow. "How did you learn this?"

He reaches into his case. "I told you Petteri sent me some things. First, this was mine that I've been saving forever. I want you to have it." He hands her a 1924 Oxford University yearbook with two scraps of paper sticking out. "Open it to that first marker."

She flips the page of the well-worn book, and her breath catches in her throat. "It's Papa's handwriting." She reads the inscription and smiles through her tears. "Aww, he really valued your friendship, Dad. What's this other page?" She flips to the next marker to reveal two dozen small headshots of the junior class. Her breath quickens as she scans the page for Jens's name. "Here he is. Oh... Look how young he was. I wonder why he didn't have one of these books?"

Helen peers across the table. "He had a couple of annuals, but they got left behind when we left Germany. He always regretted leaving them because they contained the pictures of so many of his good friends."

Geoffrey reaches in his case and pulls out an old magazine then offers it to Bridget. "Turn to the page I have marked. That's when Jens, Petteri, and I had our first article published in a surgical journal. We researched together and wrote on Diverticula of the Colon."

Her fingertips graze over Jens's name under the article title. "Oh, thank you. Aww, and Dr. Van Den Boom's and your names are here. These are my three favorite doctors. What a treasure this is! Thank you, Dad."

Jack raises an eyebrow. "Hey, don't you mean three of your *four* favorite doctors?"

Her eyes twinkle, and she giggles. "I apologize, my love. Of course..." The smile melts from her face. "Hey, where have you put all your food? No one else has an empty plate!"

He blushes. "Sorry. I told you I was hungry, and it was too delicious to waste."

Ada snickers. "That's true. I don't care if it is getting cold, I'm eating every bite." She cuts a pierogi with her fork and shoves a bite in her mouth.

Geoffrey pulls a well-worn reel-to-reel tape recorder from his case then plugs in the electrical cord, saying, "Bridget, Helen, I don't know if you'll want to hear this. It's an interview with Jens after he was liberated. A Dutch magazine ran a story about the liberation of Dachau, and Ambroos van den Boom actually recognized Jens in it and showed the article to his father. Apparently, he and Petteri did a lot of legwork and tracked down the reporter. They were able to secure the reporter's audio recording of when he visited the Dachau patients."

Bridget's stomach flip-flops. "Wh—when did you get this?"

"It was right before we moved to the States. The summer of '48. I contacted the Good Doctor to let him know we were coming to America so you could enter the medical program. He told me then that he'd worked on obtaining this for nearly two years and asked if I wanted to hold onto it for you. He said Helen had visited him after she was liberated, but he had no forwarding address for her. Of course, he didn't know you were living with me until long after your mama had seen him. Lovey, I—Maybe I didn't do the right thing by not showing this to you straight away. But since you hadn't ever brought up your parents or your past since we met, I wasn't sure how to proceed. I talked to Petteri about it a few times over the years. He agreed that maybe it was all just too painful for you, and we thought it would probably be best if I just held on to it until you decided to discuss it. In fact, it wasn't until one of our later conversations that he told me that you believed your papa was killed in your home. I'm so sorry if I've hurt you by withholding this, Lovey."

Bridget stands and throws her arms around Geoffrey's neck. "No, Dad, you did exactly the right thing. I—I just... I wasn't ready to talk about any of it. You were right; it was too painful. I was so angry at my mama for abandoning me and moving to Hong Kong with my brother—" She looks to Helen. "I'm sorry, Mama, but that's what I thought. Anyway, any thought of my family and all I'd been through made me so furious, I couldn't stand myself. I just wanted to be yours and Mum's daughter and pretend the rest never happened. I think that's why, when you and I left the camp and you took me to the Netherlands to find my diary and other treasures, I didn't ask to stop and see Dr. Van Den Boom. I knew if I saw him, he'd bring up my mama and papa, and I didn't want to have to think about them. As far as I knew, my papa was dead, and my mama was dead to me. I just couldn't... I mean—I love you and Mum, but I do also love my other parents and—" She wipes the tears from her cheeks with the back of her hand. "I'd really like to hear it, please."

Geoffrey looks across the table. "Helen?"

Helen nods. "Yes, I—I do too." She takes a deep breath and snuggles into Maurice's waiting arms.

Geoffrey pulls a yellowed sheet of paper out of an envelope and hands it to Helen. "This interview is in Dutch, but Petteri transcribed it for me. Here's the translation."

Helen's hands tremble as she unfolds the paper.

Geoffrey's eyes glisten with tears, and he sniffles. "Okay. If you need me to stop it, just say so." He presses the play button, and the tape reels turn. Within seconds, a young man's voice starts to speak on the staticky recording:

"Goedenmiddag. Mijn naam is Kees Janssen." – Good afternoon. My name is Kees Janssen. – "Today is Tuesday, the eighth of May, nineteen hundred and forty-five. I'm here today at the Dachau concentration camp barracks hospital set up by the American Medical Corps after the American troops liberated the camp on the twenty-ninth of April. Since I've been here, I've been looking for any Dutch-speaking patients to talk to me, and I've come across a patient who is also a doctor. Despite his obvious malaise, when I got here this morning, I found him helping the Americans tend to other patients. Sir, can you please tell me your name and when you arrived at Dachau?"

"I'm Dr. Jens Breitman. I arrived here on the second of January, 1944."

Bridget's heart skips a beat. *Papa, I never thought I'd hear your voice again.* She looks to Helen. Tears stream down Helen's face as her index finger follows along on the translation sheet.

"So, Dr. Breitman, you've been here more than a year. Can I ask, sir, how much weight you've lost since you arrived?"

"I weighed a hundred and thirty-two pounds when I was arrested. I weighed eighty-three pounds last week when the hospital here was set up."

"Have you been feasting on lots of good food since the Americans came?"

"No."

"No? I don't understand."

"When you've been malnourished for so long, you have to gradually introduce solid food. Otherwise, the results could be fatal."

"I see. I had no idea. We've only recently learned about some of the horrific conditions here. Can you tell our readers how you managed to survive for so long?"

Jens coughs. "I think for any of us who managed to survive, it was certainly due to sheer stubbornness, determination, and a strong constitution. I also often recalled the generosity of all the friends who helped my family stay hidden, and those memories helped me stay strong when things looked bleak. I would love to thank them personally, but... with the war still going, I'm afraid they may be targeted. But they know who they are, and to them, I'd like to say I'll be eternally grateful for all you've done for me and my family."

"Wow. It sounds as if you had a lot of good people helping you before you were brought here."

"Yes. I've also personally made some good friends since I've been here who have helped keep my spirits up during times when I felt I couldn't go on any longer. Do you mind if I thank them by name?"

"Of course not. Be my guest."

"Thank you. Well, let's see, first, there was Rudolf Schubert. He and I rode here on the train together. He gave me his jacket to make a tourniquet for my leg where I was shot by the Gestapo when I was arrested. After we got here, he was always willing to share anything he had. We lost him in February when he succumbed to tuberculosis. Then there's Wolfgang Jung. He participated in the Sunday Cabaret. He had the most amazing voice. Every week, just knowing we'd get to hear him sing gave me a little slice of freedom. I would close my eyes and imagine I was home listening to the radio with my family. It was the best hour each week. Wolfgang was forced to go with some of the others a few days before the Americans got here."

"Wow. You really made some meaningful friendships while you were here."

Jens pauses to cough. "Yes, well, I have a couple more. Maurice Kugelman will always be my hero. He was a kapo, and he was able to get me a job working in the kitchen when I arrived. When we were being registered, I heard rumors that doctors would likely be executed because the S.S. didn't want any of the prisoners to become aware of what the S.S. physicians might be doing. Maurice then saved my life a second time when he got me released from having to march with the others a few days before our liberation. I don't think I would have lasted a day if I had to go out on foot." He gasps for breath and coughs.

"Finally, there's Klaus Pfeiffer. He's here in the infirmary, but I'm certain he'll be heading back to his family soon. There were times when I was literally unable to stand another moment, and Klaus was always there to let me lean on him while we were on work detail so that I wouldn't be beaten or executed for falling down on the job. Sometimes in the kitchen, we had to lift more than our weight in pots of water or gruel, and there were so many times that I didn't have the strength to do it. But Klaus always pitched in and helped me out. He's a stellar man, and I'll be forever indebted to him."

Bridget looks up at Maurice's face, drenched in tears. He pulls Helen closer as they continue following the transcript.

"Earlier, you mentioned that you had a family? Did they come here with you?"

"I have a beautiful wife who will be forever my true love, a lovely fourteen-year-old daughter who is my best little brown-eyed girl, and, by now, I have either another pretty little girl or a handsome son who should be approximately thirteen or fourteen months old. God willing, they're in the Netherlands or somewhere safe." Jens pauses for a coughing fit.

Bridget squeezes Geoffrey's hand then looks to Jack as he reads over Helen's shoulder and blinks back a tear.

"Well, Doctor, it sounds like you have a lovely family. I take it you haven't been able to contact them yet?"

"No, not yet. I've tried, but the communications here are still limited."

"Is there anything you'd like to let them know through this interview?"

"While I was here, I frequently looked at pictures of them in my mind and imagined what my new son or daughter might look like by now. I want them to know that there hasn't been a moment since I left that I haven't thought of them in my waking hours or visited them in my dreams when I slept. I'll love them until my dying breath and beyond. I want them to never doubt that."

"Well, I'm sure you're anxious to get home to them."

"Mr. Janssen, I'm afraid that won't be in the cards for me. I have both dysentery and malaria, not to mention tuberculosis. I don't expect I have much longer on this earth, but at least I will die free. It's important to me that my loved ones know that." Jens's cough overtakes him, and he makes some hacking sounds followed by the sound of retching.

The sound of movement proceeds the reporter's uncomfortable voice. *"All right, that concludes my interview of Dr. Jens Breitman. Now, moving along..."*

Geoffrey hits the stop button and takes a deep breath. "Well, I hope that at least brought you some peace, Lovey. I know it was upsetting."

Bridget wipes her face with her napkin. "No, it was good. I mean, I never thought I'd hear Papa's voice again, so it was—I really appreciate all that Dr. Van Den Boom must have gone through to get this for me. And you. Thank you, Dad." She hugs Geoffrey and kisses his cheek.

Helen sips her wine then says, "Yes, that was difficult to listen to, but I think it ended well, considering. I mean, I'm glad he at least expressed some happiness at the end. Not even the Shoah could break my Jens's spirit."

Geoffrey furrows his brow. "Shoah?"

Maurice wipes the tears from his eyes and shakes his head. "Shoah is the Hebrew word for catastrophe. It's what we call the Holocaust. And, yes, Jens was indeed a good man. One of the best I've ever known. I'll never forget him."

Ada scrapes the last bite of pierogi from her plate then pauses mid-bite. "I only met him a few times, but he always had a sterling personality. And his letters to Geoffrey always brought a smile to me face. So, it's simply incredible, Maurice, that after you left Dachau, you went searching for Helen and found her."

Maurice manages a crooked smile. "It actually didn't happen that way at all. It was sheer dumb luck that I happened to meet Helen. Truth be told, I didn't even remember her name from Jens talking about her because he usually just said 'my wife.' I moved to Scotland after the war, then I moved to America a few years after that and settled in Wisconsin where I had a friend who offered me a job in his restaurant. A few months later, I started having digestive problems that I thought were ulcers, but my doctor did some tests and sent me to the Mayo Clinic for an evaluation. We were afraid it was some sort of reaction to chemicals I was exposed to in Dachau. Anyway, that's where I met Helen; and, of course, by then she was no longer AnneHelene. It was about a month after we started dating that I mentioned that her last name was also the last name of a friend I had in the camp; and we talked more and realized her husband and my friend were one in the same." He wipes his face with his napkin and stands. "Hey, let's not forget I promised you all some sernik for dessert. I'll be right back…" He heads to the kitchen while Helen collects the dirty plates.

After Helen disappears around the corner, Ada moves to another chair and cups Bridget's face in her hands. She says, "Lovey, I'm so sorry. I know this must be so difficult for you, just finding your mama and hearing your papa's voice after all these years and learning that what happened to them and your brother was not what you'd always pictured. Part of me wishes you would've been able to talk about all this when you came to us, and then maybe it wouldn't be so painful for you now. But I must admit, I'm equally glad that you put all this behind you for a few years. Perhaps that was why you were able to focus your attention on your medical dreams, and you gave Geoffrey and me so much joy being our daughter."

Bridget's eyes fill with concern, and she grabs Ada's hands. "Mummy, I'm *still* your daughter, right?"

"Well, of course you are, love. You'll be ours forever. Our feelings haven't changed one bit. Right, Geoffrey?"

He rubs Bridget's shoulders. "I should say not, Lovey dear. We're both so chuffed with you. We always have been. I don't know where our lives might have taken us if you hadn't come along when you did. You're our diamond gal. Our true treasure."

A sense of contentment washes over Bridget, and she closes her eyes and recalls her first few days of living with the Andersons.

# # #

16 August 1945

Lief Dagboek (Dear Diary),

I'm writing this in Dutch because what I have to say today must never be seen by any other eyes. Today started off as a very special day. I've been here in England for just over two months, and this morning, Mum and Dad took me to the Magistrate and formally adopted me. Never again will I be Renate Brigitte Breitman, the poor Jewish orphan. I am now officially Bridget Anderson, daughter of two parents who adore her.

After we left the courthouse, we went to a portrait studio and had our first professional family portrait made. Dad requested several poses with all three of us, some of myself with just him, some with Mum and me, and some with me alone. It wasn't until we got home that I realized that all the pictures of Mum and Dad's first child, Hazel Bridget, were removed from their frames. By this, I mean that EVERY SINGLE PHOTO with Hazel included are simply gone! I suddenly have the eerie feeling that once we get back the photographs we took today, they will be housed in the numerous empty frames throughout the house where Hazel's photos once took residence.

This kind of confirms the strange suspicion I've had ever since I got here that I was brought here to be a changeling of sorts. To tell the truth, I kind of find the whole thing unnerving. I mean, I love Mum and Dad because they cared enough to rescue me and take me in, and already, they are talking about my education and what they can do to make sure I realize my dream of becoming a surgeon. But, by the same token, I can't help but remember when we learned our dear Otto had died, my former family never removed pictures of him. In fact, everywhere we moved after we lost him, one of the first things we did was find a place to hang my brother's photos so that we would always feel as if he were there with us.

How else could I possibly interpret such a strange incident as these creepy empty frames? How am I not supposed to be made to feel like a stand-in, a surrogate, a replacement daughter? It makes me feel almost as though I should be celebrating Hazel's death or the Blitz that claimed her because, had she not died, I most surely wouldn't be here sleeping in her bed, living in her house, and kissing her parents goodnight.

# # #

CHAPTER THIRTY-TWO

Long after midnight, Bridget's dreams transport her to the past. She watches in horror as Jens, all skin and bones, sits hugging himself with his head bowed while Führer Hitler injects Jens's carotid artery with tuberculosis bacterium. Bridget attempts to scream, but before she can utter a sound, a loud crash causes her to spin around to find Gunter Hetzel, dressed in his S.S. uniform, throwing plates at Helen who is tied to a pole. Gunter laughs every time a dish hits Helen in the head, and with blood pouring down her face and pooling around her feet, her head falls forward, snapping her neck. Bridget shields her eyes with her forearm and turns away, but the loud buzzing of numerous planes, diving then climbing in airspace theatrics, causes her to duck and cover her head. She squeezes her eyes closed, but the buzzing grows louder and couples with the sound of cracking. She imagines someone is being repeatedly beaten with a leather whip, but when she opens her eyes to peek, she finds Jack smacking his lips as he downs an entire barrel of thin soup meant to feed thousands of famished prisoners. The prisoners start chanting, "Sprengen die Hindenburg! Sprengen die Hindenburg!" *Blow up the Hindenburg!* Jack then takes every loaf of the prisoners' bread and shoves them down his throat, one after the other, making them disappear faster than a magician. His body grows and grows, until it finally reaches the size of the famous Zeppelin, then he explodes, sending bits and chunks of engorged flesh and tissue flying in all directions.

Bridget, helpless against the horror, screams, "Jaaaaaaaaaccckkkkk!" But her voice is soon drowned out by the upsurge in the buzzing of the diving aircrafts. She jumps out of the way of a bomber headed straight for her then hits the floor with a thud.

She gasps as she wakes, sweat pouring down her face. *Bollocks. Not again.* She pulls herself to her feet and covers her ears with her hands as she cringes. *I've never heard him snore this loud! Must be because he stuffed himself like a pig tonight.*

She smacks his shoulder. "Crikey! What the bloody bollocks are you harboring in your throat? Let it out, for Pete's sake!"

His eyes spin as he sits up and grips his upper arm. "What? What happened?"

"You ate too much! I'm sleeping in the other room!" She grabs a fresh set of pajamas and wraps her robe around herself. As she slides her feet into her slippers and heads out, his sawmill opens for business again. She rolls her eyes and closes the bedroom door.

She heads to the bathroom and washes her face and neck then changes into her clean PJs. As she settles in the guest bedroom, snuggled under a warm blanket, her dreams return, this time of her own doppelganger. She starts off as a young girl running into the room to play with Otto, but when she gets there, he's already playing with a girl that could be her twin. "Otto, what are you doing?" she asks.

He fails to look away from his playmate as he says, "Renate, leave us alone. I'm playing with Hazel now."

Time fast-forwards to a period after Otto's death, and she witnesses Jens ask Hazel to be his surgical assistant in the Netherlands. He then gives Hazel the silver ring, Chirpy Bird, and the diary. Then, instead of being shot, he takes Hazel's hand, and they board a boat to Hong Kong. She then finds herself in England with the Blitzkrieg dropping bomb after bomb after bomb, and the close to deafening noise pierces her ears. She looks around at hundreds of dead bodies, all children, and upon closer inspection, they all have her face, and each wears a shirt with *"Hazel"* printed on the front. Horrified, she races out of the building only to find herself on an old brick road. She sees Baby Josef as he looked in Helen's water color painting, bundled in Otto's old blanket, sleeping with a contented smile on his face, snuggled in a basket hidden in an alcove near the Dutch print shop. She attempts to sneak over to the child to collect him in her arms; but as she gets near, Führer Hitler steps from behind a wall and guffaws as he pours kerosene on the child and asks Dr. Steve Slater for a match. Dr. Slater throws back his head and cackles as he ignites a torch then places it in Hitler's hand, and Hitler lights Josef on fire. Bridget screams, "Nooooooo!"

She turns and runs then ducks into a doorway to hide. As she closes the door, she realizes she's in Dr. Kurt Heissmeyer's medical office in Neuengamme. Moments later, Gunter Hetzel stumbles in, wearing his S.S. uniform, and he falls to his knees. Sweat pours down his blanched face, and he clutches his stomach, saying, "Please help me. I'm in so much pain, I can't stand it."

Bridget folds her arms as she towers over him. "You just wouldn't believe me. I told you this place used prussic acid. It's probably ruined your health. It's probably also why your Vater's lungs are bad. Or maybe it's just fate stepping in to repay you for all the inhumane, sadistic medical experiments you sociopathic Nazis did on all those people!"

Gunter's eyes narrow, and he winces as he clenches his teeth. In a low, purposeful tone, he says, "Those so-called experiments never happened! They were just a figment of a hyperactive imagination used as anti-German propaganda by the Untermenschen!"

A wry smile forms on Bridget's lips. She loads a syringe then injects Gunter in the carotid artery with succinylcholine. Within seconds, he melts, spread-eagle on the floor, his fear-filled emerald eyes watching her.

She rubs her hands together. "Ah, Herr Hetzel, you wonder what's happening? Well, the injection I just gave you will temporarily paralyze you. Though you'll be unable to move, don't worry... you'll still feel *everything* I'm about to do. Now, let's get you up on this table so I can give you a proper lobotomy."

Bridget hears herself scream as she sits straight up. She attempts to wipe her sweat-drenched brow, but her blanket, twisted around her body, prohibits her from moving. "What the hell? I've haven't had so many nightmares since I moved to England." She wiggles her arms free then swipes her hands across her face. She turns on the bedside lamp and blinks as her eyes adjust. She squints at the clock. "Bollocks. My pyjamas are soaked. It's after five thirty. I might as well get up. It's certainly not worth trying to sleep any longer just to deal with these bloody nightmares."

She steps in the shower and allows the hot water to pelt her face like a warm massage, moving her blood, waking her up, and washing away her dream-induced tension. Once she's ready, she rolls her eyes as she passes the master bedroom and heads downstairs. *Sounds like the sawmill is still going strong.*

She pulls on her coat and heads out to her car. *Must get coffee.* As she pulls out of the driveway, she turns on the radio.

"...Yesterday, eleven United States Army soldiers and one South Vietnamese noncom were released by Cambodia. The group was captured on July 17 when their boat strayed into the Cambodian waters, and they've been held as prisoners ever since. A twelfth American, who was captured on November 28 when his helicopter made an unauthorized landing, was also freed. Also, yesterday, Eastern Air Lines Flight 47 was hijacked, and one hundred and fifty people were taken hostage as the Philadelphia-based flight's original destination of Miami was diverted to Havana. The hijacker was taken into custody by Cuban police, and the remaining passengers and crew were taken by bus to Varadero, a Cuban beach town, where they were sent by plane back to the United States..."

"Oh, how I wish Barry Arnold was among those released." She changes the station to music and sings along to "Crimson and Clover" with Tommy James and the Shondells, "Ruby Tuesday" with The Rolling Stones, and "Purple Haze" with The Jimi Hendrix Experience.

At seven o'clock, she pulls into the hospital employee parking lot, only half-filled to capacity, and gazes at the pink sky growing brighter as the fiery sun peeks over the horizon. *I need that coffee right now.* She grabs her lab coat and purse and hurries inside to avoid the bitter cold. She nods at President Johnson's photo, peeks at Carol's empty desk, and turns right at the elevator in search of caffeine. She hums along with Frank Sinatra as he sings "Have Yourself a Merry Little Christmas." Her smile grows as she inhales the rich, nutty fragrance of fresh coffee. Stepping into the sparsely occupied cafeteria, she scans the various breakfast items behind the glass. "Mmm, everything looks delicious. I can't make up my mind."

The food service worker offers a friendly smile. "Take your time, Doctor. We won't see much action here until about seven-thirty."

Without looking up, Bridget says, "Hmm. Well, I know I want the largest cup of coffee you have. And let's see... I think I'd like some scrambled eggs and a cherry cheese Danish, please. Oh, and this will be to go."

"Yes, ma'am. Coming right up. I'll send them down to the cashier."

Bridget moves down the line and gives the cashier three one-dollar bills. "Here you go."

The cashier rings up the food and says, "That'll be $2.11. Just a moment for your coffee. It's still brewing. And here's your change, Doctor." She slips a handful of coins into Bridget's palm.

Bridget slides her plate to the end of the counter then steps aside to wait for her coffee. Moments later, Dr. Steve Slater comes through the otherwise empty line with a glazed doughnut on a small plate. He hands the cashier a five, and she gives him four singles and a couple of coins. He steps beside Bridget and says, "Good morning. I guess you're waiting for coffee too."

Bridget's stomach tightens, and she fabricates a smile. "Yes. I wish I could get it intravenously."

He chuckles then winces and touches his fingertips to his temple. "Ooh, I've had a wicked headache since last night. Nothing I've taken has seemed to cut it. So, you didn't come see me about Hetzel yesterday."

Heat creeps up her neck. "Oh. Yes, I'm very sorry about that. With the blood shortage and then the staff shortage from the flu, I got really busy. Uh, Jack did give me your message that it was an allergy or a severe intolerance to the G.I. cocktail."

"Right. The anticholinergic in the cocktail."

"Well, I've got his surgery scheduled for eleven this morning, so I appreciate your help." *Where's the bloody coffee?*

"Good. You just make sure that Heeb maid stays away from him, and my bet is his ulcers won't flare up nearly as much. Those Shylocks really need to know their station in life and stay there." He squeezes his eyes closed and raises his shoulder to his ear for a few seconds. "Damn this headache. If I've contracted this flu, I'm going to be pissed."

Screw you and your head pain! I'd love to shove a dagger in there to help it along. She squeezes her hands into fists and thrusts them in her coat pockets. "You know, the Jews have been through enough to last for many generations to come. Between torture, starvation, the barbaric medical experiments, and the gas chambers, not to mention the millions of men, women, and children who lost their lives—"

He waves his hand, and his eyes narrow. "Oh, come on, Doctor! You wouldn't actually count the number of roaches that were exterminated in a Harlem tenement; you'd just be grateful they were gone. Besides, I already told you, my uncle was there, and he said none of that ever happened. It was just propaganda. You're a scientist, Doctor. You, of all people, should know better."

Bridget's jaw drops. "So, I suppose you don't believe all the medical experiments on human guinea pigs there were carried out either?"

Dr. Slater rolls his eyes. "Yes, I know medical experiments were done there, but they were conducted on a population that was already ill with tuberculosis and other communicable diseases. The physicians that tested their theories there were medical geniuses. They took a small population of people who were already slated for certain doom, and they offered experimental treatment protocols that at least gave them an against-all-odds chance of being cured. They probably saved many lives. I'm sure TB would be even more rampant today if they hadn't had the good judgment to test their theories on humans rather than rodents."

Acid swells in Bridget's gut, and her knees turn to jelly as the food service worker steps between them and places both coffees beside their plates, saying, "Here you go, Doctors. Have a good day," nodding her farewell as she returns to the growing line of customers.

Bridget takes a deep breath, and her nostrils flare as she forces a tight smile. She takes her coffee and plate, saying, "If you'll excuse me, Doctor, I have a full day." She leaves without waiting for a reply.

She makes her way to the elevator and resists the urge to hum along with Eartha Kitt singing "Santa Baby." Bridget pushes the call button and takes a sip of coffee then grimaces. *Ugh! Black coffee. I didn't even get cream and sugar because I allowed that rotter to chase me out of there. I don't know how Papa ever dared to remove shrapnel from that Gestapo man's leg.* She boards the empty elevator, presses seven, then takes a deep breath. *Yes, I do. Because Papa said his feelings were his own, and no one else had the ability to steal his happiness.* She presses six and starts humming the remainder of the carol with the hospital's piped music.

She steps off on the sixth floor and heads to the Community Room's coffee station. She splashes cream in her cup then spoons in some sugar before taking a sip. *Mmm. Much better.* Still standing, she eats her scrambled egg while she watches some women from a ladies' club assemble Christmas stockings for the pediatric patients. Her smile returns, and she wraps her Danish in a napkin then tosses her plate in the waste can.

As she heads back toward the elevator, she makes an unexpected detour to the maternity ward. She stops at a window and peeks at the new babies sleeping in their acrylic bassinets. Rearranging her lab coat over her arm, she shoves her Danish into her coat pocket then raises her hand to the window and smiles at an infant swaddled in a sky-blue blanket. A lock of auburn hair clings to his forehead under his blue knitted cap. His long eyelashes flutter in his sleep, and she watches as his mouth forms an O as if sucking an invisible nipple. Her heart melts.

"They're so sweet at that age, aren't they?"

Bridget gasps as she turns to find a pediatric nurse at her side. "Oh, good morning, Joyce Ann. Yes, they are darling. This little chap reminds me of someone I knew a long time ago." She nods to the baby and taps the glass with her fingertip.

Joyce Ann adjusts her white cap. "Well, come on in and see him. Babies love to be held, and we don't have nearly enough hands around here to cuddle them all as often as they'd like." She pulls open the door and gestures for Bridget to go in.

"Oh, well, I—"

"Here you go, Doctor. Let me takes these things from you..." Joyce Ann sets Bridget's coffee and lab coat on the counter then helps her remove her coat and hangs it on a hook. "...and you just have a seat in this rocking chair." She picks up the sleeping infant and places the bundle in Bridget's arms.

The baby's nose wiggles, then he resumes sucking the invisible nipple. Bridget relaxes as the infant melts into the crook of her arm. *What a darling lad. He looks so much like Josef.* In a flash, her mind is transported back in time.

# # #

31 March 1944

Drogi Pamiętniku (Dear Diary),

I think I'll be able to write a little more frequently here since I get to actually come outside after dark and sit under the stars. It's nice, sometimes, to have a little place all to one's self. My baby brother smiled today for the first time, and I was the one holding him when it happened. I couldn't have been prouder. Mama clings to him so much of each day and night that sometimes I think they might actually be conjoined.

It's so rare that I get to spend more than a few moments holding Josef that I'm surprised he even recognizes me. Regardless, his smile today was genuine. His bright eyes danced as they looked right at me, and his sweet, pink lips grew into the biggest grin I'd ever seen. It made my heart swell with pride to be his sister. I also realized that since he'll never get to know his older brother, it will be up to me to let him know just how special our dear Otto was and how much Otto would have loved him.

I can't wait for this stupid war to be over. Maybe then, Mama will actually allow me to spend some time with my brother and get to be as close to him as I was to Otto. But for now, I think I shall try to sneak some more frequent cuddles with our sweet Josef and volunteer more often to give Mama a break. Wouldn't it be grand if I could teach him his first words? And if I could teach him the different languages that Papa taught me, we could have our own little secrets between us. (It's too bad Otto was never able to catch on to anything other than German. He would have definitely loved having secrets with me right out in the open in front of Mama.)

# # #

Joyce Ann removes a baby bottle from the warmer, startling Bridget from her thoughts. "Would you like to feed him, Doctor?"

Bridget gasps. "Oh. Yes, of course." She takes the bottle and inserts it in the baby's eager mouth. He begins to suckle as if he's been starved. Bridget's lips curl into an amused smile.

Joyce Ann sits in a rocking chair beside them. "You're a natural at this, Dr. Castle. Maybe someday you'll have time for a family."

Bridget maintains her gaze on the infant. *It's funny. People just always assume a woman with a career is too busy to have children. I'd love a baby to carry on Papa's and Otto's and Josef's names.* She sighs. *But of course, with all the chemicals I was exposed to, I'd hate to pass any birth defects on to a child and have them carry that horrific legacy with them. Not that I could ever get pregnant anyway, what with my menstrual cycle being forever lost in Auschwitz.*

Joyce Ann takes the empty bottle from Bridget's hand. "Do you want to burp him, Doctor?"

"Hmm? Oh, I'm sorry, but I really need to get started on my day. I have a surgery in a few hours. Thank you for allowing me the pleasure of feeding this sweet little chap." Bridget stands and places the baby in the nurse's arms.

"Yes, ma'am. You feel free to come back any time. These babies can use all the love we have to spare."

Bridget grabs her coat, her coffee, and her lab coat then nods and heads out. She stops back by the Community Room and tops off her cup then heads upstairs to her office.

* * *

CHAPTER THIRTY-THREE

Bridget finishes her coffee and pastry as she thumbs through a small stack of messages left under her door. *Let's see, medical equipment sales... That's rubbish. This one wants to sell me a subscription to another surgical journal... No, thank you. Ah, what's this?* She crumbles the first two notes and tosses them in the garbage, and her heart warms as she reads the third: *"From Pete Keene: I got the marshaller job at Logan, and I'll be moving in with Lloyd this evening. I can't thank you enough! When I get my first paycheck, please allow me to take you and your husband to dinner."*

She places her hand over her heart. "Aww, that's splendid. I'm so happy for him." She makes a note on her calendar to call Mrs. Romano and Lloyd later to thank them, then she stands.

She locks up her office and heads down to the fourth-floor nurses' station. "Morning, Brenda. How's the Turner girl doing?" She plucks a roll of Wint-O-Green Lifesavers from her pocket and takes one then silently offers the roll to the nurse.

Brenda waves her hand. "Good morning, Doctor. No, thanks. Susan's doing remarkably well. Her vitals were perfect all night and this morning. Her mother spent the night, and Susan ate every bit of her chicken and rice lunch yesterday. She also had two cups of split pea soup for dinner."

"Oh? Remarkable. Has she finished her breakfast yet?"

"No, ma'am. Breakfast hasn't been delivered yet. Dietary's still short-staffed."

"I see. Well, let me take a look at her, but I'm leaning toward letting her have a full general diet. I'll let you know."

"Yes, Doctor."

Bridget heads to the child's room. "Good morning, little one. How are you feeling today?" She rubs her cold stethoscope between her hands to warm it.

"I hungry. Read!"

Mrs. Turner stifles a giggle and says, "Susan, let's not be rude. The doctor needs to visit you first, then I'll read your new book."

Bridget peeks at a small stack of books including *The Snowy Day, Mr. Rabbit and the Lovely Present,* and *Go, Dog, Go!* She chuckles and says, "Oh, did we get tired of Mr. Lyle Crocodile?"

The muscles in Mrs. Turner's neck tighten, and she lowers her voice. "Please don't mention that one. I'm so sick of it, I could scream." She clears her throat. "Susan, tell Dr. Castle what your new book is called. We haven't even read this one yet." She holds up a book featuring two small boys with a woman and an old man on the cover.

Susan's face glows as she says, *"Tikki Tikki Tembo!"*

Bridget's eyes twinkle. "Wow, that sounds very interesting. You'll have to let me know what happens." She takes the child's blood pressure and listens to her heart and lungs. "All right, Mrs. Turner, Susan's doing just fine. Better than fine, actually. I've got her on the surgical schedule for Monday to remove her drainage line. She'll still have the halo for another five weeks or so, then I have no doubt she'll be as good as new."

Tears form in Mrs. Turner's eyes, and she covers her mouth with her hand. "I can't thank you enough, Dr. Castle. I was so afraid we'd lost her. And you letting me stay here with her now means the world."

"Is your husband and the rest of your family still staying at the hotel?"

"Actually, he's out today looking for a short-term rental close to the hospital. We weren't sure how long we'd be here, but just buying our meals out was getting so expensive."

"Will the two of you be okay with your jobs?"

"Oh, I don't work. Not since the twins were born. We live in Hartford, so it's only a couple of hours away. My husband's almost out of vacation time, so he's going to have to head home and just come back on the weekends and for Christmas. My mom will stay on and keep Melissa while I'm here with Susan; then, during visiting hours, we'll switch off so I can spend some time with Melissa."

Bridget makes a note in the patient's chart then jots on a prescription pad and hands the paper to Mrs. Turner. "Here. This is the name and number of a friend of mine. Her name is Mrs. Romano, and she owns the pizzeria over at Quincy Market. She has a garage apartment close by that she rents out, and I happen to know that the current tenant is moving closer to his new job at Logan Airport tonight. You might give her a call and mention my name. Ask if you can use the place. She's a very nice lady, and if you like Italian food, she'll make sure you don't go hungry."

"Are you serious? That would be a godsend. Thank you!"

"You're quite welcome. I'm going to be talking to her later this afternoon, so I'll let her know to expect your call." Bridget turns her attention to the child. "All right, little one, you be a good girl, and enjoy your new books." She heads out and pauses at the nurses' station, saying, "Yes. Regular diet for Susan Turner. I made a note on her chart."

"Very good, Doctor."

"All right. Have a great day." Bridget heads to the elevator and pushes the call button to go upstairs. The doors open to Jack and a middle-aged man chattering like magpies. She steps on and says, "Well, good morning, stranger."

Jack's eyes grow wide. "Ah, there's my beautiful bride. Dr. Walsh, may I present my wife, Dr. Bridget Castle. She's the head of our Neurology Department. Honey, this is Dr. Willard Walsh. He's the head of G.I. over at Fairfield County General Hospital in Danbury."

Dr. Walsh presents his hand to shake Bridget's. "Pleasure to meet you, Doctor."

Bridget smiles. "The pleasure is mine. Jack, is he here for..."

Jack tips his head. "Yes, he's here for an interview. He was originally scheduled for Monday, but he was out here today to pick up his nephew for the weekend, and he stopped in to see the layout here. I happened to run into him down in the cafeteria, and we got to talking. I asked if he might just like to have his interview today."

The elevator stops on the seventh floor, and Bridget says, "What a lucky coincidence. Best of luck to you, Dr. Walsh."

"Thank you, Doctor."

The men step off, and Jack says, "Hon, we're going to talk in my office for a while. Then, if Dr. Walsh is interested, we're going to take the tour then head down for some lunch. Do you care to join us?"

"No, thanks. I'm still on my rounds, and I have surgery at eleven."

Jack's forehead creases. "Sorry, I forgot. Good luck."

"Thanks anyway, my love. I'll see you this afternoon. Ta ta." She pushes the button for the fifth floor.

As the doors close, Dr. Walsh says, "Your wife has a lovely accent." The comment brings a smile to Bridget's face.

When the elevator stops, she makes a beeline for the nurses' station. "Good morning, Maryann."

"Morning, Doctor. How can I help you?"

"I need statuses on Barnaby, Alexander, and Hetzel, please."

The nurse scans a clipboard. "Ah, yes. Barnaby couldn't be better. Vitals are perfect. No complaints. That kid's on top of the world."

"That's wonderful. How about Mrs. Alexander?"

"Eww, she's been complaining of muscle aches, chills, and moderate head pain at her surgical site. She's been running a low-grade fever off and on. Her stomach did okay on the rice and applesauce she had for dinner; and when Dr. Redding called in last night to check on her, he recommended that she remain on the

B.R.A.T. diet and that we continue giving her Paracetamol for pain and fever."

"Okay, and her vitals?"

"Her B.P. is one forty over seventy. Temp is ninety-nine point two. Pulse is ninety-seven."

"Okay. We'll go ahead and follow Dr. Redding's advice." Let me get in there and see her straight away." Bridget heads to the janitorial closet and dons a long-sleeved surgical gown, head covering, face mask, and gloves. She steps into Room 514 and pulls open the oxygen tent, saying, "Good morning, Mrs. Alexander. How are you feeling today?"

"Hello there, honey. I've been waiting for my granddaughter to come, but she isn't here yet. Did you happen to see her out there?"

Bridget grabs the woman's wrist and feels her pulse. "No, ma'am. You're under quarantine with the flu. I'm afraid you're not allowed to have any visitors right now."

"Oh, bosh! That's silly. Can you please ask Nadine to come see me? I need her to bring me something for this headache."

"Are you in a lot of pain?"

"Now that you mention it, my back and arms hurt too. I must have spent too much time out in the garden last evening."

Bridget steps over to the wall and unlocks a medicine cabinet. She loads a syringe and injects it into the patient's I.V. line. "All right, Mrs. Alexander, I've given you something to ease your discomfort. It's mild, and it'll help you relax."

The patient's eyelids blink a few times then remain closed. Bridget watches the woman's chest rise and fall, then she removes her gloves and washes her hands. She leaves and tosses her scrub gown, mask, and head covering into the dirty linen receptacle in the janitorial closet.

She heads down to Room 502, knocks, and steps inside. "Good morning, Craig. How's my favorite patient today?"

"I'm great, Doc. In fact, I'm better than great. Remember I told you Lisa had a brother in 'Nam?"

Bridget removes her stethoscope from her lab coat pocket. "I remember. He's M.I.A." She sits beside his bed.

"Right. His name's Wayne. He was part of an operation to take down a bridge when he went missing. From all reports, it was assumed he'd gotten himself blown up. That was last April. Turns out, he was knocked unconscious. He drifted down the Mekong River and ended up in Saigon. Some locals took him in and eventually turned him over to the military, and they put him in a field hospital. Apparently, he had amnesia for months, and his dog tags were gone, so they classified him as a John Doe. A couple of days ago, apparently his Sergeant gets himself injured and gets shipped to the same hospital. He recognizes Wayne and calls him by name. All of a sudden, Wayne remembers who he is. It was as quick as that." Craig snaps his fingers. "Lisa's parents got the call last night, and they got to talk to him for a couple of minutes. He's being shipped home next week."

"Wow! That's amazing. I've always said the brain is a mysterious organ that holds more secrets than we'll ever know." She stands and presses her stethoscope to his chest. "Go ahead and take a deep breath for me." She takes his pulse, blood pressure, and temperature then says, "Well, everything's perfect. Keep it up, and we'll have you up and out of here before you know it."

"Thanks, Doc. I couldn't have done it without you."

She makes a notation in his chart then opens the door. "You keep up the good work, and I'll see you later."

She heads down to the nurses' station. "All right, Maryann, I've sedated Mrs. Alexander. She should be out until after lunch. Mr. Barnaby couldn't be better. And is Mr. Hetzel ready for his surgery in..." She checks her watch. "...ooh, about an hour and a half?"

"I'm not sure. He got an overseas call about half an hour ago, just before my shift started – Janice said she thought it was his father – and he's been in there talking in German ever since. He's gotten loud a couple of times, and I didn't want to interrupt. I figured as long as I can hear him, he's not suffering; and as long as he doesn't buzz me, he must not need anything. It's actually the most peaceful the floor has been since he arrived."

"Is this the first time his father's called?"

"As far as I know. Janice usually works overnights, and she told me she hadn't transferred any calls to him before this one. Actually, a couple of days ago, he received a box in the mail from West Germany, and he seemed pretty excited about it when I went in to take his vitals a short time later. But later that afternoon, he asked me to store it in his closet, and it was still unopened. Then Janice said last night, he asked her to get it for him. She said it had some old photos and stuff like that inside. She said he apparently tried to make a couple of calls out because he was yelling in German when no one was in there with him. Then this this morning, he got the call, and he's been in there yammering ever since." Maryann gestures to the station's switchboard. "Yeah, he's still on the phone. See, the light's still on."

"Okay. I guess I'll just wait to see him in pre-op. I know this surgery terrifies him, and his father's in poor health. They probably just want to say everything they need to, just in case things don't go as planned."

# # #

29 December 1943

Caro Diario (Dear Diary),

I can hardly believe that my papa has been gone a week today. When you lose someone you love so much, you tend to remember all the lasts you had with them: The last thing you said to each other, the last argument you had, the last time you said you loved them, the last secret you shared. For years, I replayed all my lasts with Otto. I guess because we knew he would be going away for a while to the government program, we prepared ourselves by making each last count. Of course, we had no idea just how permanent those lasts would be, but we still made each moment we had meaningful, nonetheless.

This week, I've been thinking of all my lasts with Papa, and it's just making me angry. None of them were special. Our last words exchanged was him telling me to get in the broom closet and hide and me begging him to hide with us. He gave me one of the sternest looks he ever has as he pointed at the secret door and silently admonished my hesitance. As I climbed into the dark space with Mama, I whispered under my breath (in Dutch so Mama wouldn't understand) that Papa was dwass – foolish – for answering the door. I'm so livid that he didn't hide with us! If he did, he'd still be alive.

But even more than that, I hate myself for taking every moment prior to his death for granted. If I had things to do over, I'd live each moment as though it might be our last, and then, at least, I wouldn't have so many of these regrets that will surely weigh me down like a millstone tied around my neck for the remainder of my life.

# # #

CHAPTER THIRTY-FOUR

Friday morning, Helen steps out of the shower and is greeted by the aroma of strawberry and cream cheese blintzes coupled with freshly brewed coffee. After dressing, she heads to the kitchen and plants a loud kiss on Maurice's waiting lips. "Good morning, dear. Something smells delicious."

He makes her a plate and joins her at the table. "Morning, hon. You know, I don't think I've ever seen you smile so much as I have these last few days. You even smiled in your sleep last night. Your daughter's a very special woman."

"Yes. Rena—I mean Bridget has always been a brilliant girl with a heart of gold. I just never thought this day would come. I'm so happy my search is finally over. And now, I get to go to work where I can actually see her every day and visit her whenever she has time during the evenings and weekends. It's like a dream come true, multiplied by a thousand."

Maurice chuckles. "Is that why you're dressed for work early today?"

"No. I told the kids the other night I wasn't planning to disturb either of them at the hospital. There's this patient who's having surgery today, and I want to go see him. I don't know why, but there's just something that draws me to him."

"Are you thinking of leaving me?" Maurice's eyes twinkle as he winks at her.

She dismisses his joke with a dramatic roll of her eyes. "Oh, stop. You know better than that. This man is barely older than a child. Early twenties, I'd say."

"Is this the German fellow?"

Helen sips her coffee and nods.

"Hon, you can't go see him. Look what he did to your head. He tried to kill you."

"Ack, he did no such thing. He's got a brain tumor, and perhaps he doesn't behave as he should, but there's just something about him. It's like... It's like I'm *meant* to know him."

Maurice raises an eyebrow. "And that's why you're going up there almost an hour before your shift starts? You're trying to sneak in before someone catches you... Like maybe your daughter who's asked you to stay away from him?"

Helen's cheeks turn pink. "Perhaps. But I also want to have time to see him before I have to clock in."

"And what if he doesn't want to see you?"

She stands and takes her plate and cup to the sink. "I'll cross that bridge when I come to it."

"Dear, I really think—"

"Darling, please don't try to talk me out of this. You said I was smiling in my sleep last night. That wasn't because I was dreaming about my Renate. I was dreaming about my boys. Otto and Josef were grown men, and they looked so much like their papa. But they reminded me of someone else too. When I woke, I realized they looked very much like this young man."

Maurice's face blanches, and he stands. "Helen, please don't go in there and tell him that and get him all upset. I'd hate to see him hurt you or himself if he throws another fit."

She pulls her coat on and grabs her keys and pocketbook. "Don't worry. I'm not saying I think he *is* one of my boys, just that he reminds me of them. It just makes me feel good to be around him, despite his nasty temper. I'll see you this evening." She pecks his cheek and leaves without giving him further opportunity to protest.

After a short drive to work, she stores her purse and coat in her locker then heads up to the fifth floor. As she steps off the elevator, she stands against the corridor wall and eyes the nurses' station. As Nurse Janice straightens her cap then heads to a patient's room, Helen makes a beeline to Room 529. She taps softly on the door then slips inside. "Herr Hetzel, good morning. Please don't get upset. I just wanted to—" She looks at the patient and stops short.

Gunter sobs as he hugs his knees, seemingly oblivious to anything around him. Black and white photos strewn across his blanket, bedside tray, and on the floor make the room look like a scrapbook exploded; and a crumbled letter, clutched in his hand, crinkles as his broad shoulders heave.

Helen stoops and picks up a photo of a handsome, young man in a Nazi uniform holding a pregnant woman's hand. As she offers it to Gunter, her tattoo peeks out from under her sleeve. "Are these your parents?"

Gunter glances at her arm and snatches the photo from her. "I knew it! You are a Jew."

She maintains her calm demeanor. "And I'm also a German. Why do you hate me so much? Is it because your Vater was a Nazi soldier? Did he teach you to hate people you don't even know?"

His angry façade melts as he grabs a fistful of tissues and swipes at his eyes. He sniffles and shakes his head. "No. My Vater doesn't hate anyone. It was my Mutter who hated Jews. She was in the Bund Deutscher Mädel – *League of German Maidens* – the equivalent of the Hitlerjugend – *Hitler Youth* – for females, when she was a girl. Her Vater was an S.S. Obersturmführer – *Senior Assault Leader* – and he and his family all hated the Untermenschen... Sorry, I mean Jews."

Helen raises an eyebrow. *Oh, you're sorry now?* She plucks another photo from the floor and examines the same young soldier standing in front of a house. "Is this your Vater? He's a nice-looking man."

Gunter grabs the photo and flips it upside down on his tray. "Jah, that's him."

She sits in the chair beside his bed. "I know you wish your family could be here with you. It's not easy going through a surgery all alone. But Rena—Dr. Castle is the best there is." She nudges the tissue box closer to him.

"It's not my surgery that has me upset."

"If you'd like to talk about it, I've been told I'm a good listener. I know you don't like me, but the truth is, you don't even know me. You just hate what you think I stand for."

He buries his face in his knees and starts sobbing again. "I... I don't... I just learned that I don't have any right to hate anyone. Apparently, mein own Mutter hated *me* because she thought I was an Untermenschen."

Helen gasps, and her pulse quickens. "Excuse me? I don't think I heard you right."

He looks up with red-rimmed eyes, saying, "My Vater wrote to me a few days ago. His health is bad, and he sent me this package with this note inside." The crumpled letter crinkles as he shakes his fist. "The package said 'Öffnen Sie nicht bis zum Tag Ihrer Operation.' – *Do not open until the day of your surgery.* So, I left it in the closet until late last night. When I opened it, there were all these photos inside." He gestures to his tray and bed. "I was happy to receive so many tangible reminders of my childhood. Then I read his letter. He said he couldn't risk me facing such a serious operation without telling me the truth about things. He said if I should perish before he could tell me, he'd never be able to live with himself, and if he passed away before he shared his news, he could never rest in peace."

Helen furrows her brow. "I... I see."

Gunter shakes his head. "No, you don't. For as long as I can remember, I've always been Gunter Werner Hetzel, the son of Heinz and Inge Hetzel. My Mutter, she hated the Jews. She killed herself when I was five. On my fifth birthday, actually. My Vater always told me it was because she just couldn't handle the fact that Germany lost the war. That's why I don't like Jews. Part of me always felt like, if it weren't for the Jews, my Mutter would still be alive. But I also always suspected that her death had something more directly to do with my Vater. See, even though he was a Nazi soldier, he hated it. He always said the only reason he even put the uniform on was that he was too terrified not to. When his brother was a teenager, he was recruited to join the Führer's Army, but he refused. His brother was then taken away at gunpoint, and the family never heard from him again."

Tears burn behind Helen's eyes. "Oh. I'm so sorry. I guess I'm guilty of misjudging others too. I never considered the possibility that all of Hitler's soldiers might not have wanted to be there."

Gunter sniffs and squeezes the letter. "Yeah, well, that's not the point. In his letter, my Vater told me that I'm not his son. Apparently, the *real* Gunter Hetzel accidentally drowned while Mutter was bathing him when he was only three months old. Vater says here that Mutter went into a deep depression and she was inconsolable. Vater was afraid she'd be killed by her own Nazi family if they discovered just how mentally unstable she had become. So, a couple of weeks later, while he was doing his duties – He was in the clean-up crew that came after the Jews were arrested and took whatever valuables they had before he burned their homes down – He says here that he found a baby boy hidden in a basket. The child was about the same age as his son would have been." His breath catches in his throat. "He said that baby was me! He slipped me in his knapsack and brought me home to his wife and put me in *that* Gunter's cradle then told Mutter that she was mistaken. That her baby had never drowned." He sniffs and swipes his hands across his face as he begins sobbing again.

Helen rubs his shoulder. "And this upsets you so? It sounds to me like he must have loved you very much to want you for his son."

"You don't understand. From what my Vater just wrote me, my Mutter apparently learned of this around the time of my fifth birthday, and *that's* why she killed herself. She couldn't stand the sight of me!" He runs his fingers through his hair, and his face turns scarlet as he weeps.

"Aww, there now. I'm sure there's more to it than you realize. Perhaps her depression returned for some other reason. You mustn't blame yourself."

His eyes narrow. "I don't. I blame my Vater for lying to me about this! He must be out of his mind to tell me this pack of lies. Honestly, how could a Jewish boy possibly be substituted as a *changeling?* You know what I mean? I mean, my Mutter certainly bathed me, and if I was truly Jewish..."

Helen takes a deep breath. "Herr Hetzel, a lot of babies were born in hiding during the war. With the Jews being rounded up and exiled to the ghettos and the synagogues burned down, there weren't many rabbis available to perform a bris. Plus, a lot of the men and boys were checked to see if they were trying to pass. For this reason, many Jewish families didn't have their sons circumcised at all back then."

He rubs his temples with his fingertips and squeezes his eyes closed. "Nein. It's a pack of lies! I don't know why my Vater would want to hurt me so, but I've put in a call to him, and he should be calling me back soon so I can straighten this out." He cringes and sits forward, plunging his fingers into his ribcage, sending several photos to the floor.

Helen scoots her chair back then gathers the photos from the ground. She picks one up, and the air leaves her lungs as she stares at it. "Did... did your Vater say he found you in Amsterdam?"

"What?"

"Did he find you in Amsterdam?"

"I already told you this was a lie. Some fantasy he made up in his drug-induced state from his painkillers."

Helen shows the photo to Gunter. "Is this your Vater holding you in front of this print shop in Amsterdam?"

Gunter's eyes narrow, and he snatches the snapshot from her. "That's us, but obviously, no one knows where it is. There's a fire in the background."

"And didn't you say your Vater was responsible for setting the fires?"

"That doesn't mean anything."

She plucks another picture from the floor and examines it. Her heart quickens. "And look here. This blanket wrapped around you says 'O.T.B.' What do you suppose that means?"

He grabs the photo from her and inspects it. "I remember that blanket. I found it in a trunk in the attic when I was four. In fact, that was one of the last conversations I remember having with mein Mutter. I was playing when I found it, and I asked her who it belonged to. She got angry and threw it in the garbage. I'd never seen her so upset. When I went to bed that night, she and my Vater yelled until the wee hours. When I woke the next day, excited about my birthday, my Vater told me that Mutter had overdosed on pills and was dead."

Helen's hands shake as she unbuttons her right sleeve. "Herr, Hetzel, during the war, my family hid in the Netherlands. My husband had been arrested, and it was just my daughter and myself until my son was born a couple of months later. When he was only a few weeks old, we were forced to leave the place where we were hiding and relocate to somewhere safer. We had only a few minutes' notice before we had to leave. There had been word that the Nazis were moving in, so several families were relocating at the same time we were. During part of our move, we had to travel on foot in the dark of night so the Gestapo wouldn't catch us. I was holding my infant son in my right arm, and my teenage daughter and I each held a small suitcase. Rena—my daughter tripped, and some people pushed their way between us. Everyone moved silently, and all you could hear was the sound of feet moving swiftly along the cobblestone road. It was a literal stampede of frightened men, women, and children, all just looking to find their way to safety. When I realized my daughter wasn't beside me, I moved over to the right side of the road to wait for her, and that's when someone pushed by us and burned my baby and me. I can only assume the woman had been ironing and still held the hot iron in her hand as she fled." She rolls up her sleeve and reveals a dark, trapezoidal-shaped scar. "My baby let out an ear-piercing wail, and I was terrified that we would be heard by the Gestapo. When we got to safety, I realized my son had been burned on the side of his der Hintern – *buttock*. Before I was arrested, I left my son with the owners of the print shop in Amsterdam. When that couple was arrested, they hid him in a basket in an alcove before their shop was torched, and I never saw my son again. Herr Hetzel, I'm thinking you are him."

Gunter throws back his blanket and rolls to his left side. He flips his gown up and says, "No! You must have seen my scar before. You're making that up. My family had a Jewish maid who burned me when I was an infant. That's why my Mutter had her sent to the gas chambers."

Helen's chin quivers as Gunter re-covers himself. She says, "Did your Vater tell you that? Herr Hetzel, I've never seen your scar, and how could I make up this matching scar on my own arm?"

"I don't know. Lots of people get burned by irons." His face reddens.

She unrolls her sleeve, and her pulse quickens. "Okay. Well, my first son was named Otto Theodor Breitman. I knitted him a sky-blue baby blanket with his initials in deep crimson red. He died when he was ten years old. A few years later when my next son, Josef

Wilhelm, was born, I gave him his brother's blanket. Is that not the same blanket that was in your attic?"

"You just saw the photo yourself!"

"The photo is black and white. How could I possibly know the colors?"

His face blanches, and he looks as if he's been punched in the gut. "I... I don't know. Maybe I mentioned it earlier. I'm so distraught, I don't remember what all I told you. I don't know why I'm talking to you anyway."

"Herr Hetzel—"

"What? Why are you tormenting me like this? You seem dead set on wanting to believe you're my mother, and it's just not possible! What's wrong with you?"

Helen remains calm, and her lips curl into a confident smile. "Herr Hetzel, all three of my children had a small birth defect. Each of them had a tiny bit of webbing on each of their feet between their fourth and fifth toes. It's so minor, one might not even be able to notice it upon first glance. And my little Josef had a small, heart-shaped birthmark at the base of his skull and a large freckle on his left interior ankle."

Goosebumps cover Gunter's arms as he touches the back of his head. He jumps when the telephone beside his bed rings. "That will be mein Vater. You stay here. We'll ask him..."

* * *

CHAPTER THIRTY-FIVE

Bridget, leaning against the fifth-floor nurses' station counter, watches the switchboard as the light turns off, then she and Maryann jump when a loud crash comes from Room 529. An irate voice yells, "Get out of here, you Shylock! Do you have to be hit in the head to understand you're not welcome here?" Something else crashes, and Helen flees from the room with a steady stream of blood pouring down the side of her face.

Bridget shrieks and races toward the room. "Mama! Come back!"

Helen runs the other way down the corridor and ducks into a restroom. Bridget's flaming face screws into a contorted scowl as she throws open Mr. Hetzel's door and storms into his room.

* * *

A short time later, Bridget steps into the Surgical Prep-Room. The patient stares at the I.V. dripping down the line into his arm. Bridget narrows her eyes at him and says to the nurse, "Jan, I'll prep him. You go ahead and go. Leave us alone."

"But, Doctor—"

Bridget steps closer and takes the electric clippers from her hand. "Jan, I said get going. I'd like to be alone with my patient."

The patient attempts to speak, but his words don't come. He makes a gurgling noise.

Jan backs away and says, "Yes, Dr. Castle." She closes the door as she leaves.

Bridget stands over the patient, her lips twisted into a sinister smile. She removes a loaded syringe from her pocket and plunges it into the patient's I.V. line. "Ah, so you figured out that Helen and I are related. Yes, I'm Jewish, and I'll be damned if you and your anti-Semitic beliefs are going to ever hurt my mother again! You see what I just injected you with? It's succinylcholine. I'm sure you know what that is. It will immobilize you, but you'll still be able to feel every little thing I do when I open up your skull and pluck out a chunk of your brain! That's just what your idol, Dr. Mengele, did, by the way. He performed many a surgery without anesthetic, and his surgeries weren't even necessary. They were cruel and demented." She turns on the clippers and begins shaving his head. "Oh, I know you don't believe the Nazis ever did such things; but, you see, I was actually there. I actually worked in Dr. Mengele's office and saw first-hand just what a perverted, barbaric sociopath he was."

Though he's unable to move, the patient's eyes display a flicker of recognition. And unmistakable abject terror.

Bridget's eyes narrow. "I should have told you the other day that it really burns me how much you and people like you hate Jews. And you really had no idea what kind of cruel experiments the Nazis did on people? Hmm. Those bastards killed half my family, but since you identify so well with the Nazis, you can now pay for their sins." She lets out a a calculating giggle. "Auge für Auge, Zahn für Zahn, ein Leben für ein Leben. Or maybe you'd prefer English? An eye for an eye; a tooth for a tooth... a life for a life."

She finishes shaving his head and says, "Ah, if only we had some calcium chloride to rub into your scalp and... What was that your Nazi heroes said? Kill the filthy vermin? Isn't that what you'd like to do to my mama? And now, you sick Nazi maggot, it's time for your surgery..."

* * *

CHAPTER THIRTY-SIX

A few hours later, Bridget leaves the surgical suite and heads upstairs to her office. She locks her door and pulls one of the guest chairs from in front of her desk to the closet. She kicks off her shoes, climbs up on the chair, then balances on the arms as she reaches over her head. She lifts a ceiling tile and plunges her hand into the opening until her fingers touch what she's looking for. She grabs a leather-bound book, and her face displays a satisfied glow. She takes the book to her desk and opens it. Reaching in her drawer, she grabs a Butter Rum Lifesaver then pops it in her mouth and locates a pen. She begins writing...

20 December 1968

Kedves Naplóm (Dear Diary),

I apologize for not having written in so long. I'm writing in Hungarian today because what I have to tell you must never be discovered by anyone, and none of my friends or family even knows I learned Hungarian while I was in Auschwitz.

A lot has happened this week, and I have so much to report. But first, I must tell you what happened just now. I lost a patient on the operating table. In my career as a surgeon, I've only lost two other patients on the operating table and one post-surgery. The thing is, when this happened previously, I felt positively horrible. Today, not so much.

The patient I operated on was a sadistic, Nazi-loving anti-Semitist who, if he had his way, would gladly initiate another attempt to reach the Final Solution. I've met plenty just like him in my lifetime, and they all seem to have such a deep-seeded hate, it surprises me that they can even find love for anyone. But this patient, he was one of the worst.

Papa always taught me that taking the Hippocratic Oath meant striving to do all I could for every patient – not just the ones I liked – and that there was nothing more important than keeping one's word when having taken such a solemn vow, no matter what the circumstances.

Funny thing, when I saw him this morning in the cafeteria, Dr. Steve Slater complained of a headache, but he didn't make it seem like it was anything out of the ordinary. It wasn't until later when he was in one of our shared patient's rooms that he flipped out. He started yelling and threw a bedpan at my mother's face before he fell on the floor, grabbing his head as he writhed in agony. I sent him for diagnostic tests, and that's when we learned of his cerebral aneurysm and that it had ruptured.

Oh! I guess I forgot to mention the biggest part of my day! Turns out, my other patient, Herr Gunter Hetzel from Cologne, West Germany – the patient who's also been very vocal about how much he, too, hates Jews – is actually my baby brother Josef! I still don't know yet how Mama figured out that he's my brother. (Oops! I guess I also forgot to tell you that my genetic mother has come back into my life. That will be a story for another time.)

Anyway, once Mama figured out who this patient was, she didn't hesitate to let him know it. From the limited details I heard earlier, he spoke to his Vater and confirmed it to be true. Afterward, he actually hugged Mama and asked her to stay with him until he had his surgery and then made her promise to be there when he woke up.

I guess it was about this time that Dr. Slater went to check on Gunter's ulcers, and he found Gunter and

Mama in a tearful embrace. I don't know what led up to him throwing a fit, other than he then accused Gunter of being a Jew-lover, and they started yelling at each other before Steve threw the bedpan at Mama. Regardless, Mama was so thrilled to spend every moment with Gunter, she wouldn't even allow anyone to stitch up her scalp where the bedpan hit her until after Gunter was taken down to pre-op.

Of course, these new findings meant that I couldn't perform his operation, so Jack stepped in and successfully removed his meningioma. Jack said once he got in there, it wasn't nearly as bad as the tests led us to believe. Josef – or rather Gunter will be just fine, and I'm anxiously looking forward to getting to know him and making up for all the years we lost.

Her telephone rings, and she picks it up. "Hello. Dr. Castle."

"Afternoon, Lovey, it's Dad. Mummy and I received a call earlier from Helen saying that she found your brother. I just got off the phone with Petteri to share the incredible news, and he's coming here in a fortnight to see all of us. He said he's located a few photos of Jens and a couple of pieces of your papa's medical equipment that he wants to give you."

"Are you serious? I can't wait to see the Good Doctor! This is turning out to be the best week of my life."

"I was stunned also. I never thought we'd see him step foot off the Continent. Oh, he said to tell you not to worry; he's bringing a large bag of dropjes for you."

She laughs. "I can't believe he remembers how much I used to love those candies. He always had some for me whenever he visited."

"The Good Doctor is a sterling man, to be sure. So, I called to tell you that Mum and I would like to take you and Jack and Helen and Maurice out to dinner tonight to celebrate everything. What do you say?"

She checks her watch. "We'd love to. Let me finish up here, and I'll go tell Jack."

"Right-o, Lovey. We'll meet you all at your house at six, then go from there. Okay?"

"Of course."

"Jolly good. We'll see you soon. Ta ta."

"Cheers!" She cradles the phone and resumes writing...

Anyway, as I said before, while Papa always taught me that staying true to my oath meant doing all I could for every patient, though he may not have meant to, he also taught me that family is more important than anything, including any old oath. (He actually taught me this by helping the damn Nazis and allowing himself to be taken away just when Mama and I needed him the most.)

That's why I handled Steve's pre-op myself. I injected the benzodiazepine in his line (which, of course, is just a mild dose of Valium and is standard pre-op procedure for cranial surgeries), but I told him it was succinylcholine and that he'd be immobilized but able to feel everything I did in his surgery – just like his Nazi heroes used to do to their unsuspecting victims.

Then I told him how I knew, firsthand, exactly what some of the Nazi doctors did so he'd get another eye-witness account to compare to his uncle's stories. It was about this time that the anesthesiologist, Dr. Dick Spurgeon, came in to introduce himself to the patient (as he always does), and he overheard some of what I was saying. Dick expressed a profound interest in why I might be telling such a thing to a patient, so I explained Steve's views on the Holocaust and how he felt about Jews. I don't know who was more shocked, me or Steve, when Dick told us that his wife's grandfather was killed at Buchenwald – the very camp where Steve's uncle worked.

The operation was barely underway when Steve went into sudden cardiac arrest and flatlined. With a ruptured cerebral aneurysm, the odds were stacked against him anyway, and with him having no immediate family, there won't be an autopsy. I guess, like so many Jews who were massacred by Dr.

Mengele, Steve's precise cause of death will remain forever a mystery. I mean, the aneurysm could've killed him. On the other hand, when a patient receives too much anesthesia too quickly, the results could be fatal.

Either way, what was that he said this morning? One doesn't actually count the number of roaches exterminated in a Harlem tenement; they just rejoice when they're gone.

* * *

THE END

EPILOGUE

8 January 1969

Dear Diary,

I can't believe it's already 1969. The Good Doctor left early this morning after a four-day visit. Though his visit was too short, it was wonderful seeing him again. However, seeing him again opened up some old wounds and reminded me too vividly of my last days in Amsterdam and, even more so, of my last hours with Papa.

Mama's taken a leave from her housekeeping job so she can spend every moment with Josef – or Gunter, as he prefers to be called. He is healing remarkably well, and since Jack operated on him, he's remained under Jack's care. They've really hit it off and are getting along like brothers.

But I believe the biggest news I have to share, Dear Diary, is that Gunter's doctor has invited Jack, Dad, and me to lecture and demonstrate a couple of surgeries at the teaching hospital where he works in Cologne. I haven't set foot in Germany since I was liberated from Bergen-Belsen, and frankly, the mere thought of it is making me a nervous wreck! We'll accompany Gunter home at the end of the month, and Mama and Mum have already announced that they will be joining us.

> *I have no idea how I might react once I get there, but I can guarantee you one thing... While I'm there, it will be my mission to meet Gunter's Vater, that Nazi swine, and tell him exactly what I think of him!*

* * *

To travel with Bridget and her family to West Germany, be sure to check out **The Changeling of the Third Reich Book II: The Reckoning** on Amazon. To keep up with future adventures of Bridget and her loved ones, follow the author on Amazon, Facebook (Rachel Carrera, Novelist), and X formerly known as Twitter (@NovelistRachel) for news about upcoming sequels.

If you enjoyed The Changeling of the Third Reich, **please leave a review on Amazon and/or Goodreads**. I'll be eternally appreciative.

Cheers!

AFTERWORD

As mentioned in the letter to the reader, all the news reports in this book (with the exception of the news report regarding Susan Donna Turner) really happened. Several beta readers of the book wanted to know more about how some of these 1968 news items concluded. Here are the answers:

During the 60s and early 70s, the Vietnam-era anti-war movement was the largest protest movement in United States history. The U.S. military occupied parts of Southeast Asia beginning in 1955 in an attempt to subvert communism from spreading. In 1963, when the Kennedy Administration began sending combat troops to Vietnam, the anti-war movement took a strong foothold as citizens expressed their dissent of the government's position on this "police action". With more than 3.1 million U.S. troops stationed in Vietnam during this period, the U.S. suffered roughly 282,000 deaths of military personnel by the time the war ended in 1975.

In **July of 1968**, an influenza pandemic known as the Hong Kong flu or H3N2, originated in Hong Kong, China. Within two weeks of it emerging, more than half a million cases were reported as it rapidly spread around the globe. This strain of influenza evolved from the H2N2 flu pandemic of 1957. By September of 1968, the virus reached the Panama Canal Zone and the United States. The pandemic lasted until late 1969 or early 1970 and claimed between 1 and 4 million lives globally.

On **15 December 1968**, the Philadelphia Eagles were set to play the Minnesota Vikings, but a substantial snowstorm the night before left the stadium covered in snow. Temperatures remained in the low 20s

(Fahrenheit) at kickoff, and accompanying 30 MPH wind gusts prevented the scheduled halftime Christmas pageant performers from showing up. The Eagles' entertainment director, Bill "Moon" Mullen, spotted a Santa Claus in the stands, 20-year-old Frank Olivo. Mr. Olivo had a tradition of dressing as Santa on the last regular season game each year. Mr. Olivo and Eagles cheerleaders, the Eaglettes, dressed as elves, entered Franklin Field with "Here Comes Santa Claus" being played by a 50-piece band. Because the fans were angered at the Eagles' poor performance, by the time Mr. Olivo reached the endzone, fans booed and threw more than 100 snowballs at him. Howard Cosell broadcasted the show. The Eagles presented Mr. Olivo with football-shaped cufflinks and a tie tack to compensate him for his services. The following year, they invited him to return as Santa again, but he declined. Mr. Olivo died on 30 April 2015 at the age of 66 after a battle with heart disease and diabetes.

On **13 December 1968**, Col. Francis J. McGouldrick, 36, went missing when his B-57B bomber collided with another American plane during a night strike over Laos along the Ho Chi Minh Trail. Only the body of the pilot of the other plane was recovered. After the war concluded, the crash site was excavated, and parts of his aircraft were located. However, an extensive search found no evidence of the Colonel or his crew. In 1978, President Jimmy Carter declared U.S. servicemen who were listed as "missing in action" to be reclassified as "killed in action". A funeral with an empty casket and full military honors was held for Col. McGouldrick at Arlington National Cemetery. His wife passed away in 1980, never having known what happened to her husband. On 3 September 2013, the Colonel's daughters were notified that his body had finally been located and positively identified after an extensive dig the previous year yielded DNA-testable material.

On **16 December 1968**, Dr. Lloyd Bailey, a Republican elector from North Carolina, cast his vote for George Wallace rather than for President Elect Richard Nixon. Dr. Bailey, an ophthalmologist from Rocky Mount, North Carolina, achieved notoriety when he became the 145th faithless elector in the country's history. Though his vote meant that President-Elect Richard Nixon received only 301 electoral votes instead of 302, Dr. Bailey's actions did not affect the outcome of the election. The doctor, who was a staunch conservative, made several excuses for his bold actions at first but later admitted that he did so because Nixon intended to appoint Daniel Patrick Moynihan and Henry Kissinger to government positions. This admission caused Dr. Bailey to be known as a "protest elector" and shortly thereafter prompted calls for electoral system reform.

On **17 December 1968**, 11-year-old Mary Flora Bell was sentenced to life in juvenile detention after she was convicted of killing two boys in separate incidents. On 25 May 1968, the then 10-year-old girl strangled 4-year-old Martin Brown in the upstairs bedroom of a derelict house. A couple of days later, Miss Brown and a friend knocked on the door of Martin's mother's door, asking to see her son. When Mrs. Brown told them they couldn't see Martin because he had died, Mary said, "I know he's dead; I want to see him in his coffin." On 31 July 1968, 3-year-old Brian Howe went missing, and after an extensive search, his body was discovered next to a broken pair of scissors. He had been strangled, and his body and genitals had been mutilated by Miss Bell and her friend. A detective recalled that on the morning of Brian's funeral, Miss Bell stood outside laughing and rubbing her hands together as his tiny casket was walked outside. The detective knew if he didn't arrest her right away, she would "do another one". At the trial, it was discovered that Miss Bell was an abused child herself. Her aunt recalled the day she was born when her mother yelled at the nurse who attempted to place the baby in her arms, "Take the thing away from me!" Prior to the trial, it was determined that Miss Bell suffered from psychopathic personality disorder. Because of this, she was cleared of the murder charge but convicted of two counts of manslaughter on the grounds of diminished responsibility. Her friend was acquitted of all charges. To date, Miss Bell is Britain's youngest female killer. She was sentenced to a Red Bank secure unit in Newton-Le-Willows, Lancashire and remained imprisoned until 1980 when she was 23.

On **17 December 1968**, Gary Steven Krist, a prison escapee, and his accomplice, Ruth Eisemann-Schier, disguised themselves as police officers and knocked on the door of a room at a Rodeway Inn in Decatur, Georgia. The room was occupied by 20-year-old Emory student, Barbara Mackle, and her mother, Jane Mackle. Barbara was suffering from the H3N2 flu, and her mother came to drive her home for Christmas break. The kidnappers chloroformed, bound, and gagged Jane and took Barbara at gunpoint. They drove to a remote area near Duluth and buried her alive inside a fiberglass box fitted with an air pump, a battery-powered lamp, food, and water laced with sedatives. Two plastic pipes provided additional outside air. The kidnappers demanded half a million dollars from Barbara's father, Robert Mackle, a successful land developer in Miami. However, the ransom drop was disrupted when a police cruiser drove by. While the second ransom drop was successful, the kidnappers abandoned their car which was traced back to a George Deacon who built ventilated boxes for a living. Armed with this information, police were able to track Eisemann-Schier and Krist, and three days after the ordeal began, Miss Mackle was located, suffering only from dehydration.

316   THE CHANGELING OF THE THIRD REICH

Krist was located on 20 December 1968, in a Florida swamp. Eisemann-Schier's role in the crime led her to being the first woman listed on the FBI's ten most wanted list. She was located in Norman, Oklahoma on 5 March 1969. Both were imprisoned and released a few years later. In 1971, Miss Mackle wrote and published a book about her experience entitled *83 Hours Till Dawn* which was made into two television movies.

On **18 December 1968**, President Lyndon Johnson was admitted to the Bethesda Naval Hospital after being diagnosed with the H3N2 flu. Coincidentally, Vice President Hubert Humphrey who was visiting Phoenix was forced to cancel his planned speaking engagements after learning that he, too, was infected with the flu. This marks one of the rare times in history when both a U.S. President and his Vice President were simultaneously incapacitated. Just eight days prior to his hospitalization, President Johnson hosted a state dinner for the Apollo 8 astronauts. Apollo 8 launched on 21 December 1968, and the President spoke to the astronauts from his hospital bed. Upon learning that the Apollo 8 Commander, Frank Borman, became ill while in space, President Johnson feared he may have infected the crew. The President remained hospitalized until 22 December 1968.

On **19 December 1968**, Eastern Air Lines Flight 47 was hijacked. Seven flight crew members and 147 passengers and were taken hostage as the Philadelphia-based flight's original destination of Miami was diverted to Havana. Aircraft hijackings between Cuba and the United States began in 1958 and have continued as recently as 2003. However, air hijackings between the two countries were at a height between 1968 and 1972, when more than 130 aircrafts were diverted. The hijacker, Thomas George Washington, abducted his daughter from his ex-wife and boarded the DC-8 with her. After the plane was airborne, he gave the stewardess a note which demanded that the captain reroute the flight to Havana. He claimed to have a gun and nitroglycerin. Mr. Washington was eventually convicted of interfering with a fight crew which earned him a 2-year sentence in federal prison. This was a far lesser charge than air piracy. At the time it was committed, this Flight 47 hijacking set the record for the largest number of air hostages taken.

To conclude, as the infamous CBS Evening News newscaster of the time, Walter Cronkite, might have said, "And that's the way it is…"

THE RING ON THE BOXCAR

The same boxcars that were meant to hold eight horses or 40 soldiers during World War I (the Great War), were used by the Reichsbahn (railroad) to hold between 80 and 120 Jews as the Third Reich transported them to one of the six death camps, 900 concentration camps, or 44,000 incarceration sites throughout Europe.

The Florida Holocaust Museum was fortunate enough to procure Boxcar #113 0695-5 from Poland. This was one of the original cars used to transport human cargo to places such as Auschwitz and the Treblinka Killing Camp. When the museum took possession of the car, they pressure washed the interior, and a little girl's gold ring fell out from between the slats. The museum displays the ring as a tribute to the child who hid it there.

The first time I saw that ring, I knew the little girl who hid it left it as a way of saying, "I was here." And I was determined that she *would not* be forgotten. Her ingenious plan of leaving her ring as a message inspired me to honor her by giving Dr. Bridget Castle the same brilliant foresight.

(Photos by R. Carrera)

ACKNOWLEDGEMENTS

First of all, it wouldn't seem right to write a book about the Holocaust without acknowledging the six-million Jews who were mercilessly murdered in this reprehensible genocidal catastrophe. To their loved ones, I can only offer my most profound and heartfelt condolences. I hope this book serves as a means to help educate people as to at least some of the atrocities their loved ones were forced to endure.

* * *

Next, I owe a debt of gratitude and offer my deep appreciation to the following individuals who encouraged me throughout my creative process:

My children, Stefani Daugherty and Jeremy Carrera, who listened to endless hours of my story weaving long before I ever decided to memorialize a full-length tale in writing.

My sister and best friend, Michelle Chestnut, a devoted historian, who made several road trips with me in the name of research and who was my sounding board whenever I got stumped.

My son's brother from another mother, Brad "Moose" Seay, an aspiring writer who's always been happy to act as a beta reader for me.

My good friend and fellow author, Leslie Noyes, who encouraged me to "publish already".

My dear friends from across the pond, Mike Steeden, a fellow author whose father was a prisoner of war in German Stalag VIII-B, and his lovely wife, Shirley Blamey, who inspired me in ways they cannot imagine.

My dearly departed grandparents who raised me, Pete and Toby Hathcox, who taught me to love both reading and writing and who nurtured my creative endeavors and inspired me with their stories of life during the Great Depression and World War II. As far as this story goes, Grandma's tales of her brother who was a prisoner of war in German Stalag IV-B and Grandaddy's anecdotes of when he attended pre-med at Emory at Oxford before the war helped paint a vivid picture of how Bridget's life might have unfolded.

David, the British gentleman who volunteered at the Florida Holocaust Museum in St. Petersburg in October, 2019. He led a thirty-minute tour and said he'd be happy to answer any questions along the way. Two hours later, he was still just as happy to answer my questions as when we started. Unfortunately, I was so busy taking notes on all he said, I didn't catch his last name, and when I returned to ask him, Covid restrictions had displaced him from his job.

And finally, my sweet lady girl, Cleo, the best Devon Rex cat in the world. She was my co-writer and beta listener, and she loved to help me type and edit. Sadly, she died before publication, but the magical warmth of her presence and the special memories she created will live on.

* * *

Printed in Great Britain
by Amazon